Starlight Starbright

A Novel by
Clifton LaBree

Published by
Fading Shadows Imprint
New Boston, New Hampshire

Paperback ISBN-13:978-0-9746450-9-4

Cover and Picture by Vivian LaBree

FORT LEWIS SERIES

Fort Lewis is a fictional Cree Indian village in the vast Canadian boreal forest on the shores of the beautiful Lake Diamante. It has a Hudson Bay Store, a Catholic Church, a Royal Canadian Mounted Police barracks, and a newly-built infirmary. The Crees are in a transition period trying to adapt to modern civilization. The infirmary was established by Bright Cloud, a beautiful Cree nurse who saw the need for a medical facility to care for her people. For centuries they have survived the brutal winters with plunging temperatures and deep snows. They had traditionally followed the reindeer herds which provided them with sustenance and shelter. Survival has been their greatest achievement. It's a tribute to their woodland skills, undaunted courage, and a triumph of the human spirit.

The four books that make up this series portray a Cree family in cataclysmic events during World Wars I and II, the Korean War, and the Vietnam War. The series pays tribute to the brave men and women who served to defend our right to live as a free people. The beauty and tranquility of Fort Lewis helps to heal their troubled souls. The families return every summer for renewal and spiritual growth.

Book 1 – Edge of Tomorrow

Book 2 – Starlight Starbright

Book 3 – Give Me Tomorrow

Book 4 – Beyond the Horizon

Dedicated to my wife Pauline, and my family, with thanks for all their support and encouragement

Chapter One

Mark could feel the searing heat of the bullets as they tore through his flesh, momentarily lifting him off the ground. The impact halted his frantic flight towards the Japanese machine gun emplacement as it blurted its message of death in a staccato of fury. He held in his right hand a small satchel charge of explosives armed and ready to explode on impact. Before Mark fell to the ground, grievously wounded, he threw the satchel into the gun pit with every ounce of strength his ravaged body could summon. The ensuing explosion showered his inert body with debris and shattered body parts of the enemy gun crew. Before the dust settled, Mark's men had enveloped the enemy's position, finishing off those enemy soldiers who survived the explosion. A steady line of troops then began pushing inland from the beach to take advantage of the breach Mark had opened in the enemy's defensive line.

A Navy corpsman spotted Mark and quickly ran to his side. Seeing that the wounded marine was his regimental commanding officer, the young corpsman spoke to him in a loud voice so that he could be heard above the deafening din of the battle raging around them. "I'm gonna turn you over, Colonel, to see how badly you're hit." The young corpsman knew that Mark had been seriously wounded because his back and the ground beneath him were already saturated with blood. He felt no response from the inert Colonel as he turned him over on his side. It was critical that he stop the flow of blood that was spurting from Mark's body at an alarming rate. The corpsman immediately began applying large pressure bandages to the bloody back area, calling out in desperation for additional help from whomever was available. He knew the colonel needed a blood transfusion just as soon as they could get his body to a more sheltered spot away from the exposed gun emplacement site. It might already be too late, but he was determined to try! Another corpsman nearby answered the call for help with a stretcher. They quickly placed Mark's body on it and made a frantic dash for the relative safety of the water's edge.

A voice called from afar as one of the corpsmen secured Mark's hands to the stretcher. "Is that Colonel Leroux?" Both men knew that the voice was that of the Assistant Division Commander, Brigadier General Arlo Korsman. "How bad is he hit?" he demanded.

The noise of the artillery and naval gunfire over their heads made normal conversation impossible. Brigadier General Korsman ran to the stretcher and knelt down to see with his own eyes what was happening. The colonel's bloody figure lying at his feet was just one of hundreds of casualties. The invasion of a relatively insignificant island in the middle of the Pacific Ocean was going to be a costly enterprise, reflected the sturdy officer. Many sad letters would be going out to hundreds of parents across America. Suddenly, the stocky general felt the heavy responsibility of the grim business he was a part of. But this particular casualty gave him a sick, wrenching feeling that slammed him like the physical impact of an exploding shell.

"He's bleeding heavily, Sir. I think it's pretty bad, and if he doesn't get plasma soon, he'll surely be gone." Both corpsmen worked feverishly to get a needle into the Colonel's arm so that they could connect him to the life-giving liquid suspended from a piece of twisted metal from that had once been an amphibious tractor.

"I can't believe what he just did!" cried one of the corpsmen. "He sure as hell stopped that bunker that was creating havoc on the beaches."

"Yes, he stopped it, but what was he doing up here in such an exposed position?" the General asked of himself as much as anything else. He was in that frustratingly difficult situation when the plan of operations becomes just a piece of paper and the events on the ground are in the hands of the few that are controlled by the situation that confronts them. In other words, he was unable to do much about what was taking place, except pray.

Naval gunfire was answering a call for support on the front, rapidly firing over the heads of the invasion force. The heavy shells sounded like locomotives making a swishing sound as they passed alarmingly close overhead. It was an eerie sound that blended with the small arms fire and the mortar sections of the infantry as they tenaciously engaged the enemy in a brutal duel of life and death. The noise never seemed to stop, but when it did diminish in intensity you could hear the cries of the wounded, American as well as Japanese, scattered all over the battlefield. One marine close by called out for his mother until he haltingly stopped in mid-sentence, and remained silent.

The battle scene was one of organized confusion, with maximum violence of man and machines against man. The high pitched clamor alone frightened most men. If a person was normal, he was scared. Fear could be an invaluable ally on the battlefield. It never failed to heighten the senses making every soldier more keenly alert to what was going on around him.

Earlier, Colonel Mark Leroux had acted on his own instincts when he saw that the two lead battalions of his regiment were being savagely torn apart by enemy bunkers that had escaped unscathed from the pre-invasion shelling by the Navy. One bunker in particular was at the center of the advance inland. The machine guns and mortars in the bunker had effectively stopped the two battalions by killing most of the company commanders and several of the platoon leaders. Tragically, all of the battalion commanders had been lost before the men ever got ashore. It was a miracle that there were enough men left to form a perimeter line at the high water mark on the beaches. Mark quickly evaluated the situation and went among the remaining men, organizing them into an attacking column. Dazed by the horror they had already witnessed in the past few minutes, the survivors cautiously followed Mark's calm resolve as he led the way up the hill towards the deadly Japanese weapons that prevented them from getting off the coastal plain into the more protective cover of heavier vegetation just yards ahead of them.

The corpsmen were able to start blood plasma flowing into Mark's battered body and looked for a landing craft that was returning to the ships anchored off the beaches. The colonel's only hope, they both agreed, was the professional medical help available on the hospital ship resting at anchor nearby. One of the corpsmen took a small piece of paper and wrote that Mark had been given a large dose of morphine and blood plasma. His condition appeared to be doubtful. The paper was then taped to Mark's chest so the surgeons aboard the ship would know what had been done for him. Mark had not made a sound since he was hit, but in a moment of relative silence when the guns all seemed to stop at the same time before resuming their thunderous mission, Mark slowly opened his mouth and started to say something that the corpsman heard distinctly:

"Bright Cloud..."

It didn't make any sense to the corpsman, but the way Mark said it touched the young sailor with a feeling of helplessness as they sat on the sand with the cacophony of the battlefield surrounding them. Stretcher bearers eventually came to help carry Mark to an empty spot on the deck of a departing landing craft. The ramp of the craft retracted and the vessel slowly backed away from the violent shore. The white hospital ship was anchored close to the beachhead, allowing for easy access of returning craft and quicker treatment for the injured.

The mercy ship was a beehive of activity filled with state of the art medical equipment and a large contingent of well-trained surgeons. An unprecedented number of casualties had already preceded Mark to the ship. The prevailing mood of the attendants was that of professional urgency and all the wounded men had to take their turn regardless of rank. The staff was anxious to give each person the care they needed, yet they remained unhurried and methodical. Each of the wounded men was routinely given a thorough check to determine the extent of his wounds before he was shunted to the appropriate operating rooms where white-robed physicians calmly applied themselves to the grim task of trying to put broken bodies back together again. A large cart filled with dirty, blood-soiled uniforms that had been cut and removed from the young men who had already gone through surgery, gave silent testimony to the magnitude of suffering and pain taking place on the small tropical island.

Mark's condition warranted immediate action to control the bleeding, so he was wheeled to a waiting team of surgeons. He had not regained consciousness since the bullets tore at his flesh, but when one of the nurses whispered in his ear and asked him if he could hear her, he lightly squeezed her hand and said with a garbled voice, "Bright C-C-Cloud..."

The nurse could not understand what he meant, but the compelling way he uttered the two words broke her composure. Tears ran slowly down her face as she looked at the waiting surgical team shaking her head!

The circle of light beneath the powerful lamps hanging overhead illuminated Mark's bloody and mutilated body so that the surgeons could accurately assess his true condition. There was a sense of urgency; yet, there was an air of calm competence that filled the room with hope. They were witnesses to unprecedented violations of the young bodies that came before them. The cleanliness of the surroundings in the white operating room was in stark contrast to Mark's blood-stained uniform that dropped to the floor as they hastily cut it away. This initial medical station frequently determined the wounded man's chances for life or death. It could also determine the patient's quality of life, as he would know it, from this moment forth.

A thorough check of Mark's body indicated that he had a total of five bullet punctures in his upper body torso. One went through his left arm shattering the lower bone near the elbow. Two of the shells had gone through his body and exited with what appeared to be clean wounds. A fourth had penetrated to the right of the heart beneath the collarbone and the fifth bullet went straight through the chest cavity possibly breaking a rib bone and damaging a portion of his lungs.

The latter two shells had seriously threatened Mark's life. The spleen was completely destroyed by one of the cartridges. Internal bleeding was massive and he was balancing on the edge of death while the surgeons explored the full extent of the damage. The last wound that the surgeons had to deal with was made by the machine gun bullet that had partially nicked Mark's spinal column and severed several of the nerves that ran within the protective covering of the spine. The surgeons were able to splice some of them together, but only time would tell if the union was successful or not. They gravely hoped that they were not too late and that nerve function would eventually return. If not, then the use of Mark's legs, and possible other body functions, would be in doubt.

Eventually Mark's bleeding was arrested. He would not have survived the trip from the beach to the ship if it had not been for the life-sustaining value of the blood plasma administered by the corpsmen on the beach. Generous amounts of the new antibiotic drug, penicillin, had been administered along with heavy dosages of pain killers. Mark's destroyed spleen had been removed completely and the ragged puncture wounds to the lungs sutured. The final procedure on the spine was finished and the long incision finally closed.

While Mark's hospital bed was being wheeled out of the operating room the head surgeon remarked candidly, "This patient might make it, but he's got a rough road ahead of him. He's the oldest and highest ranking combatant we've had in a long time!" In an adjoining room a team of bone specialists set Mark's arm while he was still heavily sedated, and placed it in a preliminary cast. He was now in the hands of his Creator. All that mortal man could do, had already been done!

Mark was placed in a special recovery room designed to monitor his condition so that the nurses could give him the individual care demanded by the nature of his wounds. His body was wrapped like a mummy in a museum. His left arm was suspended in midair by a small rope that went over a pulley attached to a mast fixed at the head of his bed with a small weight hanging on the lower end of the rope. He was still unconscious and had remained that way ever since the machine gun bullets struck him. On the second day after the operation, Mark began to receive visitors from his command. One by one the concerned men filed past his bed, self-conscious of their disheveled condition in such sterile surroundings. They paid silent homage to their commander, who still remained unconscious. One of the men, a burley sergeant with his stripes barely visible under a heavy coating of grime and dust, lingered apprehensively at Mark's side and stood silent for a while. When he finally spoke, it was from the heart, "I'm sorry, Sir. I hope you make it..." Silence filled the room as the sergeant studied the ashen pallor on Mark's face. The young sergeant continued in a sober tone: "I wanted to thank you for all the help you've been to me and the guys. The nurse told us that they don't know if you're able to understand what we say, so in case you can hear, we all wanted you to know how much we appreciated all the times you went to bat for us. I ain't much at words, but it's important that you know we're rooting for you. Semper Fi, Sir."

As soon as Mark's old regiment came off the battle line for rest, the men started to come to the hospital ship in a steady stream. Most of the visitors were enlisted men with a sprinkling of officers. They all had a common purpose - to give respect and thanks to the one man that had been the most responsible for molding them into who they were. Mark had a very unique and personal way of leading his men. Respect and concern for the men was a way of life for him and the men reciprocated in kind. He was a "by-the-book" commander who tempered it with common sense and compassion. Whenever Division, or other headquarters, was out of line in placing impossible demands on his men, he was the first to cry "foul" and protest against any unjust treatment. Loyalty always flowed from the top down.

Perhaps Mark's greatest strength was his strong sense of duty and an honest admiration for the accomplishments of his men. He never strutted like many officers who do it to show their importance and to impress the men. He simply never commanded like most other officers. Instead, he asked in his normal quiet way for this and that whenever a job needed to be taken care of, and it was done skillfully and without hesitation. The men would have gladly done anything he told them to do, and most of all, they appreciated the way he asked them instead of demanding that it be done. His most pleasing attribute was the ability to recognize and reward good work. His calm demeanor earned the respect of most men, but the latter trait of rewarding effort endeared him to the men in his command forever.

Several days after the operation, a small group of marines stood in awkward silence around Mark's bed. They all had worried looks on their drawn young faces. They had grown old beyond their years. A corporal, young in age, but old in what his eyes had seen, noticed a star on the collar of the man standing next to him and he called to the men, "attention, officer on deck."

The general that had silently joined the group told the men to stand easy and continue as they were. "I've just come to see an old friend of mine, too. I know what he means to all of you men. I also know the kind of an officer that he's been. I'm luckier than most of you, because I've been able to call him a friend for many years. He's a very special human being, and we all pray that he'll come out of this okay. If we lose Colonel Leroux and other good men like him in the process of beating the enemy, what have we really gained in the long run, except a very high price for victory?" General Arlo Korsman paused and looked at the men in the room. "I didn't intend to intrude, marines, please excuse me. Continue as you were." With those few words he turned to leave the room and went to the nurse's station.

"Nurse," the general asked of the Navy captain on duty. "Could you tell me any more about Colonel Leroux's condition, and who was the doctor that operated on him?"

"The head surgeon was Commander Henning and the normal surgery room team, Sir. His prospects are not known for sure. He was hit pretty bad, as you already know. His arm is shattered and movement in his legs is uncertain. He still has a massive amount of infections that have been difficult to control, and his lungs keep filling with fluid. Until he regains consciousness, we're uncertain about his legs, and what his chances are." The nurse was searching for something on her desk. She found the slip of paper and continued: "Colonel Leroux hasn't been conscious since he was wounded, yet every once in a while he'll say something that seems so strange. It sounds like he was saying a bright cloud. When he does say it, he seems to be very emotional."

"I can tell you what the words mean. Bright Cloud is the name of his wife. She's a Canadian Cree Indian, and a graduate nurse. I've known both of them for a number of years. Theirs is a story-book-love that would make your heart sing. His wife, Bright Cloud, is one of the loveliest persons I've ever known and they're devoted to each other. The only positive thing that will come of this whole ordeal, if he survives, is that he won't have to go into combat again. We pray for that."

"Of course we do, Sir." The nurse interrupted his moment of reflection. "I'm glad to hear about his wife. It may help us in his recovery. I don't believe that the Doctors can help you with any more information than I've already given you, General."

"Thank you. Would you please notify my headquarters if there's any significant change in his condition?"

"Yes Sir, it would be my pleasure."

"Thank you again, Captain." General Korsman, the doughty Finn with the solid build and the penetrating blue eyes, left the hospital ship as if he was carrying a heavy burden, and returned to his temporary headquarters ashore. He was bone-weary and wanted to sleep for a week. Even though the battle raged on the island with increased fury, he felt compelled to write Bright Cloud while the visit to the hospital ship was fresh in his mind. He retired to his walled tent near the water's edge and started a letter that he dreaded to write. He turned on a lantern above his field desk and laboriously started…

United States Marine Corps

Somewhere in the Pacific

March 9, 1944

Dear Bright Cloud,

I don't know of any other way to tell you except straight out. Mark has been seriously wounded in combat and I know that you will not hear from him for some time. Consequently, I am the messenger of bad news for you and your family. It goes without saying that he is getting the best medical attention that is in our power to give a wounded man.

So far, I don't know yet, what all of his injuries are, but you should be prepared, when that time comes to be strong. He was struck with a full blast from a Japanese machine gun while leading some of the men from his regiment. One company in the regiment was in the first wave to get ashore and had lost most of its officers in the first few minutes of the assault. The men were badly demoralized and confused while still on the beach. It might have been a greater disaster than it already was, if Mark had not come among the men at that time. He set a course of action that rallied them, leading

9

them off the bloody beachhead. They were magnificent, Bright Cloud, I've never seen anything like it in my career. With that calm positive way he always had with his men, they followed him through murderous fire from the pillboxes in front of them up to the more sheltered coastal plain and overran several enemy strong points which was the beginning of our breaking their heaviest line of defense on the shoreline. When the men saw Mark fall, they angrily threw caution to the wind and plunged forward to obtain their objectives.

I can honestly tell you that the men did not accomplish what they did for any of the reasons most people would like to think about, such as for the flag, or for the Marine Corps. No way, they did it for Mark, who had worked with them for months. I'm so proud of the regiment's performance! There is something very special about the way your husband turned a decimated unit into a dynamic force with just a few words and his presence. It was an achievement of the human spirit. You have every reason to be proud of his actions. I know that I am.

I've made a career of serving my country in the Marine Corps, and I've met many courageous men who have earned my admiration. None have inspired me to any greater respect than your husband, Colonel Mark Leroux. It has been my privilege to not only be his commanding officer, but to also be his friend.

I can only imagine what this letter is doing to you, Bright Cloud. I've been praying for Mark and I want you to know that you are not alone, even though thousands of miles separate us. Rest assured that I will notify you immediately of any change in Mark's condition.

I'll always cherish the memories of many pleasant days with you and your beautiful family. Let us pray together that God will be kind to us and that we can all be the way it was before the war started.

Be strong, Bright Cloud.

An old friend, Arlo Korsman,

Brigadier General, USMC

By the time Arlo had finished the letter to Bright Cloud, his exhausted body cried out for relief, so he stretched out on the small cot his aide had set up for him. It wasn't just the lack of sleep that was making him tired; it was the daily worry and responsibility for the hundreds of lives that he was losing on an insignificant speck of land in the middle of the Pacific Ocean. Blessed sleep came at last and released him from the unthinkable things that had increasingly made his nights such a difficult time to endure. The battle noises were not as intense at night, for even the enemy had to sleep sometime. Early in the morning, Arlo was awakened by a bomb blast from a Japanese plane that usually dropped a few bombs to keep the Americans from sleeping. He was not surprised; it seemed to happen every night. Getting back to sleep was hard to do. He had traditionally done some of his best thinking and planning on such dark, sleepless nights. Sometimes it could be a welcome release from the reality of the moment.

The image that instantly came to Arlo's mind was that of Mark Leroux as he had known him during the First World War. It was only natural to place his wife, Bright Cloud, at his side because they were such a remarkable twosome! He could vividly remember the first time he saw Bright Cloud. Even after all the years it still brought a smile to his face. Mark had written to him that he had married the most beautiful woman in the world. Arlo was happy for his friend.

* * *

Mark had arranged to meet with Arlo in Washington, D.C. for the ceremony and burial of the Unknown Soldier in the Arlington National Cemetery on November 11, 1921. Arlo was stationed, at that time, at the large Marine Corps Base in Quantico, south of the city a few miles. Arlo remembered that day as if it was yesterday. It had provided him with one of the most moving experiences of his life. The American tribute to the unknown soldiers, killed in France during the

11

First War had special meaning to Mark and his new wife, Bright Cloud. Her brother was one of them.

Mark had served with distinction as a company commander of an Army regiment in France during the War. One of his platoon leaders had been a young Canadian Cree Indian with a lieutenant's commission in the U.S. Army. His name was Lieutenant Joseph "Flying Eagle" Mann, a Reserve Officer Training Corps graduate of the University of New York at Syracuse. The two men soon became very close friends. Once, Mark led a patrol into "no-man's land" and became surrounded by the Germans as he was trying to return to his own lines. Flying Eagle recognized that his company commander was in trouble, so he launched himself over the top to help break up the German intrusion and bring Mark to the safety of the Allie's trench line. It had been a close call for both of them. Flying Eagle was seriously wounded in the leg by a German bayonet during the violent encounter, and had passed it off as insignificant. That next morning at dawn, the Germans started to shell their positions with gas cartridges. Mark had quickly put on his gas mask in time to avoid the deadly mustard gas. Some of the soldiers ran wildly from the lethal gas cloud, blinded and gasping for breath while their faces turned a bright purple. Their final seconds of life were filled with grotesque agony. Flying Eagle was one of the unlucky ones. He was too late with his life-saving mask and succumbed to the wispy yellow-green fumes. A few seconds later, Flying Eagle, desperately trying to breathe, was at the center of a direct hit from a large caliber artillery shell. He was instantly obliterated. Mark observed his friend's body evaporate into small particles and could not understand or accept the circumstance of such a courageous man's ignoble death. Mark, consumed with anger and agony, passed out from the trauma of such a personal tragedy.

Whatever was left of Flying Eagle was collected and buried in a common grave with several other unidentifiable soldiers. Mark's last job as a marine after the war had been to bring a Distinguished Service Cross to Flying Eagle's family in the Canadian northern wilderness as a token of appreciation for his sacrifice. Mark met Bright Cloud at this presentation, and eventually married her after a stormy courtship.

Arlo was as surprised as Mark to learn that Flying Eagle's wife had died giving birth to a baby girl while he was overseas in France. Bright Cloud took over the responsibility for the small child. She and Mark adopted her when they married at her ancestral tribal village in Canada. When Arlo first saw the little girl she was about four or five years old. He had made reservations in advance for them at a hotel in Washington as soon as he learned of their proposed trip to the city. Since he had just recently purchased a brand new automobile, he was more than anxious to show it off to an old friend and his family. He had picked them up at the train station.

Mark recognized Arlo in his forest green uniform, standing on the station platform surveying the passengers getting off the train. Arlo could still picture Mark stepping down from the train with a little girl in his arms and a strikingly attractive lady in tow. Mark met Arlo halfway across the platform flushed with excitement and anticipation.

"Arlo, it's good to see you. It's been a long time, hasn't it?" The two friends shook hands with unreserved smiles on their lips.

"Time has been good to you, Mark. You look trim and in great shape." Bright Cloud had not said a word.

"I've been writing to you about a miracle that came into my life, and here she is, my wife, Bright Cloud." Mark was a short, slender young man with a friendly smile and a confident air. He set the little girl down on the platform, but kept her in check by holding her hand. "Honey, I'm proud to have you finally meet the best friend a fellow could ever ask for, Major Arlo Korsman."

Arlo was impressed. The lady before him was beautiful. She wore a rose colored dress with a white lace collar around her neck and a small tight fitting white hat with a partial veil that almost touched her nose. Arlo could still remember that her eyes, beneath the veil, were a luminous deep brown. "Forgive me if I stare, Bright Cloud, but I was not prepared for such a lovely lady. Mark had written about you, but your presence exceeds my expectations. Congratulations, the happiness that you and Mark share is becoming to both of you."

Bright Cloud was excited about the meeting. She looked into his eyes and said with sincerity, "Mark has talked a lot about you, so I feel as if I already know you. A friend of Mark's is my friend also. It's nice that you can meet us like this." She firmly grasped Arlo's hand.

"I can see why my friend chose you for his wife." Arlo's first and most lasting impression of Bright Cloud was her gracious naturalness. He also remembered her voice. Words, which she took the time to enunciate carefully, seemed to flow effortlessly from her mouth. She smiled easily, especially when she glanced at Mark. They were a delightful couple, and Arlo envied what they shared together.

"I told you I was a lucky man!" Mark smiled with a twinkle in his eye. "We must not forget another important member of our family. This little lady is called Bright Star. We call her Star for short, and sometimes we call her by her English name of Dawn. Do you want to say 'hello' to daddy's friend?"

Little Bright Star clung desperately to Mark's leg not knowing exactly what to make of the tall man in uniform. Arlo kneeled down to her level and held out his hand to her. "I'm proud to meet you, little lady. If I'm a friend to your dad here, then you and I can be friends, too. Is that okay with you?"

Star reluctantly took Arlo's hand and studied his face for a moment. She was sizing him up to be sure that he was acceptable to her. She had eyes like Bright Cloud. Her ancestry was obvious. Bright Cloud had braided her black hair in two long strands and tied a red ribbon to the end of each. Her small round face looked innocently at Arlo and finally said, "Hello." She was adorable!

Bright Cloud was quick to clear up some hesitation that she saw on Arlo's part. "You should know, Arlo, that Mark and I have adopted little Bright Star. We're her parents in every way except in conception and birth. We've never wanted or tried to hide that from her. As a matter of fact, we encourage her to be as proud of her ancestral heritage as I am. She has the blood of Cree chiefs running through her veins, and she should hold her head high with dignity. I've always cared for and loved her as if she was my own flesh and blood." Bright Cloud glanced sideways at her husband beside her and clasped his hand. "God bless my gentle Mark, he's been wonderful. He has loved and accepted her from the very beginning. You can see who she clings to for protection."

14

"Being the family that we are, I'm called Daddy or Dad. Flying Eagle is called 'Papa'. Bright Cloud is called Mother, and Star's maternal mother is called 'Mother Minnie'. We hope that by honestly facing this situation we can avoid some awkwardness when we talk about each other, and I hope that we've set a good tone of respect for everybody involved," Mark declared matter-of-factly.

"I'd say that you've done the right thing. I admire your honest approach. Star has every right to be proud of her legacy," answered Arlo, impressed with such a forthright attitude. But then, he thought to himself, it's what he would've imagined from Mark. Now that he had met Bright Cloud, it's also what he would expect from this remarkable lady from the North Woods.

"I see the bags are piled on the luggage cart. Why don't we pick up yours, and we can get you settled into the hotel where I've made reservations for you. The Capital City is already filled with visitors anxious to participate in tomorrow's services. I'm staying at the Marine Barracks, just a short distance away."

"Sounds good to me, Arlo," said Mark, selecting two of the bags, and handed Star off to Bright Cloud. "You can be on point and we'll follow." The two men chuckled with each other.

"Now I can tell you that I have a surprise. I just purchased a brand new auto car last week. It's a Hudson Super Six, four passenger coupe. It's an extravagance that I indulged myself with. My first one. This will be the first time I've had four people in it, too." In his enthusiasm to show the car, Arlo set a rapid pace to the parking lot that actually made Star run to keep up. She giggled excitedly with Bright Cloud as they made their way through the crowded train station.

The shiny green paint on the automobile was spotless, like Arlo's uniform. "Wow, Arlo, this is a beautiful one. I'm glad you got it. You work hard and deserve some rewards in this life." Mark walked slowly around it, nodding his head in approval.

"You and Bright Cloud can ride in the back seat. Bright Star can sit up front beside me. I'll be the chauffeur for your visit to our fair city. Do you want to sit up here with me, Star?"

15

Star nodded her head in agreement and said "Yes, Sir." Her eyes shone brightly at the prospect of being in the big shiny car. She was comfortable with Arlo's inherent kindness.

"I love the smell of a new car," said Mark, settling into the back seat beside Bright Cloud. "We've been using Aunt Maddie's old Nash. She doesn't want to drive anymore, so we purchased it from her with the understanding that we would drive her whenever she wants to get out, which isn't very often."

"I'll always remember your Aunt Maddie's hospitality. She's a grand lady. Give my regards to her when you return."

"She remembers you as a young man with a large appetite," Bright Cloud laughed from the back seat.

"I plead guilty. That lady could charm anyone with her cooking. I know that she liked to have people eat heartily at her table and I just tried to show my appreciation!"

Arlo proudly maneuvered his new car to the entrance of the busy hotel where Mark and his family were going to stay. The lobby was crowded with people from all walks of life. There was excitement and anticipation in the air about the ceremony the next day. They stopped before the large reception desk to register. Mark set the suitcases on the floor and looked around for a clerk to wait on them. Arlo was standing a short distance to his right along the counter, and announced himself to a passing clerk. He said that he had made reservations several weeks ago. The clerk looked over a register before him and caught the attention of Arlo with a quick nod of his head to meet him further down the counter. Once out of hearing distance from Mark and Bright Cloud, the clerk announced to him what was wrong.

"Major, it seems that there is some terrible mistake with your reservation. When I took the reservation from you, I was not aware that the party would include an Indian woman and an Indian child. It's highly unusual to accept them; we have other guests to consider..."

Arlo could not believe he was hearing what the clerk said. His immediate reaction was one of quiet resolve. He quickly answered the very properly dressed clerk with a calm measured response. "Let me make myself crystal clear, so that you don't misunderstand and end

16

up getting hurt. It's not my intention or desire to cause a scene in a crowded hotel lobby, but if you don't go over there to that family and graciously welcome them to your hotel, I'm prepared to break every bone in your body for insulting me and my friends. Unless you want to be looking through your belly button, I better hear an apology real quick! Do you understand?"

The look in Arlo's eyes told the clerk he meant what he said. The broad shoulders and solid arms testified to Arlo's ability to carry out his threat. So, the meticulously attired clerk swallowed hard and muttered a reply, "Maybe I can make an exception..."

"That's more like it. The best suite in the house, too, or we meet again, friend."

Arlo's smile frightened the clerk more than his words. It conveyed a message of deadliness that could not be avoided. The clerk briskly walked down the counter to Mark and Bright Cloud, and with a newly discovered air of hospitality, announced: "The suite reserved for you is one of our best with a panoramic view of the Potomac River; you should be very comfortable."

After getting settled into the hotel, Arlo suggested that they go to dinner at the Army and Navy Club, where they could have a quiet meal in pleasant surroundings before taking a tour of the capital city after dark.

"This is a beautiful city at any time, but it really glows and shows its special qualities at night under lights." Arlo told them.

The hour at the Army and Navy Club was particularly relaxing to Mark and Bright Cloud, after spending much of the previous night and day on the train. Little Bright Star found it restful enough to fall asleep while stretched out on the luxurious bench seat of their dining table. Arlo was enjoying the company of his old friend and his new wife. They were his kind of people!

Bright Cloud spoke about the significance of the day ahead of them. "The Memorial for the Unknown Soldier has special meaning for us. It was you who first brought it to our attention in a letter to Mark at my village while he was in Canada. I remember that day very well. I carried the letter to Mark, who was at the center cabin doing his forestry work for the tribal council. It turned out to be special in more ways than one." Bright Cloud smiled at Mark. "I read the letter

17

that you sent. It was reassuring to know that Mark had a friend who was interested in such things. I also called you my friend from that day. You're much like I expected and hoped you would be. I knew that you had to be a good man or you would never have earned the friendship of my Mark."

"How can you top support like that?" grinned Mark, touching Bright Cloud's arm at the end of the bench. Little Star was stretched out between them with her head on Mark's lap.

"I think it's wonderful, and I'm really happy for you both. I've been busy going to school at the Army War College. I suppose I've dedicated myself to the Marine Corps more than I would if I had a family to look after." Arlo hesitated for a moment, avoiding his guests' eyes. "I thought I'd like a family of my own. There was a special girl before the war who fascinated me and dominated my thoughts. We were supposed to be married when I came home, but it didn't work out."

"I'm sorry Arlo, I never knew," said Mark, listening carefully to his friend's candid admission.

"I didn't mean to bore you with my problems. I don't know why I did. I haven't thought of it for a long time," confessed Arlo. "Now, that's enough of the past. We have a pleasant evening ahead of us."

"Hurts of the heart are the most painful to bear, and the most difficult to hide," admitted Bright Cloud. "If you two will excuse me for a bit, I'll visit the ladies room before we leave." She gently placed Bright Star, who was still sound asleep, on the seat.

"I wanted to ask you about the problem you had with the hotel clerk. Was it about Bright Cloud?" asked Mark, now that she had left the table.

"Yes, it was, but he came around to my way of thinking, so it turned out okay. You should not take it too much to heart; this is, after all, still just a southern town with all of the built-in prejudices that go along with it," explained Arlo.

"Thanks, Arlo, I appreciate your support. It's hard to imagine anyone being prejudiced against Bright Cloud."

"Mark, you've chosen well."

"You know, Arlo, seeing you in uniform again brings back memories. I still miss it at times."

18

"I wanted to talk to you about that, Mark. I had a feeling that you might have some second thoughts. There's a board currently discussing the possible organization of a Marine Corps Reserve that would be established under the supervision of the Commandant, and be subject to the same rules and regulations as the Army Reserve. This way the Marines would have a trained cadre of troops available if needed, without the large cost of having to maintain them on a daily basis. Maybe this kind of part-time marine thing would appeal to you. Think it over. I'll find out more about it and drop you a line with the latest scoop."

"Well, something like that could be interesting. Yes, let me know what the status of the program is. It's strange that you should mention this now, because I've been approached by the Army Reserve unit in Portsmouth to see if I was interested in signing up with them. I'd prefer to keep my Marine Corps commission if I decided to make a commitment to do something like that." Mark's enthusiasm was not lost on Arlo.

The possibility of duty on a part-time basis appealed to Mark. His last year in the military had given him some strong feelings of inadequacy, and he wondered if that would have any lingering affect on his ability to contribute to the effectiveness of whatever unit he might be assigned.

Arlo had an answer for that situation. "It may be that the best thing you could do is to go back in and work these feelings out to your own satisfaction. If you need a recommendation, I'd be glad to provide one for you, but your record stands on its own merits, Mark."

"I appreciate the offer, Arlo. I started doing better before I left France, but it was really Bright Cloud and the wonderful people of her village that helped me the most. They did it by giving me a purpose in life and having faith in my ability to achieve what I started out to do. They made me feel needed. It was important to me then."

"I'm sure they all contributed to your sense of well-being, but the strength and discipline to use that situation to your own advantage originated with you in the first place. Those same traits of character and industry are what will always make you a good officer, Mark. Many veterans who were burdened beyond their ability to cope with the situation ended up as alcoholics with a restlessness that remained with them for the rest of their lives. Some even went so far as suicide to end their pain. I would say that your accomplishments in rising above such infirmity are a tribute to your own strengths, as well as the help of your lovely wife."

"You speak of angels and you hear the flutter of their wings," exclaimed Mark, smiling at Bright Cloud's return to the table.

Shortly, they ventured into the crisp night air for the anticipated tour of the Capital City of Washington, D.C. Arlo was fantastic as a tour guide. He had served in the city for the past year. The casket with the body of the Unknown Soldier was on display in the Rotunda of the White House. They had planned to go through the reviewing line but changed their minds after seeing such a large crowd waiting in the rain. Bright Star was wide-eyed at all the sights around her. Arlo slowly drove them past the White House and the Capitol building, both ablaze with lights. Their majestic beauty filled them with pride. The Lincoln Memorial, which had the power to reach out and touch everyone who visited its marble simplicity, worked its magic on the visitors. It was as if they had just walked into a great cathedral and felt the presence of God. The newness and the majesty of the evening's sights captivated all of them. However, as unforgettable as that night was, it was the next day that was destined to become indelibly etched forever in all of their hearts.

* * *

Awakening a second time that evening, Arlo knew that light of day was near at hand. The sound of gunfire increased; small arms fire filled in between the larger detonations of the naval rifles. His first thought while getting up from the cot after another restless night, was not the responsibility ahead of him, but the hope that this would not be the day he would have to write that final letter to Bright Cloud.

Chapter Two

Bright Cloud was a tall slender middle-aged woman with long black hair and copper complexion, reflecting her Cree heritage. She was beautiful by any standard applied to her. She sat on the rocky Maine coast watching the churning waves throw themselves upon the jagged rocks in their relentless assault upon the shore, only to be repulsed and fragmented into smaller segments, returning to the restless swells reappearing again in rhythmic fury. Today the sea was especially restless and forbidding. She could not free herself of the frightening thought that something terrible had happened to her beloved Mark. She tried to not let the darkness of despair rule her life. It would be easy to let her imagination run wild with unbearable thoughts. Her faith in the future was based on a deeply held belief that her prayers for his safekeeping would be answered. Prayer usually brought peace to her troubled soul. The worst part was wondering and never knowing for sure what was taking place on the other side of the world where Mark was fulfilling his duty.

She asked nothing for herself except the opportunity to share the rest of her life with him. She was not complete without him. The ominous feeling churning inside of her, and the realistic potential for tragedy that was a constant companion in her life was especially troubling today. She intuitively felt that something had gone astray...

One thing that gave Bright Cloud comfort during the long lonely vigil, was her ability to escape to a time and place that was more reassuring, never failing to fill her heart with joy. Many years ago, in the Canadian northlands of her people, the Crees, Bright Cloud had found contentment and satisfaction with a life she had made for herself before she met her husband,

Mark. She had worked hard to become a nurse and was rewarded with the thanks and appreciation of her people, and others of the northlands who sought her healing touch. Her life changed abruptly when a young American officer came to her native village and presented a medal to her family that had been earned by her brother, Flying Eagle, on the distant killing fields of France during the First World War. Flying Eagle had served with Mark as a young Army officer. She fell instantly and completely in love with Mark, and the orderliness of her life at the infirmary as she had always known it until that time, was shattered.

The helplessness and frustration of being unable to do anything about her misgivings, now that Mark was overseas, reminded Bright Cloud of the time when she and Mark confronted Flying Eagle's twin brother, Red Fox, one cold winter day. He had kidnapped a nurse from her infirmary at the tribal village and fled northward with his captive. Mark and Bright Cloud had doggedly pursued Red Fox and his band of thieves in a raging snowstorm and were forced into a difficult situation when she had to make a choice between the two men. Without hesitation Bright Cloud made the choice to save Mark from her own blood brother by firing her rifle three times to stop the appalling vision of Mark about to be struck down by a raised ax in Red Fox's powerful hand. She reacted to the magnitude of her act by fleeing the scene as fast as she could, only to be unexpectedly shot by a companion of her deranged brother. Mark, thinking she was dead, had been so distraught by his own failure to protect her that he heeded the angry and threatening warning of Bright Cloud's father, Running Deer, to leave the village. Bright Cloud awoke from the coma caused by the wound shortly after Mark had left the tragic forest scene. When she was told that he had gone back to his homeland on the coast of Maine, she was plunged into a deep abyss of despair. She felt lost and alone and withdrew to a private purgatory of her own creation.

The emptiness that she felt today sitting on the cliffs near their home, was similar to what she had experienced after the tragedy of killing her brother, Red Fox. For days afterward

Bright Cloud lived in such a tortured state of despair and hopelessness that she privately feared for her own sanity. She was responsible for the death of Flying Eagle's twin brother, and at the same time, had lost the one person who had touched her heart. The irony of the situation was devastating to Bright Cloud's fragile emotional state. Before she met Mark, no man had ever earned the respect and love she willingly gave to him. She had believed in their dreams for the future, and they were cruelly wrenched from her when she needed them the most. At times she questioned her faith in God.

Bright Cloud recalled that earlier time of her life to be the most painful period she had ever experienced. The bleak winter of suffocating snow had enveloped the land, and she saw the homeland she had always loved, as a prison through her dejected frame of mind. The dynamic forest had been laid bare to show its simple severity, its haunting beauty, its infinite sadness, and its unlimited strength. For the first time in her life she had seen the forest as Mark saw it and respected its capacity to be many things to many people. Today, on the shore of the turbulent Atlantic Ocean, Bright Cloud thought that the sea was a lot like her native forestland. She looked into the angry greenish-blue waters with an overwhelming sense of sadness and apprehension for the future. The pounding surf seemed to be telling her something she really did not want to know...

Letters from Mark came periodically in uneven batches because of his location in the Pacific. He wrote daily whenever possible, and the letters were an opportunity for a celebration within her heart. They represented the high point of her days. The letter she received yesterday was full of love for her, as usual, but between the lines she had the feeling that he was trying to prepare her for something that he could not or did not want to write about. Her stomach tightened into painful spasms every time she read the letter. What he did not write filled her with anxiety. She knew he was keeping something from her. He did, however, tell her that the regiment he was commanding was scheduled to go back into combat again soon. Probably by the time she received the letter, it would be over. The fact that she did not receive a notice from any War Department office was at least encouraging, she thought.

Bright Cloud had worried less about Mark after his promotion to full colonel and subsequent command of the regiment, because he should be in less exposed places behind the front lines. She shuddered at such a thought and immediately felt guilty, because someone's loved one had to go in harm's way if the war was to be won. She honestly believed that Mark had spent enough time in combat under fire. She lived each day torn between extremes of hope overcoming a chronic panic, and of acts of faith that allowed her to rise above doubts and depression.

* * *

It had been that same way with Bright Cloud twenty-three years ago, when she was numb with fear that Mark had left Canada and herself forever. Bright Cloud's father, Running Deer, felt responsible for her emotional depression and withdrawal into a world of her own making. He had lived long enough to see the tragedy of two of his children violently taken away from him, and now he was terrified at the prospect of losing his beloved daughter, who was a source of great joy and pride, not only to him but to the entire village. He realized his error in sending the young American away from the village. Afterwards, when he had taken the time to think rationally about the situation, he knew in his heart that Mark had displayed courage and wisdom. Even though Bright Cloud had been forced to make a difficult choice when she killed Red Fox, Running Deer also knew that he could not have done any better if faced with the same decision himself. Now, by sending Mark away, he had wounded Bright Cloud possibly beyond her capacity to recover, and he was destitute to find a solution to the monstrous situation he helped create. His foolish pride had caused enough hurt, and he was anxiously looking for some way to make amends for his impulsive behavior.

Bright Cloud did not realize it, but her father had spent as many sleepless nights as she did, worrying over her depressed condition. She found out later that he had talked about many of these things to their dear friend, Inspector Clough. Between those two men and the saintly village priest, Father Dumont, a plan was developed and anxiously presented to her. She could still feel the thrill that flowed through her body on that memorable day. Her father wanted to know if she would like to go with him to Mark's home in Maine. An apology was owed to Mark. Running Deer said that he had an obligation to apologize in person. The Inspector said that he would be glad to arrange the trip and accompany them. No trio ever anticipated a trip with as much happiness and hope for the future as Bright Cloud and her two escorts.

She did not know, at the time, that the Inspector intentionally went along with them because he was concerned about Bright Cloud's mental state. He was worried about the long-term effect of her responsibility for Red Fox's death, as well as her anxiety about Mark. Even though it was done to save Mark from a savage death blow, it would have been a bitter lesson for any person to have to live with.

The formidable Inspector Gerard Clough, Bright Cloud affectionately recalled, had been a staunch friend for many years. He never failed to be a champion for her requirements at the infirmary. She looked to him for support in many ways, and she could not recall a single instance when she was disappointed with his response. She never spoke to anyone about it, but her women's intuition whispered to her inner self that the Inspector was probably in love with her. They were about twenty years apart in age which she expected was the reason that he never declared himself. His relationship with her was always respectful and circumspect, and he never stepped beyond that threshold of familiarity. Bright Cloud's feelings for Inspector Clough had always been that of a trusted friend, and he returned that trust with the same sense of fairness and integrity he was respected for throughout the North Woods.

The infirmary was the local terminus of the North Country's "bush telegraph", and Bright Cloud was frequently told about things that happened in the forest long before the police or the tribal council members had the same knowledge. Large numbers of patients sought help and treatment for a variety of medical problems. The Inspector was acutely aware of the phenomenon, and to his credit, never asked her to compromise or betray the trust that the patients placed in her. She had that special gift of making each patient feel at ease and comfortable in her care. The message of dispensing care to all who needed help was freely circulated throughout the wilderness. The Inspector respected the air of informality that existed at the infirmary and saw to it that the other police officers did nothing to upset it. Sometimes, when certain information was crucial for a person's welfare, Bright Cloud would let him know about it. However, she always received prior approval from the source of the information before she related it to the authorities. It was an understanding that worked well and benefited all who were concerned.

Bright Cloud always felt that Inspector Clough was as much concerned for her safety as for her happiness, and that made her feel special, but she never had the same feelings for him that she shared with Mark. Nothing compared to the total commitment that she gave to Mark. It made her feel happier than she had ever been in her life, and the Inspector seemed to be genuinely content about the situation.

One example of the policeman's approval was manifested in the efficient way that he made preparations for the trip out of Lac Diamante for Quebec City, where they stayed overnight at the prestigious Chateau Frontenac. It was a little bit extravagant on their budget, but the Inspector rationalized that it would be a memorable experience for both Bright Cloud and Running Deer. The plane ride had been a thrilling undertaking that was also frightening at times for the two and remembered for the rest of their lives. Running Deer was a short, wiry man filled with energy and spirit for his age. He was particularly amazed by the limitless expanse of forest and lakes that stretched out to the horizon as far as the eye could see. The crystal clear sparkle of the lakes and streams glistened in the afternoon sun as they broke up the pattern of dark green forest that seemed to go on forever. The immensity of the forest could not fail to make any person feel insignificant. Bright Cloud was so anxious to see Mark again that she didn't remember much about the trip. She was still living within her own private world, but the closer they got to the Maine coast, the more she seemed to break out of her protective shell of silence. The train came to a stop at a station with the large wooden sign announcing their arrival at Wells, Maine.

So many doubts and fears raced through her mind that she was on the verge of being physically sick when the taxicab turned into a driveway and stopped beside a large white house. Instinctively, Bright Cloud knew that it had to be the house of Mark's Aunt Maddie. She haltingly looked around to see if she could catch a glimpse of Mark before she showed herself. He was nowhere to be seen. Her heart beat wildly out of control as she recognized what had to be the house of Mark's father located across a small field from his Aunt's home. She noticed an elderly white-haired lady burst excitedly through the front door to greet them.

"I hope you didn't have any trouble finding the house," Aunt Maddie exclaimed, approaching the taxi.

"No trouble at all, madam. I'm Inspector Clough, the person who called you on the telephone. I appreciate the invitation that you have so graciously extended to us." The Inspector helped Running Deer from the automobile and continued, "This is my good friend Running Deer."

Aunt Maddie shook both of their hands with an approving nod of the head and a twinkle in her eyes. "Welcome to my home. I was so glad and relieved to receive your call. It was most welcome."

Bright Cloud reluctantly held back for a moment to brace herself, then accepted the Inspector's helping hand down from the taxicab. She straightened herself and looked directly at Aunt Maddie with an apprehensive smile.

"It goes without saying, this has to be Bright Cloud. My gracious," exclaimed Aunt Maddie, reaching out for Bright Cloud and embracing her enthusiastically. "I would have known you anywhere, young lady. Mark has done nothing but talk about you. Now that I see you, I can understand what he meant."

Bright Cloud could not help herself, the last few words from Mark's Aunt Maddie opened the relief valve she had kept closed for a long time. She cried from relief that her ugly thoughts would not come true. "I'm sorry to be so emotional..." Bright Cloud tried to explain, but the tears continued to flow from her large brown eyes. She clung to Aunt Maddie as if she had just been saved from drowning.

"Let them come, my dear. I would be the same way if I was in your shoes, but let those tears be tears of happiness, because you have won Mark's heart, and it would appear that he has won yours, also. Come, let's go inside the house. I have a lunch ready for you and have just put on a pot of coffee in case you would like some refreshment after such a long trip. I must confess, I knew you would be here at this time. The station master is an old friend of many years, and he called me when you left the station."

"Thank you for your generosity..." Running Deer was desperately searching for the right words, when Aunt Maddie came to his rescue.

"Everybody calls me Aunt Maddie. My real name is Madeline, but most of the children had such a hard time saying it when they were young, including Mark, that we all settled on Maddie. Through the years it just seemed to stick." She led the way into the house gently directing Bright Cloud with a motherly arm around the waist.

* * *

Bright Cloud absent-mindedly watched beyond the angry surf, and was woken from her reverie by the large waves striking at the rocks below her. She imagined that this must be the same spot where Mark watched the shore when she came that first time. Over the years, she thought, several events in her life stand out as truly momentous and unforgettable occasions. Her wedding day was at the top of the list she recalled with a tug at her heart, and the birth of their son, DJ (Daniel Joseph), was a joy that all of the years could never dim. She also had wonderful memories of Mark's promotions in the Marine Corps, but they all fade compared to the memory of the

28

happiness she treasured when she first found out that Mark shared the same feelings for her. Their love had been renewed and reaffirmed.

* * *

Aunt Maddie had not told Mark about the phone call from Inspector Clough, or about their anticipated trip to see him in Maine. Instead, she tried to encourage Mark to develop a better outlook for the future. She did not want to burden him with any new hopes until they were a definite reality. His heart had been torn from his chest when he first arrived from the North Woods after Bright Cloud's tragic wound. There had not been time to talk about everything with the Inspector when he called her, so she decided to not tell Mark anything, just in case something had gone wrong with their travel plans. A few days more would not unduly hurt him, she imagined. In the meantime, she joined the Inspector in the conspiracy to plan a most wonderful surprise remembered by all.

He thought that she was having a bridge party or Bright Cloud found out later that Mark had promised to make himself available on that day in case Aunt Maddie needed something done. Some other affair with her friends, because she had been cooking all day. Mark had no idea what was planned for him. He continued to believe that Bright Cloud had been killed by her brother's companion... The passing weeks had not eased his depression, and that was why his Aunt Maddie refused to let him know about everything planned for the day until they could became an answer to his prayers, instead of a distant hope. Mark never failed to be comforted by the endless display of energy and consistency of the vibrant surf.

He found Aunt Maddie anxiously looking for him as he walked up the path from the shore. She seemed to be unusually excited, but he thought nothing about it. Bright Cloud had regained her peace of mind by the time she had eaten a small lunch in Aunt Maddie's kitchen. It was hard not to be swayed by her gracious, loving ways. Everyone around the table agreed to a plan in which Mark would meet Running Deer and the

Inspector first, so that they could say what they traveled so far to say. Bright Cloud would be held back until last.

She could clearly recall every word spoken on that day, especially when Aunt Maddie told Mark that someone wanted to see him. Bright Cloud could see Mark's back as he spoke with the two men in the parlor. She had to use all of her iron discipline to not reach out and take him into her arms. When he did turn and look at her standing in the doorway, he stared in disbelief and cried out to her.

"Bright Cloud...I can't believe my eyes," Mark stammered with a gasp. He took her in his arms and held her next to his heart. "I thought I had lost you forever, dear God, if this is a dream, please don't wake me!"

"No, Mark," she answered as her lips eagerly sought his. "I'm real. Don't ever leave me again."

* * *

The memories could still send shivers through her body the same way they did on that exceptional day. They shared twenty-three years of happiness and not once had either of them raised their voice in anger at the other, or gone to bed at night with an unkind word that had not been apologized for. They did not agree on everything, but both respected the other's position, and they worked out their differences as quickly as possible in a spirit of cooperation. The magic of all the years together filled her heart with pride at the gift of love they shared. She could not imagine life without Mark!

Bright Cloud glanced at her watch and calculated that the mailman must have dropped off the mail by now. She was hoping for another letter from Mark, and DJ. The well-worn path from the coast climbed slightly uphill towards the house. She breathlessly ran the last few feet to the mailbox, knowing that there was something inside, because the rural carrier always left a small strip of cloth outside the mailbox door to let her know that mail was in the box. She opened the door in eager anticipation of good news from Mark. There were three letters inside the box. One was from Mark, one from their son DJ, and one from General Korsman. The last one gave her a chill, even before she opened it. Her trembling fingers selected Mark's letter to be opened and read first. She continued to walk up the driveway as far as the kitchen steps and sat on the large granite entrance to devour the words her husband wrote.

My Darling Bright Cloud,

It's been a while since I took pen in hand to write you. Things have been pretty busy for me and the regiment. We've been undergoing some rigorous training exercises, which is about all I can tell you.

You must know that you're always on my mind, no matter what's going on around me, and I sure wish that I could be with you. I have so many precious memories of us together, but I think the one that comes to my mind the most, sweetheart, is the time you, your father and Inspector Clough came to Maine that first time. The Red Fox ordeal was a difficult one for us both, especially for you, Darling. I know how much courage and determination it took for you to do what you did, and my respect for your strength of character is greater than ever. I thought you were out of my life for good until you showed up like an angel from heaven in Aunt Maddie's living room. I was on the brink of madness at that point. I was responsible for you and I had failed miserably to keep you safe. Then, God answered my prayers for another chance by bringing you back to me.

You've been the fulfillment of all my dreams and hopes, Sweetheart. I return to our own special Memory Lane time after time as a refuge when we are apart. In my mind I can escape from the present and find sustenance and hope in the thought that when our job is finally completed, I can come home to you. It's difficult here, especially the responsibility of having to write letters to the families about the death of their loved ones. I haven't figured out any way to tell a mother that her son is not coming home, and make it sound easy to accept. I worry about the families left behind. My letters to them must be a cruel experience. Consequently, I spend a lot of time making sure that the regiment is trained

31

properly, so that our casualties are held to an absolute minimum. We are here for now and we will do what has to be done to end the war, but my God, these boys are so young! I only hope that the country and our people are worthy of their sacrifice, and that they appreciate what is given up by these young men for our nation's safety and freedom. I admit, it weighs heavily on my mind every hour of the day.

I'm sorry if I sound morbid today. We just finished a burial ceremony for the latest round of casualties for the regiment. I leave a little bit of myself in every man's grave. I'm constantly reviewing my own performance to see what I might have done differently, and how I can improve anything to hopefully save some lives tomorrow. Maybe it's for the best that the American people don't know what takes place here in the combat zone, because it's impossible to describe what the men go through...

Just before I started this letter, I had a talk with a young rifleman in the second battalion. He reminded me a lot of DJ. I could tell that he was bothered by something, so I sat beside him to see how he was doing. It seems that he was afraid of combat, and he was even more afraid of that fact being known to his buddies. My Lord, we are all petrified in combat and I told him so. I hope I put some of his anxieties to rest. He was dumbfounded when I told him that everybody was afraid. I also told him that if one of his buddies tells him that he is not scared, then his buddy is either crazy or lying.

I don't like it when I go on and on about my problems, Sweetheart, so forgive me for a certain amount of self-pity. If something ever happens to me, I want you to know that my last thoughts on this earth will be for you and DJ, and our precious Star. Goodnight Sweetheart, I send my love to you by way of the stars and the moon.

All my love,

Mark

P.S. I received a letter from DJ today and it was good to hear from him. I pray we can clean this mess up before he has to get into it! I've also heard from Star the other day. I'm a lucky man to have such a fantastic family!

The letter from Mark reassured her some, but its overall tone left her unsettled and nervous just the same. Her Mark was going through hell, and more than anybody else in the world, she knew it from the letter in her hands. The letter from Arlo Korsman was one that she dreaded to open. She knew it had to contain some news that Mark could not tell her. Trembling fingers tore at the envelope. As she read the words in front of her, an empty sinking feeling flowed through her body like an electric shock. She felt detached from things around her. Mark's tragic situation was something she did not want to hear right now. She slowly devoured every word a second time, dropped it on the ground by the steps, as if it burned her hands, and ran aimlessly into the pine grove next to the house. Bright Cloud did not shed a tear, but a steady chant of high-pitched sounds flowed from her throat that would have made strong men tremble. At first it was a low moan increasing in pitch and frequency. Even she was amazed that it had come from her own lips. Her feeling of detachment was complete. She felt trapped, angry at those who put Mark in harm's way, and more than anything else, she was helpless to do anything about his injuries.

Sheer exhaustion finally stopped her flight, and silenced her unearthly screaming. She collapsed against the trunk of a pine tree and sank to the ground, oblivious to her surroundings. It was as if she also felt the same wounds that had injured Mark on a tiny island half a world away. Finally, the rage within her subsided and tears ran freely down her bronze cheeks until there were no more tears to shed. Hours later a cool breeze from the ocean sent cold shivers through her body. She slowly picked herself off the damp ground shaking dried pine needles from her dress and aimlessly walked back towards the house. Her pragmatic nature had taken control of her emotions by the time she reached the kitchen steps. There was one thing that she should be thankful for - no letter had come from the War Department. That simple revelation gave her some hope. If Mark had been killed, she would have been notified before this time.

Returning to the letters on the steps, she picked them off the ground before she entered the house to read them one more time at the kitchen table. DJ's letter raised another dark cloud over her weary head, and she wondered just how much a family has to give up for the war?

West Point, New York

March 20, 1944

Dear Mom,

You'll be surprised to receive a letter from me, whereas I usually just wait for the weekend to call on the phone. I had a strong desire to write and tell you that I will be finishing my training here at the Academy very shortly. You will be reading about it sooner or later, so I figured that I should let you in on the scuttlebutt that is making the rounds at the Academy. My class is being graduated and commissioned early because we're needed to fill replacement billets that are open. I know that both you and Dad hoped for the war to be over, and me safe with another year at school before I had a chance to enter combat. I must tell you in all honesty that I relish the opportunity to take my turn to do what I've been trained to do - fight for my country.

You are probably worried about all of this, Mom, but I've been given the finest military education in the world, and I will be proud to make my contribution to the war effort, just like Dad. Please don't worry about me, Mom... (I know that you do, but I have to ask anyway.)

I often think about Dad and his achievements. I admire him more than any other man I've ever known. I only hope that I can be half the soldier he has proven himself to be.

I believe that I'll have a short furlough before being shipped overseas or assigned to a new unit, so I'll let you know more about our situation when I have the information. Say "hi" to Star the next time she calls or you write to her. Tell her that her brat brother sends his love (ha-ha)!! When I call to tell you the exact time that I'm coming home, would you please make me a custard pie? I can taste it now...

All my love to you Mom,

DJ

P.S. I'll write Dad myself to keep him informed. Thanks, Mom, for being who you are and for being someone that I have always been so proud to call my mother. Love you.

The letter was typical of DJ. It only increased her worries about him; yet, at the same time, it made her proud of such a fine son. DJ didn't say anything about her, but Bright Cloud knew that a high school classmate of his had been corresponding regularly with him, and would probably be pleased to know that he might be home in a short time. Bright Cloud made a mental note to call the girl tomorrow.

Chapter Three

Brigadier General Arlo Korsman, exhausted from lack of sleep and the strain of worry, watched the small American flag slowly climb to the top of the makeshift pole and unfurl in the wind with a snap that brought a lump to his throat. At last, the marines could declare the island secured from the fanatical resistance of the Japanese Army. They would leave the blood-soiled island as soon as the Army came in to relieve them.

The marines had done their job. Everyone had said that it could not be taken, but Arlo's crack division had proven them wrong. His faith in their courage and abilities had never faltered. The costs had been higher than expected. The number of white Crosses and Stars of David grave markers at the Division cemetery on the island was a grim testament to the ferocity of the combat. His young warriors had wrenched a virtual fortress from the enemy and given the world a standard of valor that would live as long as mankind valued courage and dedication to duty. Arlo said a few words in his booming voice as he stood beneath the undulating flag.

"The world never thought we could do it, men, but we have achieved the impossible with courage and skill and a devotion to duty that are beyond my ability to describe. I'm proud to be your commanding officer. It's been an honor and a privilege to lead such a fine body of men during this perilous time. As long as the world admires courage and dedication to a cause, then your deeds of valor will be remembered by your children and by your children's children, and inspired by your indomitable will.

"We've won a great victory here; yet, the price has been alarmingly high. Some of you have paid more than others, and we will never forget those brave comrades who have gone from our ranks. What we accomplished here, and the ones that we leave behind are destined to be a part of our legacy for as long as we live. Freedom has never been free. As sad as the losses are to each and every one of us, the sacrifice of our brave dead should motivate us to hold our heads high with a promise to live the rest of our lives to be worthy of our fallen brothers.

"I want to remind you that we, the victors, should not forget that there are thousands of mothers in Japan that are weeping for their sons who will never come home. Be charitable to them. God bless all of you."

General Korsman was notified that the Army garrison troops were being off-loaded from the large transports anchored beyond the coral reefs that surrounded the island. As soon as they finished unloading, the marines would be able to utilize the same transports that would take them to an area where they could train for the next operation. They had earned that opportunity to replenish not only their lost and destroyed equipment, but their emotional sanity as well.

The hospital ship where Mark was being cared for was also preparing to move away from its anchorage position when Arlo made a final visit to say good-bye to his wounded men. Mark continued to be prominent in his thoughts. Two days before, Arlo was told by the doctors that Mark was slowly losing his battle to stay alive. His lungs continued to fill with fluid. The dangerously high fever no longer responded to medication. There had been too many bullet holes in his body, and the new antibiotic, penicillin, could not keep up with so many sources of infection. The hospital staff expected him to die within hours. There had not been any meaningful response from him since that first day. Mark was losing his biggest fight...

Arlo boarded the ship with a heavy heart. It was common knowledge throughout the Division that General Korsman had a tender side beneath the gruff exterior. He really did agonize for those who had been wounded or killed in action. As deep as the torment was for the rest of the men, he had always looked upon Mark as a younger brother, and concern for him was deeper, more profound, and personal. "I must be getting old," Arlo thought, climbing the steps to the ship, "these past weeks have been the longest of my life. I feel exhausted; yet there's no end in sight to the killing and maiming of our young men. I hope I can hold out long enough to see it all stop."

Arlo entered a ward full of wounded men and was surprised to feel an air of optimism in the room. Several men in wheelchairs had a crap game going at the far end of the ward. Arlo was bolstered by their defiance and courage in accepting whatever fate had in mind for them. They all knew that they were going home, and almost anything could be tolerated if it translated into that magic order, "being sent stateside". Midway down the row of beds, a young seaman sat upright in his cot and watched General Korsman approach with a look of hostility on his face.

"Good morning, sailor," Arlo greeted the man with respect. He always found it difficult to approach a wounded patient, because he did not want to sound superficial or intrusive. Most of all, he did not want to sound glib. "You Seabees have done a great job here."

"Knock off the palsy bedside manner, General, I'm not in the mood for it!" The viciousness of the response caught Arlo off guard. The sailor continued without any interruption, "I didn't see many officers out there on the airfield when the going got real rough. How can you know if we did a great job or not?" The wounded sailor defiantly mocked what Arlo had said.

"You're right, son, I wasn't up there dodging the bullets, but I've been in places like it in the past." Arlo was not going to enter into an argument with the young man. He knew that the sailor was speaking out because he was afraid. Then, Arlo noticed that both of the sailor's legs had been removed. Only short stubs were visible beneath the sheets.

"When the going gets rough, the officers get scarce."

"I disagree with you, sailor. Man for man the officers in this command have shown great courage in carrying out their duties. Rank has nothing to do with courage or sharing of risks. If you have the time, I'd like to tell you about a very special officer who's losing the fight for his life, just down the passageway from you, as we speak."

"I've got the time, General, its about all I do have," said the sailor, shrugging his shoulders in resignation.

Arlo recounted the story of Mark's performance on the beach, and how he was apprehensive about what he would find. He left the more reflective seabee with these parting words, "I wish you all the luck in the world, son, as you try to put your life back in order. I'm very proud of you, and you're in my prayers."

Arlo saluted him and started to continue down the center aisle of the ward when the sailor called after him.

"Sir, I meant no disrespect towards you, it's just that I got to feeling sorry for myself, and sometimes I'm scared. I've heard about the Colonel on board and the word is out that he isn't going to make it. I'm sorry, Sir. Some of the guys in the ward told me what he did. He had a damned lot of guts, didn't he? One way or another, I'll be able to get around. At least I'm alive. The Colonel deserves better. I apologize for my outburst, Sir. I was out of line."

"You carry on, Son. Don't let the bastards grind you down. Promise?"

The sailors lips parted in a smile answering in one word, "Promise!"

Arlo left the ward, and anxiously sought Mark's room. The ship was alive with activity. The crew was preparing to leave the anchorage for Pearl Harbor where they would transfer all of the patients to a land facility. The intensive care rooms were still full of seriously wounded men.

"Excuse me, Captain. Can you tell me if there's any change in Colonel Leroux's condition?"

The naval nurse, stationed at the deck nurse's center, recognized General Korsman. "General Korsman, I'm sorry, there's not any change from the last time you was here. In fact, his condition has gotten worse. We're using everything we can to hold his fever down, but the points of infection are just too many. The human body can only stand so many intrusions... My candid opinion, Sir, is that he will be gone by the time we set sail for Pearl."

Arlo heard the words, but refused to believe that Mark would be lost to all of them. He asked for directions to the room.

"It's the small room directly behind you, Sir. We moved his bed so that he could be in the sun next to the window. It might make him more comfortable." the nurse soberly pointed out the door.

"Thank you for your thoughtfulness, Captain. I want to be with him a few minutes."

"Of course, I understand, Sir."

Arlo removed his hat and quietly entered the room. Mark was lying flat on his back, with his eyes closed. My God, Arlo thought, he already looked dead! His skin was still mustard color from the atabrine tablets they all took for malaria treatment while they were in the tropics. Mark's face was drawn and more emaciated than the last time. Arlo put his ear down to his friend's mouth to see if he was still breathing. It was heavy and labored. The ominous rattle of phlegm in Mark's lungs frightened Arlo.

"Old friend, I'm not sure if you know that I'm here or not. Maybe I'll never have another chance to let you know how very special our friendship has been to me." Beads of sweat formed on Mark's face, creating small rivulets that emptied on the clean white pillow case. He seemed to be burning up inside.

Arlo continued softly, "If it's God's will that this is your time to answer the call, then good-bye, Mark. I shall miss you more than I can ever tell. All the years we've spent together have been swell. Semper Fi, Colonel!"

Arlo left the room and went directly to the boarding stairs. Anxious steps took him down to the waiting launch. He did not want to see or talk to anyone just now. A wave of sadness came over him that was so powerful, he had to bite his lips to prevent himself from giving in to the emptiness that drained him. The ride to the shore provided precious time for him to compose himself for the duties ahead.

Later, in the early hours of the next morning, Arlo was still working at his field desk. One of his duties and privileges was to make recommendations for those men who had performed deeds worthy of medals. The Division staff agreed that Mark's conduct warranted the receipt of the nation's highest award for bravery - the Medal of Honor. It had to be earned for "conspicuous gallantry and intrepidness above and beyond the call of duty". Surely, Mark's actions fit the description "above and beyond."

Arlo had just completed writing the recommendation for Mark when he was interrupted by a commotion among the men outside his tent. Throwing the tent flap open, Arlo saw a strange white glow of light above the hospital ship, and a more intense concentration of light rays angled down from the sky toward one side of the ship. The rest of the anchorage area was blacked out and nothing could be seen except the glow at the hospital ship. Then, as quickly as it came, it was gone. Darkness enveloped the offshore cluster of ships once more.

"Some goofball just shot off a flare gun from the ship," speculated one of the men outside the tent.

Arlo tried to make some sense of the affair and called for his aide-de-camp to check with the Navy Task Force commander for an explanation of what they had just seen. The requests by the marines ashore for gunfire support had been over for almost twenty-four hours. Personally, Arlo thought that it had been a star shell inadvertently fired by a careless gunner. A few hours after the illumination incident, Arlo's aide entered his tent with a message that the Navy could not find a ship that had a discharge of any type of weapon at that time.

The waters off the crowded beach were alive with barges and amphibious tractors hard at work unloading the endless array of supplies for the Army garrison troops from the ungainly transport ships. Arlo had already given the embarkation orders. It was just a matter of waiting for the Army to complete its transfer. He estimated that the Division could be loaded within twenty-four hours. They had very little equipment that was good enough to be reloaded on the ships, so he had negotiated with the Army to trade some of their new equipment to be left on board, in exchange for the Marine's used stuff already present.

The unsettled feeling that had come over Arlo since the unexplainable glow on the water, was still with him and he could not get it out of his mind. Consequently, he decided to make one more trip to the hospital ship before it left the anchorage. He located an Army "duck" that volunteered to take him out to the ship. Once on board, he went straight to Mark's room where he found several doctors gathered around the bed.

"General Korsman," greeted the same Naval nurse he had met previously. "I'm glad you came before we weighed anchor for Pearl Harbor. Come with me. The doctors will be a little bit longer with Colonel Leroux. I want to talk to you in private."

"Is something wrong, Captain?" questioned Arlo, assuming that his fears had at last become reality.

"My office is just around the corner, Sir." She motioned for him to take a chair, and then proceeded to reassure him that everything

41

was okay with Mark. "There's nothing wrong, Sir. Last night something happened on this ship that's unexplainable, and has the staff of the hospital in a strange state of bewilderment."

"Yes, continue," pleaded Arlo impatiently.

"It was near the end of my watch at about 1:30 AM, when a bright light appeared in the Colonel's room. It startled me at first, and by the time I got to the room, all I saw was an intense beam of light shining through the window illuminating the Colonel's body. Then it disappeared as quickly as it came."

"I saw the same light from the shore, Captain. I was convinced that someone had fired a star burst or a flare gun by mistake," Arlo explained matter-of-factly.

"The Captain of the ship claims that neither of those guns had been fired by mistake. He has contacted every ship nearby for confirmation on that issue. They're all emphatic that it was not from them. I cannot explain it, Sir." She was still flushed with excitement and was anxious to tell her story.

"There has to be an explanation, Captain. They just have not found it yet..."

"That may be, General, but there's more. Last night I personally took Colonel Leroux's pulse, temperature, and blood pressure and duly recorded them about a half hour before the presence of the strange light. His breathing was extremely labored and heavy at that time. The congestion in his lungs was slowly drowning him in his own fluids. I estimated that he was only hours from death.

"This morning, my shift replacement took his vital signs again and found everything normal. No lung congestion, no fever! It's a miracle that I cannot understand." The nurse watched General Korsman for his reaction to the startling revelation.

Arlo was slow to comprehend the significance of what he had just been told. Her excitement was contagious though, and he allowed himself the opportunity to be optimistic about Mark's condition. He let out a sigh of relief and confessed, "I can't believe this is happening." He wanted to hug the nurse.

"The doctors are evaluating him now. He still has some difficult and serious wounds to manage, but at least the secondary problems of fever and infection don't seem to be an issue at this time."

"Thank God," exclaimed Arlo. If this thing had happened to anybody else except Mark, he would not believe it. In the past, he had witnessed incredible happenings involving Mark and his family, and had reasons to believe that the incidents described by the nurse were feasible. He did not volunteer any information to the Captain about his earlier experiences, for he too saw it as a miracle. It helped him to understand that God does work in strange and wonderful ways. He needed to hear the news, almost as much as Mark needed to receive the gift of life. These past two weeks Arlo had been a participant and a witness to some of the most ferocious combat that man has ever experienced. He was beginning to doubt that a God really did exist.

"There's more, General. What I'm going to tell you has been confirmed by an observant lookout on the destroyer that was anchored for the evening on our port side. They usually surround us with ships for the evening in case of submarine attack. An officer from another destroyer to our stern also saw the same glare of lights. They both claimed that while the bright light was focused on the window where the Colonel's bed was located, they also saw a large bird, a bald eagle, perched on the lip of the window casing. The light remained for several seconds and seemed to be coming from the heavens. Later in the morning, after it became light, several lookouts from the fleet observed an eagle circling the ship for about twenty minutes at a great elevation. It eventually left on a northeasterly course.

"Some of the ships in the fleet went so far as to train antiaircraft weapons on it in case it turned out to be a Japanese trick of some kind." When the nurse finished, she was breathless. She was also surprised at the lack of response from the General. He remained so calm, almost as if he disbelieved her story.

"Captain, the story you've just told me is something that I'm pleased to hear. Surely it's a miracle, as you put it, and I'm relieved that my old friend is going to have another chance. Yet, I'm not too surprised that it has happened to him. He has a special angel that looks after him and his family. Without going into great detail, you may be interested to know that Colonel Leroux has an adopted daughter called Bright Star, whose father was his wife's brother. This brother was a brave warrior who saved the Colonel's life in World War I, and was killed shortly after the episode took place. Before he died, he wrote a letter home to his sister that said, 'if I am killed, tell Bright Star that I will always be as close to her as death allows...' It's a tantalizing promise that your imagination can run away with. Especially when I tell you that his Indian name was Flying Eagle!"

"Oh my Lord!" the nurse shrieked. She thought to herself, maybe she was involved in a miracle in progress. She responded unconsciously to a loud knock at the door, "Come in."

"Sorry to interrupt, Captain," a doctor in white surgical robes entered the room. "Excuse me, Sir. I didn't mean to intrude."

"Not at all, Doctor," Arlo reassured him.

"Dr. Henning," the nurse said, rising from her chair. "This is the Assistant Division Commander, General Arlo Korsman. General Korsman, this is our head surgeon, Commander Henning." The two men shook hands.

"It's my pleasure, Commander. How's Colonel Leroux doing this morning?"

"I can't explain his turnaround, General, except to say that it's unusual in every respect. Even if the Colonel had somehow been able to overcome his fever and infections on his own, it still would have taken days for his lungs to drain and become clear. They're working as good as any normal lungs can with a bullet puncture through one of them. His congestion has disappeared. It is beyond any question, a miraculous phenomenon. I cannot explain, nor do I understand it."

"Has he regained consciousness yet?" asked Arlo.

"Not yet, General," answered the Doctor.

"May I see him now?"

"Of course. We're finished with our examination for the time being."

Arlo could feel something different in the room that was not there yesterday when he had checked on Mark's progress. The warm sun radiating through the window gave an air of hope and optimism, where there had been fear and sadness. Mark's complexion was about the same. In time, the atabrine tan would disappear, giving him a more natural coloring. For now, the gaunt look on his face reflected the ordeal he had experienced. Arlo looked closely at his friend for any recognition or acknowledgment that he was aware of who was in the room with him.

"You've caused quite a stir around here, old friend." Arlo took Mark's uninjured right hand in his own. It was cold and unyielding to his touch. "I'll have to write to Bright Cloud and tell her the good news about your recovery this morning."

The magic words "Bright Cloud" made a difference. Arlo felt Mark put pressure to his grip. Encouraged by the response, Arlo continued in a gentle voice, "Mark, what would you like me to tell Bright Cloud? Today the ship sails for Pearl Harbor. No more combat for you, old man. I won't be able to stop by and see you for a while, but you'll still be in my thoughts."

Mark opened his eyes for the first time since he had been wounded on the beachhead. At first he seemed confused with the white walls and ceiling of the room surrounding him. He had a little trouble focusing his eyes on different objects and it took a few seconds before he recognized Arlo standing beside him. There was a look of desperation in his eyes that alarmed Arlo. At first Mark registered relief at the sight of Arlo and squeezed his hand in recognition. Then, a frightened look of panic came over him as he realized how seriously he had been hurt. He looked pleadingly at Arlo for answers.

"Don't be frightened, Mark. You're in good hands aboard a hospital ship. No more combat for you, you're going home..."

Mark hysterically pointed to his legs with his right hand and struggled to cry out in a dry, scratchy voice, "My legs... I can't move my legs..."

Alarmed at Mark's panic, Arlo called for a doctor or anyone that could hear him. Mark was hysterical and kept pointing to his lifeless legs by the time the deck nurse and Dr. Henning rushed to his side. He repeatedly screamed that he could not feel his legs. Arlo tried to reassure him, but Dr. Henning eased him aside so that he could check Mark's eyes with his pocket light.

"I'm going to give him a shot to calm him down, and ease any pain he may be feeling right now. This kind of a response may be upsetting to you, General Korsman, but it's a most gratifying one for me to witness. It's important for the seriously wounded men to come to grips with their condition as soon as possible. It may seem cruel and harsh, but the alternatives are even harder in the long run. We don't want to remove hope, but it's important to be realistic about expectations. That way we can be honest when we talk to them about therapy treatment that might be involved and eventual recovery. Colonel Leroux should survive if all of his vital indicators are correct. Now, we've got to concentrate on his primary wounds and take them one at a time. It's impossible to predict the outcome, but his initial response is encouraging."

Mark rested easier after the sedative took effect. Arlo felt better having seen the outburst from Mark, and listening to the doctor.

"I've got to get back to my command now. I want to thank you, Doctor, for clarifying things about Colonel Leroux. His wife will be pleased to get the letter I'll write shortly. As for you, Captain, you've been a wonderful source of enlightenment and encouragement. Thank you for your courtesies. I leave my men and my old friend in capable hands. Good-bye and 'bon voyage' to Pearl Harbor."

Arlo left the ship in a buoyant mood. Mark was going to survive!

Chapter Four

The outpost village of Fort Lewis was located in the Canadian northern forest wilderness. Bright Star sat at a table in the Fort Lewis infirmary reading the letter from her mother. Dressed in a white nurse uniform which accented her dark complexion and slender lithe figure, she read the words over and over, hoping she might have missed something that would be reassuring or that her father would be okay. The world was tearing itself apart, she lamented, and now the tragedy taking place so far away was touching her family in a very personal way. The general tone of her mother's letter was one of subdued hope that the shattering news would soon change to something more positive. Bright Star suddenly felt nauseous and faint. It seemed ironic that a gentle man like her father, should be the victim of such violent actions.

Before receiving the letter, Bright Star was preparing for a short journey to the lumber camp belonging to the tribal council. Some workers had been hurt when a team of horses nervously reacted to confused commands and pulled a loaded scoot of logs over a stump and dumped them onto several unsuspecting workers. The letter was dropped off by one of the young policemen from the nearby barracks just as she was leaving the infirmary. She took time to read what her mother had to say. It left her drained. She wanted to scream in protest that this should not be happening to her family again. How much does a family have to keep giving, she wondered bitterly? Sacrifices and hardships should be shared equally, not borne by a select few.

Unnoticed by Bright Star, a tall muscular figure in the green field uniform of the Royal Canadian Mounted Police filled the door entrance, pausing for a moment before entering. "Are you okay, Lass?"

Bright Star hesitated to answer. The letter had completely unnerved her. "Yes, Inspector, I'm okay, I guess. I'm afraid. My mother's letter brings bad news about my father. He's been seriously wounded, and they don't know what his chances are for survival..." The words were difficult to say. She was thankful for Inspector Clough's reassuring presence.

"I'm sorry to hear it, Lass. My old American friend has certainly had his share of hard times. Does your mother say what happened to him?" There was concern in the Inspector's voice, for he and Mark had a friendship that went back to the First World War, when they had met in France. The Inspector had been a Canadian Army officer serving as an observer attached to Mark's regiment.

"Only that he was hit by several machine gun bullets while he was leading his men off the beach. Arlo wrote to Mother, and he praised Father for his actions."

"I can well imagine that his actions would be extraordinary. He's that kind of man. The quiet ones seem to find that extra measure of guts when it's needed the most. I don't have to tell you, Lass, what he means to me." The inspector sat in the chair beside her at the small table in the infirmary kitchen.

"I know that you two are good friends, Inspector. My father holds your friendship very close to his heart." Star placed the letter in front of him and said in a wavering voice. "You're welcome to read it; Mother writes about you, too."

The Inspector reached into his tunic pocket for his reading glasses. At sixty-five years, he should have retired from the police force, but these were not normal times, and able-bodied men were impossible to recruit with the war on. He was happy and capable of continuing in the same capacity where he could make a contribution. He immediately recognized Bright Cloud's flowing handwriting style:

My Dearest Bright Star,

I don't want to needlessly alarm you, but, if you are standing, you should sit down before you continue with this letter. Your father has been seriously wounded and is at a military hospital somewhere in the Pacific. I received word from General Korsman about his condition, and all he could say was that we should prepare ourselves for the worst. I don't know what that means right now, but I am afraid.

Evidently your father was wounded while leading his men in assault across a beach. I don't know where it is, but Arlo was generous in his praise of your father's actions. I'm sure he did what he had to do, because that is the way he does things. I'm sure you're as impatient as I am for more details after reading this letter.

I'm so sorry to bring this kind of news to you, our dear little girl who has grown into such a lovely young lady. Your mother and father both are very proud of you and the dedication you bring to your work. I know how difficult it can be at the infirmary, dear daughter, and I pray for you every night. I can't think of the infirmary without remembering all of the dear souls who have passed away such as your Grandfather and Father Dumont, who was a saint. Of course, our dear old friend, Inspector Clough, has been a part of the North Woods for an eternity it seems. Would you please tell him about your father's condition?

I hope that you are not overdoing, Star. Take some time for yourself. I worry about you the same as I do over DJ and your father.

All my love,

Mom

PS: DJ sends his best to you. I do hope that he is writing to you!

Inspector Clough passed the letter to Bright Star, remaining quiet for several seconds before he spoke. "My Yank friend will certainly have my prayers that his burden will pass and he'll get better. I know that it's a bitter message to receive, Lass, but he's made of strong stuff and he has a way of overcoming things.

49

"I stopped by to see if you wanted any company going out to the lumber camp. Maybe I can help. I don't mean to belittle the importance of what we've just learned about your father. God knows it would be easy to give up at such times, but keeping busy is the better way to handle things we cannot control. Worrying until one is sick will not help." Inspector Clough had watched Bright Star grow from a small child into an adult over the years. As a nurse, he praised her ability to function with grace under trying conditions. The look he saw on her face when he came into the room frightened him. She seemed so alone and lost that he was immediately concerned and afraid of the worst. It would be impossible for him to erase her pain, but he could show her that he shared it with her.

"You're right, Inspector. I'll get my medical bag next to the door. I didn't mean to delay as long as I have."

"You don't need to apologize to me, Lass."

Bright Star grabbed a jacket from a hanger behind the door, while the Inspector picked up the black medical bag. Watching her tuck her long black hair under the jacket's hood reminded him again of Bright Cloud. "My Lord, you're the picture of Bright Cloud when she was your age. It would be easy to confuse you for her, Lass."

"You're always saying that to me, and it never fails to make me feel good." Bright Star smiled at him as they fell into an easy walking pace on the trail to the camp.

"I remember the time," the Inspector started all of his stories lately with those same words. "Mark was injured on the trail and I carried him to the infirmary and your mother became so distraught over his condition that her true inner feelings surfaced. I knew from that time just how much she cared for him."

"I've heard that story before, but this is the first time I've heard it from you, Inspector." Star had trouble keeping up with the long legs of her self-appointed protector.

"It seems like only yesterday, yet I've grown old and you've blossomed into the flower you always promised to become."

"Inspector, your compliments are outrageous. If you're not careful you'll make my head swell 'til it bursts."

"It's the truth, so help me, Lass. I made a pact with the good Lord not too long ago, that if he would continue to bless me with good health in my older years, I vowed to not hold back, as I was frequently apt to do in my younger days, but speak my mind as I saw it. You, also, have a big heart like your mother and that wonderful spirit that touched us all whenever she was around."

Star blushed under Inspector Clough's barrage of praise, and reached out to link her arm with his. "I'm beginning to understand now why Mother and Father hold you on such a pedestal." It was the Inspector's turn to blush this time.

The well-worn pathway was much the same as when Mark and Bright Cloud first met after the First World War. Mark had stayed at the center cabin further along on the trail. He always called it the center cabin, because it was approximately at the epicenter of the tribal lands being managed for logs and pulpwood. The cabin had served Mark as living quarters and an office while he developed the first forest management plan for the Cree tribal forest tract. Segments of the plan still helped to regulate the patterns and intensity of forest harvesting taking place today.

The subtle fragrance of cedar floated in the early spring air mingling with the ever-present perfume of balsam and spruce. The forest, dormant for the long cold winter months, was now responding to the longer days of sunshine and returning to life again. Warmer weather was on its way to the North Woods. You could feel and smell its renewal of life now that it was released from its winter blanket of snow. It was a good time to be in the forest.

It was still too early for the spring flowers to bloom, but the first manifestation of an early spring breaking through the harsh winter months was the appearance of small fire-red plants, called fireweed, springing to life in open locations with a southern exposure. At a distance, one would almost think there was a forest fire. Its crimson hue reflected the warming rays of the sun to announce the first tangible evidence of life. Sometimes the small climbing plant will grow on one or more sides of a cabin, giving it a colorful coat of blazing red.

The Inspector and Bright Star approached an area of the forest tract that was sacred to the Cree Indians around Lac Diamante. It had special meaning to Star. Her paternal father, Flying Eagle, was killed during the First World War in France. She never knew him, but he was still a powerful influence in her life. Mark and Bright Cloud, Flying Eagle's sister, had taken over the role of parents to Star, and she could not imagine any parents being more loving and nurturing than the two people she called Father and Mother. They gave freely of themselves for her sake, and instilled an appreciation of her natural Cree legacy and heritage. She had been encouraged to complete the nursing curriculum at the same school that Bright Cloud attended in Syracuse, New York.

"I can always tell whenever I come near the cenotaph," declared Bright Star solemnly. "I feel as if my real father was watching over me. I know that his spirit is present. I can feel it when I come here, Inspector."

"I have no doubt that you do, Lass. His spirit is finally at rest. I feel the serenity and peace at his cenotaph, too. It's in contrast to the feeling that I have when I'm around the grave of your uncle, Red Fox. His spirit is not at rest and you can feel the tensions that seem to emanate from the grave. Maybe you've felt the same things yourself."

The Inspector was referring to Red Fox's grave near the first waterfall on the Diamond River near the outlet of Lac Diamante. It was a secluded location where the rapids interrupted the smooth flow of water in the river. A fine misty fog usually filled the air after the noon sun failed to penetrate the protective grove of large spruce trees. Sometimes, during the first years following his death, and when the evening noises were hushed in the forest, the dark figure of his father, Running Deer, could be found kneeling beside the grave. Gentle sobs would rise from the glen to mingle with the continuous trickle of the water among the rocks. Running Deer continued to ask himself, until he died a few years afterward, what had he done wrong that could cause a son of his own blood to be so alien to those values the Crees held so sacred. Bright Cloud had also visited the scene frequently, seeking forgiveness for being the instrument of her brother's death.

It was not uncommon for violent lightning storms to take place in the area between the grave of Red Fox and the cenotaph of Flying Eagle. It was almost as if the spirits of the twin brothers were angry at each other, and still fighting as they frequently did in real life. They were identical twins, almost impossible to tell apart by physical features. Yet, they were worlds apart in emotional disposition and character. Red Fox had a violent temper which always got him into trouble. He saw no advantage in working hard like everybody else, instead, he chose to bully those weaker than himself. When he became a young adult, he was attracted to the easy money of the illegal whiskey trade. He was cunning and relentless in pursuit of his chosen endeavor, managing to stay just one step ahead of the law. His capacity for brutality and insensitivity was the talk of the village. Everyone was afraid of him and avoided his path when he was around.

The cenotaph beside the trail was created by the village people at Fort Lewis to honor one of their own. It was a memorial to the memory of a brave warrior buried somewhere in the fertile soil of France. Here, in this sacred place, the people had expressed their appreciation, by selecting a dozen or more large cedar and spruce trees that were killed by the trapped water of a beaver pond. The trees selected were as large as trees ever get near the permanent frost line in the Canadian forest. The young men of the village had climbed to the top of the trees and pruned off every branch from the extreme top to the bottom of the tree. From a distance the spires looked like giant needles protruding from the swampy ground.

The trail ran easterly along an elevated dry strip of ground adjacent to the wet area. Several years ago Mark and Bright Cloud had carved Flying Eagle's name on a large cedar log lying beside the trail where Bright Star and the Inspector paused for a rest. Bright Star walked over to the cedar log, knelt down beside it and took a small object from a shelf chiseled into the wood and reverently held it in her hand.

"Why do you leave the cross here, Lass?" asked the Inspector.

"The cross was made by my dead father when he was very young and is one of my most precious legacies. He gave it to his sister, the one I now call Mother, as a sign of remembrance. She, in turn, gave it to my father as a token of her love. When I was old enough to understand the significance of it, we all decided that it would be proper to consecrate this holy place with a part of him. So my father carved a pocket into the log to protect it from the weather." Bright Star's supple bronze fingers held it briefly to her lips and replaced it to its secure resting place.

"I've heard the story about the cross. I didn't realize you had left it here at this special place." The Inspector gently took her by the arm and started along the trail.

"Yes, we must not delay any longer. The men are waiting..."

Bright Star's sense of duty urged her on to where she was needed, but her thoughts and prayers were with her mother and father, so far away from the forest wilderness.

* * *

Bright Cloud, devastated by the news about her husband, faced the news as best she could. It was the most traumatic period of her forty-six years. She was searching for anything that could give her some hope. Every day she watched for the mail delivery hoping for more information. At bedtime, she knelt in prayer and pleaded for his safety and recovery. The ritual of her evening prayers were comforting, but she still felt that her world was coming apart and there was nothing she could do to prevent it.

Sweating hands and cold chills accompanied her tortured soul as she took her private thoughts to her God. "Oh my God, I've never asked you for very much for myself, but tonight I'm begging you to hear my cry for help. Be with him and let him know that my love is stronger than ever. Please give me some sign that you're hearing my plea for his welfare. If you can grant us what I beg of you, my God, I will make any sacrifice you ask of me. My beloved Mark deserves some consideration, for you must know how good a person he really is. He has given of himself more than most men.

"If you've been pleased by any actions in our lives, then reward us now and bring him back to us. No one is more loved by his family, or more worthy of your compassion. I may be selfish asking you for the gift of Mark's life, but I need him, and Bright Star and DJ need his gentle influence in their lives.

"Hear me, dear God, let our love be his armor. If I'm too late and Mark is already gone, give me the strength to carry on as he would want me to do. Forgive me for what I'm going to say now, but if Mark is already dead, then you had better show me how you justify the loss of such a good man. In all honesty, Lord, it would test my faith in you."

Later, Bright Cloud had just returned from an exhausting night of work at the small hospital in York. Since the news of Mark's injuries, she had requested work at night so as to be home when the mail came. She did not want to lose any time from the precious life-lines the letters provided. Mark's letters continued for a few days after Arlo's, and it helped considerably to maintain the hope that her prayers were being answered. Shortly after her supplication on behalf of Mark, she was troubled trying to clarify the significance of a strange feeling that had suddenly come over her. She did not understand. It had been with her throughout the evening at work. She felt relief and a consciousness of euphoria that she had not experienced for a long time.

Several days had gone by since Bright Cloud wrote to Star. She was starving for news from Arlo, or anybody else, about Mark. Uncertainty was always something Bright Cloud had a difficult time accepting, for in the absence of facts, her imagination ran rampant among a plethora of ghastly possibilities.

DJ was coming home, yet, she could not rejoice because she knew that it was probably the first step towards his eventual introduction into combat, like his father. She was so distraught over it that she even contemplated the possibility of taking him to Fort Lewis and forcing him to stay there out of harm's way. In her heart she realized it could not work, but she honestly admitted thinking about it. The family would never condone such a cowardly act. She realized that it was wrong, but it was one of several thoughts which came to her mind when all that she wanted to do was keep her family together.

The faithful old Model A Ford of the mail carrier stopped at the mailbox several days after the bad news about Mark, and with a single honk of the horn, chugged on its way. Bright Cloud heard the horn and ran as fast as she could out of the house to the mailbox. She was rewarded with a thick envelope from Arlo. Anxious fingers tore at the seal and opened it. The first sentence leaped from the paper directly to her heart. Hungry eyes consumed what was written as she retraced her steps toward the house. Halfway back she clasped the letter to her breast, lifted her head to the heavens and shouted, "Thank you Lord for answering my pleas. Thank you..."

Dear Bright Cloud,

I bring you good news. The life-threatening stage of Mark's injuries is over...I repeat, <u>Mark is out of danger</u>. I rejoice with you Bright Cloud. I have just left his bedside on the hospital ship. He was distraught over the extent of his injuries, but he was at least awake and talking. They don't know whether he will be able to recover the use of his legs (especially his left one). You should not be too concerned right now, just wait and let therapy and time take their course. Now is the time for patience and fortitude.

The doctors all agree, Mark was near death. They expected it within hours. Then a miracle took place that still baffles them. I would not know what to make of it myself if it had been anybody except Mark. The power of that special spirit or guardian angel that watches over you and your family is a source of inspiration to me. I was a witness to its existence, and it was easy to understand what must have taken place on the hospital ship last night when Mark was balanced between life and death...

Arlo continued for several pages telling Bright Cloud exactly what he saw and what the doctors and nurses did that first day. She knew...she had a feeling that something was taking place when the miracle occurred. She could not explain it, but she knew that something unusual was taking place. Tears of joy and thanksgiving rained down on the letter from Arlo. The letter gave Bright Cloud back her hope and faith. She must thank Arlo for being such a true friend. Over the years his friendship had remained steadfast, and whenever Bright Cloud prayed for Mark's safety, it was only natural to include Arlo in the same prayers.

Bright Cloud felt compelled to write to Bright Star as soon as she could to relieve her worry and to tell her about the good news. DJ could be told when he arrived at home from West Point. She was anxious to share the message from Arlo with all of them.

The gratitude she felt in her heart for Arlo's generosity towards all of them, was tinged with sadness. She thought that he had to be a very lonely person. His rise to higher command within the ranks of the Marine Corps had been possible, partly, because of his total commitment to the service he loved. In many ways, he was a tragic figure. He had no family to spend time with and no one to share his daily trials and tribulations. Bright Cloud personally knew about the tragedy that would have been a tortured ordeal for anyone to bear. Yet, Arlo continued as he always had with a heavy heart and a lonely future. He never looked for pity from others, and he never wallowed in self-pity. Mark and Bright Cloud saw a difference in him after the calamity. He didn't laugh as often or as heartily, and he drew a protective shield of silence to hide his pain and hurt from prying eyes.

Touched with thankfulness after receiving the letter from Arlo, Bright Cloud could not help herself from thinking how it all came about, and how she and Mark were an important part of the story. At first, to everybody's delight, it introduced Arlo to a world of happiness. It seemed only yesterday, when the promise of the future loomed bright and full of joy.

* * *

The summer of 1926 was the first summer that Mark left home for two weeks of training at Quantico, Virginia, with his Reserve Marine unit stationed in Portsmouth, N. H. The year before, Congress had passed the bill which established and authorized the Marine Corps Reserve. Mark was an early volunteer to the unit formed in nearby New Hampshire.

He was fortunate to have been well trained in military science, and to have commanded a company of soldiers in the war. His services were in demand by the Army and the Marine Corps. Arlo had been instrumental in obtaining a reserve commission for Mark as a company commander in a reserve infantry battalion.

In the beginning, Bright Cloud had not been pleased to think that Mark's service in the reserves could take him away for long periods at a time if a crisis developed. However, she accepted it, for Mark's sake, because he seemed to feel better about himself once he became part of the military establishment again. She kept her misgivings to herself.

Arlo had been assigned to the department of Reserve affairs as a staff officer stationed at Quantico, and when Mark's battalion went to Quantico for summer training that first year, Mark stayed with Arlo.

After the training period was completed, Arlo had planned to take some furlough time and accompany Mark back to Maine. Bright Cloud and the children had already left on their annual summer pilgrimage to Bright Cloud's ancestral home at Fort Lewis in Quebec Province, Canada, after waiting for Star's school to finish for the year in mid-June. Mark and Arlo intended to follow as soon as they accounted for all of the reserve company's equipment and returned it to their secured places in Portsmouth.

Arlo had traveled extensively with the Marine Corps, but he had never been to Canada. The two men took a train from Wells to Quebec City, where they stayed one night at the spectacular Chateau Frontenac, before taking another train further north to Lac St. Jean. There they hitched a ride on a Royal Canadian

Mounted Police plane to Fort Lewis. They had both left their uniforms in Wells and outfitted themselves with more suitable clothes for the wilderness they were about to enter.

The Mounted Police plane slowly circled the lake the same way it had when Mark first saw the small island of civilization in an expanse of swaying spruce and fir trees. The float plane gracefully touched the clear blue waters of Lac Diamante and headed to a wharf that jutted out from the western shore. Mark and Arlo were the only passengers. However, there was a large amount of supplies on board for the Mounted Police station adjacent to the dock.

Inspector Clough was standing on the shore waiting for them. As soon as the pilot shut down the engine of the plane, the Inspector ran to the aircraft to welcome Mark and Arlo.

"Ah, Yank, you're a sight for these tired old eyes. It's been a long time and not a day has gone by that you've not been in my thoughts." The Inspector reached out for Mark's hand and clasped it in both of his with a genuine show of affection.

"I see that you've brought a guest to our shores, and I'm assuming that you're Major Korsman. I'm Gerard Clough, welcome to Fort Lewis. We don't get many visitors here, and an officer in the Marine Corps is most welcome."

"Thank you, Inspector Clough. Mark has been telling me a lot about your country. I'm favorably impressed with its pristine beauty." The two men silently sized up one another and were pleased with what they saw.

"Mark told me that you had served in the Canadian Army during the Great War," Arlo said, feeling the intense scrutiny of the policeman. "I was in France when the war ended. I had a chance to observe some of your Canadian troops in combat, and I was impressed with their discipline and dedication."

"You're kind, Major. We Canadians usually get a little tongue-tied when others compliment us, but I will agree with you. The Canadians accept authority much better than you Americans, who are uncomfortable with it. I had a chance, as a Canadian observer and liaison officer with the U.S. Army, to see them perform. They were marvelously full of spirit. My friend Mark happened to be in one of the units that I spent some time

59

with. He was a credit to the uniform that he wore." He affectionately put an arm around Mark's shoulders.

"You guys can knock off the mutual admiration stuff," laughed Mark, looking around the lake shore and spotted a small figure running along the path that ran through the village. "I was about to ask where is everybody? I can see little Star coming now."

"Bright Cloud is not at the infirmary. Earlier this morning a young Cree came in from the bush with a frantic tale that his wife was having their first baby and was experiencing difficulty. Bright Cloud offered to return to their cabin with him. I sent Constable Gillespie with her to carry some supplies and to help where he can. Michelle is at the infirmary with Bright Star and little Daniel Joseph."

By the time the Inspector finished telling them where Bright Cloud had gone, an exuberant eight-year-old Bright Star ran across the dock and literally jumped into Mark's waiting arms.

"Daddy, I saw the plane come in. Miss Gurney said it was probably you!" It had been almost a full month that she had not seen him, and she was breathless with excitement. Her coal black hair was neatly done in two braids that came to the center of her back. Two red ribbons tied at the end of the braids told Mark that Bright Cloud probably did her hair. The ribbons were a trade mark of hers. Star had not paid any attention to Arlo until she curiously looked over Mark's shoulder with her large brown eyes and recognized who it was. She had never seen Arlo when he was not in uniform and it took a moment to register with her just who he was.

"My little girl is growing up. I'll have to tie a rock on her head to stop that from happening," teased Mark, setting her down on the wharf. "Do you remember Daddy's friend, Arlo Korsman?"

"Yes, I remember him with the shiny green automobile."

"That's right, Star. It was a few years ago when we all went to Washington, D.C. You've grown since then," Arlo crouched down to her level and held out his arms to her. Star smiled at him and responded to his gesture by giving him a perfunctory hug about the neck. "The last time that we met, young lady, an event took place that I will remember for as long as I live. Your father has invited me to come up here to try my luck fishing some of these beautiful lakes and to enjoy the magnificent scenery. Since this is your village, maybe you can show me some of your favorite places, okay?"

"I get tired climbing up the top of lookout rock, but it's my favorite spot. I can take you there if you want to go."

"I'd be delighted to go sometime after we get settled in, young lady. That's a promise," responded Arlo.

"She's a jewel, just like Bright Cloud," said the Inspector with pride and affection. "Sometimes I think I'm young again, and she is Bright Cloud. This bundle of energy needs only to look at Bright Cloud to see whom she will look like."

"I've been thinking the same thing, Inspector," Mark agreed. "Why don't we carry our luggage over to the cabin and stretch our legs for a change. You can carry my bag, Star."

She approached the suitcase with expectations of moving it, but it was much too heavy for her. She looked up at Mark, who was watching her with a silly teasing smile on his face, and scolded him with playful distaste, "Dad, I can't carry that!"

They all stepped off the wharf towards the pathway which meandered through the village behind the cabins built on the shore of Lac Diamante. The Royal Canadian Mounted Police Station was on their immediate right at the end of the wharf. The Inspector said good-bye to the group as they passed the entrance to the station.

"I'll see you two later on after you've gotten squared away in your cabin. I'm happy to see you again, Yank. That goes for you too, Major. If my arm is twisted real hard I could probably be forced to show you my secret fishing holes on the lake. I hope you enjoy your stay."

"Thanks, Inspector," said Arlo with a smile. "I'll try to twist your arm later."

"See you later, old friend," said Mark with a wave of his free hand. "I'm glad you had a chance to meet Inspector Clough."

"I can understand why you talk so much about him. Wow, he's unlike most policemen I've ever met. The village is lucky to have one like him." Arlo watched the long strides of the retreating policeman, and was impressed with the latent strength and power that a keen observer could detect beneath his calm demeanor.

All of the cabins were built from logs, except the large church Mark pointed out. It was constructed of lumber, with cedar shakes on the exterior. The white cross on top of the two-story steeple made it the tallest structure in the village. The infirmary building was located next to the church. A small addition had been built since Mark's last visit to Fort Lewis.

"I like the improvement to the infirmary. Michelle must find the additional room and privacy a welcome change. I know that Bright Cloud always complained about the lack of space." Mark was glad to be back. It was a second home to him and it never failed to bring him contentment and peace of mind.

The trail brought them to the bridge over the spring. Water was still flowing into the large pool below the path. Large trees sheltered the bridge and pool area where the sun never broke through the protective sentinels of spruce. A soft mist usually rose from the water's surface.

"This spot is pretty, but it must be ten degrees colder in here than out in the open," remarked Arlo.

"It's always a friendly reminder of how far north we really are." Mark pointed to the next cabin on their right, and said, "This cabin was Running Deer's and Bright Cloud's when I first came to the village. It's now used by two older members of the tribal council. Our destination is the newer cabin next to it. The council had it built for Bright Cloud and myself a few years ago as an expression of their appreciation. They maintain it in case we want to come at any time of year. You can see the large pile of dry firewood against the south wall. The people have been great to us. I love it here."

Star had already run ahead of them and was smiling at Mark and Arlo as they turned into the path leading to the door. On the door was a piece of paper that said "WELCOME HOME MARINES". Bright Star could not contain her enthusiasm.

"Mommy and I did the sign to surprise you both," she said wide-eyed and happy over the occasion.

"I'll say it's a surprise, Honey. Thank you for being so thoughtful. I missed you and mommy and DJ just as much as you missed me." Mark reached down to give her a big smack on the cheek. "It's nice to be missed, huh, Arlo?"

"That's for sure, Mark."

They all stepped inside to the great room, which was the central and largest room in the cabin. It contained the kitchen area and a large fireplace built against the north wall. On each side there were two rooms used as bedrooms. The configuration of the cabin was quite typical of most of the structures at Fort Lewis. A large tavern style table sat in the center of the great room in front of the massive stone fireplace, the focal point of the cabin. It was tastefully decorated with fruits and nuts and colorful wild flowers placed on a table cloth made of dyed deerskin beautifully decorated with quills and beads attached to its border.

"This room is yours for the duration, Arlo," Mark announced, walking over to one of the doors on the right. "Bright Cloud and I have the one beside you. The view of the lake is great and the sun rises over the lake giving the rooms first crack of its warming rays."

"I always wanted to have a log cabin on a pond or lake I could use as a retreat," admitted Arlo, checking the room. The bed was freshly made up and towels were laid out on top of a rustic dry sink with a large ornate water pitcher and wash basin. "I'm glad you asked me to come along."

"What you see is Bright Cloud's usual touch. We're both happy to share some time with you up here in the clean air of the North Woods. We have to give up some conveniences, but the tradeoff is well worth it. We lug our water from the spring by the small bridge we just came over. The toilet is a two-holer on the north side of the cabin."

"My room is over there," announced Bright Star, pointing across the great room. "Do you want to see it?"

"I'd love to," answered Arlo, taking her hand across the great room to a smaller bedroom than the adults slept in. It had one window filled with sunlight facing west. Bunk beds were built into one corner of the room. Across from them was a simple wardrobe constructed from a wide shelf about six feet high running the length of the room with a wooden rod serving as a clothes hanger. Bright Star's clothes were neatly organized on hangers, with some folded and piled on shelves built on each side. The walls were decorated with some children story book characters, but mostly they were covered with beautifully ornamented deerskin hides. A black bear pelt served as a rug on the floor beside the bunk bed. Beside the window was a table filled to overflowing with books and magazines for children. The room had a warm secure feeling.

"This room is very nice, Star. When I was a little boy about your age, I had to share a room with three older brothers, and it was kind of crowded. I see you have lots of books. Do you like to read?"

"I like to read, but I like it better when my mother and father read to me. Sometimes my little brother sleeps in here with me; then I can sleep on the top bunk," answered Bright Star.

"I've only been here at Fort Lewis for a short time, and my reaction to being closer to nature and further from the rat race is one of relief," Arlo said, turning his attention to his host. "It's so quiet here, Mark, that you really can hear yourself think."

"After you've been here for awhile, Arlo, you'll be able to better understand why we're reluctant to return to the beach at the end of the summer. It's always hard to leave. The winters here are extremely severe. It's the winters that define the character of the Cree people. Unless you know what winters are all about in these latitudes, it's impossible to understand these hardy survivors. The winter season shapes and limits every decision and every action." Mark reached for a match to light a fire in the stove that had been set up with kindling wood earlier in the morning by Bright Cloud. He had just closed the lid on top of the stove and set on a pot of coffee, when a knock came at the door.

Mark leaped for the door and came face to face with an old friend. It was Michelle Gurney. "Michelle, I had a feeling it was you."

"Mark, I'm glad to see you again." Michelle grasped Mark and embraced him briefly. "You look as youthful as ever. Married life seems to agree with you and Bright Cloud."

"You must meet an old friend who has consented to spend some vacation time up here with us. Michelle, this is Major Arlo Korsman. Arlo, this is a one of our angels of the North Woods, nurse Michelle Gurney. Michelle is from New York State."

"It's my pleasure to make your acquaintance, Miss Gurney."

"It's so nice that you could come for a visit. Mark and Bright Cloud have spoken often of your friendship. Now I can put a face to the name, Major."

Chapter Five

Bright Cloud's spirits soared after reading the encouraging letter from Arlo about Mark's improved condition. It was thoughtful of Arlo to be so considerate of her worried state of mind. She reflected on Arlo's first visit to Fort Lewis with mixed emotions.

Arlo was a sturdily built, blue-eyed Finn with blond hair which he kept neatly trimmed. He carried himself with confidence and pride and was an impressive looking man in his uniform. Women were naturally attracted to him for his good looks. Even though he was comfortable in a group of people, he preferred to be by himself or with close friends. Mark learned years ago that Arlo was essentially a shy, pensive person who avoided boisterous company or loud parties. Mark and Bright Cloud agreed that he would make a wonderful family man if he could only meet the right woman who would appreciate his fine qualities.

During the war Mark found that the men who had served under Arlo had a nickname for him; "Freddie the Fearless Finn". It was a harmless thing that men often do for commanders they respect. It was intended to portray Arlo as the stalwart leader that he was. It also sounded good to the men who used it discreetly. When Mark told Arlo about it, he laughed and said he had never heard that epitaph, but suspected something more derogatory and explicit.

Bright Cloud founded and built the original infirmary at Fort Lewis with the help of several other people in the village. The Catholic Church agreed to take over its administration and be responsible for its staffing. Father Dumont, who married Mark and Bright Cloud in 1921, had been influential in obtaining supplies and assisting Bright Cloud in developing a set of rules and standards for the operation of the medical facility. Every person that sought treatment was accepted at no charge. The "wilderness telegraph" soon flashed the word that competent and compassionate aid was available at the simple infirmary for those in need. It had grown over the years since Bright Cloud first opened the doors into one of the most respected institutions in the far north. Bright Cloud looked forward to their annual return to the village during the summer months. It was a duty she could not deny.

Mark was able to make a living in Maine as a consulting forester dealing with the large forest holdings of absentee owners. He also did some selective harvesting of his father's forestlands in Wells, and planned all of his work so that he could be with the family in Canada after the annual summer reserve training session. Mark enjoyed the ties to the military, but the highlight of each year was the annual trek to the North Woods. He was anxious to share his enthusiasm for the area with Arlo.

The summer of 1926 was an important year for the wilderness north country of Canada. Gold had been discovered in Manitoba, yet there was an influx of gold seekers throughout the region. The most feasible way to get to the uncharted areas was by float plane in the summer months and planes equipped with skis in the wintertime. Mark and Arlo were lucky to be able to hitch a ride on the regular Royal Canadian Mounted Police plane which serviced the barracks at Fort Lewis. Inspector Clough left specific instructions at Lac Saint Jean headquarters for them to assist Mark and his family whenever possible. Planes were difficult to hire because they were all busy ferrying gold-miners to the outer reaches of the Dominion.

Arlo's first introduction to Michelle Gurney was a surprise. Mark had told him how he had met Michelle on the train ride from Washington to Portsmouth before reporting to Arlo at the Portsmouth Naval Yard for his separation papers. Arlo had been under the impression that all of the workers and nurses at the infirmary were nuns. He was impressed with Michelle from the first moment he saw her. There was a quality of strength and perseverance about her that he liked.

The community and population that Michelle Gurney served demanded much from her and the small volunteer infirmary staff. Anytime a call for help was received at the infirmary, Michelle was ready to go, even to the most remote portion of the forest. It did not matter if it was a cabin or a teepee, she willingly volunteered her services. She was a young lady with an independent streak who stood up well to the rigors of the region, even in wintertime. She was the most resourceful nurse in the group and was frequently called upon to administer care and procedures beyond the professional abilities of most nurses. The absence of a doctor's services meant that they had to do the best they could for the patients. It was not long before she developed a reputation for professional competence in setting broken bones. She was looked upon as a true angel of mercy by the people she served. Her skills were equal to Bright Cloud's.

When Bright Cloud left Fort Lewis, after the first year of her marriage to Mark, the main responsibility for the infirmary's work was placed upon Michelle's shoulders. She carried the burden with the same dedication and tradition established by Bright Cloud, but she was unprepared for the physical demands and the long hours that the job demanded of her. Common sense soon indicated that she had to have more help. The requests for assistance were growing all the time. Father Lamontagne, who had replaced Father Dumont as the tribal administrator, was receptive to her request and was able to locate the services of two more nurses. It was a well organized facility where all of the members worked in an atmosphere of harmony.

The years continued to mount for Michelle without any break from her demanding schedule. She was showing visible signs of exhaustion one summer when Bright Cloud returned. She firmly demanded that Michelle take some time off each summer so that she could rest and be better prepared to continue when Bright Cloud was ready to leave in the fall.

Michelle was preparing for her annual leave when Mark and Arlo arrived at the village. She heard the plane land on the lake. Young Bright Star was helping with the linen laundry at the infirmary and gleefully stepped outside to watch the plane idle to the long dock. Once Star was certain who was inside, she was off at a run to greet Mark. Michelle waited for the return of one of the nurses before she left the infirmary to stop at Mark and Bright Cloud's cabin.

Michelle warmly embraced Mark, and was pleased to see that he was doing well. She was surprised to see another man standing behind Mark, who quickly introduced them to each other.

"I hope that Mark has not built me up to be someone I'm not," exclaimed Arlo, reaching for Michelle's outstretched hand.

"I think Mark has probably been truthful, Major," answered Michelle playfully.

"Please, call me Arlo."

"I will if you'll call me Michelle instead of nurse."

"It's a promise," answered Arlo, feeling comfortable in her presence. "Mark has assured me the best fresh water fishing I've ever had. I'm looking forward to my stay for a couple of weeks."

"You'll see that I wasn't pulling your leg," commented Mark, still holding on to Bright Star. "The coffee pot is perking, would you like to join us, Michelle?"

"Yes, that would be fine. Neseka, one of the new nurses, has come in from a call, and she'll be at the ward for the rest of the evening. If I remember, Mark, you make a strong cup of coffee, so I'll take only a half cup. Sometimes when I can't hear it, he calls my coffee 'troubled water.'" Michelle's wide smile was mirrored in her eyes. There was an informal unassuming manner about her that was comforting.

Arlo took a seat at the table opposite Michelle. Bright Star poured the coffee.

"Each year that goes by I'm surprised at how much Star has grown," Michelle commented watching the young eight-year-old return the pot to the stove. "Come, dear, and sit beside me. I don't get much of a chance to see you, because I always leave soon after you arrive. Now I can see with my own eyes what my heart always told me when you were a little girl. You're lovelier with each passing year."

Bright Star blushed and hid her face behind cupped hands and grinned from ear to ear.

"Now she'll be insufferable to order around," teased Mark, watching his daughter with pride.

"What part of New York do you come from, Michelle?" asked Arlo.

"I lived in a small town on the banks of Lake George in the Adirondacks called Diamond Point. I have a brother and a sister who live nearby. Their children are growing so much I hardly know them now. My parents are both dead. A very dear cousin lives in the old family house where I stay, and she dotes on me all summer long. I get spoiled easy, and have to return to Fort Lewis for a reality check!"

"I'm from a farming community in Minnesota. My parents passed away several years ago. I lost two brothers in the war, so there wasn't much use for the old homestead. I eventually sold it and made the Marine Corps my home and family. My parents were first generation immigrants from Finland."

Before anyone could say another word, Bright Cloud bolted through the door breathless and excited. The first person she saw was Mark. She ran and embraced him with a sigh of relief. The past two weeks had been a long separation.

"Welcome back home, Honey," she whispered in his ear. She was surprised to see Arlo in the room, and exclaimed, "Arlo, how pleasant it is to see you here." Bright Cloud released Mark and gave Arlo a friendly hug.

"Your husband has been bragging so much about the good fishing up here, that I came along to see for myself," Arlo smiled.

"I'm so glad you came. It'll do you good to get away from your military duties for a while and relax. I heard the plane circling overhead and came as quickly as I could. Constable Gillespie has been very helpful on this call. He carried all of the supplies to the accident and waited to escort me back to the village. The workers were not badly hurt."

"It hasn't taken you long to get back into the swing of things, Bright Cloud," said Michelle with admiration. "Sometimes I feel guilty leaving you every year the way I do."

"Nonsense, Mike." Bright Cloud always called Michelle by that nickname. "Nobody knows any better than I, just how draining this job can be. If you didn't take some time in the summer months, you would soon be worn out and sick from the grinding routine. You've earned the break. Don't let me hear that kind of talk from you," scolded Bright Cloud.

Michelle reached out to put her arm around Bright Cloud's shoulder and said, "Thanks for being my friend and for being so supporting of my efforts here." It was a simple statement that touched everyone in the room.

"It should be I who thanks you, Mike."

"I don't know if Mark has ever told you, Arlo," interrupted Michelle, turning to him across the table. "But I owe my life to these two special friends. The incident took a lot of courage and strength of character, and I'll always be thankful for the gift of life."

"I've heard about it," Arlo responded. "Mark told me a few years ago. Sometimes desperate situations demand desperate decisions that are formed from our inherent character. I can understand what took place and why it ended the way it did. At the time of the incident, you're correct, you were blessed with friends of high character who acted on instincts formed from that character."

Bright Cloud, aware of where the conversation was going, changed the subject by announcing, "I can see that the stove is warmed up. Bright Star can help me get supper ready. Everyone must be starved. Why don't you ask Neseka to take over for the evening, and you join us, Mike? It will be fun to be all together again." Bright Cloud looked at Michelle with pleading eyes.

"Sure, you're right, it'll be nice to do that. I'll help Neseka set up things for the night, and be back in about an hour," replied Michelle. "Welcome back, Mark, it was nice meeting you, Arlo."

"Thanks, Michelle, it's great to be back," answered Mark.

"Meeting you was my pleasure, Michelle," said Arlo, following her lithe form out the door.

Later that evening, after a traditional supper of baked whitefish and fresh biscuits topped off with a warm gingerbread cake, everyone sat around the snapping fire. The weather outside started to deteriorate rapidly. It frequently changed in a short period of time in the northern latitudes. Rain started to fall in sheets driven by swirling winds that created small tornado-style water whirlpools. Arlo could not remember ever experiencing such an intense rainstorm in the summertime. The winds tore at the eaves of the sturdy cabin as if it wanted to shred everything in its path. The rain pelted the windowpanes with tiny rills that ran sideways across the glass.

Mark and Bright Cloud's four-year-old son, Daniel-Joseph, was brought to the cabin by the family who was caring for him. He was an active child who had a tendency of becoming the center of attention. An atmosphere of informal fellowship permeated the great room.

"Wow, it sure is coming down out there," declared Mark. "I'm glad we're inside while this one blows past us."

"It reminds me of some of the storms we used to experience in the North Atlantic when I served on a Navy cruiser for a year," said Arlo.

Michelle was holding DJ in her lap after he had run himself out of energy. He was valiantly struggling to keep his eyes open, but it was a battle he was slowly losing. Michelle claimed the only rocker in the cabin so that she could have the enjoyment of rocking him to sleep. Bright Cloud, seeing that DJ was finally subdued, got up from her chair next to Mark and motioned Michelle to bring him into the bedroom. They disappeared for a few seconds and returned empty-handed. Bright Star took the cue of bedtime from DJ's surrender, and said goodnight to everyone in the room. Bright Cloud conceded to Michelle the opportunity to accompany Star into her room to say her evening prayers.

Mark placed another log on the bed of coals in the fireplace and lit his pipe from a small flaming branch. Arlo usually smoked cigarettes, but tonight, he had bent under Mark's persuasion to try one of the new pipes in the cabin with his old standard pipe smoking mixture, Half and Half. Arlo stepped up to the fireplace to use the same firebrand Mark had in his hand. Arlo noticed the plaque on the mantel for the first time. A small caliber revolver was mounted on a rustic cedar shake. Closer examination of the revolver by Arlo, pointed out a damaged cylinder with a piece of steel broken from one of its jackets.

"That revolver saved Bright Cloud's life, Arlo," said Mark gravely looking at the firearm. "The revolver absorbed a Winchester 30-30 caliber rifle bullet that would have tore Bright Cloud apart if it had not been in her parka pocket. I decided to mount it where it would be a daily reminder that we have much to be thankful for, and of how God watches over us in ways we could never imagine. It had to be a part of His plan."

"I remember the scene as if it was yesterday," recalled Michelle staring at the fire. "I found Bright Cloud lying still on the ground with blood flowing from her mouth. The ground beneath her was stained bright red. I was so frightened for her. When I felt for a pulse, I could hardly contain my happiness, for she had a strong heartbeat that told me things were not as grave as we all feared. She had bitten her tongue when the bullet slammed her against a nearby tree. That was the source of blood in the mouth. The pistol stopped the bullet from doing anymore harm to our Bright Cloud. That day is one we can never forget."

Arlo listened to the story that he had heard from Mark, but he was interested to hear it from Michelle's perspective. She spoke about the event with reverence and respect. Bright Cloud did not volunteer anything more to the story. It was a bittersweet experience. She took Mark's hand and unconsciously squeezed until it turned white from lack of circulation and looked into his eyes with tight-pressed lips.

The storm continued outside unabated. Arlo surmised, correctly, that the circumstances surrounding Michelle's abduction by Bright Cloud's brother, Red Fox, was still a painful subject to her. Still, Arlo could not help admiring the courage and determination that sustained Bright Cloud with the strength to shoot her own brother when she was faced with the reality of having only two options available to her. Her love for Mark had been demonstrated in a very tangible way. The tragedy was now a part of their legacy to each other. Arlo had a chill thinking about the incident. The wild wind blowing violently outside, reminded him that many tales of tragedy are acted out in the wilderness, with no one aware that they ever took place. The north guards its secrets well.

The room had taken on a more somber air and Arlo took advantage of the silence to watch Michelle. She seemed lost in her thoughts staring at the flickering flames of the burning log. He realized he had not met many women who have earned his respect and admiration. Bright Cloud was one who had earned it with her sterling character. Looking at Michelle across the room, he imagined that she, also, was one who possessed similar reservoirs of strength. She looked tired and drawn, but that did not hide the tilt of her chin and the proud determination that motivated her. He guessed that she was about 30 or 31 years old. She was an inch or two shorter than Bright Cloud, and maintained her athletic trimness. The work at the infirmary demanded a cool head and an agile body to withstand the physical and emotional aspects of the job.

Michelle wore her sandy brown hair pulled tight against her scalp to a round bun at the back of her head. Arlo thought it made her look older. She was a very attractive lady with a finely chiseled nose and luminous hazel blue-green eyes which betrayed a trace of sadness. Her mouth was full and sensuous. Most of the time she spoke her mind regardless of the consequences if she was convinced that she was correct on an issue. She was not cruel in stating her position, and those who knew her, soon realized that it was her trademark of strength and plain speaking honesty. Arlo would have given anything to know what thoughts passed through her mind as they sat basking in the warmth of the fire.

After the children had settled down in the adjacent rooms the conversation turned to the problems of Indian children in white society. In particular, DJ was the subject of discussion. Bright Cloud asked Michelle about something that was frequently on her mind. "Mike, how do you think white society is going to feel about DJ? I think often about how he's going to be perceived and accepted. He's a part of both cultures, and at the same time belongs to neither. I pray we have not made his life more difficult by being different. He and Bright Star are two of the reasons we come north every summertime so that they can experience, first hand, both cultures as they actually are. What do you think, Mike?"

Michelle continued to look at the dancing flames of the fire a few seconds before answering. "If I had a daughter like Star and a son like DJ, I would count my blessings everyday. Some will call DJ a `half-breed', but most people are decent and honest in their relations with others. I would take the position of glorifying his uniqueness. It would not be impossible to imagine that children like him have the best of both cultures in their blood, hence are superior, compared to their white or Indian counterparts. But since we live in an imperfect world, some people will perceive him as being inadequate in some ways and inferior to those who enjoy a self-imposed sense of superiority. When everything has been said, I think we're our own person and we should be judged by what's in our hearts and minds. Those two gifts from God have nothing to do with race, culture, nationality, or gender. They define who we are to others and to ourselves. That's what we should be measured by, and we should discipline ourselves to ignore the bigots of the world, for they're an insignificant minority."

"Bravo, I could not agree more," boomed Arlo with enthusiasm.

"You're right, Michelle," Mark admitted. "I think Bright Cloud and I both feel the same way. You have a special talent for putting it into simple English."

"It's just common sense," replied Michelle matter-of-factly.

"I remember a time, years ago, when you used those same words with me," remembered Mark. "I had asked your advice about my feelings for Bright Cloud, and what the future held for us. I'll always remember your reply, which was to fight for our love with all my strength and to not let anything stand in my way. I've always thought it was the best advice I've ever had from a friend."

"If you keep on like that I'm going to cry, and I don't want to cry in front of you or Arlo." Mark had touched a sensitive side of Michelle and she spoke from the heart. "I think of you and Bright Cloud, and your wonderful children as a part of my family. I envy the love you share with each other, and at the same time I cherish being included in your circle of friends. Sometimes I question whether I made the right choice for my life," confessed Michelle, hiding her eyes from the glances of those in the room.

Bright Cloud sprang from her chair as if she was shot from a gun, and took Michelle in her arms. "I haven't appreciated how lonely this life must be for you, Mike. Forgive me if we've offended you or intruded into your private world. I would die before bringing any hurt to you. Please forgive me, dear friend, I've been insensitive to your feelings."

"Of course, there's nothing to forgive, Bright Cloud. I'm just exhausted and maybe feeling a little sorry for myself tonight. I didn't want to display my emotions this way to your friend, Arlo. It's been such a pleasant evening being all together like this that it made me realize how important friends are to me." Michelle apologized and announced that she should be returning to her cabin. It was still raining hard outside even though the wind had moderated some.

Realizing that she came to the cabin without any coat, Michelle asked: "May I borrow a coat for a dash to my cabin?"

"I have a light all-weather coat on my bed," volunteered Arlo, already on his way to the bedroom where he had stored his things. "May I have the pleasure of escorting you to your quarters? I have a powerful hand torch to light the way."

"Yes, that would be nice, thank you."

"My cabin is the first one on the left after we go over the bridge at the spring," Michelle told Arlo as they walked along the path lit up by his flashlight. "You're going to get yourself soaked."

"It's nothing really. This jacket is all the protection I need. Tonight has been special to me, and I'm sorry to know that you're going to leave Fort Lewis so soon. I don't mean that you haven't earned the right to some relaxation...'

"I understand what you mean," Michelle said, linking her arm around his. Arlo was moved by the gentle touch of her hand. Shortly, they arrived at the front door.

"This is the same cabin I've had since I first came to Fort Lewis. I arrived a few days ahead of Mark's initial visit after the war. It isn't much, but I've been comfortable and safe here." Michelle released Arlo's arm and reached for the door latch.

Arlo followed Michelle into the cabin and held the torch for her to find matches to light the lamp on the table in the center of the room. The room was immaculate and filled with the subtle scent of bayberry.

"Thank you for walking me home, Arlo. Forgive me for letting my feelings show. I don't do that very often and I'm sorry. It's been swell tonight. I enjoyed it and I hope to see you tomorrow."

"Without sounding too familiar, may I take the liberty of saying how much I admire what you have done with your life? Your dedication to the native people is inspirational." Arlo was searching for the right words to depart, and settled for a simple, "I look forward to seeing you again tomorrow."

"Goodnight, Arlo. Thanks for those kind words."

"Goodnight, Michelle."

Chapter Six

Preoccupied with his own personal thoughts, Arlo walked slowly around the deck of the Naval command ship. The seas were calm and a light breeze drifted from the small islands to the starboard with the delicate scents of exotic tropical flowers. It was midnight and the sky was ablaze with light from the full moon overhead. Streaks of sparkling incandescent rays shown in the wake of the ship beside them as it forced its passage above the dark depths of the sea beneath the gray hull. They were headed for the Solomon Islands off the coast of New Guinea. Having been relieved by the Army, the Marines were in desperate need of rest and refitting.

"Pardon me, Sir," interrupted a young navy signalman. "We've just received a message from CinCh POA, General Korsman."

"Yes, sailor."

"You've just received a warning order to report to Pearl Harbor as soon as you deposit your brigade at Guadalcanal. Written orders will follow, Sir."

"Thank you. Signal my acknowledgment."

"Aye, aye, Sir."

Arlo retired to his quarters. A number of things weighed heavily on his mind. One picture in particular that never left his consciousness was that of Michelle as he remembered her on his first visit to Fort Lewis. He could almost smell the spruce and balsam fir fragrances as they wafted across Lac Diamante. Michelle was different from all the other women he had ever met. Memories of that idyllic time in their lives was a welcome retreat. Every event in his life was measured and defined using that period of time as a bench marker. That evening Arlo succumbed to the flood of memories that he kept close to his heart.

* * *

The year of 1926 in the Canadian wilderness was special to remember. Mark and Bright Cloud were up early on the first morning of his trip to Fort Lewis. Arlo dressed quickly and anxiously cracked the bedroom door. He had slept longer than usual.

"Good morning, Arlo," greeted Bright Cloud cheerfully. "I hope you slept well."

"I can't believe I've slept this late in the morning."

"It's only 8:30. The nights are so still and dark up here that it's easy to lose track of time," commented Mark, sipping his second cup of coffee. "But that's the whole point of coming here for a vacation. You throw away the clock and let your body find its own natural rhythm."

Bright Cloud was already fully dressed and ready to leave the cabin. "You two should relax today. It'll do you both good. You've earned it. I'll be busy for most of the day. I'll see you later this evening." Bright Cloud gave Mark a kiss on the cheek and left the cabin with a wave of her hand.

"Help yourself to coffee, Arlo. There's plenty to eat. If you trust me, I volunteer to be the chef of the day."

"Coffee and one of those bran muffins will be plenty for now." Arlo said, pointing to a pan of muffins on the top of the cast iron cook stove. "I'm going to try my luck fishing in the lake this morning. Do you have a boat?"

"Not a rowboat, but we do have a canoe, which was a gift from Running Deer before he passed away. It's a light craft and it handles like a cork in the water. It's under the eaves on the back side of the cabin. I think I'll spend the day checking with the Tribal Council to find out what's going on with the Tribal lands. I'll keep an eye on the kids too, so you take the canoe and enjoy the water, Arlo. If you get lucky, maybe we can have fish for supper again tonight. I never get enough of it."

"I'll do my best."

Arlo found the canoe in good shape. He was like a kid on his first try with it and hoped that no one was watching his efforts to paddle the craft in a straight line. He had used one a long time ago on a lake in Minnesota, so he expected that it would be a short time before he got the hang of it. It was like riding a bicycle, you never forgot. Within a couple of hours, he was able to reach a level of skill that pleased him. The water was smooth and inviting. By midmorning he had already filled his fish bag to overflowing with large whitefish and lake trout. Mark had been right about the quality of the fishing on Lac Diamante!

He had satisfied his fishing urge and decided to explore the eastern outlet of the lake. The day was perfect. Arlo pointed the canoe to the east away from the cabin. The sun warmed his body enough so that he was actually sweating from the vigorous workout. There was a feeling of freedom about this place, and he surrendered to its desolate vastness. His powerful frame pulled the light craft over the glistening water with ease.

As he came closer to the eastern shore, Arlo noticed a movement out of the corner of his left eye. He headed towards what he thought was a person waving to him. The closer he came, the more surprised he was to see that it was Michelle Gurney standing on a small rock formation that jutted out from the shore.

"Hello, ashore!" hollered Arlo to the trim figure dressed in white, precariously standing on the edge of the rocks holding a black satchel in both hands.

"Good morning, Arlo," hailed Michelle. "May I have a lift? I had to return to the camp last night because another one of the workers had injured himself. I've done the best I can, and the Inspector will have to radio for the doctor to stop by on his next patrol. I saw you on the lake and was hoping you would see me wave. I really could use a lift to the infirmary. I'm exhausted."

Arlo skillfully swung the canoe into a small inlet beside the rock and stepped out to help her climb aboard.

"Of course, I'd be glad to take you back to the other end of the lake," beamed Arlo, surprised at the encounter. "I've been fishing for most of the morning. My fish bag is already full."

Michelle accepted his arm to steady herself as she took a seat at the bow of the canoe facing the rear. Arlo carefully placed her medical kit on the floor in front of her. She looked tired. Small lines beneath her eyes betrayed her cheerful air and willing smile. She looked very serious this morning.

"The trail to the work site follows the shoreline for a short ways. I'm glad you noticed me. I could help you paddle if you wish," offered Michelle.

"Thanks, but I prefer to have you sit back and let me do the work. It's been a long time since I had a chance to guide a canoe the way I used to as a young man in Minnesota."

The water was deeper than Arlo realized as he stepped toward the rear of the canoe. He was balancing himself on a wet rock and started to roll himself into the canoe when his foot slipped sideways. He fell backwards into the water with a big splash. The water was not as warm as the heated air and it stunned him with its frigid temperature. He quickly recovered from his embarrassment and stepped onto the pebbled beach and let the excess water drain from his clothes. Michelle wiped a splash of water from her cheek and softly laughed at his predicament. It was infectious and he too laughed at his incredulous luck.

"I'm sorry, Arlo, I feel responsible for this," cried Michelle, pawing through her bag for a towel, which she eagerly handed to him.

"Don't blame yourself. My awkwardness caused the accident," said Arlo, wiping his face with the towel. "Wow, it's cold even with the sun out in full force. I'll be able to warm up, though, as soon as we get underway."

Michelle took a paddle to hold the canoe as steady as she could while Arlo climbed back on board. He was shivering by now, and she offered him her smock to keep warm.

"Thanks for the offer, but I'll be okay within a few minutes of good exercise on the paddle. You relax and let me be the driver," Arlo smiled at her, imagining how ridiculous he must look.

"If you insist, I'll let you," she conceded.

Arlo noticed that she had on a lightweight hood with a net attached, hanging at the back of her shoulders. She saw his interest and said, "The headnet is a necessity up here at this time of the year. It's fine on the water like this when the breeze keeps them down, but inland they're terrible, but you soon learn to adapt to them as a part of life."

"Mark has told me that it would be paradise up here in the summer months if it wasn't for the black flies and mosquitoes."

"They disappear by mid-August. Then it's pleasant for a while, but the prospect of winter overshadows one's enthusiasm for late summer. Winter comes early with a viciousness that I've never seen in the Adirondack region of New York. It's harsh for those who chose to live here. They are hardy individuals who spend most of their time preparing for winter, fighting its severity, and recovering from its deadly grip. Winter is not only a time of year, it's a state of mind that partially shapes the people's attitudes towards many things we of the western world take for granted. For instance, the presence or absence of animals available to the natives during a long winter means the difference between living or dying from hunger or from exposure to the extremes of the weather. The basic needs of food, clothing and shelter are related to the animals of the region."

"It sounds as if you respect them a great deal," inquired Arlo, getting his second wind and already warmed by the effort he was giving to the paddle.

"I do very much. They've made me feel needed, and they never fail to show their appreciation for my work."

"Have you ever thought about taking religious vows and working as a nun?" Arlo was aghast that the question, which he had wondered about, found its way into his mouth. "Forgive me, it was a personal question and totally uncalled for, Michelle."

Michelle sat watching the shore thinking about his question. She was uncomfortable with it. Her face blanched as soon as he asked it. "The answer to your question is no. I considered taking vows at one point in my life, but the calling was not strong enough within me. Consequently, I decided to do missionary work as a nurse without making any vows as a religious." The answer was direct and truthful, betraying a nervousness that she was uneasy with.

"I'm sorry, Michelle," he apologized, avoiding her searching eyes. "It was presumptuous and bold of me. Please forgive me."

"I hesitated, because I've never really asked myself that question before."

"You must be tired if you had to interrupt your night's sleep to go the work camp," remarked Arlo, anxious to divert attention away from his intrusion into her private world.

"When a runner came to my door in the night, they thought it was a more serious injury than it turned out to be. He should be fine, but I want the doctor to double check on my work. Over the years I've learned to adapt to these kind of emergencies, and I will admit, it

81

gives me a great sense of accomplishment when I'm able to make a difference. In answer to your question, yes, I'm exhausted."

Michelle's presence in the canoe was a pleasant experience for Arlo. They traveled across the water in silence for most of the trip. He watched her closely as she scanned the shore. There was an air of sadness about her this morning that reached out and profoundly touched him. It showed in her face and in her eyes. She avoided looking at him as they approached the wharf.

"If you would like, Arlo, you can run the canoe up on the beach in front of the infirmary," pointed Michelle.

Steadying herself to climb out of the canoe, Michelle was a different person than the one he had picked off the rock. Arlo would have given anything to retract the hurtful question he asked. "Michelle, I feel badly that I stepped out of line. I'm sorry if I offended you. I never meant...," Arlo was trying to find the right words. The look on Michelle's face was enough to stop him in mid-sentence.

"Thank you for the lift across the lake, Arlo. Please don't think unkindly of me, or of yourself. I've just been thinking of something which always makes me feel sad. It has nothing to do with you, and everything to do with why I chose to be a medical missionary. Please, don't ask me to explain. You've been a perfect gentleman, and I'm sorry if I've made you feel uncomfortable."

"Of course I'd feel bad if things aren't right for you," Arlo blurted out involuntarily. He hardly realized what he had said when Michelle cried out. Holding one hand to her face, Michelle hurriedly grabbed her medical bag and fled towards the infirmary steps.

Arlo sat motionless in the canoe watching her, angry at his own ineptness. Inspector Clough had witnessed the scene from his desk at the police station and naturally assumed that something had gone wrong at the work site. He ran out to the canoe.

"Is everything all right at the camp, Major?"

"Yes, Inspector," answered Arlo, glad to see the policeman again. "I picked up Michelle at the other end of the lake and gave her a lift to the infirmary here."

"Is anything wrong with her?"

"Yes, Sir, I think she's upset with me. I asked her a few questions that I now realize should not have been asked. I should have known better. I'm responsible for her sudden flight to the infirmary, and I feel terrible about it."

"You look as if you took a swim in the lake with your clothes on," said the Inspector noticing his soggy clothes.

"I did, Inspector. I tripped on a wet rock trying to get back in the canoe after picking up Michelle. It looks as if I've been a royal flop on my first day at Fort Lewis."

"Don't be too hard on yourself, Major. You better get along and find some dry clothes before you catch pneumonia."

"I do feel a chill in the air. I was going to twist your arm about the location of some good fish holes. However, on my own, I located some pretty good ones. What do you think of these beauties?" Arlo held out the string of fish he had already caught.

"I guess you don't need any advice from me, Major," smiled the Inspector with a gleam in his eyes. "However, I could be bribed with a couple of good-sized whitefish, which would make an excellent lunch for an old policeman."

"Inspector Clough, take the string as payment for your honorable services," laughed Arlo, handing him the catch of the day.

"I'm indebted to you, Major. Later, this afternoon I'd be glad to go out on the lake with you, and bring you into my trusted circle of successful fish holes. There are about a half dozen of them, and I promise to show you every one. Now, these fish have whetted my appetite, and I think the Constable has a fire going." The Inspector had an impish grin on his face as he turned towards the police station. "Have no fear, Major, I never welsh on a debt."

"I'll hold you to it."

Arlo ran to the cabin to change clothes. He was glad that nobody was there. Here he was, an invited guest to the village, and on his first day he manages to insult Michelle. He nervously smoked his pipe with long deep puffs, filling the bedroom with a cloud of smoke. He finally noticed a note on the table of the great-room, which Mark had left to tell him that there was food in the basket on the table and he would be back later in the day. Arlo wasn't hungry, just upset. He searched for some way to make amends when Bright Cloud came through the door. He watched her enter the cabin. She seemed to be preoccupied with something that was worrying her. She sat at the table without realizing that Arlo was sitting in one of the large chairs near the fireplace. She was startled when she noticed him.

"I'm sorry, Arlo. I didn't see you there," she exclaimed.

"I've been sitting here trying to figure how I can apologize to Michelle for my stupid questions."

"I just left Mike. It was not just your question which upset her, Arlo," said Bright Cloud absently looking past him at the dead embers in the fireplace. "Mike's unhappiness, today, springs from something that I'm not at liberty to tell you. However, you should not punish yourself with thoughts of responsibility for her anguish. She told me a story so depressing that I'm angry at her for not sharing it with a friend. I never knew, and I could never imagine her carrying such a burden without sharing it with someone. My heart is saddened for her. I can't tell you more, dear Arlo. Maybe I've already spoken too much. Everyone has got to be patient and understanding, or we may lose her trust and friendship. Right now she's in need of rest."

"Do you think I should go to her and tell her how terrible I feel?" Arlo sounded desperate.

"No, I put her to bed for the rest of the day, and mixed a sedative in her drinking water. It's taking affect as we speak. She needs to rest. After a long difficult winter filled with daily emergencies, she's worn out and on the verge of a nervous breakdown. I'm concerned for her long term well-being. She's particularly upset because you've seen some of the pain she carries deep within her. Believe me, ordinarily she's one of the most stable individuals I've ever known. Her judgment in a crisis has always been unfailing. Be patient, Arlo, you can see her later."

"I understand. I still can't get over the awful feeling that if I had never spoken to her, this crisis she's having might never have manifested itself."

"Perhaps you're correct, but sooner or later she would have to deal with it. It may be a part of God's plan for you to act as his surrogate and ease the burden poor Mike has carried around for so long. One never knows. I saw you talking to the Inspector as you brought Mike to the shore. He has a wonderful habit of showing up when he's needed the most."

"I traded a string of fish for the location of his favorite fishing holes," laughed Arlo.

"You may have been hoodwinked, Arlo, because the man is shameless with that ravenous appetite of his, but we love him just the same. Speaking of an appetite, you haven't touched anything I left for you. I was about to fix a cup of hot tea. Would you care to join me? I can have it ready in a few minutes."

"That would taste great after my soaking."

"Mike laughed with me about that," said Bright Cloud, using a short candle to ignite dry cedar and spruce shavings in the stove.

"Thank God Michelle has a friend like you, Bright Cloud."

Arlo spent the rest of the day on the lake fishing and exploring the shoreline. By mid afternoon he saw the Inspector waving for him to come in and pick him up. By the time the sun dropped below the large granite mountain to the west of the village, the Inspector kept his word and showed Arlo all of his lucky spots. The two men got along well. A mutual respect influenced their relationship from the first moment they met each other. Arlo was anxious to speak to the Inspector about Michelle.

"Michelle has had to fill the vacancy left by Bright Cloud, which probably was impossible," said the Inspector. "But she's done a marvelous job under difficult circumstances. She's no phony, I can vouch for that. The native Indians from the village and for a hundred miles to the north have taken her into their hearts. She gives of herself and asks for nothing in return. Within a short period of time, she is known throughout the region as an authentic angel of mercy in the same mold as Bright Cloud." The Inspector paused to fill his trusty pipe. Arlo waited in silence, anxious to know all that he could find out about her.

"Back when Michelle first came to the infirmary, Bright Cloud was uncertain how the native people would react to her. Within a short time she realized that her fears were groundless. There have been several young men who've expressed an interest in her, but so far, she has managed to avoid any kind of personal attachment to anyone. I think she works too hard. She drives herself to the limit. She started taking annual leaves only after Bright Cloud promised to come back to the village every summer. Even then, we all had to insist that she take the time off.

"When she's not actively assisting a patient, she's studying the books we've transported to the infirmary. There's a small library over there right now. I could go on for a long time praising her work and the young lady herself. I fear that the lass is going to burn out if she doesn't start to slow down. Father Lamontagne thinks the same. We watch over her as best we can. She's worthy of our concern."

"You're lucky to be served with such dedication," observed Arlo quietly.

"That we are, Major. Constable Gillespie will be mad as a wet hen at me if I don't relieve him so that he can commence his routine patrol to the north before total darkness sets in. Shall we head for the wharf, Major?"

"By all means, Inspector," answered Arlo, silently acknowledging the undeclared challenge implied in the policeman's voice.

The fragile bark canoe sped across the lake faster than it had ever been propelled before. With Arlo at the stern and the doughty Inspector in the bow, both paddled in sequence so that the craft never slowed down between strokes. The Inspector was inwardly pleased with the fact that he had finally met his equal in handling a canoe.

"Thanks for sharing your locations with me, Inspector," said Arlo, holding the canoe steady against the dock. "I appreciate your confidence in me."

"It's pleasant to see new faces up here," answered the policeman, jumping to the wharf. "Ever since you and I communicated to arrange Mark's visit in 1921, I've wanted to have the chance to meet you face to face. You've not disappointed me, Major." The Inspector started down the wharf towards the station, then turned and hollered, "The fish string was enjoyed by all of us, much obliged."

With a wave of the hand, Arlo was underway across the lake to try his luck again at a quiet inlet before darkness settled in. In the distance several dogs were barking. It was casting its spell over him and he was ready to surrender to its mystical charm. For the first time in years, he was listening to his inner self. The feeling of open space and isolation from the civilized world, as he knew it, made him feel secure and fulfilled.

Later that evening after the supper dishes had been cleared away, Bright Cloud returned to the infirmary, while Mark and Arlo relaxed in the great room with their customary cloud of smoke overhead. The fire crackled warmly and felt good. The air was cool after the sunset.

Little DJ had already been put to bed. Bright Star was allowed to stay up a little longer. She listened to the conversation between Mark and Arlo. The sun had set earlier with a large red ball, which usually forecast another good day for tomorrow. That prompted Star to plan her day.

"It looks as if tomorrow will be clear like today," she stated, looking at Arlo. "Would you like to climb to the top of Lookout Rock in the morning, Major Korsman?" There was a sparkle in her eyes that made them look larger than they actually were.

"That would be great fun, Star," answered Arlo. He was pleased to see that she was beginning to feel comfortable around him. "You'll have to go very slow or I'll never make it all the way to the top."

"You'll be able to, Daddy does it and Mother seems to climb it easier than any of us."

"If I hadn't planned to go out to the test sites with some of the tribal elders, I'd go with you," said Mark. "Bright Cloud calls it her favorite spot after the cenotaph on the trail north of the village. I'll show you that before you leave, Arlo."

"Young lady, you'll probably wear me out," joked Arlo. "But, yes, I'd be happy to let you show me what promises to be a fantastic view."

"You won't be disappointed," said Star, giving Mark a goodnight hug and kiss before going to bed.

"How about a hug for this old soldier?" Arlo held out his arms. Little Star granted his wish with a youthful flourish. "Goodnight, young lady."

Later in the evening, the glowing coals in the fireplace were slowly dying by the time Bright Cloud returned to the cabin. Michelle was with her and they announced that they were going to have a cup of tea before returning to the infirmary. Mark and Arlo agreed to join them. Tea drinking in the North Woods was a more popular custom than coffee. It was a relaxing tradition. Arlo thought that Michelle looked more rested and at ease than the last time he saw her.

"Bright Cloud put me to sleep all afternoon and part of this evening. I do feel better though. I'm glad to have this chance to apologize for my conduct this morning, Arlo. It was uncalled for, and I'm sorry you had to see it."

"Please, Michelle, it was my mistake to intrude where I have no right to do so, and it is I who must apologize to you. I'm glad you had the chance to get some badly needed rest. The Inspector shared his knowledge of the lake with me this afternoon. He's a remarkable character. I've heard many stories about his exploits, and I'm inclined to believe them now that I've met him."

"The inspector is the living embodiment of a public servant. His code of ethics and standards of performance are not just fancy words, but a way of life," Mark proudly proclaimed, thinking of the courtesies he had received from the Inspector over the years. "We're lucky that he still chooses to conduct his Fort Lewis patrol after all these years."

Bright Cloud quietly checked the two children in their bedrooms and tiptoed back to the gathering at the table. "Star just whispered to me that you're going to be given the tour of our famous Lookout Rock tomorrow."

"Yes, she seems anxious to find out if I can climb the hill as well as everybody else can," answered Arlo with a grin.

"You won't have any trouble with it," said Michelle, watching him from across the table.

"Maybe you could go along, Michelle. It would give you a chance to spend some time with Star before you leave us," suggested Bright Cloud with one of her spur-of-the-moment ideas.

"That would be great," Arlo interrupted enthusiastically.

"Starting tomorrow, I'm not going to let Mike do any work. She plans to leave the day after tomorrow with the Inspector by airplane," Bright Cloud announced with finality.

"If Star doesn't mind, it would be fun. I haven't been up there for a long time."

"Then it's settled," said Bright Cloud, pouring the boiling water over several tea bags in an enameled steel pot.

After a leisurely cup of strong tea the two women returned to the infirmary. Arlo and Mark gladly retired shortly after they left the cabin.

Star was the second person up that next morning and she proceeded excitedly to make preparations for the day ahead. Bright Cloud, who had already left the cabin for the infirmary, had prepared their lunches and put them in a small packsack which Arlo volunteered to carry. Breakfast was completed by the time Michelle showed up. The three hikers started out on their great adventure.

Michelle was dressed for the occasion with matching corduroy pants and shirt, and a sturdy pair of shoes to support her ankles for the descent. Arlo was dressed in a set of Marine fatigue duty clothes. Star was completely clothed in soft deerskin shirt and pants. Her feet were covered with heavy moose-skin moccasins. She looked like the Native American she was. All of them came prepared for the hungry mosquito population with head nets of fine mesh cloth. The day was clear with a cobalt blue sky, which was cloudless except for a few lazy cumulous puff balls that seemed to be skewered to the distant mountains.

Star led the way along the path to the bridge by the spring, where they turned due west to the right and headed directly into the massive formation that loomed before them.

"It looks like a challenge to me, Star. Are you sure we can do it?" smiled Arlo. "You'll have to go easy or I'll never keep up with you."

"Oh come on, Major," scolded Star with mock displeasure.

"We can master the climb by taking as many breaks as we need. This is a welcome change from my normal routine. It'll be a nice memory for me to take back to New York with me tomorrow," commented Michelle.

Star selected an open spot above tree line for their first break. It was an area where a rock slide had removed any vegetation that may have existed at that elevation. Medium-sized rocks were still scattered all over. Like any veteran hikers, the three were quick to seek a place to sit and rest.

"So far so good, ladies," bragged Arlo. "This old man is doing better than expected. I'd hate to show you how much I'm out of shape. Probably tomorrow, I'll be so lame I won't be able to get out of bed."

Star and Michelle both laughed at the way he poked fun at himself. He told them comical stories about some of the men he had served with, and of some experiences he enjoyed talking about with close friends. They all laughed about the time a sergeant had given Arlo a cigar to celebrate a promotion. Unbeknown to the sergeant, some of his buddies had loaded the center of the cigars with a small amount of smokeless gunpowder. Within five minutes of smoking the cigars, Arlo and the sergeant were the victims of two small explosions, covering them with a black smudge. The sergeant feared a court martial, but Arlo said he could not stop laughing about what had happened to him. As they continued the climb to the top, Arlo's thoughts, while kept to himself, were on the sergeant who was killed in action on the last day of the war in France. The war was never very far from his mind.

The views of the surrounding territory were exceptional, especially to the south, where several bodies of water could be seen. As far as the eye could see, a green carpet of spruce and balsam fir covered the landscape. From the distance the forest looked like a soft blanket of green. Michelle seemed to be enjoying herself. Arlo's outrageous stories had set the right tone for the three climbers to feel comfortable with each other. Bright Star was a bundle of energy who tirelessly pointed out some interesting features in the area. There was a relaxed, easygoing manner about Star that reminded Arlo of Bright Cloud. She was very mature for her age. Arlo credited that to the fact that Mark and Bright Cloud both talked to her and treated her as a young adult instead of an infant.

Arlo watched Michelle closely for any sign of what happened yesterday. She seemed to be in good spirits, yet she was relatively quiet. Maybe, he thought, she was just naturally reflective when the situation allowed it. The first break period allowed them to remove their headnets. When Michelle took off her net, Arlo noticed she had fixed her hair to fall loosely about her shoulders. It made her look younger. She still had that proud confident tilt of the chin which seemed to tell the world she had everything under control. Maybe she does, he said to himself, but yesterday he had uncovered something that struck her deeply, and he was concerned for her. This morning she still looked vulnerable, regardless of the air she projected.

The open-topped woven knapsack Arlo carried had a supply of candy bars, which he distributed to Star and Michelle. Sitting against a large rock, he casually remarked that he should do this sort of thing more often. He liked any opportunity that put his muscles to work.

"Did you go to France in the war, Arlo?" asked Michelle.

"Yes, I was there for over a year. I served with a different division than Mark. He served with an Army division, whereas, I was with the Marine Brigade. Thank God it's over..."

90

"What does a soldier do when there's no more war to be fought?" inquired Michelle innocently.

"There's always a war someplace in the world, or the threat of a war. We have to plan for and anticipate what's going to happen and prepare to defend against any and all threats. It's a constant cycle of training, reviewing, and training again. Hard training saves lives in combat," reflected Arlo. "We're a long ways from any serious threat of war in this beautiful wilderness." Arlo glanced at Michelle and detected a slight droop to her chin. She avoided looking at him. The old sadness is still just below the surface, he surmised.

An hour later, the three hikers reached the highest pinnacle. The vast panorama before them was worth the sore muscles and strenuous effort. Michelle and Star pointed out the different locations. The easterly bounds of the tribal forest tract were readily defined by the systematic patches of clear-cut forest. The openings were a lush vibrant blue-green mosaic of young seedlings. It was a small part of the continuous verdant forest cover of the land. The only difference was that the young new growth supported more wildlife than the older mature and stagnant stands of spruce, fir or jack pine. The openings insured a fully established crop of desirable species for the future. All that was required to secure that natural reseeding, was the presence of mature seed-bearing trees to the north and west of the cut-over area, where the prevailing wind carried seeds from the mature trees to the newly scarified forest floor. Nature did an excellent job when helped by sound forest management.

Michelle pointed to the center cabin where Mark first stayed a few years ago. Smoke curled from its chimney. She also showed the approximate location of the cabin where she had been held captive when Mark and Bright Cloud came to her rescue.

Bright Cloud had thought of everything. She had included a large thermos bottle of hot tea for Michelle and Arlo, and a small bottle of lemonade for Star. The hikers were ready to replenish their energy. They eagerly ate the lunches in the knapsack and waited for a large cloud to ponderously move away from a spot to the south. When the cloud did uncover the view from the mountaintop, Arlo was surprised to catch a glimpse of the blue black waters of Lac St. Jean, two hundred miles to the south. Star pointed a small finger to the east where the cenotaph for her maternal father, Flying Eagle, was located.

It took him a few minutes to detect the pattern of whitish-gray spires against the green background of the surrounding vegetation.

"When I first came up here, I wasn't much of a tea drinker," commented Michelle, sipping the hot liquid. "Now, I'm addicted to it."

"It does go good in these latitudes. It sits well on the stomach." Arlo watched Star eat two peanut butter and jam sandwiches with a youthful relish. She combined the inherent modesty of her race with a confident poise that was most becoming to her. A stranger could easily picture Bright Cloud as her maternal mother instead of her aunt.

By two o'clock, the three hikers decided it was time to leave Lookout Rock. The climb down was easier on the legs, but it was more of an obstacle for the feet. Good footwear was a necessity because the toes are pushed down into the ends of the shoes at an angle that can be uncomfortable. By the time they reached the level ground, they all shared a feeling of accomplishment. It had been a most pleasant day for all of them.

Mark and Bright Cloud were gone from the cabin when the three hikers got to it. Star was still full of energy and anxious to share her adventure of the day with some of her friends, so she left to visit them in the village. Arlo and Michelle found themselves awkwardly alone in the cabin after Star left.

"Why don't we go out to the lakeshore and enjoy the breeze off the water," suggested Michelle. "We won't need the headnets. I probably won't have a chance to see you again before I leave tomorrow with the Inspector."

"I'd like that," answered Arlo, leading the way out the door. "I want you to know that I've really enjoyed my visit to Fort Lewis and meeting you, Michelle. I don't make friends easily. I guess it's my Finnish bashfulness, but I want you to know that it's been swell being with you, and I'd like to be considered one of your friends."

"I appreciate the kind words, Arlo," responded Michelle with some uncertainty. "My work has been my life, and there hasn't been much opportunity to socialize with a lot of people. Sometimes it's lonely here, and your visit has been a pleasant break from a tiring routine. I thank you for that."

"How long will you be in New York?"

"Probably until the first of September."

"I'm only allowed two weeks furlough at this time, so I'll be returning to the Washington area in about a week and a half. During the week I'm more than busy, but the weekends are generally free for me. May I call on you at Diamond Point on some weekend before the end of summer? It's not so far from Washington that it can't be managed."

The simple request caught Michelle unprepared for an answer. Arlo could see that she was having trouble. "I'm sorry again, Michelle, I meant no harm to you. I know that it may sound sudden and a little presumptuous, but if I didn't ask you that question now, I may never see you again. I admit, honestly, I would like to call on you. Excuse my boldness, and believe me, I normally am not this bold with ladies."

"I believe you, Arlo," Michelle said, trying to compose herself. She looked at the shore of the lake to hide the tears that were slowly rolling down her cheeks. "I'm flattered that you wish to see me again. I would like that too. Yet, there is something about me which you don't know, Arlo. It may drive you away from me, once you know about it."

Tears continued to fill her eyes. She wept silently into her hands cupped over her face. Arlo placed a comforting hand on her shoulder, feeling responsible for putting her in such an uncomfortable position.

"Forgive me, Michelle."

"It's me. My nightmare keeps coming back to haunt me... You're entitled to an explanation. I owe you the truth; then you must decide whether you want to call upon me."

Arlo held out his clean handkerchief to her. She took it and carefully wiped the tears from her face.

"Be patient with me, Arlo. It's not an easy story for me to tell. Especially to you."

"I promise to be patient."

"When I was a young girl in high school, I fell in love with a classmate whom I thought would be at my side forever. After graduation, he joined the Army and went overseas to France. He was killed near the end of the war. I was devastated when I heard the news. I didn't tell him before he left for France, or in any letters that I wrote to him, that I was pregnant with his child. When the news of his death arrived, I went to his parents and explained my position to them. They just called me a cheap hussy and didn't want anything to do with me or the child.

"My own family shared my shame and allowed me to stay at home until the baby was born, with the provision that I give the baby up for adoption. I agreed, because there was nothing else for me to do. I had no money and no other place to turn for help. It was a healthy baby boy. I let him go for adoption and I'm still so ashamed of it that I hate myself. All of these years I've been trying to locate my son, without success.

"I've buried myself in my work to forget and to make amends for my sins. I was able to live with it until you came along and asked me an honest question out there on the lake. I've had chances to meet young men that were interested in me. I've tried to discourage them because of my private shame. It was different when you came to Fort Lewis. Bright Cloud and Mark have talked so much about you that I was attracted to you before you ever came here.

"The shame and regret of my actions when I was younger has been a worrisome burden to live with, and not a day goes by that I don't hear the voice of a tiny baby boy crying out in the arms of a hospital nurse who took him away from me forever...I regret that decision the most."

The depth of her anguish was difficult for Arlo to witness. He wanted to reach out to console her, and was searching for the right words to say what was in his heart. Michelle naturally interpreted his silence as condemnation of her conduct, and quickly pulled herself up from the ground where they were sitting and bolted as fast as she could toward her cabin. Her choking sobs trailed back to him as he sat alone, stunned by her precipitant flight.

Chapter Seven

The emotion-packed scene had taken place twenty-two years ago and Arlo could still feel the pain today. The pulsations of the large command ship forcing its way through the calm seas brought him back to the present and reality. They were still a long ways from their destination, Guadalcanal. Wiping the perspiration from his brow, Arlo laid back down on his bunk and tried, once again, to sleep. A busy day was ahead of him tomorrow, but he could not deny the memories that filled his heart.

* * *

Arlo sat motionless and stared blindly across the sparkling waters of Lac Diamante. It was almost dark before he could gather the strength to return to the cabin after Michelle's flight from his presence. Mark was standing over the stove, lighting a fire in it.

"My, God, Arlo. What's wrong?"

"I think I've hurt Michelle terribly," cried Arlo, the depth of his distress showing in his voice. Mark had never seen Arlo look so beaten.

"Talk to me, Arlo. Is she okay? What happened?"

"I don't know if she's ever told you. I think she told Bright Cloud yesterday."

"Bright Cloud would never tell me anything that was told to her in confidence, unless she was given permission."

"Well, Mark, then you can get the story from Michelle or Bright Cloud. I'm not at liberty to repeat it, either. It's enough to say that she's been carrying a terrible hurt around with her for many years."

"Poor Michelle, she certainly needs a friend!"

"You can say that again. When she told me her story, I knew that she was expecting an answer from me. I just clammed up and sat there like a dumbbell saying nothing."

Always one to use attack as a defense, Mark's advice to Arlo was short, to the point and predictable.

"If your feelings tell you that you're wrong with the way you handled it, then don't let another moment go by. Go to her cabin and tell her what you honestly think, Arlo."

"You're right, Mark, I'm just not thinking straight," called Arlo, shaking his head as he left the cabin with flashlight in hand.

Two knocks at Michelle's door were answered by a feeble voice which he barely recognized. "Come in."

The interior of the cabin was dark except for a short candle almost burned out on the table at the far side of the room. The same voice spoke again from the darkness. "Who is it?" This time Arlo recognized it as belonging to Michelle.

"It's me, Michelle. I came to say what I honestly feel. May I speak freely or do you prefer that I leave? Please don't doubt my sincerity in being here," pleaded Arlo.

"I'll be right out."

Arlo saw a light flicker beneath her bedroom door. The door opened and revealed a disheveled Michelle. She deliberately walked into the room, holding a kerosene lamp in both of her hands. They were unsteady as she placed it on the table and turned to Arlo.

"I apologize for how I must look. Please sit down."

"I didn't come to judge you on the basis of your appearance, Michelle. I came to tell you that I don't stand in judgment of your actions either. When you told me tonight, I was searching for the right things to say when you ran off so suddenly. I'm not quick with my reflexes like some people. My immediate response to your story should have been what was in my heart. I can honestly tell you that I think you're the most courageous person I've ever met. To think that you've carried your guilt for all these years is remarkable. If God is going to judge you for something you were forced to do, then He's not the same God of compassion that I've always believed forgave us for our human transgressions. If He can forgive you, why can't you forgive yourself?"

"It's not that easy, Arlo. I'm ashamed and angry at what I did, and I miss my son! I did a terrible thing after a weak moment of passion, by letting him go."

"Nonsense. You took the only way available to you at that time in your life. You could have endangered yourself by having an abortion, but you made the right decision not to do so. Good Lord, Michelle, stop beating yourself up for past mistakes. We've all got failures of one type or another that are a part of our past; we have to bury them and get on with our lives. We learn from the experience and come out of it wiser than ever. I'm sounding like a preacher now, and it's not my calling, but don't you think you've paid enough for your actions?"

"I don't know how to answer that, Arlo. These past two days have been very difficult for me, as you already know. I haven't gone through this kind of soul searching for years. I was worried how you would perceive me if you heard the truth. I'm not sorry I told you. It's a part of my life, and I cannot separate it from me."

"You shouldn't have to, Michelle. I came to you tonight because you're going to be leaving in the morning, and I probably won't see you again. You never did answer my question. Would you object if I call on you while you're in New York State for the summer?"

"That would make me happy, Arlo. Please do."

The few minutes they had been talking around the small table, Arlo could already detect a change in her. Her voice was stronger and her hands stopped fidgeting with the soiled handkerchief she kept folding and unfolding. He could not see her eyes distinctly, but she was not crying the way she was when he entered the cabin.

"I may not see you in the morning before you leave, so I wish you a `bon voyage' and happy landings. I promise to see you within a month, probably on the weekend, at your place in New York. By the way, can you give me directions to where you're staying?"

"Certainly, I'll get a pencil and paper." Michelle returned to the table and wrote out directions from the center of Lake George village to the house where she would be staying.

"Thanks, Michelle," said Arlo, standing away from the table. "I'll be looking forward to seeing you again."

"I'll be awaiting your visit, Arlo."

She led him to the door and stepped aside for him to pass. He was reluctant to say good-bye. Arlo turned at the threshold to look at her one last time. Her lower lip was trembling. He took her into his arms and kissed her. She returned it.

"Whatever happens, young lady, you're not alone. I admire your quiet courage, Michelle. Please, don't do this to yourself anymore."

"I can't believe this is happening to me," cried Michelle, resting her head on his broad shoulder.

"Let's count our blessings and not rush it too much. I've seen one miracle in my lifetime, and I think I'm living another one right now." He squeezed her in his arms and slowly kissed her again before releasing her.

"Until next time, Michelle."

"Until next time, Arlo. Thank you for coming back tonight."

Arlo could not recall the walk to his cabin after that magical encounter with Michelle. All he remembered is that he walked on clouds for days. The first time he went to New York State to visit her was still crystal clear to him, after all the intervening years...

Arlo had traded his Hudson for a new 1926 Nash Advanced Six four-door sedan. He was anxious to try it out on a long trip, so he drove it to upper state New York to see Michelle as he had promised when she left Fort Lewis. He traveled as far as New York City from Washington, D.C. on Friday evening in mid-July. Early Saturday morning he finished the trip to Lake George, where he had lunch at the busy part of town next to the southern end of the lake, studying the map Michelle had drawn for him while he ate.

He found Michelle's place without any trouble. It was beautifully located on the western shore of Lake George, which reminded him of Lac Diamante in Canada. Michelle was staying at the old Gurney homestead with her brother's family. The house was what he had always referred to as a New Englander style, similar to the ones he had seen in Maine and New Hampshire with a high pitched roof to shed the heavy snow loads that were normal for the area. The white house had a neatly trimmed lawn in the front with several large sugar maple trees planted in a line along the road frontage. An open porch ran across the front and down the right side towards the shore of the lake.

Arlo pulled into the driveway and approached the front door with his stomach tied in knots. He rang the door bell and knocked several times, yet nobody answered. Suddenly a young boy about seven or eight years came running around the corner of the house, spotted Arlo at the door and stared in wonder at the sturdy marine.

"Wow," exclaimed the child, running to the back of the house.

Arlo was amused at the boy's reaction to him and still remained apprehensive. He was ready to step down to the driveway when a woman appeared from around the corner of the house.

"May I help you?" she asked.

"Yes, ma'am. I'm looking for Miss Michelle Gurney. Do I have the right address?"

"You certainly do, Major," answered the woman with a slight flush at her cheeks. "Michelle will be surprised. I'm her sister-in-law, Laura Gurney. The over-active young man you just scared is my son, Philip. You must be Major Arlo Korsman."

"Yes, ma'am. It's my pleasure to meet you. I'm earlier than I expected. I left Washington after I completed my work for the week and stayed over at New York City. It's beautiful up here in the Adirondacks."

"I hope you enjoy your stay. Come, Michelle is out back with the children. We just completed a rowboat ride on the lake."

Laura Gurney led the way across the large lawn behind the house. He saw Michelle sitting on a small wharf with a couple of rowboats tied up to it. She had not noticed him until Laura called to her.

"Arlo," cried Michelle, startled by his presence. She had never seen him in uniform before, and it took a moment for her to recognize him at a distance. She leaped from the wharf and ran towards him. "You did come after all. When you wrote me that this might not be a good time for your work, I was disappointed. I'm so glad things worked out for you to make it." Michelle reached out for his hands. He eagerly grasped them.

Michelle was a different person from the one he left on the shore of Lac Diamante. She was vibrant, energetic and full of enthusiasm. She had picked up a slight tan since she left Canada, and it was most becoming to her. She wore her light sandy colored hair loose about her shoulders, pulled back around the side of her face. He was delighted to see her eyes light up when they met.

"You look like a new person. A vacation is what you needed," he said.

"Why don't you take Major Korsman into the front parlor and I'll keep these little monsters quiet out here for a while," suggested Laura.

"Thanks Laura, that would be nice. Arlo, you must be tired after all that driving. Come we'll be comfortable in the front room."

"To the contrary, I enjoyed the trip along the Hudson River. I never realized how popular this region is in the summertime. Lake George is bustling with people." Arlo said, following her into the house.

"Have a seat in the parlor and make yourself at home," Michelle pointed to the large sunny room at the front of the house. "I'll get us a cold drink. How about some lemonade and something to eat?"

"Just a cold drink, thanks. I ate at Lake George, so I'm fine."

"I'll just be a minute, Arlo."

The sitting room was cheerful and warm as the sun filtered through the white lace curtains on the windows. The mantel above the fireplace had a picture of a younger Michelle in a white nurse's uniform with a dark blue cape over her shoulders. She was smiling for the camera, but Arlo detected a tinge of sadness in her eyes.

"That picture was taken when I finished the course at the Nursing College at Glens Falls," remarked Michelle, returning to the room with two glasses of lemonade. "I can't believe you're actually here. I've thought a lot about our parting at Fort Lewis. It still feels like a dream...far away and long ago. I haven't dared to hope too much, because hopes and dreams have a way of being shattered when we least expect it."

"I really enjoyed my stay with Mark and Bright Cloud, but to be perfectly honest, I could hardly wait for this weekend to come, Michelle. I've thought a lot about that parting. I see a different Michelle here before me than I saw at Fort Lewis. I'm glad to see you're resting."

"This is the first time I've seen you in your uniform. My little Philip ran back to the rowboat to tell me that a big soldier was on the front porch. You looked strong and formidable to him, and I have to agree, you look great in your forest greens. It's reassuring to have you here, Arlo."

"The marine uniform makes every man look good. I've always tried to keep myself in good physical condition, much like my father

100

did. Several years ago, my Finnish heritage was bolstered by the fantastic performance of Paavo Nurmi, a four-time Olympic Gold Medal winner at Paris. Since then, I've been a daily runner. The military routine can be quite physically demanding when you're commanding troops, but less so when you're assigned to some school which has been continuous these past few years for me. That's why I enjoy running. It keeps me in good condition."

As Arlo was talking to Michelle, he had the strange feeling that she was holding something back from him, and filling time with small talk. She seemed preoccupied. It was not what he expected or hoped for. Her hesitation became more evident when he suggested that they take a ride in his new Nash around the lake.

"I'm sorry, Arlo. I must apologize for being so distracted at this time. I'd love to go for a ride with you, but I must tell you something first. I've been busy these past few days, as you will soon find out. I'm expecting a visit from a private investigator by the name of Lawrence Ralston who's been trying to locate the whereabouts of the baby boy I put up for adoption. I know that it may sound crazy and foolhardy, but my desire to find out all that I can is so strong, I can't help myself. He should be here anytime now. I beg of you, please don't judge me by these actions..."

Arlo could understand her yearning for such information and did not prejudge her motives. He was not a person who habitually judged other people unless he had sufficient reasons to do so.

"I told you once, I don't stand in judgment of the natural desire of a mother to want to find out all that she can about her son. However, I'll say one thing as a caution for you. How do you know he wants to be found? What about the delicate position of the people who've provided him with a home and loving parents? And finally, what do you do if you come to a dead end? There has to be a point when you have to admit that enough is enough, Michelle. I applaud your efforts, and admire your spirit in pursuing what your heart tells you is right; however, it should not become a lifetime career. Reality has to guide you. When you made the decision to give up the child, as difficult as it was to make, it has to be honored for the sake of the other people involved."

Michelle looked at him with misty eyes and said, "I've said those same words to myself, Arlo, believe me."

He opened his strong arms for her and she readily sought their comforting support. She drew strength from him. For the first time since the child was born, she felt that she was not alone.

"I'll promise you one thing, Arlo. If this investigation runs into a blank wall, and we cannot find out anything about him, then I'll put this chapter of my life behind me and get on with the future. As a matter of a fact, your advice to me at Fort Lewis was the motivation for contacting the detective. I felt that I had to make one last serious attempt, and then I'd let it rest in God's hands and stop searching."

"I think it's a wise decision, and I support you. I'm not your enemy on this subject, Michelle," said Arlo, embracing her.

"I know. You could never be that to me. I feel bad dragging all of this out between us again. I've been so anxious for your visit, and it isn't fair for my past indiscretions to come between us. Thanks for being so understanding."

Feeling safe in his arms, she looked up at him and returned his kiss. "I've been thinking of you all the time since you left Canada," Arlo whispered in her ear.

Michelle was about to answer him when her sister-in-law, Laura, intruded to announce the arrival of Mr. Lawrence Ralston in the driveway. Arlo suggested that she see him alone, but she was adamant that he stay with her. Lawrence Ralston turned out to be a well-dressed professional who apologized for his inability to produce any information that would be encouraging for Michelle. He told both of them that the adoption laws in the State of New York were very strict in order to prevent what he was trying to do. However, he had several ways, which he did not reveal, of determining basic information. The full results of his exhaustive efforts was that the child had been taken by a couple who settled into the Finger Lakes region of New York. Their last name was Stevens, and the baby boy had been christened in the Catholic faith as John Stevens. The family was involved in a tragic house fire a couple of years ago which took the lives of the two adult Stevens. The baby boy survived and was apparently uninjured in the fire. He was subsequently adopted by a couple whom he had been unable to locate. To determine the identity and whereabouts of the new couple could be very difficult, if not impossible, and very expensive.

Arlo was proud of Michelle when she told the detective to present her with a bill, which she would pay forthwith, and that further investigations were out of the question. Now she had reached the turning point that Arlo mentioned earlier. She knew that it was time to turn her energy towards those things which she could control. Though she was disappointed, and felt sick at heart, there was a small sense of accomplishment, even relief, at reaching this pivotal milestone in her life.

Michelle showed Arlo some of the strong determination which helped to define her. From the moment she dismissed the private detective, a new revitalized person seemed to take her place. Her life had been rooted in the past, dominated by her inability to keep her own flesh and blood. Now, she could stop looking backward and concentrate on the future, which promised to be very fulfilling.

Saturday they visited the old Fort Ticonderoga ruins north of Lake George. The picnic lunch Michelle packed was shared while they sat on some of the old ramparts of the Fort with a view to the east and north across Lake Champlain. It was a pleasant day for both of them. The evening was spent at Lake George watching a moving picture show called "The Jazz Singer", with Al Jolson. It was the very first talking movie show. Price of admission was fifteen cents apiece.

The weekend passed quickly for Michelle and Arlo. Late Sunday afternoon Arlo told her that as much as he would like to stay with her, he had to start back to Quantico, Virginia. They both knew that the weekend had been special. The visit confirmed what had been dormant in each of their hearts since Fort Lewis. Their being together was "right", even though the time they had known each other was short.

Just before Arlo left her in the driveway, he brought up a subject that would always be a part of his life as a member of the country's armed forces. He could be sent anywhere in the world on a short notice. A large percentage of the Marine Corps was already stationed in several countries in South America fighting insurrections and securing American Legations in danger. There was a rumor in the air that the Corps was going to China. Arlo warned Michelle that if that rumor proved true, then he would be going as commanding officer of one of the battalions in the brigade.

Michelle had never considered this aspect of Arlo's career. The possibilities were frightening to her, and she responded slowly, "If it happens, we'll just have to accept it. I understand that you're obligated to follow orders. It frightens me to think about what could happen..."

"Bad things can happen to any of us anywhere, regardless of what we're doing or where we're doing it," Arlo tried to reassure her.

"I'd still be concerned for you and worry."

"I know that, and I'm flattered that you feel that way, Michelle. The life of a soldier is not as predictable as an ordinary citizen. My career is important to me and I would not want to change it unless I was..."

"I would never ask you to change what you're doing on my account," interrupted Michelle.

"What I'm trying to say, Michelle, is that the Marine Corps places demands on officers such as myself that are frequently unfair. That's part of the job. I'd like to see you again and I want you to know precisely what you're getting yourself into with me. I'm doing very badly asking you to be patient with me. Demands placed upon me when I don't have a choice is a part of what I do and who I am. After telling you these things, am I being too pushy if I ask you to understand my position and wait for me?"

"Arlo, if you didn't feel the commitment to your calling that is so evident in you, then I would respect you less than I do." She continued almost in a whisper, "Yes, I'd understand and wait for you if that's what you want. Your visit here at Lake George has only reinforced the feelings I carried with me from Fort Lewis. I think we've started something that is very special, and I shall pray for us."

Arlo heard the words he was hoping would come from her lips. He embraced her with both arms and, for the first time in his life, felt complete.

"I'm almost afraid to believe this," Michelle cried softly. "What if I wake up tomorrow and find it's only a dream?"

"It's for real. If you'll wait for me, I promise to come whenever I can and as often as I can, because I've fallen in love with you, Michelle."

"I'll wait for you forever if that's what is needed, Arlo. I love you too, and thank you for being the person you are. Until next time, Arlo..."

"Until next time, Michelle..."

* * *

Arlo was jolted back to the present by a loud throbbing klaxon announcing battle stations. He was out of his bunk in a hurry, instinctively reaching for his life preserver and helmet. He could hear the scurrying of feet beyond his door. The klaxon kept sounding its irritating warning. By the time he got out the door, the loud speakers announced that all battle stations were manned and ready.

The bridge was a beehive of activity. Arlo knew better than to interfere with the operations, so he just stood off to one side near the Captain's chair, out of the way. The officer of the bridge, a young Navy Captain, saw him and acknowledged his presence to the crew. "General officer on deck. We've sighted two Japanese submarines, General. The destroyers are trying to make contact again. In the meantime we're traveling in an exaggerated zigzag pattern."

"Thank you, Captain."

The ship's Captain burst through the door excited by the situation developing with the convoy. He gave several orders to the officer of the bridge and seriously studied the charts on the plotting table. Satisfied that he had done everything possible to prepare for the worst case scenario, he nervously walked over to Arlo and climbed into his bridge chair. It could be a long night.

"I get nervous when we're in convoy with troop ships," confessed the Commodore. "There are enough destroyers and destroyer escorts to make a fence around the troop transports, General. However, you can never tell for sure where the subs are. The Japanese Navy doesn't have many submarines left. We were unlucky to pick up whatever is out there."

A loud explosion rocked the ship, interrupting the Commodore in mid-sentence. Two other blasts sounded simultaneously, rocking the ship several degrees off center. A quiet pause made it possible to hear the sirens of the sleek destroyers to the starboard, who were the first to draw blood. They jockeyed for the best position to deliver the finishing blow to the enemy below the surface.

Wham, wham, wham, wham, sounded the depth charges being fired from the dancing destroyers. Arlo was fascinated by the virtuoso performance beside them. He could see the mountain of water that rose with each explosion. After one destroyer had fired its pattern of charges, it turned sharply to the starboard allowing one of its sister destroyers to zero in on the target and fire its own pattern of depth charges. The command ship was rocking like a cork in the water from the powerful detonations. The agile escorts fired a hundred depth charges before they signaled all ships in the convoy.

"Jap subs found, Jap subs sent to Davy Jone's locker. That is all."

"That was a dazzling display of powerful teamwork, Commodore," said Arlo, impressed with the short violent action.

"It was a sight to behold, wasn't it, General Korsman? Would you believe it if I told you that the crews of all of the destroyers out there are reservists? They make me feel proud."

"I would believe it, Sir. Those of us who are career professionals are a small part of our military capabilities. The lion's share of it is done by those citizen soldiers and sailors we're all so proud of. So far in this war, they've taken on two of the most professional and most powerful militaristic nations of all times, and licked them every time, at every engagement when the playing field was reasonably level. We have a right to be proud of these men."

Arlo left the bridge to check on his brigade staff below decks. In order to comply with his recent orders to proceed to Pearl Harbor, he would have to rely on his staff to see that the men were well taken care of and settled into the new encampment. If he was lucky enough to catch a plane to Pearl Harbor as soon as they landed, he calculated that he might be able to beat the hospital ship carrying Mark to the large naval complex on the island of Oahu in the Hawaiian Islands.

As soon as the convoy dropped anchor off the coast of Guadalcanal, a Catalina flying boat was ready and waiting for him. He and his aide boarded the two-engine aircraft and were whisked away from the stinking jungle island of Guadalcanal. The lumbering airplane was unable to make the full distance to Pearl Harbor without refueling, so it landed in the Gilbert Islands at Tarawa. It was a welcome opportunity for the occupants to stretch their legs and catch a cup of coffee. Arlo and his aide visited the large cemetery on the island and reflected on the high cost of victory. Men from the armed forces were not the only casualties of the war, thought Arlo. His beloved Michelle was still among the missing!

By the time they finally landed at the seaplane base at Pearl Harbor, they were starting the day all over again. They had crossed the International Date Line and landed on the same day as they started.

Arlo reported to the Headquarters of the Commander in Chief of the Central Pacific Command the next morning. Security was tight. Arlo had a little bit of a problem getting past the sentry, because the picture on his ID card no longer resembled the same person who had gone through more than two years of constant combat. The huge complex was alive with activity. Everybody moved at a quick-time tempo. He was rushed to the office of the Deputy Chief of Staff for Operations. A stern-looking Rear Admiral reviewed the status of those operations now under way and those still in the planning stages with Arlo. His brigade had just passed from General Douglas MacArthur's Command to that of Admiral Nimitz, Commander of the Pacific Ocean Area Command.

Arlo's Brigade was scheduled to be a part of the operation now being planned for the assaults of Peleliu and Guam. He was ordered to Pearl Harbor to contribute what he could to the proposed scheme of maneuver for the two islands. On his return to Guadalcanal, Arlo would act as a courier for the proposal conceived by the CinCh Pacific Ocean Area, and authorized by the U.S. Joint Chiefs of Staff in Washington.

The marines were glad to be back under Naval supervision, where many felt that they were more appreciated. Arlo could agree up to a point. Serving under MacArthur and the Sixth Army's commander, Lt. Gen. Walter Krueger, had given Arlo some hope that he might be a part of the eventual liberation of the Philippines. General MacArthur had made it clear to everyone concerned that he was going to return to the Philippines, one way or the other, as soon as possible. It was also common knowledge among the higher echelon of commanders that the most obvious command to make the initial strike would be the Sixth Army, which Arlo's Brigade had been a part. Consequently, Arlo was not as happy as some of his marines to leave the Sixth Army.

He had a personal reason for wanting to be a part of the organization that liberated the Philippines. His beloved wife, Michelle, was in the Philippines, possibly on the island of Leyte. He didn't know if she was alive or dead, prisoner of war, or still free in the central mountain regions of Leyte operating with Filipino guerrilla groups. His gut feeling was that she was in the mountains or the vast jungle regions instead of behind barbed wires. His hope and daily prayers was that she was alive regardless of where she was existing. He did not dare to let his imagination wander any deeper.

As soon as Arlo finished his business with the staff officer, he looked up the Army Liaison Staff to the Pacific Ocean Command, which happened to be across the hall from where he had just been. He desperately wanted to learn all he could about current information available from the Philippines. As soon as he walked through the door he knew that luck was with him. He came face to face with two Army Colonels who had been classmates with him at the Staff and Command School at Fort Leavenworth, Kansas several years ago, Col. James Ready, and Col. Henry "Hank" Thomas. Arlo breathed a sigh of relief, for he was among friends.

The star on his shoulders brought them to attention. Col. Ready was the first to recognize Arlo. "General Korsman, it's been a while, Sir!"

"It's great to see you again, Jim, and you too, Hank," exclaimed Arlo.

"Those stars on your shoulders look really good, General. I guess advancements in the Army are lagging behind the Marine Corps a bit," added Hank, saluting Arlo and then grasping his outstretched hand.

"Please, forget the star and call me what you always did, 'a goddamn cocky marine.' I come as a friend, not as a general officer," smiled Arlo.

"You haven't changed a bit," laughed Jim, offering Arlo a chair beside a large table covered with papers, charts, etc.

"The amount of paperwork generated by this command is out of control. If I'd known, I would've invested in stocks of paper companies," added Jim in his relaxed easy-going manner. He was a short stockily-built officer with bright eyes that were constantly observing those around him. He had a reputation of being on the intellectual side. Staff work was his strongest and most productive assignment in the Army. He could quote minute details of several complex operations once he had reviewed them. He also had a tendency to take a firm stand on any issue he believed in regardless of the consequences. He was a serious professional and Arlo got along well with him at command school. They had kept in touch over the years, but had never served together. James Ready had a great sense of humor, and a tendency to do things his own way.

Colonel Hank Thomas was a tall, slender Texan who did things by the book. He did not talk as freely as Jim, but when he said something, he meant it. He was more taciturn than Jim, and more meticulous, with a tendency to perfectionism. A wise commander must have seen in the two men what Arlo had always known: they complement one another. Their work had an element of genius with a flair noticeable only to the astute observer. These two men, in Arlo's estimation, were both intelligence producers "extraordinaire".

"What brings you to this neck of the woods, Arlo?" asked Jim. "We've been following the progress of your brigade for several months. You've had some hard nuts to crack and you've performed very well. Congratulations!"

"Thanks, Jim. We've been able to take our objectives even when the costs have been high. I haven't totally reconciled in my own mind, if what we've accomplished is worth the price we had to pay," answered Arlo with honesty.

"I'd feel the same way if I was in your shoes," said Hank, watching Arlo closely. He thought Arlo looked tired and drained.

"I can't tell you how glad I am to be in the company of two friends, and I would love to reminisce with you, if you have some free time tonight. Right now I've come to ask you something that's very personal and has me at my wits end, because I've heard nothing in the past two years about my wife. If you've got the time, I'll tell you what I can."

"Of course we've got the time, Arlo." Both Army officers nodded in unison. "What can we do to help?"

"As you may already know, I was stationed in China as a battalion commander with the Fourth Marines in 1940 and 1941. When things started to heat up, the regiment was ordered out of China to the Philippines. My wife, Michelle, was with me in

Shanghai. As soon as we got word of our eventual withdrawal, I sent her, along with several other dependents, to the Philippines to keep them out of danger. Admiral Hart, Commanding Officer of the Asiatic Fleet, changed my orders and sent me to Pearl Harbor after Michelle had already left for Luzon, and before the Fourth Marines left mainland China. I was here at Pearl Harbor doing staff work when the war started, while my wife was still in the Philippines. I've had only one letter from her which was dated November 30, 1941. She landed safely in Luzon, and was going to examine some Missionary medical facilities in the company of several other nurses, in the rugged central mountainous region of the island of Leyte. She wrote that her boat was not scheduled to arrive for another ten days to take her to Hawaii, and that she was going to visit the mission while waiting.

"I've been going crazy trying to find out anything about the situation in the occupied areas of the Philippines. That's why I'm here. I need your help!" Arlo lit a cigarette and waited anxiously for the things he had just told Hank and Jim to register.

The two Army colonels looked at each other in disbelief. "I'm not sure that you realize what our liaison job is all about. We coordinate raw intelligence from the Southwest Pacific Command and the Pacific Ocean Area Command. Everything we do is classified, Arlo. Surely, you know what that means. However, may I suggest that we get together tonight at the Army-Navy Club for a drink and dinner?" asked Jim.

"That sounds like a great idea if you can spare the time before returning back to the Canal," said Hank, grasping Arlo's shoulder.

Arlo had the feeling he was being brushed off, but he knew these two officers better than to think that he was getting the "bum's rush".

"I'm going to be able to stay here for a couple of days, guys. Tonight at the club sounds good to me. I want to visit some of my wounded men tomorrow. They're coming in by hospital ship from New Britain. I've been authorized to take off a whole week, but I'm also anxious to get the next operation started, so that my men can be ready. I won't take up any more of your time. So until tonight at seven."

"Tonight at seven, General," smiled Hank with a parting grin and salute. Jim silently and respectfully saluted also.

Arlo returned the courtesy and walked to the door wondering if he had come to the right place to seek information about the Philippines. He wished that he had talked to General Kreuger's Chief of Intelligence before leaving Cape Gloucester. The Sixth Army should have the most recent updates on the situation. He was disappointed that the opportunity was no longer available to him.

Arlo and his aide settled into a civilian hotel on the outskirts of Honolulu which had been taken over by the Navy for rest and relaxation of its weary mariners. Both of the men were eager to shower and change into clean uniforms in preparation for the evening ahead. Arlo's aide asked permission for the night out, and Arlo was more than glad to grant him a well-earned respite from his duties. The hotel room provided an excellent view of the harbor below. He could see the white hospital ship slowly making its way through the channel under the guidance of two tugs. His compliment of wounded men were finally safe in the harbor where it had all started on December 7, 1941. He was thankful for their safe journey to this piece of American soil. Now they could begin the tedious task of rebuilding their broken bodies and twisted souls.

Arlo took his time getting dressed for the dinner engagement with his Army friends. He retrieved his wallet and pocket watch from the bureau top and placed them in his pockets. Michelle, who was never far from his thoughts, had given him a lock of her hair several years ago. It was carried safely in his pocket watch beneath the cover which also contained a portrait of Michelle as she looked when they first got married. He gently placed the single curl to his lips, and, for a short moment, could feel her presence reach out to him. It was an act of love that only served to highlight his anguish. Carefully tucking the precious lock of hair under the cover, he closed the lid.

The Club was a short distance from the hotel, so he chose to walk along the shore and enjoy the brilliant red sunset that monopolized the western sky. Sunsets in the Pacific are spectacular events. The waves were drenched in an orange hue reflecting from the fading sun. They seemed to be alive as the water danced beneath the gentle trade winds. The sweet smelling breeze filtered through the leaves of the tall palm trees that lined the walkway. The towering palm trees framed a picture that could have been taken straight out of a travel brochure for the tropical island paradise.

Loud music and merriment drifted across the still air as Arlo approached the Army-Navy Club. The sounds emanating from inside the club were a contradiction to the sounds Arlo was accustomed to hearing in the combat zone. He could not help but think that such merriment was inappropriate for a staging area so close to the fighting front. Perhaps his self-imposed solemnity set himself apart from more frivolous activity, but it was not his disposition to party extensively even when everything was going right for him. The music only made him more aware of his emptiness and longing for some shred of information that he could cling to.

"Good evening, General Korsman," greeted Jim Ready, sitting on a bench beside the boardwalk. Arlo was startled at first; he had been walking along absent mindedly in his own private world as usual, and didn't notice his friend.

"Hi Jim," responded Arlo as Hank Thomas joined them from the Club. "It's great having this chance to be with you guys."

"The Club is packed right now," said Hank, grasping Arlo's hand once again. "Why don't we take a walk along the beach where our conversation can't be overheard?"

"Sure," answered Arlo, thinking it was somewhat unusual, but gladly followed the two officers across the wide stretch of smooth sand towards the splashing waves.

"What we're about to tell you, could get us court-martialed for sure and maybe even a firing squad if the wrong people were to find out about it," stated Jim in a deliberate calculated manner. "Arlo, the questions you have every right to ask, cannot officially be answered given all of the secrecy placed upon all information received from the Philippines. We did not want to say anything at the office. Who knows...? The walls may have ears..."

"Jim is right," continued Hank soberly. "As you may not know, there has been a rather sophisticated intelligence gathering system established by one of General MacArthur's staff members, General Courtney Whitney. What we're about to tell you, cannot, repeat, cannot, go any further."

"You have my word on that, guys," promised Arlo gravely.

"That's good enough for us, Arlo. We've been pumping in supplies and equipment by submarines on a steady basis for the past two years to several different partisan groups on all of the islands, including Leyte. Clandestine radio networks have also been established all over the islands. A lot of individuals who have successfully evaded the Japanese have been retrieved from under the enemy's nose by the same submarines that have been supplying the organized resistance force of Filipino and American soldiers. To make a long story shorter, we have just taken a close look at all of the intercepts received from Leyte in the past several months." Jim paused to catch his breath. Arlo remained spellbound beside him.

"We've come across some information which may pertain to your wife, Arlo." Col. Hank Thomas watched his marine friend closely and stopped walking. "Jim and I believe that your wife is alive and with a guerrilla band in the central mountains of Leyte. A wounded Army Air Corps pilot was rescued by guerrillas when his plane was forced down close to shore. We were able to review his full statement, because he was picked up by a submarine which had been in contact with that particular band of freedom fighters. He was badly injured in the crash. His description of three nurses who cared for him is quite complete. One of them is a sandy-haired white woman of average build who set both of his broken legs. He never knew any of the nurses' names. In time of war names can be dangerous ammunition for the enemy, so most people avoid letting anyone else know their true identity. This nurse spoke English well, appeared to be well educated, and wore a wedding band on her left hand. We think she could be Michelle."

"How can I ever repay you two for this gift of knowledge?" cried Arlo excitedly.

"There's more," Hank continued. "Earlier in the campaign, this particular group of Filipino and American service men provided us with a rough roster of their members. There were approximately one hundred able-bodied fighting men and twenty women with them. Ten of these women were nurses. Only two of them were Caucasian and capable of speaking English. One of them was listed on the roster a year ago, as a 'friend of Flying Eagle'."

"My God, that's her," exclaimed Arlo. "That has to be her. It couldn't be just a coincidence. No one except a select few know about Flying Eagle. By giving that description, Michelle was able to notify us of her safety and at the same time hide her true identity. Anyone familiar with me and my friends would recognize the significance of the name of the dead Canadian patriot." Arlo was filled with appreciation for two friends who would ignore the dangers to their own careers, in order to put his worst fears to rest.

"We've just one request to make of you, Arlo. It would be possible to approach this young airman, who is at a hospital here, with a picture of Michelle to confirm his description of her. In view of the sensitivity of the information we've just given you, we suggest that you do not seek him out for confirmation or anything else. Word could get around that you're not in the loop of those who need to know this information and all hell could break loose for the bunch of us."

"I'm willing to accept your judgments completely. I won't make contact with this airman. You have my word on that."

"What we've told you is a reasonable interpretation of all of the information we've reviewed, Arlo. I think we're right in our assessments. There is a slight possibility that we could be wrong," admitted Jim. "There's one more thing that we have a hunch about. It's only a hunch, so take it with a grain of salt. Hank and I both think that when General MacArthur hits the Philippines, the first target will be the island of Leyte. Also, to help ease your worries about the coming invasion, each Army division has an attached complement of highly trained Rangers, who will make deep penetrations into enemy territory to free prisoner of war compounds and to make contact with several groups of freedom fighters, such as the one we believe Michelle is with. The presence of these battalions of Rangers will help to insure the safety of the friendly guerrilla bands and prisoners of war before the Japanese have a chance to commit their infamous massacres when all seems lost to them. If I were in your shoes, I would be relieved to learn that this type of capability was going to be the vanguard of MacArthur's efforts to free the Philippines."

Arlo was speechless in the company of these two honorable officers. He felt as if a great burden had just been eased from his heart. From the shore, possibly from the Army and Navy Club, the hauntingly beautiful strains of the song "Blue Hawaii" was being played on a steel guitar. The plaintive melody flowed across the beach and filled his consciousness with a profound sense of loneliness. The music blended with the breaking of the surf in such a way that it touched all of them. Arlo, in particular, had all he could do to control his emotions.

Jim felt Arlo's discomfort and mentioned a good-natured bit of reality. "Now, Arlo, you know as much as we do. If anything new comes along that you should be made aware of, we'll find a way to inform you. This conference is closed and never took place!"

"How can I ever repay you guys? I appreciate your vote of confidence and the friendship that motivated it. I'll never forget it, thank you."

"We both know that you would do the same thing for us if the situation was different, Arlo," said Hank with conviction. "However, there is one thing you can do for two hungry soldiers. Since you're now getting a brigadier general's paycheck against our lowly colonel's pay, we've decided you can buy us a drink and a steak dinner at the Club. Are we presuming too much, General?" There was a broad smile on Jim's face as he confronted Arlo.

"Not at all," answered Arlo happily.

The three of them linked arms and headed towards the plaintive sounds of the singing steel guitar. There was a bounce in Arlo's stride that had not been there earlier in the day. The camaraderie of friends who are willing to sacrifice themselves for one another is the basis of the strongest of human ties. The trust and respect lasts a lifetime. It was a moment he would always remember.

It was past one A.M. before Arlo returned to his hotel room. The night had been filled with laughter and companionship. It would be a day Arlo would remember for a long time. His two Army friends had given him much to think about, and he reviewed word by word what they had told him about Michelle's situation after she left China. What they said was probably true. Tonight, for the first time since he left China in 1941, his worried mind was at ease. He could rest easier now, in the knowledge that his Michelle was somewhere out there and waiting for him. Maybe it was destined to never be, one never knows in wartime, but tonight he had a feeling that his dreams and prayers might come true, and they would be together again.

"Arlo and Michelle," he said aloud, staring at the ceiling from his bed. He liked the sound of it.

Chapter Eight

Early morning gunfire practice at the Pearl Harbor Navy Base woke Arlo from his deep slumber. The sound of stuttering machine guns on the ships in the harbor closest to his hotel window tore through the clear morning air, bringing him back to the reality of the war. Today he wanted to accomplish several things at Pearl Harbor before returning to Guadalcanal. The first item on his agenda was a visit to the wards where his men on New Britain Island would be starting their healing process. The atmosphere and smell of hospital rooms was depressing to him. The war had introduced him to injuries and wounds on a scale he could never have imagined before it started. He had a tendency to view each wound inflicted upon his men as a part of his responsibility. After seeing thousands of casualties in the bitter struggles for the island fortresses they encountered on their way to the Japanese homeland, Arlo had developed a hardness and a detached acceptance to the losses and to the bloodshed that was a normal part of fighting a war. Such an attitude, he thought, bordered on callousness, and that frightened him as much as anything, because nothing about it was normal or routine.

He was also looking forward to seeing Mark again and checking on his progress. After his visit with Mark, he would try to call Bright Cloud back in the states. He understood that the lines were open and that they were constantly monitored by military officials. Pearl Harbor and the Hawaiian Islands were under martial law.

Arlo took a quick breakfast at the hotel dining room and pushed off for a round of visits to the hospital wards with his aide to make notes on the progress and condition of every man they met. It was the responsibility of the company commanders to inform the next of kin of death or injury to those men under their command. Arlo usually followed up on that notification with an update about the men who had been wounded. He was certain that the letter was most welcome

116

by the injured man's family. Perhaps the brief message ignited a spark of hope in the hearts of those who can only sit at home and wonder what their loved ones are going through.

Arlo never failed to be inspired by the courage and sacrifice of the wounded men. They frequently tried to cheer him up and apologize for being laid up and away from the units they served. The walking wounded were even talking of returning to their buddies to finish the job they started. Morale was high, and Arlo was bursting with pride.

The attitude of the men strengthened Arlo's resolve to always search for new tactics and new methods of wearing down the enemy in order to save the most precious resource entrusted to him — the lives of his men. Some marine officers merely hurled their men at the enemy time and again in costly frontal attacks. The press seemed to find such commanders "colorful", and the tactics courageous and full of glory. Arlo scorned at such dereliction of a sacred obligation an officer had to ration the lives of his men as miserly as possible. Objectives had to be taken and orders had to be obeyed, yet Arlo searched every corner of his brain to find meaningful solutions for the situations he had to send his men against, so that his losses were at a minimum. That was what the schools he had attended were supposed to teach you. Some of the more popular officers covered by the press were prolific with juicy quotes. The same individuals frequently threw away their tactical manual and closed with the enemy no matter where they found him and regardless of the high cost to the riflemen on the ground. Arlo had gained a reputation of fighting "smart". His losses were always less than other brigade commanders in similar situations. His relationship with the press was straight forward and professional. He avoided them as much as he could. Those journalists who knew what they were talking about had high praise for his efforts.

The nurse on duty at the floor where Mark's room was located told Arlo to go right in. Mark had been moved from the ship and had just finished eating a small breakfast. Arlo noted the breakfast as a sign of improvement. Mark was sitting up in bed staring out the window across the ship-filled harbor. He looked as if he might have been sleeping so Arlo knocked softly on the door jamb, not wanting to startle him. Mark turned to see who was there.

"Arlo," he cried. "I was just thinking about you and Michelle. Come in. It's great to see a familiar face again. Pull up a chair if you can find one. I'm afraid I've made a mess of myself this time. They offered me a chance to talk to Bright Cloud over the phone. As much as I want to hear her voice, I don't know what to tell her, Arlo. I'm afraid of what's ahead for us. I won't be going home as the same person that she remembers." Mark shifted his glance from Arlo to the window again.

Arlo's heart went out to his long-time friend. He would have given anything to take away his fears of the future. It was a relief to hear Mark talk about his feelings. Mark's small body was sheathed in bandages and a plaster of Paris cast on his abdomen-chest area. One of the bandages on top of the cast had a red spot where one of the wounds was still draining. His left arm was held in a cast with his hand facing forward in front of his elbow. A sheet covered Mark's legs.

"You look better than the last time I saw you, Mark. You came through a bad period and rallied beyond any expectations of the experts. The doctors are still trying to figure it out."

"The nurses told me. I haven't thought much about it..."

Mark was still under the influence of medication. His speech was slightly slurred and slower than usual, but other than that, Arlo thought he looked quite good considering what he had just been through. His color was still a little pale, but he had lost that white-grayish pallor which frightened Arlo the last time he had seen him.

"This cast for my left arm is awkward," said Mark. "It makes me look like a policeman stopping traffic with my hand sticking out in front of me." A slight smile crossed his lips as he said it.

That smile was a welcome sight to Arlo. The old spirit that always filled Mark was still with him, and that boded well for the future.

"I had intended to give Bright Cloud a telephone call after I talked with you. You know, Mark, she has a right to know the truth, and it would be cruel to not tell her. Don't try to handle your recovery alone, let her be a part of it. Lean on her for support. You know more than anybody else that she'll be there for you in every way possible. The love you share can handle anything. Put it to the test and I'm sure you won't be disappointed. When I call Bright Cloud, what would you like me to say to her?" asked Arlo, watching Mark closely for his reaction.

"Well," Mark grasped for the right words. "I agree. You must tell her the truth, Arlo. You're right, she deserves nothing less. I want to talk to her. I really do, there isn't an hour of the day that I don't think of her. That's the trouble with loving so much, if one is hurt the other feels the pain also, maybe even more."

"Isn't that the main reason for sharing each other's lives?"

"I suppose...You know I can't feel anything in my legs. I can't move them either. What if I have to go home a cripple, who can't walk?"

"Do you think for one moment that you're not being able to walk would make a difference with Bright Cloud? You know better than that, Mark. It isn't worth talking about," answered Arlo sharply.

"I didn't mean that the way it sounded. I'm just full of self-pity right now. I realize that I've got a lot to be thankful for...a wife like Bright Cloud, a friend such as you, and a wonderful family... But, enough of my troubles, Arlo. What have you found out about Michelle? I include her in my daily prayers too. You're strong, my friend, I would have gone over the edge worrying about her if I'd been in your shoes. You know, I actually knew Michelle before I met Bright Cloud. It seems so long ago...we've both married exceptional women."

"Amen to that," replied Arlo, relieved to see Mark take a more positive attitude towards things. "Ever since Michelle and I got married in 1928, it has been a wonderful time for both of us. I remember the wedding took place at Lake George, but the most memorable time was at Fort Lewis where we spent our honeymoon at your cabin. Those were good days, that's for sure. I cling to their memory like a drowning man clings to a life preserver.

"Michelle is most likely alive in the Philippines. Nothing is a sure bet in this crazy war, but I believe that she has been surviving in the mountain regions of central Leyte where she is relatively safe from the savagery of the Japanese occupying forces. I still don't have any concrete information about her, but I'm optimistic that one day we'll be together again. Continue to keep her in your prayers, Mark."

"Always. This war makes things complicated. It's not just the combatants who're affected, our loved ones suffer too, when all we have ever wanted was to keep them safe. I worry a lot about DJ. He recently wrote to me that he's being graduated from West Point early so that they can fill the ranks of newly formed divisions for the war. He'll probably be sent to Europe. Bright Cloud and I both were hoping he would be kept out of this mess at school, but I guess the war has continued too long... I understand his desire, even his eagerness, to want to do his part. I'm proud of him."

"I was fortunate to be around on several occasions and see him and lovely Star become young adults. You and Bright Cloud have every right to be proud of both of them. I'm proud to be their adopted uncle."

Arlo stood up from his chair to signal that it was time to go. "I won't talk any more for now, Mark. Conserve your strength. I'm going back to the 'canal' soon to get ready for another campaign- you remember how it is. Rest well, old friend, a lot of us are in your corner rooting for you. When I call Bright Cloud, can I tell her that you'll be talking to her soon?"

"Oh, yes, I want to do that. She's my whole life..." Mark's eyes moistened at the mention of her name.

"I'll check in on you before I leave Pearl."

"Thanks. I can't tell you how much I needed your visit. Until next time, Arlo."

"Until next time, Mark."

Arlo walked through the huge hospital corridor on his way from Mark's room when he was approached by the surgeon that operated on Mark, Commander Henning.

"General Korsman, we meet again. Your friend, Colonel Leroux, seems to be progressing quite well."

"Dr. Henning, I'm glad to see that you're here. I was just thinking I should talk to a doctor about Mark's status. If I can get a line out of the islands for the mainland, I intend to call his wife. Do you have anything more that I should tell her?"

"Yes," answered the gray-haired surgeon, directing him to an empty office close at hand. "Sit down, Sir. I'll try to be as brief as I can. Everybody seems to be running short of time these days. The Colonel is going through a period of self-pity and the 'why me? Syndrome' which is perfectly normal and healthy at this stage. His spirits, as you must have seen, are not too bad. The Colonel has got a lot of self-discipline and a most determined nature."

"You could even call him stubborn, Commander," interrupted Arlo with a smile.

"Stubborn is the word, General. Strong personal characteristics are going to help secure his recovery when he confronts his limitations, which are going to be very real. At this stage we don't know how limiting his injuries are going to be. However, a full return to normal is probably impossible. His arm and elbow should mend, but there will always be some disfigurement. That's reality. His internal wounds are the most serious. He should, with good care and rest, overcome the lung punctures and the loss of his spleen. Infection is something we've got to be diligently on guard against for the next several months until his body has restored the ruptured tissue the bullets destroyed. His miraculous encounter on the ship has given us a chance to get on top of his infections and treat them whenever they're encountered. His lungs are doing very well considering what happened to them. The helping hand he received from fate, or whatever you prefer to call it, has insured his ability to survive. It was also helped by his good physical condition, which is going to serve him well. He took good care of himself in the past, and it's going to be an important factor in his recovery."

"Will he ever walk again?"

"I don't know, Sir. There's a slight chance that his spinal nerves will bridge the connection that was severed. Our knowledge in that area is very limited. I have a suggestion for you, Sir. I'm only going to be here for a few more days, I'm due back at sea. However, there are several of the best doctors in the world right here at this facility who have specialized in cases like the Colonel. I propose that you keep him here at Pearl Harbor instead of being sent back to the mainland. I know that may come as a shock to you and to him, but he's in for a long and difficult recovery, and the Navy team here, in my opinion, is the best there is."

"How long are you estimating before a determination can be made with certainty whether he will ever walk or not?"

"I'd say a year, General, maybe more. After that amount of time has passed, if some feeling can be detected, he's got a long period ahead of him learning how to walk again. This is the point where his inner resolve is going to make a difference."

"I understand what you're saying, Commander, and I've been thinking. What would be the possibility of the Colonel's wife coming to Pearl? She's a highly qualified nurse and could help him a great deal, physically and emotionally. I'm excited about the possibilities. It would perk Mark up a hundred fold."

"If she's a certified nurse, I could put her right to work. I could even pull some strings to get her a commission in the Naval Nurse Corps. It sounds like a great idea to me, General. You'd need to contact the right authorities to make it possible."

"I'd take it as high as Admiral Nimitz if I have to. Thanks, Commander, for everything. I wish you well. We're fortunate to be supported by dedicated men like you and your brethren in the Medical Corps. On behalf of my men and myself, I thank you for your efforts, Commander."

"We all have a job to do, General. I'm anxious to get this war over with and get back to Topeka, Kansas, where I belong. A landlubber such as myself has a difficult time finding his sea legs — combating seasickness is a daily struggle when I'm aboard ship."

The two men parted with a handshake and a salute. Arlo carefully thought about what the doctor had said. It made sense to him, also, that Mark stay where he is if the level of treatment is what the doctor described. Arlo was anxious to share his thoughts with Bright Cloud, so he returned to the nearby hotel. He ordered his aide to check on those things that would have to be cleared so that Bright Cloud could come to Pearl Harbor.

The phones at Hawaii were in use just as they always were in normal times, except that any calls to and from the mainland were monitored by military censors who would cut off any part of a conversation they judged to be injurious to the security of the Islands and the war effort in general. It was almost noontime now, so Arlo mentally calculated the five hour time difference between Hawaii and New England. It would be about five o'clock in the afternoon, a good time to try and reach an open line to Maine. Arlo even remembered, by heart, the telephone number for Mark and Bright Cloud at Wells, Maine, 92-W. Arlo heard the phone bell ringing.

"Hello." A woman's voice answered at the other end of the line.

"Hello, is this Bright Cloud?"

"Yes..."

"Bright Cloud, this is Arlo. I'm calling from Hawaii."

"Oh..." screamed Bright Cloud. "How nice to hear from you, Arlo. Is Mark okay?" He could detect a slight panic in her voice.

"Mark is fine, Bright Cloud. That's why I'm calling you."

"Where is he, Arlo?"

"He's at a Pearl Harbor Naval Hospital."

"Please," she pleaded excitedly. "Tell me how he is."

"You should be encouraged at what I'm going to tell you. With a phone line as long as we have between us, anything could happen to break our connection. So listen carefully. Mark is doing well considering what he went through. I just finished talking with his doctor who told me that it would be prudent to leave him where he is, because they have one of the best medical teams in the country right at the hospital he's in.

"Mark's spirits are pretty good and he'll call you soon. He needs to hear your voice as much as you long to speak to him. The most crucial part of his recovery is the threat of internal infection from his wounds. Now dear Lady, be brave. I'm telling you the truth because you have a right to know. Mark was struck by four Japanese machine gun bullets in the chest and stomach region, and one in his left elbow. His left arm is in a cast right now. He has a punctured lung and has lost his spleen from two of the bullets. One penetrated his right shoulder and nicked his collar bone. The fourth bullet in the body is the most serious wound of all. It severed part of his spinal column. Mark cannot move or feel anything in his legs." Arlo could hear Bright Cloud sobbing. "I promised Mark that I'd tell you the whole truth, Bright Cloud. I'm sorry to bring such harsh news to you..."

"I appreciate how difficult this must be for you, dear Arlo."

"One other thing. Would you come to Pearl Harbor if I make arrangements for you?"

"Oh, yes, Arlo. I'll be there no matter what."

"I knew you'd say that. I'll be leaving Pearl very shortly, but I'll telegram full instructions for you before I leave. As bad as Mark's condition sounds, it could have been worse. We can't ever forget that."

"I understand, Arlo, and I want to thank you for your thoughtfulness and your wonderful friendship. I've been very selfish thinking of myself when you must be out of your mind with worry about Mike. Have you heard anything from her?"

"All I can only tell you is that I believe she's alive and well. It will be a while yet before we know anything for certain. I live on hope and memories. Everyone wants this ugly war to end, believe me, no one prays for peace any harder than this weary old soldier..."

"My prayers are with you, dear friend. Mike is constantly in my thoughts. All we can do is have faith that our beseechments are answered. Someday, when this nightmare is behind us, Arlo, we should all get together at Fort Lewis for old times' sake. Thank you again for being such a dear friend."

"I've been thinking the same thing, Bright Cloud. Thoughts like that help to keep us going out here. It was great to hear your voice again. Give my love to DJ and to Star. Tell them Uncle Arlo thinks often about them. Be prepared to get a call from that husband of yours very soon. I'll be in touch again with details about coming out here. God bless you. Until next time, Bright Cloud."

"May God be with you and Mike. Until next time, Arlo."

* * *

Summer traditionally came slowly to the Canadian wilderness. Late May and early June of 1944 was no exception. After a long and difficult ten months of deep snow and paralyzing cold, the back of old man winter had finally been broken. The swollen tree buds and the early appearance of wild iris in the moist meadows, was the fulfillment of the promise of spring. The unbroken expanse of the subarctic green belt was coming back to life. Bright Star welcomed it, probably more than her native people. She had followed the same traditions established by her mother and Michelle and others before her. After a winter of increased activity at the small infirmary, she normally took some time away from the difficult routine and returned to the coast of Maine for a vacation with her family at Wells.

The greatest demand for medical services was the winter months. By the time the summer came along, Bright Star was exhausted and in need of rest. She had done her best to carry on the tradition established by her mother when she first founded the facility in 1919.

Several student nurses were recruited by the missionary branch of the Catholic Diocese of Quebec, which relieved the burden on the full time staff of four or five nurses that served year round. Bright Cloud had traditionally returned for the summer months, but since the war started, she felt that it was her duty to be at home in case she was ever needed by any of their family. With Mark serving overseas in almost constant combat, she wanted to send a strong message to him that she was holding the home together so that he could return to its security whenever he was able.

Bright Star felt a strong obligation to continue the legacy established by her mother. A large addition had been added to the original building at two different times, so that now they were capable of caring for up to twenty bed patients. The building itself required the services of at least four certified nurses and several aides. The outreach portion of the infirmary was the most demanding on the nurses. Not only was the extension branch physically draining, it was also the most challenging professionally. The first to pick up where she left off was Michelle Gurney, who performed tirelessly and competently. She had stayed on at the center until her marriage to Arlo in 1928.

Bright Star helped maintain the levels of excellence the center had come to expect, when she returned to the village after graduation from nursing school. She was scrupulous in keeping the center up-to-date with medical advancements of any kind that would have a bearing on problems unique to the region. She was able to establish a larger library for the center when she solicited contributions at the University of New York at Syracuse during her last months at the College. That was 1939. One improvement of which she was particularly proud, was the installation of a small self-contained diesel generating unit which provided electricity for the center. It was installed in a small well-insulated shed emitting a steady hum when it was running.

Evening shadows were just beginning to lengthen when Bright Star left the infirmary to return to her cabin, the same one that had been built for her mother and father. She was interrupted by a young Cree boy calling for her and running as fast as he could.

"Miss Bright Star, the Inspector sent me to get you. He has a telephone call for you...he's waiting..."

125

"Thank you, Andrew," replied Star, running towards the Mounted Police station south of the infirmary. Panic overcame her as she sped through the door to see a smiling Inspector Clough waiting for her.

"It's your mother."

"Hello, Mother," cried Star, gasping for breath into the phone handed to her by the inspector. "Is Father okay?"

"You'll be glad to know that your father just spoke to me from Hawaii. His spirits seem to be good considering what he's going through. We don't have time for me to explain all of his wounds, but he may never walk again and..."

"Oh, no..."

"Have courage, my dear girl. We have to be strong for him now. This is the time when he really needs us, and it's a time when I need you, young lady. Can you come home soon? DJ is due sometime this week before he's shipped overseas. I'd like to have the three of us together if it's at all possible. General Korsman has telegraphed detailed instructions for our transportation to Pearl Harbor. He used his rank to secure space on Navy transport planes flying to the Hawaiian Islands. I'm going to go to him as soon as DJ leaves for his command."

"I can leave here anytime, Mother. The student nurses have arrived. As a matter of a fact, I've already spoken to Father Lamontagne about leaving soon. I wish that I could go to be with Dad, also."

"Maybe you can, Star. We'll talk after you come. Tell the Inspector that we all miss him. I'll be looking forward to seeing you soon. Good-bye for now."

"Good-bye, Mother. I'll tell the Inspector. Hold DJ there until I get home."

The Inspector made out that he was busy reading a report, but he was drinking in every word being spoken.

"Mother sends her love, Inspector," said Bright Star, hanging up the phone.

"I thought she would, Lass. She had time to tell me a little about your Dad while I sent little Andrew to get you. It seems your father has his share of problems, but he's at least alive. That young Yank has a special place in my heart and my prayers are with him."

"I'd like to leave as soon as you can arrange it, Inspector," said Star with an excitement in her eyes.

"Tomorrow morning if you want, Lass. I understand your desire to be where you're needed. We've been blessed with your lovely presence for the long winter just passed. Now you must do what's best for your family."

"Tomorrow morning will be fine. Thank you, Inspector."

"I have one favor to ask of you, Lass. When you've had a chance to determine the facts about your father, would you drop me a line and let me know. We go back a long time, you know, and I feel as if he was one of my own. He's a special person, and I worry a lot for him."

"I think you worry about all of us, Inspector. What would we ever do without you? Yes, I'll be glad to keep in touch with you," answered Bright Star, gently kissing him on the bare forehead. "Goodnight, thank you for the phone call."

"You're welcome, Lass. I'll see that the plane is ready when you are."

The next day was cloudy and rainy but it could not dampen Bright Star's spirits. The Mounted Police plane sat on Lac Diamante with the engine warming up while she climbed aboard with Inspector Clough's help. He didn't say anything; it was impossible to compete with the noise from the plane's engine. He was saddened watching her leave, for he realized that he was witnessing the passing of an era that would never be the same again. Bright Star understood what was in his heart and tried to reassure him.

"I'll be back, Inspector, I promise," she shouted in his ear.

"I hope you will, Lass. It's a lonely place without you or your mother and father," he answered. She read his lips and waved good-bye. Inspector Clough watched the plane taxi from the dock. He felt old all of a sudden and was glad that Star could not see the moisture forming over his eyes.

A fountain of spray surrounded the plane just before the pontoons lifted from the surface of the lake and smoothed out with a steady drone of the engine. Star had flown in and out of the lake many times and she always got a thrill of seeing the water and forest drop beneath them. The pilot told her that they would land at Lac St. Jean for refueling and then continue to Quebec City, where she could make connections for a train to Portland, Maine, and ultimately on to Wells.

She had a strong desire to be with her mother. It had been a year since they'd seen each other. It had been three long years since she had seen her little brother, Daniel-Joseph, DJ for short. He was now a young man of twenty-two years. The last time they had been together was at his graduation from Wells High School in June of 1941. He was a young teenager then. There was a serious quality about him that she admired. Sometimes she used to tease him that he didn't seem to have as much fun as other friends his own age. He was popular with his classmates, and he had a wonderful sense of humor, but the serious side of his nature was always dominant.

There were five years difference between her and DJ, and she enjoyed the role of older sister who always looked out for him. She always knew that Mark and Bright Cloud were not her biological parents. No child could have been any more loved and cared for than she was by the very special people who had nurtured her since birth. She returned that love and respect from the bottom of her heart. Her acceptance was sincere and complete, and she never detected one bit of favoritism over their own flesh and blood, DJ. He was aware of her birthright, and proudly shared their common legacy.

Bright Star's pride in her younger brother grew stronger one day from an incident that took place when she was in her senior year of high school. The last school dance of the year was approaching and Star, who was quite popular in school, was asked by a young man by the name of Richard Hanson if he could take her to the dance. Richard had a reputation of being a loudmouth who boasted publicly of his many amorous conquests with certain girls in school. Star did not like him and refused his request as politely as she knew how. He retaliated the spurning of his request by viciously attacking the color of her skin and the inferiority of her race, in front of many of her friends. He finished his tirade with a demeaning parting remark, "...he didn't really want to be seen with her anyway because her skin always looked dirty to him. If they had gone to the dance he would have had to hurry home to wash so that he wouldn't catch anything from her."

The sudden viciousness of the words stung Bright Star, bringing her to tears on the school grounds in plain sight of many of her friends. DJ's seventh grade class had just started a recess period and they were pouring out of the school building in time for him to see Bright Star crying near the main entrance to the school. He rushed to find out what was wrong. One of Star's friends told him what had happened.

Bright Star was not positive about the chain of events, but several classmates told her what took place the next day during recess period in front of a large number of students. Loud-mouth Richard Hanson was still boasting how he had "put that squaw in her place", when DJ, four years younger and thirty pounds lighter, confidently confronted him.

"You've insulted my sister, my Mother, and myself and all of our ancestors, and I'm demanding an apology from you. Our skin is not dirty as you claim, and you're hardly an upstanding member of the community capable of making any judgments. You, who are not worthy to kiss the ground my sister walks on, owe us an apology."

The sudden appearance of DJ within the group took all of them by surprise. There was something serious and determined about the look in his eyes. He spoke in a slow measured way that could not be misunderstood. Richard Hanson, characteristically, looked upon him with scorn as if he was an irritant. DJ did not present a very formidable figure, but his air of resolve was making a strong statement. Both young men were about the same height, but DJ was much less experienced. He was still in the "awkward" adolescent stage of his development. They checked each other out thoroughly.

"I challenge you to be a man and apologize. If you can't take back the words you said about my sister, then I challenge you to a round or two of fisticuffs without any interference from your friends," DJ suggested with conviction and soberness.

"Okay squawman, put them where your mouth is."

Hanson was cheered on by a small number of his associates, while most of the students simply made room for the contestants to decide their differences. A small few objected about the differences in size and weight of the two young men. DJ had already decided what his strategy would be. He was not going to be the first to throw a punch, and he hoped that he had aroused his opponent sufficiently so that he would be a little less cautious than he might have otherwise been. Outwardly relaxed and confident, DJ raised his fists before his chest and face and awaited any move from Richard. Everyone remembered that DJ never took his eyes off the larger opponent, and gracefully sidestepped around him. The opening came when Hanson, irritated with all of the waltzing around, lunged at DJ and tried to connect with a wide swinging left hook which missed its mark. The momentum of the swing carried Richard past DJ, which was the instant he was looking for. DJ quickly unleashed a flurry of blows to Richard's face and neck, stunning him with the speed of the strike.

Several witnesses to the incident recalled different aspects of the confrontation, but all agreed on one thing. The first blows of the bout landed on Richard, and that fact angered him so much that he turned to see where DJ was after he had recovered his balance from the hits. Before Richard could set up his own tactic to strike back he was snapped twice in the face with rapid left jabs that hurt him, bloodied his nose and knocked him to one knee. DJ, who had not received a single blow from Hanson, stepped back to give him a chance to recover. Hansen's nose bled heavily and was soiling his shirt. The fact that DJ drew blood first so infuriated the bully that he leaped to his feet only to be met with another series of rapid left jabs. DJ continued to move in a circle around Richard. When he saw that Richard was momentarily distracted, he closed quickly with his leading left jabs and followed up with a right in an old fashioned "haymaker". Richard Hanson dropped to both knees while the students watching decided that it was enough, and separated the two of them.

Richard was spitting blood from a cut on his tongue. He had bit it with his own teeth when the devastating upper-cut came from DJ. Richard was glad to skulk away under the protection of a couple of his buddies. He was livid that he was so thoroughly out-classed by a bantam weight seventh grader. He promised retaliation in one way or another. The heaviest insult to Richard was that the beating took place in public view of several classmates.

Bright Star could have told them that DJ and her father regularly worked out in a small section of the sawmill where they had set up a regulation-sized boxing ring. Her father had impressed upon DJ many times the importance of never attacking on your opponent's terms. DJ was an accomplished boxer by the time he entered high school. The incident with Richard Hanson was still one of the legends old classmates talked about at class reunions. She was so proud of her younger brother who championed her reputation in a most public manner. She had lost track of Richard Hanson years ago.

The fight on the school grounds was an amazing event because she knew DJ to be a quiet, easy-going young man. He would not resort to such conduct unless he was sufficiently provoked. If he had ever taken advantage of others less skilled, their father would have meted out punishment of some kind that would have discouraged any future transgressions. Both DJ and Bright Star were expected to live up to the standards established by their parents. Star and DJ were always secure and content in the knowledge that their parents never deviated from the standards.

When the train left the Kennebunk station, she knew that Wells was next on the schedule. Star gathered her luggage on the seat beside her and excitedly waited for the small station to come into view. She was going home, and the thrill of arriving was still strong within her. Her family was well-liked in the small town, and even though they were inclined to keep to themselves, there was a large reservoir of good will towards the family.

Bright Star was the only passenger getting off the train, although several people were waiting to board. She didn't see the small taxi that was usually waiting for every train. The war had changed a lot of things. The elderly station master, Mr. Rollins, met her with a tip of his hat.

"Welcome back, young lady. Your mother will be surprised to see you again. My, you've grown. You look more like your mother every day. You can use my phone to call her if you'd like to."

"Thank you, Mr. Rollins. It's always nice to come back here."

She called Bright Cloud who promised to be along in a few minutes.

"I've heard the Colonel has been wounded in the Pacific. I'm sorry to hear that about him. He's served our country for many years. My nephew was with his Marine Reserve Company when it was activated. He had nothing but nice things to say about your Dad," said Mr. Rollins. "Give my best to your mother, and may the good Lord watch over your father."

"Thank you, Mr. Rollins." He disappeared around the corner to his freight shed. Bright Star watched the road leading from the village for any sign that her mother was coming. Their home was only a few minutes from the station. A small cloud of dust rising from the road to the village excited Star.

Her mother pulled into the parking lot with their 1940 Studebaker President. Bright Cloud was all smiles as she ran to greet Bright Star.

"My, you made that trip quicker than I imagined, Star," cried Bright Cloud. "I feel better already knowing that you're safe and sound here with me now." Bright Cloud thought she looked tired and drawn, holding her daughter in her arms for a long time.

"I'm anxious to find out all you know about father."

"Young lady, you've been working too hard. You look tired. I can't call you my little girl anymore, but I still worry about you. Would you like to drive the car back home?"

"I'd love to, Mother. It's something I can't do in the North Woods. I guess it's like riding a bicycle, you never forget how once you've learned," laughed Bright Star as she slipped behind the wheel of the car. They rode in silence for a few minutes. Bright Cloud proudly watched her drive the car after a year's absence as if she had never been away.

"The house hasn't changed any since last year," said Star, turning into the familiar driveway, parking in front of the kitchen entrance. "It's nice to be home, Mother, but I can't think of anything else except what father must be going through. Is there any chance that I could go with you to be with him?"

"As a matter of fact, Arlo said in his telegram that the travel privileges he has arranged for air travel to Hawaii is also extended to you."

Bright Cloud recited every word that Arlo told her about Mark's condition and the current situation at Pearl Harbor. The telegram was explicit as to how they were to make connections via Naval Air Transport Command. It was literally impossible to get across country by civilian transportation of any kind except by automobile, but gasoline rationing made that impossible, too. General Korsman had put them on the list to receive VIP treatment.

"Today must be our day, Star. DJ is due in later tonight by bus. He called from West Point last night to tell me his schedule. He'll be coming by train to Boston and then to Maine by Boston and Maine Trailways. It will be nice to see him again. He only has a couple of days before he has to report to Fort Devens, where he's meeting up with his platoon. I don't like to think what's going to happen after that."

"I'm sure he'll do a good job just like he's always done, Mother."

"I know he'll do like his father has done before him, but I still have bad feelings about his leaving for overseas duty." The phone rang as Bright Cloud ran into the kitchen to pick up the receiver. "Hello," she said nervously. "Yes, this is Colonel Leroux's wife."

Bright Star watched her mother carefully and pulled a chair from the table for her to sit in while she was on the phone. There was silence for several seconds while the voice on the other end of the line spoke to Bright Cloud. Star listened and waited anxiously to find out what was being said to her mother.

"Star," Bright Cloud said, turning around to her. "This is the Naval Air Station at Brunswick, Maine. They have a single seat vacancy for a flight leaving tomorrow to San Francisco, where arrangements can be made for a flight to Hawaii. What should we do with DJ coming tonight?" Bright Cloud was a nervous wreck. Star saw a simple solution to the problem.

"Why don't you let me go on this flight tomorrow, Mother? You can come along at a later date after DJ has left for Fort Devens. Father will understand and be pleased to at least have me with him."

"Are you up to it, Star?"

"Mother, I can rest on the way. It's a long trip with nothing to do except sit and read or sleep."

Bright Cloud confirmed with the caller from the Naval Air Station that they would be glad to take the seat available for tomorrow. The caller warned them that they would be allowed only forty pounds of baggage for the flight. Bright Star made a mental note to take a couple of her white nurse uniforms. They might come in handy at Pearl Harbor.

Bright Cloud and Star talked for hours about happenings at Fort Lewis, and the Town of Wells since they last saw each other. They talked and acted very much alike. They were extremely close and felt comfortable confiding their private thoughts and feelings. At times, they acted a lot more like two sisters instead of mother and daughter.

By nine o'clock, Bright Cloud and Star were getting tired and anxious to see DJ. Star saw a nervous restlessness in her mother, attributing it to sleepless nights and a powerful imagination which always seemed to work overtime when she was not given all of the facts about Mark. It was a natural reaction she could not control. Bright Star watched her mother more closely beneath the floor lamp's light, noticing dark circles beneath her beautiful brown eyes.

"Mother, you've got to take better care of yourself than you've been doing," said Bright Star in a stern voice. "You look tired and worn out. Of course it's only natural to be worried; I have been too. Father needs both of us now and you've got to be prepared to give him the support that you're able to give. If you're not well, that support will suffer. Now that you know what's ahead of us, be secure in that knowledge and rest more for his sake. I sound like a mother hen, but you know that I'm right!"

"You are, dear. I'm trying to do better, believe me. Calls from Arlo and your father have made a difference. Arlo was the first to bring me a message of hope. Hearing him talk about Mike was heartbreaking. He was trying to be positive and cheerful, but I could detect the lingering doubts in his voice. I don't know how he's been able to cope with the situation. I've been following the war in the Pacific Ocean more closely than Europe. Arlo's Brigade, with your father's regiment, has been at the center of some of the most costly battles. There's a lot of heart and strength in our old friend."

"Listen, Mother, I hear something outside," said Star, running into the parlor window looking out over the roadway. "It's a bus. It must be DJ."

"I can't turn on the outside light because of the blackout regulations," complained Bright Cloud. "I hope he can find his way."

"Mother, he could find his way blindfolded," said Star matter-of-factly.

A step sounded on the kitchen porch, then a light knock on the door before it was opened by a tall slender young man dressed in an Army uniform, with brown tunic and light beige pants affectionately called "pinks". On his shoulders he wore the gold bar of a second lieutenant. Bright Cloud started to cry as soon as he stepped into the room, and threw herself into his waiting arms.

"My two babies are finally with me tonight. I'm so thankful. Let me look at you, young man. You've grown taller, I swear," Bright Cloud cried, holding him at arms length.

"It's good to be home, Mom," answered DJ in a calm voice. "My big sister is even lovelier than I remembered her. It's awfully nice to see you here, Sis. I've missed you these last two years. Whenever I could make it home, you were always away in Canada. It's been a long time."

"You look wonderful, Danny," Star replied, wiping a tear from the corner of her eye. "My little brother left here a boy, and has returned a man. I'm so proud of you."

DJ retrieved his fully packed duffel bag from the porch and dropped it on the kitchen floor near the door. The visored cap made him look taller than he actually was, but Bright Cloud was correct, he had grown some these past two years. There was a relaxed confident air about him that was more than the uniform he wore. His bearing reflected a sensitivity and an integrity that generally marked certain soldiers as leaders of men instead of mere commanders. His father had that same quality. Both of them shared a quiet demeanor and an easy smile.

DJ resembled Star and Bright Cloud more than he did Mark. He had the same dark complexion, the high cheek bones, and the roman nose of the Native Americans. His Cree heritage was evident and he carried it with a dignity and pride that made him stand out among other men. The most memorable thing about him was the way he looked at you and into your thoughts at the same time. There was an intensity about his eyes that made people remember him. Some saw sadness in his look, while others saw an acute ability to read other people's minds. He was a courtly gentleman, which was unusual in a man of his age. He was a son that any parent would be proud to claim as their own.

"Before we get into anything, Mom, you've got to tell me all you know about Dad's condition. Have you heard any more news?" DJ desperately asked.

"Yes I have, Son," answered Bright Cloud, directing him to sit at the head of the table while she placed a kettle of water on the stove. "Would you like some tea and some custard pie?"

"You bet I would."

"Let me set the table with what we need and then I'll bring you up-to-date. Star just got here this afternoon, and we've been saving your favorite pie for this occasion."

135

"Mother has improved upon Aunt Maddie's recipe," beamed Bright Star stirring her cup of tea.

"I had never heard of such a dessert until I married your father."

Bright Cloud took her place at the table between Star and DJ and quietly proceeded to tell all that she knew about their father's condition and their plans to go to Pearl Harbor, thanks to Uncle Arlo. DJ heard the news without any visible display of emotion except for a tightening of his neck muscles, which was noticed by his mother and sister.

"It's hard to believe the part about the 'miracle'."

"I believe it, Son; it's similar to what we experienced before you were born."

"I can still remember that evening as if it was yesterday," recalled Star. "If a person wasn't there to witness it first hand, I suppose I would also find it difficult to believe. But it was real and powerful. I don't know how to explain it, except to take it as an act of faith. Even Uncle Arlo said that the doctors could not explain the phenomenon."

"I've never doubted your version of what happened, Star. It's just difficult, as you said, to imagine what took place if you've never experienced it personally," DJ admitted, reaching out for Star's hand and squeezing it firmly. "There's every reason to be positive about Dad, then. That's a relief. I've talked a lot about the situation in the Philippines with a couple of instructors who were there. They both informed me, after I told them about Aunt Michelle, that there was a very real possibility she could still be alive and gone underground with one of the resistance groups scattered all over the islands. Uncle Arlo can, at least, cling to a small hope that she's still alive. It's a tragic situation, but she's a resourceful lady who would not give up easily."

The three of them sat around the table and talked until well past midnight sharing old memories and incidents that, collectively, are the precious treasures of families. On this special evening, Mark's absence was heavily felt. It brought an element of uncertainty and longing to those sitting around the kitchen table.

DJ asked his mother about the high school girl friend, Allison Perkins, whom he had dated several times before going off to West Point. They had been writing to each other for these past few years, and he wondered if he could borrow the family car to take her out to a movie at the beach pavilion. He had to report to Fort Devens in three days for his assignment to a platoon being trained at the large Army base in Massachusetts. The frown that came over his mother's face spoke more than words. He told them that he was scheduled to become a part of a new division being formed in New England, destined for Europe. He had no idea where or when that would take place, and if he did, he could not tell.

The night was filled with worry and thanksgiving, a normal part of life during the war. It was impossible to do anything else. Their fears and concerns were echoed in every home in the nation. It was a time of national and personal sacrifice. The demands of the war effort permeated every facet of their lives. Mourning for lost loved ones became a collective lament taking place across the country, from the Pacific to the Atlantic.

Next morning Bright Star was the first person up. She made a large pot of coffee and sat quietly contemplating what was ahead for the family. She was looking forward to the trip to Pearl Harbor, disappointed that she and her mother could not make the trip together, but she knew that her father would be pleased to see her. Her single bag was already packed for the trip to the Brunswick Naval Air Station. Bright Cloud would have liked to take her to the airport, but she did not have enough gas coupons to make the trip. Gas rationing limited them to four gallons per week. It was never enough to do what she wanted with the car. So they, like everyone else in the country, learned to do without and planned every movement of the automobile in advance. Consequently, Star would catch the Boston and Maine bus that went by the house in time for her to make the scheduled flight to the west coast.

When it was time to leave, Star gave a teary-eyed good-bye to her mother. DJ carried her bag out to the side of the road and waited with her.

"I don't know when I'll see you again, Sis. Give my love to Dad," said DJ, fighting tears.

"I will, you can count on it. I'll worry about you until this war is over, DJ. Take care of yourself and never forget that our prayers are with you. We probably don't have much time before the bus comes, but I want you to know that no sister ever had a better brother than you've been to me all these years. I've always been proud of you, and you've never let me down." Star hugged her brother so tight she was afraid of hurting him.

"If you were not my sister, I would have wanted you as a friend, Bright Star," DJ soberly told her. He held her and kissed her black hair one last time.

The Boston and Maine bus was coming around the corner. Star accepted the bag from her brother and cried from the depths of her heart, "Come back to us when this mess is over, DJ."

"If its God's will, Sis."

Star remembered him standing straight and tall beside the road waving good-bye to her. Tears clouded her vision, but she was observant enough to see the small line of tears that slowly ran down his bronze cheeks. One final wave and he was out of sight...

Chapter Nine

Bright Star tried to read a magazine as the Navy transport plane leveled off for the flight to San Francisco. It was her first time on a large passenger plane. She had flown often in small single engine float planes like those that landed on Lac Diamante. They flew relatively close to the ground where you could see where you were in relation to the surrounding countryside. Flying among the clouds, like they were doing now, with no sight of the ground, was unsettling to her. Reading didn't help very much. Conversation with a middle-aged Navy captain sitting beside her was not feasible because of the loud intrusion of noise from the engines.

The seats were comfortable. Bright Star dropped the magazine and laid back against the head rest. She was tired, and the tension caused by the flight added to her exhaustion. It felt good to close her eyes and relax. She thought about her father. Her isolation in the wilds of Northern Canada insulated her from the intense emotional impact of the war upon families with loved ones in the armed services. That was about to change, for in a short time, she was going to be set down at the center of the war effort in the Pacific at Pearl Harbor. She could not believe what was taking place. Pearl Harbor was the scene of the cataclysmic attack by the Japanese that propelled the United States into declaring war, forcing the creation of the war-making machine which was slowly grinding the treacherous Japanese and the brutal German armies back to their original territory and ultimately to victory.

It was bad enough that the young people of the country had to suffer; it was doubly unfair for veterans, such as her father, to be caught up in two world wars in his lifetime. After the horrendous costs of the First World War, which was billed as the "war to end all wars," it was sad to contemplate that maybe their sacrifice was for nothing. Now the world was at each other's throats once again, on a larger scale than before.

Bright Star had studied everything she could find about the Tomb of the Unknown Soldier in Washington, D.C. The concept for the memorial appealed to her and she gained strength from the fact that it had very personal meaning to her. Thoughts about that special day came vividly to her mind while the steady drone of the plane's engines lulled her into a more relaxed state of mind.

* * *

Her Uncle Arlo Korsman had filled her in on many interesting aspects of the selection of the Unknown Soldier's remains. The Tomb of the Unknown Soldier had its humble beginnings on Memorial Day, May 30,1921, when the Congress of the United States authorized the removal of one dead soldier's body from each of the American National Cemeteries in France: Belleau Woods, the Somme, St. Mihiel, and Meuse-Argonne. The four bodies were unknown American soldiers who had fallen during the fighting in France. Bright Star's biological father, Lieutenant Joseph "Flying Eagle" Mann, USA, had been buried at St. Mihiel along with several other unidentified bodies. The remains were placed in identical caskets and honored at the City Hall of Chalons-sur-Marne, France.

U.S. Army Sergeant Edward Younger, a wounded, highly decorated soldier, was chosen for the privilege of selecting one of the four caskets before him. Sergeant Younger was given a spray of white roses from the people of France and instructed to make his selection by placing the bouquet on the casket. Those who were present remembered that he slowly walked around the four caskets three times before stopping in front of the one he selected. Slowly and respectfully, Younger placed the flowers on the lid of the selected casket. He claimed later, "...he was drawn to that particular casket." The spray of flowers accompanied the casket to the United States, and was buried with the remains of the soldier in the crypt prepared for the memorial.

Many tributes were given to the Unknown Soldier by the French people and government before it left the soil of France, in appreciation for their sacrifice. The casket traveled from Chalons-sur-Marne to a waiting American cruiser, the USS Olympia, which had the solemn task of transporting the body to Washington, D.C. The casket was under constant guard by a group of 40 hand-picked marines. Uncle Arlo had told her that he knew the officer who commanded the escort contingent, a Captain Graves E. Erskine. The marines maintained their constant vigil until the casket was taken by the U.S. Army at the Navy Yard dock in Washington, D.C., on November 9, 1921.

It was a cold, raw and rainy fall day when the Unknown Soldier's last remains returned to American soil. This time, he came in honored glory as a symbol for thousands who were left behind in France. At one minute intervals, the "sorrow gun" was fired in salute while the body was carried to dockside where members of the Third Cavalry placed the casket on a caisson pulled by six black horses for the trip to the Capitol Building where it was placed on display in the Rotunda of the Capitol. Thousands of men, women and children formed long lines that continued well into the night to pay their respect to the fallen soldier. It was a solemn moment in American history.

At 8:30 AM the next morning, three years after the signing of the Armistice that ended World War I, the casket was removed from the Rotunda and carried, again by caisson, across the Potomac River via the Aqueduct Bridge, to Arlington Cemetery three hours later. The ceremony was viewed by tens of thousands, and listened to on a new electronic marvel, the radio. The President of the United States, Warren G. Harding, and many dignitaries attended the ceremony. President Harding conferred the Medal of Honor upon the Unknown Soldier with the following tribute, "They died that others may live..."

Bright Cloud, Bright Star, Mark and Arlo were standing on the top steps of the Amphitheater with a perfect view of the memorial ceremonies. Her father took turns with Uncle Arlo holding her above the crowd so that she could see better. She could still recall the playing of the military bands and singing of the song, America. She could still remember the wailing of many mothers in the crowds around them. One part of the ceremony stood out as particularly poignant, even to such a young spectator as Bright Star. She recalled that a Native American Indian, Chief Plenty Coos of the Crow tribe from Montana was the most eloquent spokesman of the day.

Chief Coos spoke in a booming voice that could be heard by all present. His few simple words were said with great dignity and came from the heart. He called upon the Great Spirit of the Red Men "...for the hope that the dead should not have died in vain, that war might end, and peace be purchased by such blood as this..." He then removed the feathered war bonnet from his head and placed it over the casket along with his coup stick, a symbol of his high office. The aged Chief, with the finely chiseled facial features, stood silently before the crypt of the Unknown Soldier, and raised his hands in supplication to the heavens. It was a moment of powerful emotions that had passed into the legacy of the Nation, and is now an integral part of the legend of the Tomb for all eternity. The casket was lowered into the crypt while three salvos from the saluting batteries were fired. The bottom of the grave was covered with soil from France in appreciation of his sacrifice. The spray of white flowers from France was also interred. By mid afternoon, the ceremony was finished and the dignitaries were leaving the hallowed ground they had just consecrated. The Unknown Soldier continued his lonely vigil as the most sacred memorial in the Capital City.

* * *

Bright Star was as moved, today, by the magnitude and power of the national ceremony, as she was that day, many years ago. It made her appreciate what sacrifice was all about and how much it cost in anguish and sorrow for a whole generation. She searched her purse for a handkerchief to hastily wipe her moistened eyes. The Navy captain, sitting beside her, noticed what she was doing, and asked her in a voice that could be heard above the din of the engines.

"Are you all right, Ma'am?"

Bright Star, self-conscious of her emotional state of mind, answered quickly, "Yes, I'm fine. Thank you for asking, Sir."

"We'll be landing in Chicago in a few minutes to refuel the plane. If you need something maybe I can be of some assistance while they're servicing the aircraft."

"Thank you, but that won't be necessary, Captain," answered Star, taking a closer look at the tall distinguished officer at her side. He wore the rank of a Navy Captain on his shoulder epaulets, his left breast was covered with ribbons. He was probably as old as her father. There was a relaxed and friendly air about him. It was just too difficult to carry on a conversation while the plane was airborne, so

142

she was content to lean back in the seat and keep her thoughts to herself. The sailor continued to read the book that he had been reading ever since they left Brunswick.

The plane started its descent into the Chicago airport. Star watched out the window as they came out of the high clouds. Below her was the metropolitan Chicago area all aglow in its evening dress of colored lights. It was an island of light in a sea of darkness. The plane's navigator walked through the passenger compartment to announce the refueling stop of about a half an hour. A Red Cross canteen truck would come alongside of them with coffee and refreshments. Restrooms were available in the building closest to the plane.

Hot coffee sounded good to her. The plane had been flying at a high altitude and the cabin was cold. She was glad that the pilot had warned her, before the flight, to have a coat nearby. Even though it was warm on the ground, the rarefied air among the clouds had chilled her so that she was shivering. As soon as the plane came to a stop, the pilot shut down the engines.

"What a relief it is to be quiet for a change," commented the Captain, watching Bright Star more closely. "It's unusual to have a civilian on this type of flight."

"I'm on my way to Pearl Harbor to be with my father, who was seriously wounded at Cape Gloucester. Arrangements were made for me and my mother, who will be making the trip in a few days when room becomes available, by an old family friend. He's a General in the Marine Corps, so maybe his rank helped to make it possible."

"Generals have a way of getting things done. I'm Captain Fred Spencer, and I'm going to Pearl Harbor, also. How about stretching our legs and helping ourselves to a cup of java."

At first, Star didn't know what he was talking about. She had never heard coffee called java. "It'll be a welcome relief, Captain Spencer. I'm Dawn Leroux. I'm not accustomed to flying in large planes like this."

"It's a pleasure to meet you, Miss Leroux."

Bright Star excused herself as soon as they walked down the boarding stairs. She searched out the location of a restroom in the large administrative building adjacent to the Red Cross canteen. When she returned, Captain Spencer was just finishing off a large cruller with a satisfied smile on his face. She accepted the coffee and ham sandwich graciously offered by the young lady manning the canteen truck, and stood next to Captain Spencer as she ravenously ate the lunch.

"I'm heading back to Pearl Harbor to take my place in the headquarters of the Pacific Fleet. I just completed a short furlough at home in Bangor, Maine, after a convalescence period. I got blown off my own destroyer bridge, hurting my back enough so that they don't want me to command another Navy ship again, at least not for the present. It was nice to see my two children and my wife. It had been three years since I last saw them. My daughters are young ladies now; I hardly recognized them. I'm glad to be back in the war at any position. I'd much rather be a major player in the war effort than at home manning a desk."

"You sound like my father, Captain Spencer."

"How badly is your father hurt?" he asked.

Star recounted what had happen to her father. She also described his service in the First World War, and how it resulted in his marriage to her aunt Bright Cloud and the adoption of herself. It was a story she loved to tell. She thought that it was one of the most romantic love stories she had ever heard. Since she was a central party to the marriage, it was also a story of her youth. She secretly hoped that she could be as lucky as her mother in finding someone to share her life.

"I'd like to try some volunteer work at Pearl Harbor. I'm a registered nurse, and it would only be proper for me to contribute if I can."

"Believe me, Miss Leroux, if the Navy finds out you're a nurse, they'll have you in a white uniform before you can blink your eyes. There's a dire need for them ever since the war started."

A five minute warning announcement prompted Star and Captain Spencer to return to their seats for the final leg of the journey. They both carried onboard another cup of coffee "for the road". They mutually agreed that casual conversation was difficult at best in the flight, and that they would have more time to talk at San Francisco. In a way, Bright Star was content to have the time to herself.

She was a little surprised with herself, thinking that maybe she talked too much to a total stranger even if he did remind her of her father. This trip was giving her an opportunity to examine her own

144

goals in life. Ever since she left Fort Lewis, a question in the back of her mind kept asking, "Where are you going from here, Bright Star?" She had gone out on dates in Maine with several different boys. They were all part of the pleasant remembrances she had of that era of her life. None of them were any more than adolescent dates. College had been a time of hard work, but she also met and enjoyed several friendships that were continued to the present time. No relationship had ever taken on that category of being "special".

She had been so busy and so committed to medicine and the infirmary, that it left no time for her to enjoy the company of a young man. Many had expressed an interest in her, but time was so limited when she was at the infirmary, it was impossible to even think about such things. She was now twenty-seven years old and some times she was embarrassed when friends would ask her if there was someone in her life. She wasn't lonely; there wasn't time to be lonely. Neither was she looking for companionship, but she often wondered how nice it would be to share her life with someone the way her mother and father were nourished by their love for each other.

The most memorable experience of her life still lingered in her heart with a clarity that time had not diminished. The incident took place the evening after she and her mother and father had attended the dedication ceremony of the Tomb of the Unknown Soldier with Uncle Arlo. She was only four years old then, but the evening had been indelibly imprinted upon her memory.

* * *

Star remembered that she was tired and a little restless after the speeches. They remained on the steps of the amphitheater next to the large columns in front of the crypt. The day had been damp and cold. In her light coat pocket, Star could feel the small wooden cross that her father, "Flying Eagle", had carved when he was a little boy. He had given it to Bright Cloud, who had, in turn, given it to Mark as a symbol of her love for him. He had carried it with him as a good-luck charm for several years. When Arlo had written to them about the coming ceremony, and it was agreed that they would all attend, her parents decided that it was only fitting that Bright Star be given the crucifix as a part of her legacy. She had no idea that the tiny wooden cross would leave such a mark on her.

145

As soon as the large crowds receded from the gravesite of America's Unknown Soldier, Star walked across the terrace to the grave. Across the top of the lid the war bonnet of Chief Coos rested among the flowers which smothered the crypt. Her father and Uncle Arlo soberly saluted the grave while she clung to her mother's hand. At that time she had a feeling of familiarity which she could not understand. She didn't hear voices, but she heard and felt something inside herself that made her feel sad and hopeful at the same time. Her mother's tears were slow to come, but they gave her a release and a sense of peace that left her speechless. A young soldier in his immaculate uniform passed back and forth with his rifle on his shoulder, and his eyes riveted straight ahead. He respectfully guarded the final resting place of the remains of a soldier who was destined to be a symbol for all who died unidentified on the battlefield. The Tomb sent a message of hope to mothers everywhere that maybe, just maybe, their loved one could be the young man so gloriously honored on that day. The simple words, "Known Only to God", sustained the hope of thousands who had lost a loved one. Wailing mothers and sweethearts covered the marble stones with tears.

After the ceremony, Uncle Arlo drove them across the Potomac River to their hotel where they enjoyed a leisurely evening meal. The adults were not as talkative as they had been before the ceremony... Each was remembering the events of the day and its importance to their lives. Even Star, at her young age, was struck by the dignity and solemnity of what she had seen.

"Arlo, would you mind going back to the Tomb?" Bright Cloud had asked. "I'd like to see what it's like at night under lights. Unless you have other plans for the evening."

"My time is your time while you're here, Bright Cloud. Strange, but I was thinking of something like that. As soon as you're ready," answered Arlo, sipping his coffee.

"I'd like that too," commented Mark with a pensive look on his face. "This is a day I'll always remember, thanks to you, Arlo. You've made it all possible, and we thank you for your thoughtfulness. I hope this pleases Flying Eagle, he's been in my thoughts all day long."

"He's been in mine, too," added Bright Cloud soberly.

"It's fitting that Chief Coos should be one of the participants. I think Flying Eagle would approve of that. I'm glad you suggested going back tonight, Bright Cloud. I have a strong feeling about returning, also," Mark replied, taking her hand in his own.

Arlo thought that Bright Cloud looked particularly lovely tonight. Her eyes were aglow with excitement, yet there was a reflective reserved demeanor about her that was most flattering. Serenity radiated from her. She drew glances from everybody in the dining room, but she was oblivious to everyone except her husband. Arlo had caught a glance of the hotel clerk, who had made a slight scene over her presence as a guest, across the room. They made eye contact with each other and the clerk acknowledged him and his party with a smile. He thought it ludicrous how any person could object to such a lady. His friend, Mark, had made a wise choice.

Bright Cloud excused herself and Star from the table so that they could go upstairs to their hotel room for a few minutes. Once there, Bright Cloud combed Star's long hair, and had her change into a warmer coat for the cool damp evening air. When they returned to their dining room table, Mark and Arlo had a cloud of cigarette and pipe tobacco smoke surrounding themselves.

"We're all set," declared Bright Cloud cheerfully.

Darkness blanketed Arlington National Cemetery with a stillness and a silence that was in stark contrast to the scene of a few hours ago. Noise from the bustling city below penetrated the hillside area. Arlo parked his new Hudson off the roadway leading to the amphitheater.

The Tomb of the Unknown Soldier faces east from the amphitheater overlooking the Potomac River below. The lights from the Lincoln Memorial and the Capitol Building were also visible in the distant background. The Tomb had been specifically selected to be on the same east-west axis as the Capitol and the Lincoln Memorial. It was the symbolic heart of the City of Washington, D.C. The field of honor, represented by Arlington National Cemetery, is filled with the spirits of those brave souls whose deaths have made it possible for the Nation to survive and prosper. A person never feels alone on this hallowed ground. The silence speaks in many ways to different people. Bright Star remembered feeling comfortable and welcome in the sacred sanctuary.

147

The evening was cool and damp, the same as it had been all day. Bright Star placed her hands in her winter coat, looking for the wooden cross, as they walked slowly towards the amphitheater. Sadly she told Bright Cloud that she had left the wooden cross in the pocket of her other coat back at the hotel room. She felt bad about her forgetfulness.

"That's all right, honey," Bright Cloud consoled her. "Your real father would understand. He died so that you could have a safe place to live. Your real mother, my dear gentle friend, Minnie, gave up her own life so that you could come into the world. They understand and you shouldn't worry about those things you didn't mean to do."

Star remembered that those words made her feel good. Bright Cloud had that rare gift of being able to make people around her feel that way. Standing on the steps, where they had watched the ceremony earlier, they saw the dimmed city lights in the distance, while the crypt of the newly buried Unknown Soldier was flooded with small lights along the walkway for the guard. Star felt a strong pull to approach the Tomb. A force she has never been able to describe to anyone, guided her feet down the large granite steps to the flat terrace below. Mark, Bright Cloud, and Arlo followed her. The soldier guarding the Tomb maintained his ritual pace back and forth, back and forth. He marched twenty-one steps to the right of the Tomb, and returned to the center. He then paced twenty-one steps to the left of the Tomb, and started it all over again. The cadence never varied, regardless of the weather or the number of onlookers. It was symbolic of the twenty-one gun salute given to honored dignitaries. It was the highest tribute of the Nation. The American Unknown Soldier had entered the lofty realm of the world's most honored.

The four of them stood in a straight line near the carpet walkway for the guard. There was nobody else around the terrace except the four of them and the soldier guard, when a powerful beam of light shone from above onto the gravesite. The war bonnet and the multitude of flowers still rested on the top lid of the crypt. The strong beam of light traveled the full length of the monument then traveled westerly towards the end nearest the guard and themselves. The light stopped at the edge of the lid and became more brilliant.

Star remembered that she screamed and pointed to the object beneath the brilliance of the beam of light. It was the small wooden crucifix that she had forgotten in her other jacket back at the hotel room. Each of them stared in disbelief at what they saw, unable to speak or to move.

The column of light moved from the cross, poised on the edge of the cover of the crypt, moved overhead to Bright Star, and showered her, for a few seconds, in a blinding ray of light, then slowly returned to the gravesite. It did this movement two distinct times, the second time passing directly in front of the soldier walking his post. The light continued for several seconds and disappeared as rapidly as it had started. They were transfixed and hypnotized by what had just taken place.

In the distance, the rhythmic pacing of marching boots could be heard. The formal changing of the guard was about to take place. A squad of ten soldiers marching in single file stopped at the center of the Tomb of the Unknown Soldier. They were commanded by a sergeant major with so many hash marks, which indicated years of service, that neither Mark nor Arlo had time to count all of them. The exchange was formally and respectfully made. The young soldier that had been a witness to the light, took his place at the rear of the column as they marched off for their barracks at nearby Fort Meyers.

The three adults, Mark, Bright Cloud, and Arlo, remained speechless for a long time after the soldier left. They were still trying to analyze the significance of the incident they had just witnessed. Bright Star watched the marching line of soldiers disappear. In a flash before Bright Cloud could restrain her, Star ran across the walkway and retrieved the wooden cross from the edge of the lid of the Tomb.

"It's the same cross I left in our room before we came here tonight. It was in the coat that I wore during the day," remarked Bright Star, bewildered by the event that had taken place. "Does this mean that my real father was trying to tell us something?" She had the innocence and honesty of a child, but at that moment she showed a wisdom equal to the adults with her. She understood the significance of the miracle of the light.

"I think your father, Flying Eagle, was trying to tell you that it's possible his earthly remains could be buried in the grave of the Unknown Soldier," Mark told her, kneeling down in front of her. "Whether that is true or not we can never know for sure, Star. What we've just experienced could be your real father's way of telling you

149

again, that he'll always be with you, and as close to you as death allows. You've heard your mother and I mention those very same words to you, because they are what he wrote in his last letter. When you're older, sweetheart, these things will be easier for you to understand." Mark swept her off her feet and held her in his arms. She clung tightly to him, her small hands clasped behind his neck with her head resting on his shoulder.

"You're a lucky little girl, Star. You have so many people that love you. Even though we can never be sure that his physical remains are buried here in this holy piece of ground, we can at least feel confident that his spirit and the spirits of all of the other unknown soldiers are here at this memorial.

"You should also feel proud of the fact that a grateful Nation has taken the time and effort to build a memorial worthy of their accomplishments. You and I cannot see those spirits, but they are all gathered here to say, 'thank you for remembering us.' Flying Eagle is certainly among that special group of heroes. This is one of the most sacred and beloved places in our country, and it's most fitting that we honor our lost patriots in this way. Now, the cold marble grave there beside us will forever be the site of our own special sign of love and inspiration. You and the small cross, that Flying Eagle carved when he was a little boy, will have a special place in our hearts for as long as we live."

Bright Cloud had not said a word. Her facial expression was a mosaic of emotions. The grandeur and power of what they had just seen, left her in a state of reverence for the privilege of being present. She joined Mark and Bright Star in a three-way hug.

Arlo, too, required a few minutes to reflect upon what had happened. He agreed with little Star and with the things Mark had spelled out to her. He knew a lot about Flying Eagle as a soldier. Tonight added one more dimension to the legend of the remarkable Cree warrior. He had been profoundly moved by the experience.

"When we're through here, I'd like to visit the barracks at Fort Meyers and speak to the guard that was on duty. What do you think, Mark?" asked Arlo.

"I was thinking the same thing, Arlo. Whenever you're ready," answered Mark, putting Star back down on the ground and holding tightly to her tiny hand.

They left the Tomb of the Unknown Soldier and drove to Fort Meyers on the western edge of the Arlington National Cemetery. Arlo parked beside a guard box. He and Mark approached the gate and were challenged by the sentry on duty. They asked to speak to the Officer of the Day, whom the guard called on his phone from the guard hut.

The Duty Officer was a young first lieutenant who had just been told what happened at the gravesite after the soldier got back to the barracks. The Lieutenant invited them inside if they wished to speak to the guard in person. Mark told him that he was more interested to find out if any such incident had taken place with anybody else. The young guard was an alert soldier who answered all of their questions completely and sincerely. The Lieutenant added that none of the other guards in the company have noted any similar happenings in the daily log that they maintained from the first minute they took possession of the Unknown Soldier's body at the dockside of the Washington Navy Yard. The Navy and Marine Corps had started the log in France, and there is nothing in their notations about any such demonstration happening...

* * *

Bright Star fell asleep shortly after the plane left Chicago. When she did open her eyes, again, the cabin was full of sunlight and the plane was starting its descent to San Francisco. Captain Spencer watched her wake up from the long slumber with a smile.

"Young lady," he shouted. "You slept very soundly. You reminded me of my daughters, who can sleep under any conditions."

"I thought about everything before I fell asleep," admitted Bright Star sheepishly.

"Don't feel bad about it, Miss Leroux. It's a gift that I envy. I understand that our wait at San Francisco will be only long enough to change into another plane. We'll be on our way to Hawaii within an hour!"

Chapter Ten

Pearl Harbor is a name that generates strong feelings. Pearl Harbor is as much an emotion as it is a large United States Naval Base located within the relative safety of the Island of Oahu in the Hawaiian Islands. It was the nerve center of the war effort in the Pacific Ocean against the empire of Japan. It was more than a collection of buildings and military supplies stored in large warehouses. Here, on American soil, the Japanese struck swiftly and cowardly in a sneak attack that would live "in infamy," as President Roosevelt claimed.

Little did the Japanese dream that the euphoria of their first victorious assault would become a wake up call to the American people. The devastating bombing strike rallied them behind a cry of "Remember Pearl Harbor." It touched every household and every heart in the nation. At the beginning of the war the United States had a very small standing military compared to the awesome capabilities of the forces arraigned against it. Japan and Germany possessed two of the best and most powerful military forces in the world. The American people rolled up their collective shirtsleeves and rose to counter the threat ahead of them, unafraid and confident of the outcome.

History will record that their noble effort in every theater of war, and in every instance where American forces met the enemy (German or Japanese) and the opposing forces were relatively evenly matched, American forces, composed of citizen-soldiers, defeated the professional armies of the enemy every time they met in battle! The success of the Japanese attack at Pearl Harbor was a fiery victory that eventually came back to haunt them.

Bright Star had plenty of time to rest and think about her father during the long flight to Hawaii. As soon as her two-engine plane landed in San Francisco, she was whisked onto a larger four-engine plane, and shortly thereafter, was headed for the Hawaiian Islands. It was the Navy's version of the Army's B-24 bomber, which they called the Privateer. The plane was filled to capacity and much quieter than the smaller one. Normal conversation could take place without any difficulty.

Captain Spencer was helpful to her while making their transfer to the larger plane. They sat beside each other again, with Star enjoying the view from the window beside her. "Are you excited?" asked Captain Spencer, noticing her interest in watching the continental land mass fade from view behind them.

"Yes, Captain, it's all happening so fast I can't believe it's true. I caught a glimpse of a palm tree at the airport. It's the first time I've ever seen one. My travel experience has been very limited. The contrast to my native land of northern Canada is indescribable. It's literally a different world."

"You're right, young lady," answered the Captain, amused at her enthusiasm. There was a child-like innocence about her that viewed the world as a new adventure full of wonderful things just waiting to be discovered. Her bronze complexion complimented her yellow dress. She was one of the loveliest young ladies he had ever seen.

The dark sea below stretched endlessly in every direction. They had been flying for about an hour since takeoff, when Bright Star noticed small dots sprinkled on the water below. The dots grew more numerous as they continued their flight to the west. Eventually the dots covered the water all the way to the horizon. Looking more closely, Bright star could detect a small white spray accompanying each dot. She concluded that they were ships traveling the same direction as the plane.

"Oh look, Captain Spencer, the ocean is full of ships," she exclaimed excitedly. "I could never imagine so many ships in one place at the same time."

"It's a convoy leaving the United States. It could be a part of an invasion force, or it could simply be a portion of the constant supply train that accompanies our forces as they push closer to Japan proper. It's quite a sight! When the war ends, and it will end sometime, we'll probably never see such a spectacle again. You're a witness, Miss Leroux, to a part of our mighty war-making capacity against Japan. It's a remarkable achievement. It makes one proud to be an American.

Sometimes it's hard to keep one's eye upon the big picture, when we're concerned personally with our own individual problems. Even though the price we have to pay to defeat the enemy is painfully high, we must not lose sight of the fact that the alternative, enslavement, would be much harder to bear. There are worse things than war," said Captain Spencer as much for himself as for Star.

The long hours of the trip passed without incident. Captain Spencer surrendered to a sleep that was deep enough for him to snore several times. Star was amused at his loud rattling noises. She did not sleep from San Francisco to Pearl Harbor, but she did relax and contemplated a number of things. One decision she had definitely reached, was that she was going to volunteer her services as a nurse, if that was possible. She was determined to do her share. She knew her father well enough to know that he would be proud to see her help wherever she could make a contribution. Once she made up her mind on the subject, she felt content with the decision and relaxed a little easier for the rest of the trip.

The plane landed at a large airport near Pearl Harbor Naval Base. The field was a beehive of activity. Star was overwhelmed with the number of men in uniform. Several things were taking place simultaneously. Large cargo planes were being loaded and unloaded at the same time, while others were landing and taking off. The tempo almost took her breath away!

"Welcome to our world on the edge of the battle zone, Miss Leroux," said Captain Spencer. "The rush and frenzy of activity never ceases. May I help you?"

"I don't know, Sir," Star answered, standing on the tarmac beneath the plane. She looked lost and confused.

"You'll be fine, young lady. Here, I'll carry your bag. You follow me. It's not as bad as it seems. It just takes a little getting used to."

"Thank you," answered Star, appreciating his guiding hand.

They walked through a portion of the terminal area that was stacked with mountains of military material and supplies before they entered a crowded waiting room. It seemed as if everybody was going in a different direction. She was glad to follow the kind Captain Spencer as he wove a passage through the sea of bodies. At the far end of the building, he directed her to an empty bench.

"Why don't you sit here and watch both of our suitcases, Miss Leroux. I'm going to check on a couple of things and I'll be right back. Don't move from this spot."

"I'll stay here," answered Bright Star excitedly.

"Don't worry. We'll soon get out of this madhouse," Captain Spencer reassured her.

"Thank you."

Captain Spencer left her at the bench and disappeared. There were so many young men in different uniforms, that she could not keep them all straight. In front of the bench was a long solid wall filled with just telephones, and endless lines of soldiers, and sailors waiting for their turn to use them. She felt self-conscious, because she was the only woman not wearing a uniform. She soon noticed Captain Spencer making his way back to her.

"Everything is all set. You follow me and I'll explain the situation."

Star dutifully followed in his footsteps to a street filled with cars of every description. Captain Spencer stopped at a gray sedan with "U.S. Navy" painted on the door.

"This is for you, Miss Leroux. The driver will take you to a hotel that has been requisitioned by the Navy for the use of dependents and guests. You have a room reserved there in the name of your friend, General Arlo Korsman," Captain Spencer set her suitcase in the back seat and took a notebook and pen from his breast pocket. "This is the address where you'll be staying. Your father is being treated at the Pacific Fleet Hospital at Pearl Harbor. You won't need any pass to get in the gate, but you will need some sort of personal identification."

"I have a driver's license from Maine and a copy of my nurse certificate with me..."

"That'll be fine. Now, I must leave you, Miss Leroux. I hope you find your father improving satisfactorily. It's been a pleasure traveling these many miles with you."

"How can I ever thank you, Captain?"

"You already have, young lady."

"May God be with you, Sir," Bright Star replied, shaking his hand. "I appreciate your kindness."

"You remind me of my daughters, and I'd like to hope that a stranger would help them if they needed it. I wish you the best of luck, Miss Leroux. Good-bye."

"Good-bye, Captain Spencer."

The sailor driving the car casually pointed out different things of interest along the way. The most dramatic was the wreckage of some of the ships sunk during the December 7th attack by the Japanese. She questioned him about the location of the hospital, and was pleasantly surprised to learn that it was within a half mile of her hotel. The hotel was just as busy as the waiting room at the airport. She had no way of realizing how much her Uncle Arlo had done for her, until she found out what a tremendous demand there was for rooms. His rank and prestige helped to make an impossible situation, plausible. She was amazed that all arrangements had been made in advance in his name. She was given VIP treatment from the moment she stepped up to the registration desk.

A small suite on the third floor was assigned to her and her mother. It was composed of a large bedroom with two double beds and assorted furniture which included a comfortable couch and upholstered chairs. The second room was a sitting room with a kitchenette and a small stove and refrigerator. It would be possible for them to make some meals for themselves. The item most appreciated by Bright Star was a private bathroom. She knew her mother would be glad for that luxury. The dining table and chairs were positioned in front of two double windows which looked out over the harbor. She could see far out across the water where several ships were at anchor. The blackened hulls tilted from the water at unnatural angles still contained the bodies of hundreds of drowned sailors that were never recovered.

Bright Star checked her wrist watch, which had been set to the proper Hawaiian time at the suggestion of Captain Spencer. It was now five-thirty. She was determined to see her father as soon as possible and was glad to have a chance to walk after being cooped up in the airplanes for so long. Her legs welcomed the exercise.

The walkway to the hospital was crowded. Here and there she saw a wounded serviceman, among the throng, who was able to walk. She spotted several men with upper body bandages, and some with heads wrapped in layers of gauze bandages. She tried not to stare so as to not make them feel any more uncomfortable than they already were. Slowly, she was being introduced to the world of the fighting men that carried with their bodies, the full measure of pain and suffering. It was a sobering introduction to reality. The sight of so many injured men galvanized her determination to do her share.

The entrance to the Pacific Fleet Hospital was a long pathway lined on both sides with palm trees. They captured her imagination as she stopped to stare at them. She found it hard to believe that she was actually in the tropics. Beneath the trees were large beds of blooming flowers in a variety of colors. It was beautiful, she thought. It was proper that a hospital be as beautiful as possible. She was excited to be here.

The information desk was manned by several young sailors who told her how to get to her father's room. It was on the sixth floor. The nurse's station at the sixth floor was right in front of the elevator. When Bright Star asked to see Col. Mark Leroux, the Navy nurse in a white uniform stared at her.

"May I see some identification please?" asked the nurse.

"Of course," answered Bright Star, opening her small purse to get her driver's license and her nurse's certificate.

The Navy nurse methodically looked at both of the documents. A different attitude came over her as she returned them to Bright Star.

"Welcome, Miss Leroux. Your father will be surprised to see you. He has no idea that anyone was coming so quickly. I'm Lieutenant Jennifer Barkley, and I'm pleased to meet you. I've been your father's nurse since the hospital ship brought him to us. He's a wonderful patient. You'll really pick him up. He's talked about you a great deal. Now that I see you, I understand why he's so proud of you."

"Sometimes he talks too much," she replied, all smiles.

"If you'd like to put that nurse's certificate to work, any hospital would be glad to have you, Miss Leroux."

"That thought has crossed my mind. I'd like to talk to you about it later if you don't mind, Miss Barkley...or is it Mrs.?"

"Why don't you call me Jenny. Everybody around here does."

"If you'll reciprocate by calling me Dawn."

"It'll be my pleasure, Dawn. Your father is down the hall here to my left in room 627. There are three beds in there. His is against the window where he can look out at the Koola Mountain Range to the northeast. One bed is empty, the other one is occupied by a badly burned sailor who came in on the same ship as your father."

"Did you have a chance to meet General Korsman, when he was here?" asked Bright Star.

"No, I didn't, but one of the other nurses on duty remembered him."

"He was my father's commanding officer and a very dear friend of the family. I was just wondering."

"Your father's probably still eating his supper. Enjoy your visit, Dawn."

"Thanks, Jenny, I'm really excited to be here."

Mark was having trouble chasing some of the peas on his plate with a fork. Frustrated and a little impatient, he gave in and used a spoon to scoop up the rest of the unruly peas. He had a feeling that someone was watching him. The nurses did that often so he paid little attention to it, except that it "felt different" this time. Turning his head towards the door, he thought he was having a dream. Bright Star was quietly watching him eat. At first, he thought it might have been Bright Cloud, but the smile, was unique to his beloved Star.

"Oh, my God, Bright Star!" cried Mark.

Bright Star ran to him and as carefully as she knew how, wrapped her arms around his neck. It had been three years since she had seen him. He had aged in that time. Tears came easily to her dark eyes. They were tears of happiness and thanksgiving. Whatever he had to face in the future, could be shared by loved ones at his side. She was shocked to look at him up close. He seemed so small and vulnerable lying in the bed swathed in white bandages. It wasn't the dressings that shocked her as much as the hollow look in his eyes. It sent her heart pounding. He had the look of a person who had seen too much horror. His normally brownish hair had turned white. The light blue-green sparkle that was always present in his eyes was gone, replaced with a dull gray. His eyes seemed to be set further back into his head. The more he looked at her, the more she became frightened for him. He tried bravely to smile, but it was difficult for him.

The man Bright Star saw on the hospital bed was a far cry from the cheerful smiling father she remembered. She was afraid that what she was seeing and thinking would show on her face. Her tears were replaced with a desire to comfort and help him forget the horrors mirrored in his sunken eyes. My Lord, she screamed to herself, what he must have seen to do this to him!

Pushing his food tray to one side, Mark started to speak, but found no words. Tears of frustration and anguish welled from his eyes and flowed down his angular cheeks. All he could say was, "My darling little girl, thank you for coming..."

"Mother will be coming before too long, Daddy. Only one seat on the plane was available, so I took it first."

"I'm so sorry you have to see me...like this," he apologized. "This...is...like a dream come true." Mark broke down and sobbed uncontrollably for a short time. Star was prepared to ring for the nurse in case he needed medication to calm him. All the time he was weeping, he held on to Star's arm with his right hand. His slender body twitched with each sob. It tore Star apart watching him. Mark braced himself and leaned back into the mattress holding him in a semi-sitting position.

"Don't you dare apologize for your condition, Dad. Uncle Arlo has kept in touch with Mother. We're so proud of what you've done. Don't you forget, I'm a nurse, and a very good one, too, thanks to you and Mother. Right now, we've all got just one important task ahead of us, and that's to get you well again."

Bright Star calmly told him why her mother didn't come when the first seat was available. She told him about DJ and how good he looked in his uniform. A smile formed on his lips replacing the frown. An hour had passed since she came to him and she was already encouraged by the progress she witnessed. The color of his cheeks was fast loosing that ashen white pallor that so alarmed her when she first walked into the room. She came to the conclusion that he had given up. Her presence was helping him to find hope all over again, and it was rejuvenating him right before her eyes!

"My arm in this crazy looking cast is really not as bad as it may appear. The doctors think it will mend so that I'll be able to use it. They told me to expect it to be slightly disfigured, but, that's not the bad part..." Tears came again when he tried to direct her attention to his legs. "I don't have any feeling in them, honey. I can't move them either...what if I never walk again?" Panic returned to him. Bright Star took her index finger and firmly pressed it into his trembling lips.

"Hush, Dad. We cross one bridge at a time, and only when we're ready to cross it. Right now, we've just got to be thankful that you're alive. You need time for your body to repair itself. Later, we can look at what's ahead. You're not alone. We'll do the best we can. In the meantime, you had better eat all of the veggies on your plate."

The remark drew a smile from him. "You sound just like your mother, Star. Thank God, you've come." Mark reached out to touch her cheek.

"You look more like my Bright Cloud as the years pass. I'm a lucky person to have such a wonderful family care for me."

"Remember, Daddy, you have a special guardian angel who looks after you, too."

"Why don't you pull up a chair and place it where I can look at you," directed Mark. "You've got to bring me up to date about everything since we last saw each other. Tell me about Mother and DJ, and all the gang at Fort Lewis, especially Inspector Clough. Don't just tell me the news, I want to hear all of the gossip, too." Mark was feeling better by the minute, now that his lovely daughter was at his side.

Star sat and held his hand while she filled him in on all the things she could remember happening back home. She was content, at last, catching occasional glimpses of the strong father she remembered. His eyes were beginning to lighten up and he was more attentive to conversation.

It was late when Bright Star returned to her room at the hotel. So much had taken place these past few days. She was literally halfway around the world from the remote settlement of Fort Lewis. It seemed much longer than just a week since she left in the small R.C.M.P. float plane from Lac Diamante. When she was at Fort Lewis, working in the infirmary, it would have been impossible for her to imagine what it was like in the middle of the Pacific Ocean. There was something magical about Pearl Harbor. It had an attraction for her that was real and tangible the moment she arrived. Maybe it was the frantic pace of an active base near the war zone and the energy that emanated from the sea of people around her.

The telephone lines were busy and would remain that way for the rest of the night, so Star was unable to let her mother know how her father was doing. She decided to write a short letter in case her mother was delayed in getting a seat on a plane out of Brunswick. If she was by chance still at home, her message of hope would be welcome news, and could put her worst fears to rest.

The next morning, Bright Star awoke with a plan of action on her mind. After a fresh change of clothes and a hearty breakfast at the hotel dining room she made an appointment with the Director of Nurses at the Pacific Fleet Hospital. She had not told anybody about her plans. She was unsure of them up until this morning.

The Director of Nurses, Captain Somers, was a middle-aged woman who looked as if she was pushed to the limit of her ability to cope with the many responsibilities placed upon her. She wore a white Navy uniform and had captain bars on her blouse collar. The Director sat calmly reviewing the form that Star had filled out. She had a formal indifferent air that did not encourage familiarity.

"Your qualifications and experience are most impressive, Miss Leroux. We're always short-handed these days and we would be proud to have you join us. However, there are some problems." Captain Somers paused a second and avoided looking at Bright Star. "The regulations for the Navy Nurse Corps has certain restrictions, and I'm not sure rather you could qualify for a commission in the Navy, at this time."

"How am I not qualified?" asked Star, stunned by the statement.

"It has nothing to do with your training or professional qualifications."

"You mean it has everything to do with my racial origin," stated Star angrily. She had run into this sort of thing before and it made her indignant that it should be a factor when the need was so important.

"Please don't take it personal, Miss Leroux."

"How can I not take it very personal?" replied Star sharply.

"If it was just up to me, I'd put you in uniform this morning and have you in one of the wards by mid-day. I sincerely apologize for this discussion. You're more qualified than most of the nurses already in uniform at this facility. The fact that your father is a patient here and an officer in the Marine Corps makes the regulations that much more embarrassing for me. May I ask you to be a little patient with me so that I can check with my superiors? Forgive me. You deserve a straightforward answer, and I'm unable to give it to you today. Could you come back again tomorrow morning?"

"Yes, I'll be back tomorrow morning," answered Bright Star. She walked from the office feeling let down. A burning rage was starting to simmer within her. All she had done was offer her services to help where help was needed, and she was put off because of her Cree heritage. She felt used and discriminated against, and that was always accompanied with pain and rage.

Star went swiftly from the Director's Office to the sixth floor, where she confronted Jenny Barkley at the front desk.

"Good morning, Jenny," greeted Star, unable to hide the rejection she had just experienced.

"Hi, Dawn. You look upset about something. Can I help?" Jenny Barkley was a steady, moderate person who had the gift of being a good listener. She put down the pen she was writing with, and pushed her chair from the desk.

"This morning I went to see your Director of Nurses, Captain Somers, about a job as a nurse. She put me off so that she could check the regulations. My race seems to be an obstacle to an immediate answer."

"That explains why you still look flustered. Try to not let it bother you. Easy advice to give, I know. Just recently, we lost the chance to hire several Hawaiian nurses who happen to be of remote Japanese descent. It's a mess, but it's in the regulations they have to use. Wipe that frown from your face, and step in to say 'hi' to your father. He's improved immeasurably since your visit last night."

"Thanks, Jenny," said Star, waving her hand.

There was a doctor with her father.

"Here's my girl," hailed Mark. "She brightens up any room. Dr. Henning, this is my daughter, Dawn. Honey, this is the doctor who worked his magic to keep me alive after I was hit, Dr. Henning."

The doctor turned to greet her. "It's my pleasure, Miss Leroux. Now I can put a face to your name. Are you the one called Bright Cloud?"

"No. That's my mother. I'm called Bright Star," she answered directly with a feeling of pride in being able to announce who and what she was.

"Star just flew in from the mainland last night. What a surprise! She and her mother are both registered nurses. Star has been working every year since she graduated from nursing college, at an infirmary in the northern forests of Canada. She's been doing the same thing her mother was doing when I first met her."

"That's interesting, Colonel Leroux. Do you think we could offer you a job here with us, Miss Leroux?"

Star hesitated to answer the question. "It probably is no secret by now, so I might as well tell you that I just came from the office of the Director of Nurses, where she told me that I might be unacceptable, because of who I am..."

"Who questioned you, Star?" demanded Mark, outraged at the implications.

"Do I understand correctly that you were not given an immediate opportunity to join us?" inquired Dr. Henning.

"That's correct, Sir." answered Star, going to her father's side. "Don't be angry, Father. We've been through this sort of thing before, and there isn't much we can do about it."

"Excuse me, Miss Leroux, Colonel Leroux. There is something I can do about it," answered Dr. Henning, stomping out of the room.

"I'm sorry, Honey. We've grown up and spent most of our lives together in places where it didn't matter who we were. Our nationality and race should be characteristics of pride and respect. As long as people are aware of what's in our hearts, then everything else is unimportant. I'd give anything to shield you from such narrow-mindedness. Try not to take it personally, Star. Service policies are frequently unfair. Sometime they'll change, right now, they cause an awful lot of hurt to those affected."

"It's okay, Dad," answered Star upset with herself for discussing the situation in front of him.

"Would you please crank my bed up so that I can see you better?" asked Mark. "That's fine. You know, young lady, I had a feeling, after you left last night, that you would try something like this. You've opened up a can of worms, and I can visualize that several people are wondering how they're going to handle it. Your qualifications make you a rich find for any hospital facility. Try not to worry."

"I'm not worrying, Dad, I'm just plain angry at such stupidity," lamented Bright Star with a shake of her head.

Lieutenant Jenny Barkley stuck her head in the door and whispered, "Wow, I can tell you, some feathers are being ruffled right now downstairs. Keep your chin up, Dawn. Ring if you need me, Colonel, I gotta go."

Mark could not hold back a grin. "Nurse Barkley is a delight. She has the whole floor wondering what she'll do next. She's an irascible clown and everyone loves her for her bubbling personality."

"She does seem nice. I like her..." Star was interrupted by a puffing Dr. Henning, who burst into the room with a triumphant look on his face.

"Now, Miss Leroux, let me be the first in the U.S. Navy to apologize for its nonsensical hiring policy. As of this moment, it's suspended in this facility. You may, at your convenience, return to Captain Somer's office and fill out the necessary forms, if you still want to join us on the nursing staff. If you chose to do that, I'm at liberty to inform you that you can and will be sworn in as an ensign in the Navy for the duration of the war with Japan. Your duties will be commensurate with your skills, after a short orientation and familiarization period so that you can learn how we do things in the service, and learn how an officer is expected to conduct themselves. Then, you'll be assigned anywhere in the hospital, or at any of its branches in the Pearl Harbor area. Do you have any questions?"

"Well...no, Sir," answered Bright Star, amazed at the rapid decision making ability of the doctor.

Mark's eyes brightened when he heard that his daughter could be sworn in as a commissioned officer. "Is this what you want, Star?"

"Yes, Dad, it's what I thought would happen this morning when I was brushed off. I'll be glad to accept it. I'll write Father Lamontagne to tell him what I'm doing so that he can make other arrangements at Fort Lewis for the coming fall and winter."

"That's my girl. I'm proud of your decision," said Mark quietly.

"I think we're going to get a valuable member to our staff. Congratulations, Miss Leroux. I'm late for the rest of my rounds, but I'd like to go over with you exactly what your father is up against."

"I'd appreciate that, Dr. Henning."

"I'll be leaving in a few days for another sea trip on the hospital ship. While I'm gone, a specialist in nerve surgery is going to be looking after Col. Leroux."

"I realize it may be premature, but what is your prognosis for my father's prospects of walking?" asked Bright Star watching him closely.

"That's a question no one can answer, Miss. I would venture a guess that the chances of your father walking again are fifty-fifty. I've discussed this with him in great detail, as he will probably tell you. It all depends on the condition of the nerve endings that were severed. Can they mend themselves? Maybe. How long before we know for sure? About six months or more. In the meantime, the most valuable part of your father's recovery, at least for his legs, is to continue the leg massaging therapy that we have already started. We must, I repeat, must, maintain the muscular integrity of the leg and foot muscles, even though they can't move under their own power. If we allow them to atrophy, or waste away, we've lost the game. If his nerve fibers do mend themselves, he's got to have the muscular capacity to be able to move his legs. Now that you're here on the scene, and your mother will soon be present, I'd give his chances as better than my original fifty-fifty chance. He's got a lot of heavyweights in his corner. If I were you, I'd be guardedly optimistic, but it's going to take a lot of prayers and a lot of leg muscle work."

Bright Star watched her father hanging on every word the doctor said. He was beginning to look better already, his color was noticeably improved. It was a good omen.

"We'll do what has to be done," promised Star, squeezing her father's hand.

"Best of luck, Miss Leroux. Keep up the good work, Colonel, I'll look in on you when I get back," said Dr. Henning, leaving the room.

"I think he knows what he's talking about, Star. I have faith in him."

"He certainly gets things done, I'll give him that much," answered Star. "Do you think you can handle a sailor nurse in the family?"

"A commission in the Navy is an honor for any person or family. The Navy is the winner, they're fortunate to have you. No daughter is any more loved, than I love you at this moment. You make me feel special when I call you my daughter."

"Thanks for the support, Father. I was hoping to have it..."

The more she thought about her new adventure, the more she was convinced it was right for her. "Ensign Dawn Leroux, USN." It had a nice ring to it!

Chapter Eleven

Brigadier General Arlo Korsman fumed with anger at the Pacific-Commander-in-Chief staff that could callously deposit his brigade in such a God-forsaken, rotting hellhole as Pavuvu, and expect him, or anybody else, to refit the battle-weary troops. It would take more than a division to turn the area into a suitable encampment. But, orders were orders, and Arlo settled down to evaluate what could be done with the resources they had at hand. He was an old campaigner, and he could not think of a project he had been ordered to do that had a full complement of the materials and supplies needed to properly do the job. You may want more, but reality and long experience dictated that you were expected to make do with the materials on hand.

The most important task confronting Arlo and his staff was making certain that the men were properly fed and supplied with enough tents and other necessities capable of giving them a reasonable opportunity to recuperate from the last campaign. High protein food, fruits and vegetables were vitally important and essential for their well-being. Morale increased with the arrival of several hundred green replacements for the depleted ranks. The new troops had never experienced combat and brought a more positive outlook, which was frequently lacking in veteran units.

Rest and recovery were important. Arlo also knew that prolonged idleness was a threat to the cohesiveness in any combat unit. Consequently, he developed a strenuous training program for the troops that would also help assimilate the green troops into their assigned units.

If he had his choice, Arlo would have preferred to remain under the command of the Sixth Army with Krueger, but he felt, with some pride, that the proposed operation for the First Marine Division, of which his brigade was a part, was ordered to secure the right flank of MacArthur's return to the Philippines. The marines were scheduled to

167

secure the Palau Islands which lay to the west of the Islands of Mindanao and Samar in the Philippines. The Palau Islands posed a threat to the logistical line of communications for MacArthur's forces, with the island of Peleliu representing the major threat. Besides securing MacAthur's right flank, Peleliu provided a bonus to the Allies, a usable airfield.

Peleliu was another tropical stinkhole as far as the Americans were concerned. The Solomon Islands, where they had fought so long and so bravely, was an area where malaria was endemic. Malaria inflicted as much damage upon the American troops as the Japanese Army did. Arlo was suffering with severe bouts of malaria. The disease was very democratic and spread its havoc indiscriminately among the officers and men. Every few days the high fever and chills would do what fatigue and weariness could not do - bring him to the point where he could not stand and had to seek the recuperating power of his cot. He faithfully took his atabrine {quinine} tablets and shortly afterwards wore the yellowish complexion that was a trademark of men serving in the tropics. Half of the men had the fever.

The assault of Peleliu was scheduled for the early part of September, and from the information Arlo had available to him at that time, it looked like a tough nut to crack. He relentlessly pushed for intensive training in basic infantry tactics and elementary military skills. The Solomons were a good place to practice landing exercises for the brigade. The ships were subsequently loaded for combat, which meant that the materials and supplies needed first by the attacking troops, would be loaded last in the cavernous holds of the vessels.

On the day of the invasion, Arlo's uneasy feeling about the landings was confirmed. It was evident in the early stages of the assault that it was going to be a costly and bloody campaign. The assault beachhead could not be expanded until more troops got ashore. The initial losses were heavy. Sixty percent of the amphibious tractors were wiped out within the first three hours. The original timetable for the marines to secure the islands was estimated to be about a week. After two weeks of vicious fighting, more than half of the island was still not secured, and the fanatical resistance of the Japanese was just as strong as it was on the first day.

At the end of the two week period, Arlo's brigade had absorbed all that the enemy could hurl at them. The casualty rate was alarming, and he had to come to the difficult and sad conclusion that the brigade was finished as a tactical formation. Man can only be forced to do so much. The spirit may be willing, but flesh and blood have physical limits beyond which it is foolhardy to demand what cannot be delivered. After a cantankerous conference with the Corps Commander, it was decided that Arlo's brigade would be pulled out of the line and relieved by a fresh Army division that was already acting as "floating reserve." The marines echeloned to the rear as the Army advanced to take over their positions at the front.

The change of command ceremonies was brief and meant different things to the two commanders involved. Arlo was disappointed that he could not complete the job assigned him, but wisdom told him that it was a prudent decision to let fresh troops take over the task. The Army division commander, General Miller, known to Arlo only by reputation, was well respected for his abilities in the war zone. Miller accepted the grim responsibilities with mixed feelings. His division was ready for the assignment, for they too had trained long and hard, but combat meant more casualties, and that fact of life was never taken lightly by any commander.

"I wish you the best of luck, General Miller," said Arlo. "I hope your losses are lighter than ours."

"I've followed your tactics carefully, General Korsman. You've performed with an elan and tenacity such as I've never seen before. A hearty well-done to you and your marines. We'll do our best to maintain the standard of excellence you've established."

"Thank you, Sir."

Arlo was one of the last officers to leave the beach. His aide, Lieutenant Mathews, finally caught up with him on the last landing craft as it backed from the bloodstained beach.

"I have a message for you, Sir."

"Thanks, Mathews," answered Arlo, so weak that he had to hang on the rail. Beads of sweat peppered his forehead. Lieutenant Mathews had never seen his boss look as sickly as he did, trying hard to look inconspicuous in the landing craft.

"Look, Sir, you'll never make it up the rope net to the ship's deck in your condition. May I order a sling to be dropped down for you?

You've got to get some rest. Our show is finished, so let the Navy do its job for now."

"I hate to let the men see me like this." The decision to be slung aboard the transport ship like a sack of flour was repugnant to Arlo, but he was too weak to argue the point. "Have them send down a sling then."

One of the large cranes on the deck dropped a slim line with a boatswain chair attached to the end toward the rocking landing craft below. Arlo reluctantly allowed himself to be strapped in and slowly hoisted to the deck above. The men didn't pay much attention at first, but when they saw who it was, a spontaneous cheer rose from their lips that could be heard throughout the anchorage area. Lieutenant Mathews gave Arlo a look as if to say, "I told you so."

Once on board, Arlo was quickly taken to the ship's sick bay, where he rested for a short time checking the messages that Lieutenant Mathews passed on to him. One was a notice of his relief from command of the brigade ordering him to Pearl Harbor where he would report to the Commanding Officer of the Tenth Army, who was planning the campaign against Okinawa, one of the Japanese home territories. His new duty assignment was to act as Tenth Army deputy chief of staff. The last message was a notification of his promotion to Major General, effective immediately. Arlo was not able to grasp the significance of the messages. His body was wracked with the shakes and chilling fevers that made him delirious.

Lieutenant Mathews was fearful for his commander and asked the transport Captain to transfer Arlo to the hospital ship that was nearby in the anchorage. The transport ship did not have a doctor on board, and the loyal aid wanted the best for his charge. Arlo was unaware when the transfer took place.

* * *

Meanwhile, far from the scene of death and destruction of the combat zone, Bright Cloud, full of sadness and despair, watched DJ wave from the window of the Boston and Maine bus as it disappeared around the curve. She unknowingly bit her lip trying not to be emotional. Seeing her only son pass from view on his way to war, hurt so much she couldn't cry. It was impossible not to be scared. Once again, part of her world was marching toward the dreadful guns, and she was powerless to do anything about it. She resented the lonely nights ahead of her. The terror of her imagination, whenever her family was away, was beginning to take its toll. Her courage seemed to be draining from her more and more as each day passed.

Her soldier son was home for two days after Bright Star left, and Bright Cloud was thankful for the short furlough. It gave her a chance to enjoy the little boy she knew so well, and to become better acquainted with the fine young man he had become. She knew that Mark would have been so proud of him. The two men in her life were very much alike. Their relationship with each other was that of father and son, and it also had that very comfortable feeling of friendship that develops from respect and true affection. Probably DJ had a more soldierly bearing than his father, but they both had that rare quality of being comfortable and at ease with the responsibility of command. Confidence in their abilities and respect for those whom they commanded was at the heart of their unique aptitude to the profession of arms.

Bright Cloud always had a feeling of helplessness and loneliness when Mark left for combat duty. The parting of her son was different today. She felt like screaming and running after the bus to make it stop, so that she could bring her son back where he would be safe. She was fully aware that she was reaching the limits of her courage to deal with the long days and longer nights of uncertainty. Every trip to the mailbox was getting harder and harder. The anticipation of tragic news was with her, night and day. Bills in the mail box were a welcome relief.

Walking aimlessly back to the house, Bright Cloud sat on the kitchen steps and reflected upon what was taking place around her. She had a strange feeling that would not go away. It was unlike anything she had ever experienced. It could not be denied. The realization came to her, sitting on the steps with her head in both of her hands, that she was being tested. A premonition of tragedy was so strong, that it was consuming her. It was testing her faith. She had to get control of her imagination. Mental pictures of the possibilities were becoming unthinkable...

The coffee cups she and DJ used just before he left, were still sitting on the table. She lifted the one he had used to her lips and let the tears, bursting to be released, come at last. She could still hear his voice within the kitchen walls where the family had spent so much of their time together. "I have so many happy memories growing up in this place and in Fort Lewis, Mom," DJ had told her. "Thanks for all of them. Before I leave, I want you to know that the thing I've always been the most proud of, is the love that you and Dad have for each other. That gift has been the glue that bound all of us. I hope that Allison and I are going to be blessed with the same thing. Be sure and tell Dad that I think often about him. Now that I know what's expected of officers who lead men in combat, my admiration and respect for him has increased. Tell him that I'll do my best."

Bright Cloud knew that she could not sit idle, she had to do something with herself, so she phoned Brunswick Naval Air Station to ask if there was any seat available soon. She was in luck. One was assigned to her for the next morning. She quickly checked the bus schedule, and informed them she could make connections and to reserve it for her.

The next day Bright Cloud was on her way to San Francisco. It was as new and exciting an experience for her as it was for Bright Star. When she arrived at San Francisco, she was told that the next plane to Hawaii would not leave until the next morning, so she was temporarily quartered in a guest house at the airfield. Like Bright Star, she too was thrilled at seeing her first palm tree.

The airport was filled with planes landing and taking off. Next to the airport, several large transport ships were simultaneously being loaded with swinging cranes lifting heavy bundles from the wharf to the cavernous openings of the ships. Lines of trucks waited to be unloaded by the cranes. The dynamic activity was fascinating to watch. Instead of chaos, there was an orderliness to the frantic pace around her. Bright Cloud felt caught up in the industriousness of the gigantic effort. Young men swarmed over the area doing their individual jobs like part of a well drilled team. She thought it was like a colony of ants where teams of workers all labored for the same goals.

That night in the guest house, the fatigued Bright Cloud was asleep as soon as she laid her head on the soft pillow. Late at night a loud noise woke her and she had trouble getting back to sleep after the disturbance. Memories of Mark flooded through her mind warming her heart. A big part of their life together had been shared by the children, so it was not unnatural for her to recall almost minute by minute, DJ's last visit. It brought a smile to her lips.

DJ had been dating a high school classmate, Allison Perkins, through the four years of high school. Bright Cloud thought they were a lovely couple. They attended most of their senior year activities together. The senior prom was the final event of the year before graduation. They had dressed formally for the prom. Bright Cloud and Allison's parents also knew that there was something very special between them. Both glowed in each others company. DJ was quiet and reserved by nature. He did not readily reveal his feelings to those around him. However, whenever he looked at Allison, his eyes brightened and a look of contentment and approval shone all over his face.

Allison Perkins was a vivacious young lady who could never hide her feelings for DJ. The young couple were relaxed and comfortable with their relationship. They shared the same values and enjoyed doing many of the same things together. One of their favorite pastimes was hiking, which they undertook whenever time and weather cooperated. Even though they were both young in age, there was something firm and solid and mature in their attraction for each other. DJ, tall and slender, towered over Allison, who was short and petite. When they walked together, she almost had to run to keep in step. They had a mutual fondness for music. Whenever she came to the house, DJ always asked her to play something on Bright Cloud's piano. His favorite was "Danny Boy", and whenever Allison played it for him, he was moved by the sad, haunting lyrics of the traditional Scottish folksong.

The day after DJ came home from West Point, he asked his mother if he could borrow the family Studebaker to take Allison out to a movie at the Wells Beach Pavilion. He spent a couple of hours washing and cleaning the car and taping the upper portions of the car's headlights and tail lights with black friction tape so that they did not show too much light. It was all a part of the local blackout regulations that were rigidly enforced on the seacoast for driving at night. German submarines lurking off the coast at night, could readily see the full glare of automobile lights. The lower half gave off enough light to drive slowly, but not enough to reflect out to sea. The same regulations applied to inside house lights. Nothing could show on the outside of the house, which meant that curtains had to be taped tight to the windows.

DJ also drained the old crankcase oil from the Studebaker and replaced it with fresh oil. Every automobile owner took those steps necessary to maintain their vehicles the best they could; there were going to be any more new cars until the end of the war. He used to help his father do many of the chores around the house, and that included maintenance of the family car. Since his father wasn't available, he took it upon himself to do some of those things that would help his mother the most. He also rotated an almost bald tire to the trunk as a spare, and placed the better spare tire on the car. Tires were a priceless and scarce commodity since the war started.

Allison Perkins was going to a normal teaching school in Portland while DJ went to West Point. They corresponded regularly with each other. Her parents were as favorably inclined towards him as his parents were towards Allison.

When DJ came home from the movies that night, Bright Cloud thought he was such a handsome young man in his well-pressed uniform. He was excited about what had happened that evening, and bursting to tell his Mother that he had given Allison an engagement ring, which she tearfully accepted. Bright Cloud was not surprised. She expected it sooner or later, and was happy to see how excited he was.

DJ confided to his mother that he did not want to rush Allison with marriage, so he thought it would be better to wait until the end of the war. When Bright Cloud had time to speak to DJ about Mark's wounds, and the possibility of a drastic change in their lives as a result of the injuries, he was silent and reflective for a few seconds. Bright Cloud realized, afterwards, that he had her feelings in mind when he answered. "Mom, I've tried to think of Dad exactly the way he was when he went off to war. I know that we must face reality and accept what's happened to him. I'm glad that, finally, he's in the safety of a hospital, where he doesn't have to take the risks we all knew he took. You may not realize it, Mother, but I've been having a difficult time dealing with what's happened to Dad, and until I come face to face with it, I just as soon keep at a distance for now. I want to confront my new platoon with fresh courage, and not be inhibited with thoughts of what might happen. I think about Dad all the time.

174

He's always in my heart, the same as you. For now, I want to remember him the way he was. It's not that I can't face reality, there's plenty of time for that. It's just that I want to be able to take over my own command and not be troubled with thoughts or fears of the calamities that are waiting for any of us. If something happens to me, I'd want you to remember me that way, and not dwell on the tragedy that's always possible in war." With those words, her only son left her standing beside the road and went off to war to do his duty.

Morning started with an early wake-up call from the San Francisco Naval Guest House. Bright Cloud, usually an early riser, was caught sound asleep when the call came. She had lain awake for hours in the night again. A quick coffee and donut at the Red Cross canteen truck sitting on the tarmac beside the large plane being readied for the transocean voyage, made up her breakfast. She literally ran up the stairs in order to make it before the door was shut and the portable stairs rolled away from the aircraft. The only seat that remained empty was an aisle seat on the port side of the plane, midway of the fuselage, slightly behind the wing. In the seat beside her was a navy chief petty officer, already sound asleep and snoring profusely. He reeked of alcohol. Bright Cloud made up her mind to ignore it and tried to relax for the long nine-hour ride ahead of them.

The steady hum of the four powerful engines created a soothing sound for most of the passengers. The plane was filled with servicemen from every branch; enlisted men and officers were evenly scattered throughout the cabin. Bright Cloud could not see any other women on board. She sat two seats from the entrance door on the left side of the plane and felt a cold draft coming through a small gap beneath the door. She had a jacket with her which kept her body warm, but the draft chilled her legs. A young seaman, acting as a flight attendant, gave a talk on what to do in case of an emergency landing at sea. It was a routine briefing given on every flight over the Pacific Ocean. The plane had enough life jackets for every person. They were under their seats and inflated automatically from a small pressurized canister attached to each one. The only exit available for the occupants of the cabin was the side entrance door. In the event of an accident, he advised everyone to get through the door as soon as possible and jump into the water. The life preserver could be inflated once they were outside. The escape procedure talk left Bright Cloud

175

apprehensive and sober. She took the time to try hers on and to make sure it could be done in a hurry. The chief beside her remained asleep.

Four hours out from San Francisco, Bright Cloud was enjoying a ham sandwich she picked up from the Red Cross Canteen Truck before boarding the plane. The young chief petty officer beside her had tossed and turned aggressively for the past couple of hours. Unable to find any position that was comfortable to him, he sat up straight and begrudgingly checked his life preserver under the seat.

"I apologize for my thrashing, Ma'am," he admitted, recognizing that his seat companion was a woman.

"There's no need to apologize, young man," she responded with an understanding smile. He looked as if he was frightened of something. Bright Cloud was no stranger to that look of forlorn hope, and her compassion naturally reached out to him. "I picked up a few sandwiches for the trip from the canteen truck at the airport, would you like one? I'd be glad to share them with you."

"Thank you. I'm afraid I overdid some drinking at Frisco. Something to eat would be great if you can spare it."

"I have a ham and cheese, or a peanut butter and jelly. Take your pick, or have both of them. I've just eaten and will be fine until we get to Pearl Harbor."

"Peanut butter sounds great, I haven't had one in a long time."

"I also have an extra Coke. If you're like me, peanut butter needs something to wash it down," grinned Bright Cloud. That remark drew a long smile to his face. She saw, in that instant, that he was just a boy, not much older than DJ.

The young sailor, Collin Montgomery, tore into his sandwich as if he hadn't eaten for a long time. His uniform was in need of a good pressing, and close examination would show that he was also in need of a shave. His fair skinned face helped to hide that fact. Bright Cloud came to the conclusion that he was probably recovering from an overindulged "night on the town".

Bright Cloud could see the wing from where she sat, and the circular shadows above the wings made by the two propellers. She stared in disbelief. First, the outboard engine stopped and the propeller ceased to mark its blurred circle. Then, she noticed the blades on the remaining inboard engine suddenly stop turning, also.

Before the significance of the stalled engines registered on her, Chief Montgomery alerted her.

"We're in trouble, Ma'am," he cried aloud, reaching under his seat for the life preserver. "Put your preserver on quick, and tighten your seat belt as tight as you can stand it, now, Ma'am. Do it now. We're going down!"

His alarming cry was followed by a hurried announcement from the attendant, who told them to do the same thing. They had a fuel problem, and if it could not be corrected, they were going to land on the water. Each passenger should protect their face and head by holding it on their laps with their arms folded around it. There was some pitiful moans from the passenger cabin, but Bright Cloud was impressed at how calm most of them remained. She was petrified, and frantically rummaged through her large carrying bag for those important items that she did not want to lose if they crashed into the water. She stuffed her pockets with anything she thought might come in handy.

"Don't be afraid, Ma'am. We're close to the door." Chief Montgomery whispered calmly in her ear.

Another engine quit and the plane listed toward the port side and started to lose altitude rapidly. The cockpit door was open and Bright Cloud could hear the pilot giving coordinates and SOS signals to anyone out there who could receive the message. She was scared and prayed that this was not her time to die. Her family needed her, now more than ever.

The young ensign piloting the plane remained calm and confident that he could bring the stricken plane into the water with minimum rupturing of the aircraft itself. He planned to bring the tail of the craft into the water first to slow the forward momentum before the heavier front of the plane slammed downward into the breakers.

Frightened by the water spray that blanked out the window beside her, Bright Cloud heard the loud bangs and tearing sounds as the heavy converted bomber plowed into the ocean and started to disintegrate. She felt her seat being torn free from the floor as screams of hysteria and terror filled the compartment. Bright Cloud was knocked unconscious from a heavy blow to her temple. When the plane finally came to a standstill, shrill voices screamed for someone to open the door. Chief Montgomery had been wrenched out of his seatbelt. The full force of Bright Cloud's body, still attached to the seat, acted as a projectile, crushing him against the back of the seat in front of them, which miraculously remained in place. His body throbbed with pain, but he was still conscious when the plane finally came to a stop. His survival instincts saved Bright Cloud's life. He could see that she was still strapped in her seatbelt harness, so he reached around her limp body to release the catch, and at the same time, pulled the tab on her life preserver air supply to inflate it. Half carrying and half pushing Bright Cloud, he scrambled for the door which was closed. He kicked it as hard as he could — nothing happened. The door refused to budge. The hysteria all around the cabin motivated him to take drastic action. He hurled his already broken and battered body as hard as he could against the steel door, opening it against a three foot wall of water that rushed in as soon as it was opened. The Chief then grabbed Bright Cloud's inert body and flung it into the water beyond the door and desperately jumped in after her.

The sudden plunge into the cool water revived Bright Cloud. She thought that she was drowning. She gasped for air and swallowed sea water, petrified when she came to the surface. The life preserver kept her afloat. The screams of terror coming from the plane behind her were short-lived and made her feel guilty that she was already free of the coffin-like fuselage. The door was three quarters below the water mark in a matter of seconds. Most of the people had gotten out and were bobbing in the water when the plane disappeared below the surface. No more sounds came from its interior as it made the final plunge to the deep. Those last cries of desperation from the ones who were unsuccessful in getting out, was something Bright Cloud would carry with her for the rest of her life. They rose to such a high crescendo, that they sounded inhuman. Seconds after the plane sunk out of sight, a deathly silence settled over the scene. It was almost as unnerving as the screams from the victims trapped in the sinking fuselage.

Stunned and still in shock, Bright Cloud noticed a rubber life raft floating nearby. She swam towards it and hollered to others that she had a raft. The gentle swells on the surface gave her a chance to see other survivors as she rode upon the crests of the waves. A solitary voice erupted from the stillness of the dark water.

"Is there anyone injured or in need of help? Try to locate as many of the rafts as possible. We released at least seven of them. Bring them in a circle so that we can lash ourselves together," hollered the young pilot.

"I've got one raft," answered Bright Cloud. "I'm coming towards you with it."

Five of the rafts were carefully maneuvered into the circle of survivors. The pilot, in keeping with the tradition of the Navy, took charge by asking everyone to climb into the rafts. There was a possible danger from sharks. One by one, the rafts filled up with terrified passengers. Bright Cloud held her raft as steady as she could while others climbed aboard. Chief Montgomery swam beside her.

"Ma'am, it's time for you to climb aboard. Make room for the lady, folks," he announced to the inhabitants of the raft. He helped her climb up and followed behind her.

Bright Cloud was chilled by the sudden breeze blowing across her wet body and she started to shake uncontrollably. Her head throbbed with pain. She could feel a lump on the right side of her head. As soon as she settled into the relative safety of the life raft floor, she checked herself for any broken bones or open cuts. She was still in a state of shock, like everybody else, but her instincts served her well. The magnitude of what had just happened would not sink in until later.

Bright Cloud looked around to take stock of things. Altogether, they had five rafts. She announced that she was a nurse and asked loudly if anyone was badly hurt. Nobody asked for her help, so one by one, she voluntarily checked over the inhabitants of her raft. There were four men besides the Chief and herself. She looked at Chief Montgomery with grave concern. He had saved her from the sinking plane. He was lying on the floor of the raft with his head propped against the rubber side, breathing heavily and erratically. Phlegm bubbled from his lips. Bright Cloud came closer to him to check his body for broken bones, wounds and possible internal injuries. "Chief Montgomery, I'm a nurse, and I want to help you. Where does it hurt? Can you tell me?" There was no response from him, yet she could see that his eyes understood what she offered.

"If you can understand me, answer my questions with a yes or a no. Blink once for no, and twice for yes. Are you in any pain?"

The chief blinked twice. A small stream of bubbles ran down the corner of his mouth. It was crimson red. Bright Cloud carefully felt his chest cavity and reached as far under him as possible, searching for an indication of his injuries, without moving him unnecessarily. His upper body was reasonably protected by the inflated life preserver. She thought it would be unwise to remove it. She pointed to the chest area, "Does it hurt here?"

The Chief blinked twice.

"Do you hurt anywhere else?"

The Chief blinked twice, and pointed to his chest and his left leg. Evidently, she thought, his chest hurt him when he talked. She was feeling helpless. He probably had a punctured lung and had to be handled very carefully or he could bleed to death. Most likely he was bleeding internally. His left leg protruded at an unnatural angle. She had seen similar injuries. It was a compound fracture of the left leg just below the knee cap. A puddle of blood was already forming under him. The pain was almost unbearable to him.

"Do I have your permission to set the broken leg, Chief?"

He blinked only once.

"If the Chief can be persuaded to give me his permission, I honestly think that I can set his leg. I've done it several times over the years. I'll need someone who's strong and willing to do exactly what I tell them to do, without flinching. Does anyone want to volunteer?"

"I'll help," answered a young baby-faced sailor with light blond hair and a frightened look in his eyes. Bright Cloud thought that he looked too young to be in the service, but he had two stripes on his arms, which indicated a maturity beyond his youthful looks.

"My name is Mrs. Leroux. We've got to help the Chief with his fractured leg as soon as possible. There's a danger of infection and a very real danger of jagged bone fragments severing an artery if the bone is not realigned. Chief, do you understand what I've just said?"

He blinked twice.

"I'm going to ask you again. Setting the leg is going to be a very painful procedure. In my opinion, it should be set immediately. It's got to be done sometime, and the pain will be worse if it's delayed. The pain should diminish shortly after it's realigned. Will you give me permission to put the break in its proper place, Chief?"

Chief Montgomery hesitated a moment and slowly blinked twice.

"You're a brave man, son. Now we're all going to review what has to be done. If we do it only once, he won't suffer from a prolonged ordeal. Therefore, we owe him our best effort."

Bright Cloud pulled a small first aid pouch from her jacket pocket and took a small pair of scissors from it. She proceeded to cut the pant leg all the way past the knee bone and rolled it up underneath the knee joint so that it did not obstruct what had to be done. A piece of bone had already pierced the flesh at the break. Bright Cloud gently felt it to determine rather it was a part of the lower bone or a sliver that might have been severed upon impact. She was sure it was an unattached sliver and deftly pinched it with her experienced fingers and removed it by pulling the large splinter of bone through the puncture in the skin which bled profusely. The onlookers blanched at the sight of the injury.

Bright Cloud warned all of the others that she would need their help, and asked them to gather around the Chief with a man on each side of him, so that they could hold his arms down. She directed the blond volunteer to position himself so that he could brace his feet against his fellow sailors and push as hard as necessary to hold the injured leg. Another man should be available to hold the Chief as still as possible when the manipulation of the leg started to take place. The blond sailor had the important task of pulling the injured leg as hard as he could so that the muscles were stretched, like an elastic band, extending the severed bone beyond the actual break, and holding it there until Bright Cloud told him to slowly release the pressure. She would guide the severed bones back together while the muscles were stretched to the limit. She warned the blond sailor that he should not let up the pressure until she specifically told him to do so.

"Chief, I think we're ready to do it," said Bright Cloud reassuringly in his ear. She wiped his brow with her dry hand. "Bear with us, son. It won't take long. You men holding him down, be prepared for sudden moves that could contribute to a worsening of the Chief's condition. Be very careful of his chest area; he may have a punctured lung. Is my assistant ready to pull the leg?"

"Yes...Mrs. Leroux, whatever you say."

"Close your eyes, Chief Montgomery, and say a prayer to whatever God you pray to. All together men, hold him as firmly and carefully as you can." Bright Cloud looked into the eyes of her helper and found him willing. "Very slowly, brace yourself so that you can feel comfortable doing it. Then pull with all the strength you have, son. I'll tell you when to stop, and I'll tell you when to maintain steady pressure on the leg. Finally, I'll tell you when to ease up. Ready?"

Everyone muttered in agreement. The volunteer sailor straddled the leg and braced his feet against the thighs of the two sailors holding the Chief's arms and started applying steady pressure to the leg. The Chief could not help himself; the pain was more than he could bear. He uttered a blood-curdling cry that was sustained for several seconds, and then passed out unconscious.

"Now, while he's still unconscious, keep pulling. It'll take quite a bit of effort to start the movement. Keep up the steady pressure...keep pulling..." Bright Cloud was having trouble feeling the fracture on the underside of the leg. At last, she could feel some movement under her experienced fingers. "We're almost there. Keep pulling...hold steady right there while I move the foot into position...steady, steady...now start easing up...slower, slower...that's fine. You can let go now, young man."

All of them were sweating from the tension and exertion of the operation. There was a visible sigh of relief when it was over.

"Thank you, gentlemen. You all did a wonderful job. I'm proud of you..." Bright Cloud clutched her blond headed helper's arm. "What is your name anyway, son?"

"My name's Robert Holden, Jr., Mrs. Leroux." The name sounded familiar to her, but in the excitement of the moment, she could not place it.

"My thanks to all of you. Does anybody have anything that could be used as a splint?"

Nothing was available aboard the raft, but somewhere in a raft alongside them, a voice hollered out that he had a service belt knife in a sheath which could help. Bright Cloud agreed and it was passed over to her.

"If you gentlemen will excuse me, I can use the cotton material in my dress to bind up the Chief's leg with the knife. It's no time for false modesty." With that statement, Bright Cloud proceeded to cut her dress off up to the waist. She had a white slip under the dress. Then she tore the dress material into four inch strips and started winding them around the injured leg. When it was all over with, the survivors turned their attention to their own predicament. The dark blue water extended as far as they could see in every direction, and there wasn't a ship in sight!

"I calculate that we lost seven men," shouted the pilot to the tense frightened group in the rafts surrounding him. "There were twenty-nine people on board when we left. I count twenty-two heads in the rafts. The SOS's we sent out were answered, so we have only to wait and stay together until rescue finds us."

"I ain't going anywhere," answered a voice from one of the rafts.

Bright Cloud watched her injured patient with increased concern. His color was turning from a flushed red tone to a pale-gray, and his pulse was getting weaker and erratic. She prayed that rescue would be in time for the grievously wounded sailor. His life's blood was steadily seeping from wounds she was unable to treat. A flood of emotion came over her when she admitted to herself that the gallant Chief Montgomery was slowly dying in her arms.

Chapter Twelve

Newly commissioned Major General Arlo Korsman was in no condition to celebrate his promotion from Brigadier General. Ever since his transfer to the hospital ship, several days ago, he had drifted in and out of a deep coma. Profuse sweating stained the white sheets on his bed so much they had to be changed twice a day. The malaria strain he had contracted was a very virulent one. He went through all of the classic symptoms of severe chills, followed by a high fever which produced excessive sweating and, frequently, deliriums and comas for various durations of time. It was a serious disease that produced body temperatures which could be life-threatening.

Arlo was more severely affected by the debilitating disease because his natural resistance was already at a low level when he contracted it. The result of a prolonged period of lack of sleep, poor food, and the steady strain of commanding combat troops in a long series of battles. Worry and grief about his beloved wife, Michelle, also contributed to the daily ration of anxiety and worry. Only his powerful will and determination kept him functioning on the job until the ravages of malaria finally overwhelmed him. One week after being transferred to the hospital ship, he was still experiencing bouts of delirium and extreme abdominal pains. His weakened state was aggravated by the frightening discovery that he was passing blood through his urine. It was a symptom which manifested itself in most of the more serious malaria infections.

One day, while the ship was heading towards Pearl Harbor, Lieutenant Mathews, Arlo's young aide, brought Arlo a communication from the Headquarters of the Commander-in-Chief, Pacific Ocean Area. Arlo had eaten lightly that morning and was in fairly good spirits when he opened the dispatch to read...

Dear Major General Korsman:

Congratulations on your recent promotion. Your performance at Peleliu was exemplary and we are proud of your hard-fought achievement. We are sorry to hear about your problem with malaria, and hope you have a speedy recovery. We are, also aware of your new posting to the staff of the Tenth Army and wish you the best of luck with General Simon Buckner. You and he should get along well – the two of you are cut from a similar cloth.

You may be interested to know that a lot of progress has been made in our analysis of recent intelligence. We have arranged for your clearance to receive most of our intelligence reviews and you will be placed on our list of people who have a 'need to know'. Your position on the staff of the Tenth Army makes your new clearance category possible. For now, rest easy and try to relax as much as the situation allows. We are in possession of positive information that corroborates an earlier hunch on our part. You are familiar with that interpretation, and we hope that you can derive some peace of mind and security with this recent information.

We'll see you when you arrive at Pearl Harbor. This message was sent to give you some positive hope in your recovery process.

Respectfully,

Col. James Ready, USA

Col. Henry Thomas, USA

The communication left him feeling better than he had in ages. With the new position ahead of him, he was beginning to feel a sense of great things happening at a faster pace. The thoughtfulness of his two friends again touched him at a time when he was vulnerable and in need of a lift. He would not soon forget their generosity. He fingered the communication pensively and rang the bell beside his bed.

"What can we do for you, General?" asked the young pharmacist mate on duty.

"Could you get me a pencil and paper, please and crank up the head of my bed? I want to write an answer to this communication."

"Aye, Sir. Your color seems better today."

"I feel better now," answered Arlo, pulling himself upright in the small bed.

"I'll get your paper and pencil, Sir."

"Thank you."

Pen and paper pads appeared shortly. "Your aide, Lieutenant Mathews, left word that he would be available as soon as he shaved and showered. Is there anything else, Sir."

"Nothing for now, son. Tell Mathews to take his time. I'm not going anywhere." Arlo then started to write:

Dear Ready and Thomas,

Your recent communiqué was an encouraging piece of news at a time when I desperately needed something positive to think about. I'm glad that my new position on the Tenth Army's staff gives me an elevated clearance status. It means a great deal to me. Thank you.

My appreciation for your kind act at a time when I know how tumultuous your schedule must be, will always be a part of my memory of our long-standing friendship. Again, thanks from an old classmate.

Arlo Korsman,

Maj. Gen., USMC

Lieutenant Mathews sent the message for his boss and returned to the room. Arlo was still weak from malaria, even though his spirits were much improved.

"What have we got ahead of us, Lieutenant?" asked Arlo, assuming that they had heard from Tenth Army, and anxious to hear about anything that came in since he was ill.

"Well, General, the Tenth Army commander, General Buckner, has sent his best wishes for your recovery. His headquarters has prepared an apartment for you at Schofield Barracks. The plans for the invasion of Okinawa will be prepared there. It looks as if it's going to be a seven division affair."

"Who's commanding the Marine Amphibious Corps?"

"I believe it's going to be General Geiger, Sir. The Army Corps commander will most likely be General Hodge."

"It's beginning to look like a big show, isn't it?"

"It could match the Normandy invasion, General," said Lieutenant Mathews, rummaging through his brief case at the foot of Arlo's bed. "I have some preliminary directives from CinchPac, Sir. However, I don't think you're in any shape to start reviewing these papers just yet. Security for the information in these documents could be compromised by medical personnel potentially having access to them. Why don't you take this opportunity on our way back to Pearl Harbor to regain your strength and convalesce, so that you can then give your new job its full attention when we get to Schofield Barracks?"

Arlo keenly watched his youthful aide. He liked the Lieutenant because he did his job without hovering around him the way some aides did with their charges. Mathews proved to be an independent thinker when the situation demanded it. His counsel about relaxing for the remainder of the trip, was a wise one that he agreed with.

* * *

In the meantime, several thousand miles to the northeast of Arlo's hospital ship, a traumatic experience for Bright Cloud was underway in a small raft in the large Pacific Ocean. Daylight had just ended with a spectacular sunset which left each of the hungry and cold survivors of the crashed plane feeling alone with their own prayers, their own individual thoughts, and fear of the unknown. That fear increased as the night progressed. Bright Cloud, frightened and shivering from the damp clothing, was still cradling the injured Chief Montgomery in her lap. She wanted to protect him from the movements of the raft as it floated on the undulating waves. Rescue, which had been expected, failed to arrive before nightfall. A long, uncomfortable night was ahead of them.

The only thing the survivors could do was wait as patiently as their dispositions would allow them. Rescue should be forthcoming upon the dawn of a new day. Everyone was remarkably quiet. There was no nervous chatter among the men, and none of the boisterous claims of being unafraid, which usually affects some members of any group. The gentle murmur of the waves splashing against the side of the rafts could have been a reassuring and peaceful sound in any other situation.

Bright Cloud had not been able to rest. She was concerned for the chief. He was dying, and she knew it. His pulse was very weak. His breathing was labored with interruptions of sharp coughs, which tore at his internal organs with every gasp. At least his leg pain seemed to be bearable. Bright Cloud was thankful for that small favor. The evening wore on without a moon to lighten their darkness. A myriad of blinking stars overhead seemed oblivious to their plight. It was a long night.

About mid evening, Chief Montgomery stirred in Bright Cloud's arms, and started to speak, with great effort, between coughing spells. "Ma'am...I'm sorry for the trouble I've caused you." Bright Cloud squeezed his hand to reassure him that she was listening.

"I got really drunk at San...Fran...cisco. I went crazy. My wife took up with...another man...for two years...I almost went AWOL because...of it. Would you do something for me?"

"Of course I would, Chief," Bright Cloud whispered softly in his ear.

"In the inside pocket of my jacket...is an envelope...marked 'For Mom and Dad'...Would you take it and see that it's delivered to...my parents...the address is on the envelope..."

"You'll be able to deliver it yourself."

"No...Ma'am...I know I'm dying and so do you...before you mail it...would you write a letter to them and tell them what happened...to me...and have them give what's in the envelope...to my daughter...when she gets old enough to know what it means...Will you do that for me?"

"I will; I promise, Chief. I owe you my life, and I'll never forget how you disregarded your safety when you opened the door and threw me outside of the plane."

"You remind me of my mother...she was a gentle lady, too...I've seen a lot of death in the war...I know how terrible it must be to die alone...thank you for being with me...I'm awfully cold...don't feel sorry for me...I'm going to a far better place than this cruel...world...could...ever...be..."

Bright Cloud felt the grip of the Chief's hand grow weaker and weaker, until there was no response from his cold fingers. She instinctively reached for his wrist to feel for a pulse. There was none! His irregular breathing stopped and the weight of his body became heavier and heavier on her lap. The other members of the raft were silent witnesses to the scene.

In the stillness of the cool evening, Bright Cloud wiped the beads of sweat, for the last time, from the Chief's forehead. Her trained fingers groped carefully in the darkness and gently closed the lids over his staring sightless eyes. Hysteria and shock at last gripped her. She wept unashamedly. Convulsive sobs pierced the still of the night. She was comforted by the young sailor who had helped with the chief's broken leg.

"Come now, Mrs. Leroux. Be strong. The Chief doesn't need our grief right now. He's at peace where pain can no longer reach him," Second Class Robert Holden, Jr. calmly said to her. "Here, let me help you place him on the floor of the raft so that you can set against the side and relax."

"Thank you."

"That's better. We can search the Chief's pockets as soon as it gets light."

"Yes, of course," responded Bright Cloud, full of grief and exhaustion.

The remainder of the night passed without incident. The long awaited morning finally came with a large orange-red sun peaking over the endless expanse of water. Everyone's spirits rose as it showed its full ball of fire above the dark ocean. Its warm rays were welcome.

Robert Holden helped Bright Cloud remove the life preserver from the Chief's lifeless body. They passed it along to a sailor who had none. In the Chief's coat pocket, a bulky envelope was found just as he described it.

Bright Cloud unwound the small thread which bound the manila envelope. Inside was a flat velvet case which held a newly minted Navy Cross medal. The shiny gold cross had a round emblem of an ancient sailing ship within a round crest embossed in the center of the medal. The ribbon above the cross was black with a single white stripe down the center. Folded beneath the medal in the box was a single sheet of parchment paper, which stated: "To Chief Petty Officer Collin Montgomery, for conspicuous gallantry in the face of the enemy...

Tears clouded her eyes so that she could not read the full citation. The medal did not surprise her. There was something special about Chief Montgomery that made him stand tall among brave men. How proud his daughter will be to find, someday, that her father was a heroic man. She passed it around to the other members in the raft. Robert Holden paused to read the citation and a look of understanding came over him as he returned the case to Bright Cloud.

"The Chief was fortunate to have you here, Mrs. Leroux. You not only were able to comfort him in his greatest hour of need, you were also in a unique position to carry out his dying wish. May I ask you a personal question?" asked the young sailor.

"Yes, if you feel that you must," said Bright Cloud, surprised at the way the young man looked at her.

"My father, Robert Holden, Sr., frequently talked to his family about an incident in which he participated as a member of the United States Counsel in Quebec, Canada. It involved a young Canadian Indian, with the distinguished name of Flying Eagle, who was awarded the Distinguished Service Cross posthumously. A marine officer, by the name of Leroux, was selected to award the medal to the native family. The Chief's medal made me think about that occasion, and I was wondering if it was possible."

"My Lord!" exclaimed Bright Cloud. "I do remember your father, now. Yes, you remind me of him. When you told me your name, I knew that I had heard it before, but could not remember. What a wonderful coincidence! It's a small world after all, isn't it? I met your father at the presentation. Flying Eagle was my brother. It was a fateful meeting for Mark. We married two years later."

"I remember my father saying that he had met many beautiful women around the world, but none ever surpassed the natural beauty and charm of a native lady he met in the remote Canadian wilderness. He must have been talking about you, Mrs. Leroux. Forgive me for my candid comments. The beauty he saw has not diminished with age. It has only blossomed with graciousness."

Bright Cloud blushed. "You have the same gift of words as your father, young man. Incidentally, how is he?"

"He was killed in China when the war first broke out," replied young Robert.

"I'm sorry to hear that. He was a spirited young man when I met him, full of energy and possessing a wonderful disposition. He was a gentleman. My husband, Mark, and your father became good friends."

"You just described him the way most people remembered him. I loved him very much. The family was traumatized by his death early in the war. I hope that future generations will appreciate the sacrifice made by so many." Robert stared at the inert figure beside them.

"I'm not sure, Robert. Time has a bad habit of diminishing the memories of sacrifice, dedication, and noble causes valiantly won, to the point of indifference. The collective pain that we as a nation are suffering, will probably only last as long as we live. When this generation dies, its accomplishments will most likely be forgotten."

"I hope your prophecy proves wrong, Mrs. Leroux."

"So do I, Robert."

The seriousness of their conversation was interrupted by a submarine rising from the water several feet beside them. A loud round of cheers and whistles greeted the dull gray hull towering over them. The Navy Captain spoke to them through a megaphone from the conning tower. Several sailors erupted from fore and aft openings on the deck to throw lines to the cheering rafts.

"Ahoy in the rafts. Please, let my men pull you to the sub's hull and assist you down into the interior as fast as we can. There's a danger of Japanese submarines in the area. We'll talk later." The Captain traded the megaphone for a pair of binoculars and started scanning the horizon.

Bright Cloud was the first person helped aboard. "There's a dead man's body in our raft, Captain," she hollered.

"Bring him aboard then. We'll do what we have to do, later, after dark. Welcome aboard, Ma,am. We'll do our best to make you comfortable. Incidentally, my name is Captain Evans."

The interior of the submarine reeked of sweat, oil, and fresh baked bread. The crash victims were taken to a central room full of bunks amid the stored torpedoes. There, they were given a chance to

191

remove their wet clothing in exchange for clean dry navy denim pants and shirts. Bright Cloud, in contrast to her request, was given the luxury of the Captain's quarters. Her presence in the bunking area was just not acceptable to him, since they had at least three more days before they reached Pearl Harbor.

"My pharmacist mate will prepare the Chief's body for burial at sea. When he's finished, we'll wait until nighttime before we conduct a funeral service, and commit his body to the sea. It's a sailors tradition of hundreds of years. I hope you're comfortable, lady," said the Captain, standing in the doorway.

"Thank you for your thoughtfulness, Captain Evans, I'll be fine. The Chief was a courageous man. He saved my life..."

"The other survivors told me that you set his broken leg. That was an act of courage, too. Now, if I may mention it..."

"My name is Mrs. Leroux. My husband is a marine colonel in the hospital at Pearl Harbor." Bright Cloud explained carefully under his watchful eyes.

"I don't mean to be disrespectful, Mrs. Leroux, but I think that you'll feel a lot better if you put on a fresh set of one of my uniforms in the drawer beneath the bunk bed. You're welcome to whatever I have."

"I'm embarrassed to look this way in front of everybody."

"My dear lady, make no apologies to me for your condition. I admire your quick thinking and presence of mind to do what you did on that raft. So please, be our guest and enjoy the privacy of the room. You've earned that privilege."

As soon as Captain Evans left her alone, Bright Cloud did enjoy the luxury of a shower and a change into fresh clothes. The Captain's shirt fit reasonably well, but the pants were a few inches too long and had to be rolled up on the ends. She felt much better now that she was a little more presentable. Shortly after she finished dressing, a knock at the door announced that she could come forward to the enlisted man's wardrobe for food and refreshments whenever she was ready. She opened the door and followed the young sailor to the smell of fresh coffee being brewed and the mouth-watering aroma of bread being baked. She was ravenous and glad to join her colleagues in a hearty fare of chicken and mashed potatoes.

After they had eaten, Captain Evans announced that he would surface for a short funeral service for Chief Montgomery after it turned dark. The sub's pharmacist mate had prepared the dead sailor's body for his eternal resting place in a watery grave at the bottom of the sea. Ten minutes after the set of the sun, the submarine rose to the surface. Bright Cloud and most of the survivors climbed onto the deck. It was a short worship exercise: the Captain read the Lord's Prayer by a hooded flashlight. Finally the eight body bearers solemnly lifted a board, which held the remains of Chief Collin Montgomery, sending his body into the churning sea. Behind them a bugler sounded the haunting notes of taps. The martial refrain echoed across the darkness as a parting message to a valiant seaman returned to his element. Bright Cloud felt as if she had lost a part of herself. The simple ceremony ended and all of the participants returned to the sub's interior. The crew and the people they had rescued from the sea were sober and reflective for the remainder of the night.

Three days after their rescue, Bright Cloud and the other survivors were escorted to the small bridge of the conning tower, where they watched the sub approach the Island of Oahu in the Hawaiian Islands. They were presently traveling through the Kiawi Channel with the spectacular view of Diamond Head on their starboard side. It was a prominent landmark standing on the southeastern corner of the island, south of the City of Honolulu. Bright Cloud was given the courtesy of the best seat in the house, the Captain's chair, to watch their arrival at the large Naval Base of Pearl Harbor. The sneak attack by the Japanese had been turned into a rallying cry for angry Americans, "Remember Pearl Harbor"! They were still in the process of avenging the dastardly act.

The sleek submarine passed Ford Island on its starboard side and went straight to the middle lock. A bus was waiting at dockside for them. A detachment of shore patrol officers was present to make sure that the rescued victims did not wander around the base. They said good-bye to the submarine crew, who had snatched them from possible death, and catered to their every need on the journey to Pearl. The sailors of the sub represented a typical cross section of Americana. They could be stalwart warriors when the situation demanded it, or they could be compassionate life savers in the next breath. Two characteristics, known the world over, mark the typical

American fighting man — his inherent decency and innate generosity. It was a combination that the enemy was finding unbeatable.

"Thank you, Captain Evans," said Bright Cloud, leaving the submarine. "You and your crew will always have a place in my prayers. I'll send your clothes back to you as soon as I can buy new ones. Good-bye...and thank you once again for your thoughtfulness. May God be with you and your crew."

"I appreciate the kind words, Mrs. Leroux. Your presence has graced our boat. It has been a privilege to be of service. Your spirit and courage are an inspiration to all of us. Your prayers will be appreciated. Good luck to your husband." The submarine Captain saluted her and held it until she left the ship.

The bus took all of them to an infirmary on the base, where they were all given a cursory check for possible injuries. Most of the sailors were given passes to their destinations when the plane crashed. Robert Holden, Jr., was released at the same time as Bright Cloud.

"I guess this is where we say good-bye, Mrs. Leroux. My destroyer is on the other side of the base. I hope you find your husband getting better. It's been swell meeting you. After these past few days together, I find myself agreeing with my father's assessment of you. Your beauty is not just skin deep, it glows from within."

"Hush, young man. You'll make me blush and cry, and I don't want to do that. Take good care of yourself, Robert. I'll pray for you. After the war is over, if you ever have a chance, come to Fort Lewis in the summertime. Chances are, we'll be there. It would be nice to see you again."

"It's an offer I'd like to take, Mrs. Leroux," answered Robert, extending his hand towards her. Bright Cloud brushed it aside and hugged him.

"Come back to us, Robert," she softly requested.

"I promise..." he answered, walking away so that she could not see the tears in his eyes.

The shore patrol escort took her outside the main gate, where she caught a taxicab for the hotel that Arlo had prearranged for her and Bright Star. She had lost all of her belongings, except her wallet, which contained important papers and all of the cash she had taken for the trip. The large hotel was located in Pearl City. It was thrilling to be this close to Mark. She was so anxious to see him. The long lonely nights and days of separation were about to end. She could hardly wait! The desk clerk gave her a key to the room, and directed her toward it. She had the key in her hand, but knocked on the door first. A voice she knew well responded to the knock. Bright Star opened the door. At first she did not recognize Bright Cloud dressed in the oversized khaki uniform.

"Mother, I didn't know you were coming so soon," Bright Star cried for joy. "What happened to your clothes? Why are you dressed like this?"

"You wouldn't believe what happened to us. Our plane crashed at sea. I just came in with the submarine that rescued us," Bright Cloud explained breathlessly. She scrutinized Star carefully. Then she saw the ensign insignia on her shoulder boards.

"What does this mean, Star?" asked her mother, pointing to the rank insignia and the well fitted uniform of a navy nurse.

"I've decided to help out, Mother. They need help desperately, so I joined up until the war's end," explained Star. "Don't worry. I see Dad every day. Several times a day, actually. He's doing much better since I arrived, Mother. You'll be proud of him."

"Where's he located?"

"Just down the road a short walk from the hotel. We'll go there, but first, you've got to make yourself a little more presentable. Pick out a dress in my closet and I'll lay out some clean under clothes for you to put on. Lucky for you that we're almost the same size. Tell me about the crash, Mother. It must have been horrible."

Bright Cloud took her in her arms and held her tightly. "It's a miracle I'm here to be with you, Star. A young sailor, not much older than DJ, saved me after the crash by throwing me outside when I was unconscious. He was terribly injured internally. Later, in the raft, I set his broken leg and then had to watch him die in my arms. It was frightening." Bright Cloud sat in one of the chairs at the kitchen table. Star thought she looked worn out and exhausted.

"You're still in shock, Mother. Maybe we should wait until tomorrow to visit, Dad," suggested Bright Star, concerned with her mother's delayed reaction to the tragedy she had recently survived.

"No. I've come this far. I won't be put off a minute longer than is absolutely necessary. It's strange, but I haven't been affected much by the crash until I arrived here. I realize how lucky I was."

195

"Trauma and shock can come at different times after an incident, Mother, you know that. It's a natural part of coping. Your nerves and strong constitution have been keeping you going these past few days. Now that the need for a strong guard is gone or relaxed, the magnitude of what happened and what might have taken place comes to the surface. I'm going to heat some water for a cup of tea while you take a shower and get dressed. Let me take care of you for a change."

"You look wonderful in your uniform, Star. It's so good being here with you and knowing that your father is nearby." Star gently guided her into the bedroom and helped her pick out a dress for the afternoon.

"The yellow dress will look nice on you, Mother. Take your time in the shower. It'll do you good."

"Tell me about your father, Star."

"He's changed since you last saw him, Mother. I don't mean just the physical wounds. The war seems to test their faith as nothing else has done. In some cases it has destroyed their dreams and impressions of a world they never knew existed until the fighting started. The most cruel thing to watch is the men's loss of innocence and trust. The war shattered some of them completely. They aren't young boys anymore. They went from adolescence to manhood in their first battle."

"Will he recognize me?" asked Bright Cloud hesitantly.

"I didn't mean to alarm you, Mother. Of course he'll recognize you. You're the main reason he's still alive. He's older than you remember him though. I have to go on duty for a six-thirty night shift, so take your shower and there will be time for me to show you around. It's nice to have you safe with us, Mother. What would we ever do without you?" Star put her arms around Bright Cloud and gently walked her to the bathtub.

Later, Bright Cloud and Bright Star walked from the hotel to the hospital. Star felt a reluctance in her mother's attitude that troubled her. Her fears were confirmed when they approached the gateway for the hospital.

"What if my response to his condition makes him feel worse?" agonized Bright Cloud, stopping near the gate. "He's a proud man, and he'll know if I'm offended by his condition. I don't want him to

196

regret that I came to Pearl Harbor. I couldn't bear that to happen." She was close to tears. Her emotions were splintered. She desperately wanted to see Mark and be at his side, but there was a reluctance to not want to face her loved one in his changed condition.

"You're getting the jitters for nothing, Mother. Come, listen to your heart instead of your doubts, and you'll be fine. This should be a day of celebration, not a time of dread. The most important thing I can tell you is that he really needs you now, more than at any other time in his life. Forget anything else that's running through that pretty head of yours," scolded Star.

Bright Cloud smiled at her. "You're growing up, young lady. I like your spirit, but you've got to be careful talking to your mother in that tone of voice."

"I will, if she'll control her silly thoughts! Come, we're going to the sixth floor, Mother. You look lovely." Star put her arm around her mother's waist and directed her into the lobby towards the elevators.

The sixth floor nursing station was manned by Jennifer Barkley. When the elevator door opened, she unconsciously checked to see who was getting off. She was surprised to see Star with an older lady who looked a lot like her.

"Hello, Dawn," said Jennifer with her usual outgoing manner.

"Lieutenant Barkley, this is my mother, Mrs. Danielle Leroux. Mom, this is the nurse that's cared for Dad ever since he came to the hospital."

"It's my pleasure to meet you, Mrs. Leroux," greeted Jennifer warmly.

"It's wonderful being here. It's been a long time since my husband and I have seen each other," said Bright Cloud, nervously shaking hands with Jennifer.

"Come, your husband is just finishing his supper. You're everything he said you were, Mrs. Leroux."

"Thank you. Sometimes he gets carried away with things," she smiled.

Bright Star and Jennifer Barkley both stepped aside and guided her to the threshold leading into Mark's room. Mark was sitting up in his bed holding a newspaper with his right hand. The empty dinner tray sat on the shelf beside his bed. His hair was more white than she remembered. Lines that had never been present before, etched his face. The white hospital jumper over his shoulder was slightly askew, because it could not be worn normally with the left arm in a cast. Her first thought to herself was that Bright Star was correct. He had aged, and it tore at her heart. He had not seen her yet.

She slowly stepped into the room, then, as fast as she could, ran towards his bed, her heart racing... She didn't say anything at first. She just wanted to take him in her arms and tell him how much she loved him. Her movement caught Mark's eye. He expected the nurse, instead he saw Bright Cloud, as if in a dream, coming towards him with outstretched arms. Was it a trick of his imagination? He knew she was real when he heard that melodious voice of hers speaking to him.

"My darling, Mark, I'll never let you leave me again!"

Chapter Thirteen

The white hospital ship, USS Mercy, that had carried Arlo to Pearl Harbor was busy unloading its cargo of casualties at dockside. The Peleliu campaign and the Philippine assaults were straining those medical facilities located in the Pacific Ocean area to the limit. All of the hospital beds in the Hawaiian Islands were now utilized to care for the wounded men. American casualties were increasing at alarming rates by the end of 1944. An intensified fanatical resistance by the Japanese, as American forces got closer and closer to their home islands, was part of the reason for the losses. Another reason was that larger islands were being assaulted in an ever increasing effort to maintain pressure.

American forces were also experiencing, for the first time on such an alarming scale, one of the war's most drastic measures by the retreating Japanese. Kamikaze pilots, with their willingness to commit suicide using their aircraft as a bomb, added a whole new dimension to the terror of war. Once a kamikaze pilot had selected a ship or other installation as a target, he fearlessly rode his instrument of death into the unlucky objective below. The U.S. Navy's destroyers were particularly vulnerable to the new method of attack while they guarded their lonely picket outpost perimeter. Alert gunners soon realized that the only way to avoid a hit was to blow the plane out of the sky before it reached them. Naval losses were increasingly higher than the soldiers and marines on shore. Yet, the increased losses did not deter the relentless drive of the United States forces to Japan proper.

Arlo had recovered some of his strength by the time the ship reached Pearl Harbor. He faithfully walked the decks as often as he could so that he might be able to regain some of his lost stamina. He felt better now, but even he realized that it would be prudent to pace his work for a while. He was anxious to examine the planning operations underway for the largest amphibious assault of the Pacific up to that time. Before he left the Pearl Harbor area for Schofield Barracks, he wanted to check on Mark's progress at the Fleet Hospital. His aide, Lieutenant Mathews, had prepared him with a well-starched set of "tans", the appropriate light brown uniform common to all of the services while in the tropics.

After sending Lieutenant Mathews ahead to Schofield Barracks to prepare their newly assigned quarters, and to check Tenth Army Headquarters for a copy of the planning itinerary, Arlo proceeded to the hospital.

The elevator door closed with a bang on Arlo. He punched the sixth floor button. The elevator was a very rapid one that stopped suddenly at every floor level, going up or coming down. Suddenly, Arlo could feel his stomach in distress at the first stop. By the time he reached the sixth floor he was feeling nauseous. Miss Barkley recognized him as soon as he left the elevator, and saw that he was troubled about something. She went to him immediately.

"Are you all right, Sir?" she asked calmly.

"The ride up made me feel dizzy and upset my stomach. I'll be fine as soon as I sit for a minute, thank you"

"Come, take a chair and catch your breath, General. You look a little drawn. Malaria been giving you a hard time?"

"You could say that, Lieutenant Barkley," answered Arlo, relieved to sit down. As soon as he sat at the nurse's desk, an aide asked Miss Barkley for help.

"I'll be back shortly, Sir. Make yourself at home."

Arlo nodded to her, upset with himself for being so vulnerable to a simple elevator ride. While Arlo was sitting at the desk trying to look inconspicuous, he heard a voice behind his back that he would have recognized anywhere. It instantly brought him to his feet.

Bright Cloud was talking to a doctor as he walked towards the elevator door. He left her with a few parting words. "Nobody can answer your questions with any certainty, Mrs. Leroux. I'm sorry."

"Thank you, Doctor. I didn't mean to be difficult," apologized Bright Cloud.

"On the contrary, keep searching for answers. It's not impossible, and you may be correct. I just don't know right now."

"Until tomorrow, Doctor. I appreciate all you're doing for my husband." Her voice was full of uncertainty and disappointment as she watched him disappear in the elevator.

"Bright Cloud, you're a sight for an old friend to behold," said Arlo from behind the nurse's station.

"Arlo, what a nice surprise," she cried, rushing to him, embracing him warmly. "Are you feeling all right? You don't look so good."

"I'm getting over a bout of malaria," Arlo replied in a shaky voice. "It's improving everyday. It's been a long time, hasn't it?"

"It seems an eternity. I've been worried about you," Bright Cloud admitted. "How can we ever repay you for your thoughtfulness? I know that dependents are not normally allowed on the islands, so it must have been difficult for you to arrange our passage. Bright Star is working here at the hospital as a member of the Naval Nurse Corps. She's doing just great. I try to help out where I can. It has meant so much for us to be together, thank you for that. He's improving every day."

"That's good news. So Star did come with you."

"Yes, she actually came first. I followed several days later because I waited to see DJ off. He's going to Europe with his new platoon."

"I thought he would remain in school for one more year."

"They compressed the time schedule. The need for officers was urgent. I haven't heard from him yet. I'll worry until this war is over."

"I'm sure he's in good hands, Bright Cloud," said Arlo, trying to reassure her. Arlo thought to himself: if DJ is going to be a part of the destruction of Fortress Europe, he was certainly going to see some heavy combat. "I had a feeling about Bright Star, that's why I included her in your travel permits. I was uncertain about her schedule at Fort Lewis. I'm sure they'll appreciate her experience here at this busy installation."

"She looks great in her new uniform," Bright Cloud told him.

"I'm sure she does. She'll be a target for every lonely serviceman on the island. I haven't seen her since she graduated from nursing school in the Spring of 1939. Wow, that's over five years ago."

"I guess it has been that long," said Bright Cloud, smiling. "She hasn't got any steady boy friend, but many follow her with that certain look! She handles them adroitly, and I keep an eye on her..."

"I just came by to see that husband of yours. Before we go into his room, I want to share something with you, Bright Cloud. I recommended Mark for the Medal of Honor. His performance on the Williaumez Peninsula warrants the recognition. I've just received confirmation on his acceptance. It'll take a while for it to filter down through the red tape involved before Mark is officially notified, but I thought you'd like to know about it."

"That's wonderful of you, Arlo."

"What he did was truly above and beyond what any man is asked to do for his country. He earned the recognition the hard way, and I'm proud to have submitted his name for the honor."

"Thanks, dear friend." Bright Cloud watched Arlo while he spoke. She was concerned by the sadness she saw in the depths of his gray eyes. "Have you heard anything about Mike?"

"Nothing concrete, except that we're pretty sure she's alive."

Bright Cloud linked her arm in his as they walked down the hallway towards Mark's room. "I pray for her safekeeping, Arlo. I don't know how you stand it."

"Keeping busy helps some."

"I see that you have a second star," said Bright Cloud proudly. "No one deserves it any more than you do. Congratulations."

"Thanks, but I'd trade it in a heartbeat for some definite good news about Michelle."

"I'm sure you would."

Mark heard the voices in the hall before they entered his room. He was genuinely happy to see his old friend.

"Wow, two stars. A major general, at last. We can both remember when there was only one major general in the entire Marine Corps, the commandant. Congratulations General Korsman."

"Thanks, Mark. Now that your own private nurse is here, we had better see some progress on your part," grinned Arlo, winking at Bright Cloud.

"She's holding me to a strict regimen of exercises. Several times a day she massages my legs to help maintain muscle tone. I still can't feel anything...It may be too late for that."

"Hush, now!" reprimanded Bright Cloud. "No talking like that. We just don't know for sure when your feeling is going to return.

Until that time comes, we can't let your legs waste away to nothing. There is always hope that the nerves will rebuild themselves."

Hearing Bright Cloud make that statement assured Arlo that he had done the right thing by having her come to Pearl Harbor. She would not let him give up or slack off in his fight to maintain the status quo in his legs. His arm was still in a cast. Bright Cloud said it could be removed by Christmas time. The three of them reminisced for an hour or so creating an atmosphere that was comforting for all of them. The warmth and security of old friendships produced some laughs, which had its own magical formula for raising flagging spirits. Arlo laughed with Mark and Bright Cloud about the annual cribbage tally between him and the Inspector. Arlo claimed to have won with the most points for the year. The Inspector claimed that he had won based on the most number of games he had won. The room was temporarily empty, so the trio could talk freely without interrupting another patient's rest. A pharmacist mate entered the room to announce that a new patient was coming up on the elevator. He left to help push the portable stretcher through the door. Bright Star was pushing it from behind. She noticed her Uncle Arlo first. His back was turned towards the door, but she would recognize those broad shoulders anywhere. After helping the sailor transfer the patient to the bed, she turned her attention towards Arlo.

"Am I supposed to salute a general officer or what?" asked Bright Star playfully.

"Young lady," responded Arlo, turning and smiling from ear to ear. There had always been a very special rapport between the two. "As your superior officer, I order you to give your old Uncle Arlo a big hug." Star flung her arms around his neck. "Goodness gracious, my little girl has grown into a lady since I last saw her. You're lovelier than ever, Star."

"It's wonderful seeing you, Uncle Arlo. It's been a long time, hasn't it?" exclaimed Star. "How do you like my ensign bars?"

"They look great on you. I'm proud of you, but then, I always have been. Imagine, a family reunion in the middle of the Pacific Ocean, with a war going on. Miracles do happen, don't they?"

"Thanks to your efforts," echoed Star and Bright Cloud in unison.

"I've never used my rank to ask for anything special for myself, but I figured that Mark's injuries were worthy of some consideration out of the ordinary. I'm glad it all worked out smoothly."

"Uncle, what have you heard from the Philippines?" asked Star, noticing the fatigue in his eyes.

"Not much, Star. I've been at sea for two weeks and haven't heard what's happening."

"I've been reading the papers and listening to the radio everyday," said Mark. "MacArthur's return to the Philippines is well under way. He's landed on Leyte Island. After cleaning up a few of the smaller outpost islands, I expect that he'll hit Luzon next. The Japanese could do the same thing as MacArthur and Wainright had done on Bataan Peninsula. It could be a slugfest all the way."

"I think you're right, Mark," answered Arlo, noticeably uncomfortable talking about the conflict raging in the same area where Michelle could be harmed.

"You may be interested to know that we have an Army Air Corps fighter pilot in the hospital who was transferred from Schofield Barracks," added Star. "He was severely burned and needed extensive treatment. His plane crashed on a mission to the Philippines. He talks a lot about the effectiveness of the guerrilla organization that exists on many of the islands. It made me think a lot about Aunt Michelle.

"When I questioned him further about his experience, he seemed reluctant to give any specific information about them. He did say that when we finally invaded the Philippines, there would be a wide-spread outbreak against the Japanese from Filipino and American soldiers who elected to fight on in the mountains and jungle instead of becoming prisoners of war for the duration."

"That confirms what I've been told," said Arlo, wishing that he could ask Star more about the airman, but his promise to Hank and Jim made him hold his tongue. He was confident that it had to be the same pilot.

Arlo visited with Mark and Bright Cloud a while longer. He was reluctant to leave for the twenty mile trip into the higher elevations of central Oahu, where new and challenging responsibilities awaited him. Star was still on duty at the hospital until the early hours of the morning, and had promised to stop by again before they left, but the requirements of her duties made it impossible for her to get to the sixth floor before Bright Cloud and Arlo left for the evening. Arlo insisted upon escorting Bright Cloud back to her hotel after saying good-bye to Mark. She was still appalled at how fragile he had become. He looked so small in the large white hospital bed.

"Once I caught him looking out the window at the mountain range in the distance. He said to me, 'they remind me of the way a blue haze always seemed to envelope the White Mountains in New Hampshire when you viewed them from a distance. What I wouldn't give to be able to climb among those rugged peaks one more time'. It almost broke my heart," admitted Bright Cloud.

"What are his chances of walking again, Bright Cloud?"

"I keep pressing for answers from the doctors, God bless them, but they don't have enough experience to be able to predict how or when things will happen. Right now, he doesn't have any response to stimuli in either leg. That's not good, but we're not giving up. He needs more time for the doctors to be certain. In the meantime, we think positively and assume that it will return. When it does, we'll be ready for it by having his muscular system as strong as we can make it under the circumstances. His other wounds are healing satisfactorily. He did lose a spleen, but we can live without one. His lungs are improving slowly day by day. I'm not complaining, Arlo, I'm thankful that he's still alive, and that I can be here to help him when he needs it. I try not to be a bother for the hospital staff. They've been wonderful so far. They understand my concern. Whenever I can, I try to do things for them to save steps and time."

"I could never imagine you being a nuisance, lady. I feel better now that I've had a chance to reminisce and talk about old times together. It was a treat to see Star again. As she gets older, she looks more and more like you. I've always envied you and Mark with your rich family life together. I regret that Michelle and I could never have any children of our own. We certainly tried. Maybe she would not be where she is today if things had turned out differently that way."

"Thoughts such as that are not very meaningful, Arlo," Bright Cloud admonished him.

"I know, it's easy to get down in the dumps about it. I have to admit that I've found a lot of help and comfort from prayer since the war started. I was never that much of a church-going person before the war, but I'm sure it's what has sustained me for three long years. The war has at least done that for me."

"Here we are at the hotel. Would you like to come in for a while?"

"I'll take a rain check, Bright Cloud. I'm anxious to see what's waiting for me at Schofield Barracks. It's been swell seeing you and Star again. Keep me in your prayers."

"You're always there. Thanks for everything, dear friend. Goodnight. God be with you." She gave him a hug and a kiss on the cheek.

"Goodnight, Bright Cloud. I'll be in touch."

Back at the hospital, Bright Star was nearing the end of her watch. She liked the quiet atmosphere of the rooms after the patients had settled down for the night. She knew that a lot of the men were frightened and had difficulty with their own world of private thoughts after "lights out". She could feel the raw emotions of the men and worked tirelessly to help them cope with their limitations. It was different from the small infirmary at Fort Lewis, which seemed so far away from the world she now worked in. There was a family-like atmosphere at the infirmary where most of the patients knew each other, and she knew them. It was possible to relate to their backgrounds and problems, for they all shared similar hardships. The Fleet Hospital was filled with men from every possible ethnic and cultural background. The various personality traits were as diverse as the men's regional home-fronts.

The most common experience was that of being wounded in combat, with illness from tropical diseases being more numerous than she would have expected. The wounded made up at least eighty-five percent of the patients. Several wounded men were also suffering from disease, mostly malaria and dysentery. Bright Star was still finding it difficult to maintain a professional indifference to the suffering around her. Some patients reached out to her more than others, and she knew that there was a danger in becoming too emotionally involved with the men's travails. She could not ignore their pleas for compassion and sympathy like some of the nurses. She was like Bright Cloud in that respect. When she felt someone reaching out to her for help and understanding, she could not turn away from them, regardless of the emotional cost. Some of the wounded were horribly disfigured. She admired the quiet courage that many of the men showed accepting such devastating injuries.

One patient that had made an impression on Bright Star was an Army Air Corps pilot, recently transferred from Schofield Barracks Hospital to the Pacific Fleet Hospital. The Naval facility was much better equipped to handle his life threatening burn injuries. The records that accompanied him listed his name as First Lieutenant Steven Jackson, USAAC, Utica, New York. He had been blinded by the fire that consumed his plane after it was hit by enemy gunfire over the Philippines. He rode the crippled plane down to the water and was thrown out of the cockpit when it exploded on impact.

His story was one of heroism and luck. Bright Star heard it from one of the Army officers who delivered him to the Navy facility. Lieutenant Jackson was piloting his twin engine P-38 fighter plane on a bombing and strafing run over Leyte when he was hit by anti-aircraft shells. One engine was knocked out of commission, and his right leg had been ripped open, bleeding profusely. He continued to make another run against his assigned targets on a single engine, turning evasively to avoid the same anti-aircraft batteries. After the final strafing run, he headed for the nearest coast realizing that he could not remain airborne for long.

He was hit by more gunfire and managed to bring his destroyed plane down to the water a mere one hundred yards off shore. His luck started when he was thrown out of the plane in the vicinity of a guerrilla patrol preparing to go fishing. They rescued him and carried him to their hidden outpost in the mountains, where they maintained a small first aid center run by three nurses. Most of the men in the group were Filipino, but the bulk of the officers were American soldiers who had refused to surrender.

One of the nurses had supervised the setting of both of his broken legs, as well as treated his extensive burns. The fire in the cockpit had badly burned Lieutenant Jackson's upper body, and left him blind. The leader of the guerrilla battalion was an American soldier who decided to risk using the radio transmitter to contact MacArthur's headquarters, requesting a submarine to pick up the wounded airman. It was believed by all involved that he would not survive long in the primitive surroundings of the stronghold. One dark evening he was safely carried down to the shore and placed on the waiting submarine without the knowledge of the Japanese.

Lieutenant Jackson was undergoing an intensive series of treatments for burns on his face, neck, and shoulder. Some of the burned areas had become infected, and were extremely painful. There was nothing that could take the pain away from him, and even with the use of pain killing drugs such as morphine, the pain was still making him uncomfortable. In his own private world, the pain was bad enough, but the possible loss of sight was his greatest fear. His head and eyes were bandaged while skin grafting was successfully taking place around his eyes. Darkness, and the terrorizing prospect that the condition might become permanent was enough to make most anyone anxious and irritable. Lieutenant Jackson fought his battles with courage, but his patience with many things around him was in short supply. He had a reputation of being a difficult patient who strongly resented the restrictions his injuries imposed upon him. Several nurses asked to be removed from the floor so that they would not have to deal with him.

Bright Star was assigned to his ward her first week on the nursing staff. Their initial encounter was one that Bright Star did not want to repeat. She was making her rounds in the middle of the night with the medication tray. When she approached Lieutenant Jackson's bedside, she did what was by now, standard operating procedure when confronting a new patient. She calmly and clearly announced herself as his duty nurse for the evening and was there to give him his medication as prescribed by the doctors.

She no sooner announced herself to him, when he suddenly turned from his side and started flailing his arms about. He ended up hitting her a heavy blow in the chest. The blow was unintentional on his part, but it knocked Bright Star down, spilling the pills and other medications from the tray in her hand. She cried out in pain.

A wounded marine beside him spoke up. "Watch it doggie, try that again, and you'll get a taste of your own medicine. Are you all right, nurse?"

"Yes, I didn't expect it," explained Bright Star, embarrassed that she was the center of such a disturbance in the middle of the night.

"I'm sorry, nurse. I didn't mean to hit you, really I didn't," said Lieutenant Jackson, frightened at what he had done.

"You did hurt me, but you also hurt my pride, which bothers me more, Lieutenant Jackson. Let me give you a word of advice. Control those hands of yours or we'll control them for you. Now, let's start from the beginning. I'm Ensign Leroux, I'm your nurse for the night shift, and I'm here to administer your evening dosage of medicine; however, I'll have to return to the nurse's station for a resupply. I'll be right back. Next time, I'll stay out of reach when I announce myself."

"You have every right to be angry. I'm sorry, I apologize for my actions."

"If you're really sorry, use some of that resolve to never let it happen again, soldier. You hurt me, and I'm pretty tough."

"That's telling him, lady," clapped the marine neighbor.

The balance of her rounds were carried out in silence with a minimum of fuss. When she felt that she could leave the ward for a few minutes, Bright Star entered the nurse's private washroom on the floor to check herself. Lieutenant Jackson had hit her a glancing blow that started on the left shoulder and ran down across her breast. The area was already turning black and blue. She covered herself and wearily finished the rest of her shift.

The next day, Lieutenant Jackson apologized to his marine roommate and asked about the nurse he had accidentally hit the night before. Everyone in the ward had an eye for her; some thought that they were actually in love with her. When Bright Star made her evening rounds again the next night, she was on guard and warily announced her presence. Part of the medication for the evening was an injection of morphine for his pain.

"I'm going to give you a shot of pain killer to help you sleep, Lieutenant. Which arm do you want me to give it to you?" she asked softly, yet firmly.

"It doesn't matter. You can hurt me all you want, Ensign Leroux. I deserve anything after last night."

"I'm not a monster out for revenge, Lieutenant. I know that your reflex last night wasn't intentional, and I forgive you. I can even understand how you must feel sometimes. I've had a lot of experience working in the northern forests of Canada where I've seen a lot of injured men full of impatience, and even rage. However, you're the first one to ever reach out to strike me."

209

"I must have been crazy, I can't explain my actions, but I'm glad that you forgive me. I'm ashamed of myself. Sometimes..."

"I do understand, Lieutenant," interrupted Bright Star, wiping his beaded forehead. "I'll give you your shot tonight in the other arm. It should help you some."

"It does for a while, thank you." Lieutenant Jackson turned his head towards her. Even though there was a large bandage which covered part of his face, Bright Star recognized a look of supplication. "Ensign Leroux, may I ask a very personal favor of you?"

"Yes..."

"Today, I received a letter from home and I can't read it. I didn't want to bother the day nurses, so I saved it for you tonight. Would you please read it to me?"

"Yes. I'd be happy to do that for you, Lieutenant. First, let me complete my rounds of medicine distribution, then I'll be right back."

"Thanks," he answered, settling back into his pillows. He tried to visualize what she looked like. She had an angelic voice with the clipped words and enunciation of people from northern New England. His marine friend next door told him that she had a dark complexion, with black hair and medium height. He was uncertain about her nationality, thinking that it might be Spanish or Italian. She certainly had a nice touch with all of the men in the ward. Her concern and empathy for her charges was genuine and they appreciated her warm professionalism.

Star returned. "Well, I'm back and free for a while, Lieutenant. Why don't I pull the curtain around the bed so that we can be a little more private, and the rest of the ward can sleep easier."

"Thanks, Ensign. My letter is on the bed stand there somewhere. It's the first one I've had since I left on my last mission."

"The letter is dated November 1, 1944, from Utica, New York," read Bright Star clearly and slowly. "Dear Steve, You'll be surprised to hear from me after my last letter. When I wrote those awful words to you I hated myself afterwards. All I really wanted to say was that waiting for you and your return seemed more than I could bear. Jimmy Duggan is here everyday, and he has made me feel more secure with him than waiting for you to come home. You and I never got engaged; it was just a kind of casual thing. I'm sorry. What I've done makes me feel cheap and I beg your forgiveness. Jimmy and I were married last week!!

My feelings for you were always less than you hoped for, Steve. Our casual understanding was not that strong. Jimmy has been super to me and I'd like to hope that we have your blessing on our marriage.

I wish you all the best, Steve. Keep yourself safe. Yours, Marilyn {Forbes} Duggan."

"That's all there is, Lieutenant Jackson," said Bright Star. Her hands shook trying to fold the letter and place it in the envelope. "I'm sorry to bring bad news to you."

"I should have seen it coming. I half expected it sooner than this, but it still hurts..."

"In time, Lieutenant, you'll be able to look back on this incident and realize that it was for the best. That doesn't help much now though, does it?"

"Not really...," Lieutenant Jackson faced her and carefully reached out towards her. "May I feel your face, Ensign? I can't see you and I have a mental picture of what you might look like. I'd like to see if I'm correct."

"I don't object," answered Bright Star, surprised by the request. She took his two hands into her own and placed them on her cheeks.

His fingers were gentle and thorough as they searched every bit of her face. They lingered around the eyes, and traced her lips slowly. She felt a chill run down her spine.

"I was wrong, Ensign Leroux. I was sure that you would be attractive, but you're absolutely beautiful. You have wonderful bones and a sensual mouth. Forgive me if I sound too familiar. I don't mean to be. I studied sculpture as a minor in school. I can sometimes feel beauty better than I can see it with my eyes."

"You flatter me."

"Not at all, don't be angry with me. I'm just being truthful."

"And what did you major in at college, Lieutenant?"

"Education. I'm a high school teacher."

"That sounds like a rewarding profession. You'd better settle down for the night so that the medication can help you, Lieutenant. We don't want to keep anyone else up with our voices."

"Yes, thanks for tonight. I do regret last night."

"It's forgotten, Lieutenant," Bright Star took his outstretched hand in hers and placed it on his bed. "Goodnight, rest well."

"Goodnight, nurse."

Star could not get the intimate encounter out of her mind that evening. When she returned to her room her body was tired, but her imagination was working overtime trying to make sense out of what took place with Lieutenant Jackson. She had, throughout her career, been conscious and alert to the possibility of being involved with a patient under her care. She was scrupulous in keeping her professional life separate from her private affairs. Star knew that she was foolish to entertain any thoughts about a patient she had just met, but she was, also, honest enough with herself to know that those few minutes with Lieutenant Jackson awakened an interest that was unsettling and unfamiliar to her.

Bright Star didn't know the man well enough to be able to make a judgment about him. She did not want to contribute to a complicated situation, so she made up her mind to ask for a separate floor the next day.

When she reported to work the next day, several of the nurses already assigned to their own floors were busy at their stations. They had their own individual way of dealing with the various patients on their floor. Indeed, her supervisor told her, the main reason for maintaining assigned floors, as they were now allotted, was that the wounded men found comfort in routinely seeing familiar faces attending to them. Not that fraternization was encouraged or tolerated, but it helped establish a pattern of daily routines which helped the patients make the necessary adjustment to the aftereffects of their wounds. Bright Star did not press the issue any further.

She normally worked from eight in the evening to five in the morning. By the time she got to the hospital, her patients were beginning to settle down for the evening. Dinner had already been served and cleaned up, and the visitors were asked to leave by eight. Many of the men continued to read, listen to the radio, or wrote letters home, if they were able to do so. Bright Star had four wards of about ten men each on her floor. Each ward had a nurse's aide, and the four wards shared the services of two apprentice nurses or students from a local nursing school. She was comfortable with the responsibilities of her job. At the infirmary at Fort Lewis she would have had to do the jobs of the nurse's aide and the student associates, plus dispense the medicine and wash the dishes. In Canada, she was legally authorized to prescribe certain medicines to her patients. Under the rules and regulations in the United States, she was much more restricted, but she could dispense any medication if it was prescribed by a doctor. She was efficient, knowledgeable, and considered an excellent team player. She was a favorite of her supervisor and the nursing staff.

One evening, Bright Star assembled her prescribed medications, signed for them at the pharmacy, and cheerfully went about her daily ritual with the patients. Sometimes there was a new face and sometimes a familiar face was missing, usually from release or transfer to another facility, but more often than most of the staff liked to think about, death visited their wards and took the more grievously wounded men. Lieutenant Jackson was lying on his back with an impatient look on that portion of his face that extended below the heavy bandages.

"Good evening, Lieutenant," announced Bright Star. "Tonight it's another morphine injection. Do you want it in your left arm?"

"Ensign Leroux, I knew that you'd be coming. I heard your voice when you entered the ward. It doesn't matter to me which arm is used. Take whichever one is more convenient for you. I'm more concerned with the possibility of becoming hooked on the stuff. I don't need that kind of problem in my life. What do you think?"

"It all depends on your tolerance to pain, Lieutenant. If morphine is used for too long a period of time, it can become addictive. The period varies for each individual. It's one of the most effective pain killers we have, but it does have to be balanced with the strong dependency, or addiction, that some people develop with its usage. I could give you only half of the prescribed amount if you can handle only half of the relief from pain. I could also give you two aspirin every three to four hours to supplement the lowered morphine dosage. It's up to you."

"Why don't we use the half prescription tonight and see what happens?"

"That sounds logical to me," answered Bright Star, checking her instruction board. "I've also got to change your bandages and flush

213

your eyes tonight, Lieutenant, so it'll give us a chance to see how your burns are doing. I'll give you the fifty percent morphine shot now, and be back shortly to change the dressings. Your chart also calls for a heavier concentration of penicillin antibiotic to help control your infections. Be patient and I'll be right back to finish you for the evening."

"The burns will probably leave me ugly to look at," commented Lieutenant Jackson despairingly.

"Not necessarily, soldier. Try not to worry about tomorrow until it arrives."

Ten minutes later, Bright Star returned to his bedside with a tray full of supplies. She raised the head of his bed slightly, so that she could easily reach him. He didn't say anything while she cut the soiled bandages away and carefully rolled them back to expose the burned portion of his face and eyes. It was still draining and the danger of infection was very high. Once she removed the large bandage over the head, there were two small round pieces of gauze covering the eyes.

"You tell me when you're uncomfortable, Lieutenant Jackson. I'll take my time to do it slowly so that none of the bandages stick and hurt you. I think it's looking better tonight. Now that it's exposed to the air, I'm going to sprinkle some sulfa powder on the burned area. That will keep out infection while I clean and flush your eyes with boric acid solution."

"Do what you have to do," he shrugged, resigned to his vulnerable condition.

Lieutenant Jackson's eye lashes and brows had been burned away. She told him that they had already started to grow back, and that was a good sign. His blue eyes looked straight at her while she carefully bathed the eyes with the boric acid solution.

"I can't see you..." he said with desperation in his voice.

"The doctors said that's normal for this stage of your recovery. Try to relax and let the solution clean the infectious material out of your eyes."

Her gentle touch was soothing and reassuring. She was pleased to feel his tenseness dissolve while she worked on him. The doctors were unsure whether he would ever regain his full sight, but they were optimistic that partial vision could be restored in time. His legs were healing, thanks to the quick thinking and competence of the nurse with the guerrilla freedom fighters.

"Have you heard from your parents?" inquired Bright Star.

"Both of my parents have passed away. The couple who raised me were old enough to have been my grandparents. They were fantastic people and I loved them very much. I've checked into my background quite a lot and as far as I can tell, I was adopted by a young couple who were killed in a car accident when I was very small. Afterwards, the Jackson's took me into their home. They were wonderful people and I can only hope to be their equal ...Ugh..."

"I'm sorry."

"That area around my forehead seems to be the most painful part of the burn. It must have been where my goggles caught on fire."

"I'll try to be easier, Lieutenant. Tell me if it hurts you again. I've got to remove as much dead tissue as I can, so that the healing process can be complete."

"Would you consider me presumptuous to ask about your family? Or is that a violation of the nurse/patient relationship?"

"Since I asked about you, it's only fair for you to do the same thing to me," answered Star. "You may not believe this, but my father is in this hospital. He's a colonel in the Marine Corps, and was severely wounded on New Britain Island. A friend of the family arranged for us to come to Pearl and visit with him. I came first and joined the Naval Nurse Corps. My mother followed shortly afterwards. He's on the sixth floor directly below us."

"That's different."

"He's from Maine and my mother is from Canada. She's a full-blooded Cree Indian, the same as myself." Bright Star made a point of mentioning her ethnicity to the Lieutenant. His reaction was important to her.

"Is your father a Native American, also?"

"No, I was adopted. My maternal mother died giving me birth. My mother who raised me is actually my aunt. My paternal father was also a full blooded Cree and was killed in France during the First World War..."

"It's strange, but I often thought that I was alone and unique in the world. Now you tell me that you, also, were raised by people who were not your true parents. Last night I had a feeling that your facial bones reflected some native strains. You must be very proud."

"Yes, I am, although I don't consider myself any different from anybody else."

"And you shouldn't, Ensign. Only small narrow-minded people see a distinction through skin tone and culture. If we look back in our own past at many of the people we admire in our lives, it was because of what was in their hearts and minds that made them memorable. I knew, the first time I heard you talking, that there was something special about you."

"Thank you, Lieutenant, but you're making too much out of nothing. You think too much," she said teasingly.

"I have nothing to do except to think!"

Later that day, which was Bright Star's night, she woke from a sound sleep and started thinking about her parents, Lieutenant Jackson, and a number of different incidents of her past life. Suddenly, she bolted out of bed, wide-wide-eyed and exclaimed to herself,

"No, it can't be...not him..."

Chapter Fourteen

Deep in the lush jungle-covered mountains of central Leyte Island, a part of the Philippine Islands chain, an American radio transmitter was rushing to complete his transmissions before it was detected by the radio beam sensors of the Japanese Army. Anytime the radios went on the airwaves to send or receive messages, there was a real danger of being strafed and bombed by enemy planes shortly thereafter. Consequently, it was standard operating procedure to use the instrument only in times of great need, such as sending General MacArthur's headquarters important information they had requested from the guerrilla forces in the field.

Today, October 18, 1944, something extraordinary was underway and deemed worthy of the risk of retaliation against the radio station. As soon as the operator shut the radio down, several strong hands seized it and broke it down into smaller components so that they could carry it into the jungle away from harms way. Time was of the essence. The Japanese were very efficient in locating clandestine radio signal equipment. The message received was the one that everybody had been patiently waiting for. General MacArthur was about to return to the Philippines with a force large enough to evict the Japanese occupation troops. The yoke of tyranny that had been imposed upon the Islands for the past three years was about to be lifted and broken.

It was difficult for some of the Filipinos to realize the magnitude of what was taking place. The radio transmitter was relocated at the compound of a large group of Filipino and American soldiers who had refused to surrender when the Japanese overran Bataan Peninsula in 1942. Most of the members of the group were country boys who had a tendency to adapt to the countryside better than their city-born compatriots. They had wandered around the islands for months just trying to avoid capture. Major John Carlisle, a 1937 graduate of West Point, was the leader of the guerrilla group. A tall, lanky man with a serious demeanor, he had successfully evaded the Japanese and had collected a group of several hundred men who wanted to hit back at the Japanese any way they could. They were able to contact MacArthur's headquarters in Australia, where weapons and supplies were soon provided by air drop or submarine delivery on some uninhabited shore.

The group of guerrillas could not have survived without the help of the local native Filipino population, who hid them, guided them, and fed them with the full knowledge that to be caught doing so meant instant death. Not long after MacArthur's arrival in Australia, during the dark hours at the beginning of the war, he established a staff to guide clandestine operations in the Philippines. Soon a vast network of operators were in place gathering valuable intelligence and harassing the Japanese whenever possible. Each group of guerrillas was established as a company or battalion within a larger organization controlled by a central staff in Australia. Now, the time had come to strike with coordinating movements which could properly utilize the mobile capacity of the freedom fighters in the jungle.

Major Carlisle's men were ordered to act as a regular regiment of the U.S. Army's 92nd Division. Their mission was to attack and capture a large dam complex which supplied water for several towns in northern Leyte. Once captured, they were ordered to defend it regardless of the cost. If the Japanese should blow the dam, it would jeopardize operations further south. The assaulting elements of the 92nd Division planned to send a column to their relief as soon as a beachhead was established.

An important component of the guerrilla movement was the inclusion of doctors and nurses in various numbers who joined their ranks to care for the freedom fighters. They labored tirelessly, under appalling conditions to combat the plethora of diseases found in the humid tropical jungles. The lush jungle's decaying vegetation smelled so strong that it made many individuals sick to the point of vomiting. Malaria, dysentery, and other infections which defied description, were an inherent part of the environment. Torrential rains and high winds contributed to the physical discomfort of the central mountain range. Death was a constant companion in the steaming jungles.

Michelle Korsman had been an important member of the Carlisle guerrilla band for two years. She did her best to use modern medicines to heal the sick or injured. She had adamantly refused to give out her name to anyone, regardless of the circumstances, and became somewhat of a mystery woman in the group. Most members assumed that she must have been a wife to a high ranking figure; otherwise, her cover-up would not be worth the effort. Her dedicated service as a nurse was desperately needed and appreciated.

She was trapped on the Island of Luzon when the war first started and accompanied a large number of women from other countries that had been evacuated by small boat from the Manila Hotel to the more southern islands. They landed on Leyte at about the same time as the Japanese invasion started. It was impossible to even think about getting passage out of the islands at that time.

Michelle made a conscious decision. She was not going to allow herself to be taken prisoner by the Japanese. She was able to avoid detection by the enemy through the courageous efforts of many generous native Filipino families who provided her with food and shelter for the first several months of the savage Japanese occupation of the islands. In the outskirts of the town of Tacloban, Michelle was fortunate enough to make the acquaintance of a young ten-year-old girl who called herself Maria. They were hiding in a small root cellar while roaming Japanese patrols diligently tried to locate any stragglers from the Filipino or American forces. Maria had lost all of her family in an artillery explosion and suffered some hearing loss from the incident. She was able to escape to the countryside where she eventually ran into Michelle, who was doing the same thing.

In time, they heard about a group of guerrilla resistance fighters under the command of Major Carlisle, and made plans to join the partisan group. Their safety was relatively secure in the presence of the soldiers, and Major Carlisle guaranteed them that he would personally control the conduct of his men so that they could live and work in peace and safety. Michelle quickly proved herself to be a valuable member of the group. She nursed the members when they were sick and displayed her normal resourcefulness when they were wounded. She asked nothing for herself except to be left alone, and Major Carlisle kept his word by sheltering her from any of the excesses of his men.

A few of the native nurses took up with some of the men, and their lives were frequently made easier as a result of the liaison arrangement. Behavior of that kind was repugnant to Michelle who played a lonely waiting odyssey in the middle of the jungle until MacArthur made good on his promise to return. If she felt pressure from any source, all she had to do was mention it to Major Carlisle, and it was taken care of immediately. Michelle admired him for his courage and appreciated his allegiance to the code of honor he dedicated his life to on the plains of West Point — Duty, Honor, Country. She wrapped herself in that shield of armor without worry of harm.

Maria had proved to be most resourceful and diligent in gathering foods from the jungle, and she guarded the rations that the soldiers provided with tenacity. They would have gone hungry more often if it had not been for Marie's efforts.

Now that the invasion was imminent, the group under Major Carlisle would be leaving the outpost to merge with three other battalions in different sections of the mountains for the assault on the dam. That would leave the nurses and the few sick men alone and vulnerable. The Major was of the opinion that help may be coming from the invading forces, but they should not plan on it. The greatest danger was that the Japanese might find the outpost when it was undefended. Those left behind all agreed that if they were attacked, the wounded and sick would have to take their chances with the enemy. The rest would all scatter and head for the eastern coast toward Tacloban. Michelle and Maria collected everything that was valuable, filling a single small sack in case they had to leave on a short notice.

The contingency plan to disband in the event of an attack was, thankfully, not needed. On the second morning after the departure of Major Carlisle and the fighting men, a small group of soldiers clad in khaki uniforms and heavily armed, appeared in the middle of the compound.

"I'm Lieutenant Harvey of the U.S. Army," shouted the leader of the soldiers. "We come in peace to help you. We do not wish you any harm, but we will vigorously defend ourselves if threatened. Does anyone speak English here?"

"Yes, Lieutenant," answered Michelle, walking towards him. "I'm an American. Thank God you're here. We've had a long wait."

"Lady," answered Lieutenant Harvey. "I'm not surprised to find you here. My platoon is part of a larger battalion of Rangers who was briefed on the presence of your compound. We're here to give you safe passage back to our lines where you'll eventually be routed home. I'm glad that we found you so easily."

"I can't leave without Maria."

"Who's Maria?"

"A young girl who has befriended and risked her life for me, time after time these past two years, Lieutenant."

"That's all right with me, lady. Collect your stuff and everyone else left behind by Major Carlisle and the men at the dam."

"You know about the dam raid?" asked Michelle.

"Yes, we helped plan the operation. I don't mean to rush you people, but these hills are crawling with Jap troops that have been forced inland from the coast. My platoon is miles from friendly lines. Sitting here like this is getting more dangerous by the minute," cried Lieutenant Harvey.

"I'll get the others," volunteered Michelle. "Two more nurses, Maria, and two patients, Lieutenant. One can walk well enough if we don't travel too fast, and one will have to be carried."

"Yes, lady, but hurry. We're very vulnerable at this place," answered Lieutenant Harvey, nervously scouting the surrounding terrain. He gave orders for two sturdy Rangers to carry the wounded man on the litter. "Just bring your most valuable stuff, ladies. We're traveling fast and light on the return trip."

"I've traveled light for two years," said Michelle, grasping the sack holding the precious possessions of her and Maria.

The most important portion of her personal belongings was her private wallet, photos, and identification papers. They'd been the only link she had with Arlo and a life she lived long ago and far away. Leaving the bamboo shelter left her with a feeling of apprehension about the future. She had prayed daily for this moment to arrive. The jungle and its people had been a sanctuary from certain death for any Americans if they had the misfortune to be caught. The faithful Filipino people had earned her respect and affection. They had sheltered her from harm, a total stranger in their midst, solely because she represented the country that would someday return to free them from the cruel Japanese occupation. The Filipinos looked with a God-like adoration towards General MacArthur's claim of "returning".

Michelle was in no frame of mind to think about what was taking place in the Philippines. It came too suddenly. Later, when all of the excitement settled down, she would be able to look back at this day of liberation with pride in her country. MacArthur and the American people were keeping their promise. The days of Japanese occupation of the Philippine Islands were numbered.

Michelle and Maria walked near the front of the column as they cautiously threaded their way around enemy patrols and treacherous mountain terrain. Maria was walking next to Lieutenant Harvey and advising him on the best route away from the sanctuary to the sea coast. There was a feeling in Michelle's heart that she was abandoning the simple hill people of the mountains. They had accepted her as if she was one of their own. She would always remember them for their courage and inherent goodness. They reminded her of the Crees whom she served for years in northern Canada. Human kindness and unselfishness transcends all races and cultures.

Maria was content with the prospect of finding a new life with Michelle. Her dark features beamed in satisfaction as she boldly pointed out the preferred route for the column to take. She prided herself in her ability to read and write English better than many Americans her own age. She and Michelle had spent countless hours studying the English language while hiding from the Japanese in hideouts scattered all over the mountains. Michelle, always one to be doing something useful, decided to teach Maria English. The past twenty months found them both working relentlessly on writing and reading courses. Michelle reserved the evenings to work on speaking proper English. Her pupil's passion for learning was a source of satisfaction.

Maria had learned something else, too. Since they could not always talk in normal tones when they were in hiding, Michelle taught her to read lips while she spoke in a whisper. Maria's partial hearing loss from the artillery barrage which wiped out her family, was permanent. Michelle wanted to have her checked by a competent doctor as soon as they arrived at a safe haven. Maria was an important part of her life now. She could never abandon Maria, but a worrisome apprehension was always on her mind. Would Arlo accept her? She didn't think it would be a problem, but the uncertainty of his position, and their absence for these long years, was a worry that she was anxious to have resolved.

Lieutenant Harvey consulted his maps as soon as they left the steep slopes of the mountains behind. Gunfire could be heard in the distance. The air at the lower level of elevation was saturated with moisture and the heat was oppressive. All of the people in the column were wet from perspiration. Darkness was beginning to settle into the lowlands. Lieutenant Harvey decided to press on as rapidly as possible, so that he would not have to spend a night in the bush with his new charges.

Several hours later, with a full moon guiding them, the group was challenged by a voice in the night. The voice was straight out of Brooklyn, New York. Lieutenant Harvey answered the challenge. They all breathed a lot easier; they had reached the safety of American lines.

"We owe you our lives, Lieutenant Harvey," said Michelle thankfully. "You and your men have removed us from the jaws of death and we're forever in your debt. Wherever you go from here, our prayers are with you. I'm old enough to be your mother, and wherever she is, Lieutenant, I'm sure she's proud of you, too. God bless you, young man."

"Thank you, Ma'am. You, and others like you, are the reason we're fighting this war. Thanks for your kind words. I only hope that we can match the courage and determination that have sustained you these past years. I hope your passage home will be a rewarding one." Lieutenant Harvey saluted her, hoping that his men couldn't see the moisture glistening in his brown eyes.

Michelle and the others were helped aboard an army truck and transported to a landing barge for the trip to a large transport ship anchored off shore where steel stairs were dropped down along the side of the ship for the passengers to come aboard. Michelle was met at the top of the steps by the ship's Captain and an assortment of orderlies and corpsmen.

"Welcome aboard, Ma'am. I'm Captain Rutledge," he said, examining her papers. "We have a doctor on board in case anyone needs medical assistance. Our cargo for the return trip to Hawaii is wounded soldiers and sailors with minor wounds. The more severe cases are on the hospital ship to our starboard side. We want to thoroughly check each of you for insects and contagious diseases. Warm showers and clean clothing will be made available for you. I'm sorry, but Philippine nationals will have to be offloaded before we sail in the morning."

"I'm not leaving unless Maria comes with me, Captain Rutledge," said Michelle defiantly. "She lost all of her family early in the war. It would be cruel to abandon her now. I cannot allow it."

"Regulations are regulations; you, of all people, should understand that, Mrs. Korsman."

"As Captain of this ship, you have the power to allow her to stay with me. Maria wishes to remain. I beg you, Captain, don't compound the tragedy she has already had to experience in her short life. I'm not asking you to break specific orders. Would you make one exception for me? As soon as we get to Pearl Harbor, I'll set the paperwork in motion to adopt her. That's a promise. To send her back to the island alone violates the reason we're here in the first place, Captain," pleaded Michelle.

"Well done...I'll allow it, Mrs. Korsman. I have a daughter about her age and I do understand. The orderlies will show you below. The delousing and showers are necessary, so bear with us, please. Afterwards, fresh navy clothing will be distributed to you, and any food that we have on board the ship is at your disposal. Feel free to ask."

"A cup of coffee would be like a dream come true. I haven't had one in ages," remarked Michelle.

"I'll personally see to it that the stewards supply you with one as soon as you get below, Ma'am. The navy runs on coffee."

"Thank you, Captain."

The ponderous liberty ship took two weeks to make the passage from Leyte Island to Pearl Harbor. During that time Michelle was able to put herself back on a schedule which she had almost forgotten existed. Eating three meals a day, sleeping eight hours at night without interruption on a bed with clean sheets, and enjoying the daylight hours without the threat of snipers or attacking Japanese soldiers was a welcome experience. The sailors on the ship faithfully catered to their every need. She did not realize the condition she was in until several quiet days at sea. Michelle was not ill when she was rescued by the Rangers, but she had been living in a constant state of fatigue and anxiety, caused by fear and worry of the unknown.

Now Michelle did not worry about her safety anymore. Her recent past had been unpleasant, but she took pride from the fact that she survived the ordeal. It would take more than two weeks for her to shrug off the anxieties that had become an integral part of her life. If one looked deeply into her eyes they would see sadness and weariness that would take a long time to erase. There was still a spasmodic twitch to her left cheek and neck muscles. The horrific experiences had prematurely turned her hair white. Tiny lines that creased her cheeks had not been there when she left China, leaving her face more angular and drawn than ever before. It would take time for her to become the person she used to be. The sweet salt air and picture-perfect sunsets at sea were like a tonic to her soul. She fervently hoped that she would never have to experience the fetid jungle again.

The lumbering transport slowly maneuvered itself into the sheltered waters of Pearl Harbor, and tied up at a dockside lined with ambulances and other vehicles. Michelle was requested to submit to a routine debriefing session at the military intelligence offices at the headquarters of the Commander-in-Chief Pacific Ocean Area Headquarters. Michelle and Maria were met at the dock by a sailor who drove them to the office compound. Colonel James Ready met her at the parking lot. She did not recognize him until she was escorted inside and introduced to Colonel Hank Thomas.

"Now I remember the two of you. You came to the apartment to study when you and Arlo were at the Command and Staff School. That was a long time ago..."

"It certainly was, Mrs. Korsman. You may not have been aware of it, but Jim and I have been monitoring your movements for several months. You'll be pleased to know that your husband, Arlo, is now a Major General," announced Colonel Thomas.

The mention of his name started her heart pounding. "How is he? Have you seen him?" she asked passionately.

"We've seen him recently and are in touch on a weekly basis. As soon as we go over a few questions with you, Mrs. Korsman, it's going to be our privilege to drive you to his quarters at Schofield Barracks."

"You mean he's here in Hawaii?"

"Yes. We'll have the two of you together within a couple of hours."

Michelle sat before the intelligence officers with tears of joy running down her cheeks, stunned by the news of Arlo's nearness. Seeing him so soon after her deliverance was a dream beyond expectations.

"I can't believe my luck," she sobbed. "Thank you for your thoughtfulness. I'm afraid he won't want me, once he sees how I've changed. It's been so long and so difficult..."

Maria, who had remained in the background, stepped to Michelle's side and placed a comforting arm about her shoulders. "This young lady is Maria. Maria, these two gentlemen are old friends, Colonel Thomas and Colonel Ready. I would never have made it if it had not been for her. She's been a watchful guardian wiser than her years would indicate."

Michelle and Maria were both asked a number of questions that would help the intelligence community assemble more pieces of the puzzle about the situation in the Philippines. When the session was over, the four of them climbed into a staff car with Colonel Ready driving. They drove into the mountainous area where Schofield Barracks was located. The views from the road were breathtaking, but Michelle was preoccupied thinking about what was at the end of the trip.

Arlo's apartment was located in the officers quarters. The sun had just set, and the gentle trade winds swept the scent of tropical flowers into the surrounding hills. Arlo and Lieutenant Matthews were enjoying a leisurely smoke over coffee when the door bell rang. Lieutenant Matthews jumped up to answer it and greeted Thomas and Ready. Arlo heard their voices and hollered for them to come in.

There wasn't any immediate response from them, so Arlo pushed himself away from the table and turned around. There was Michelle standing in the middle of the room! He was speechless and in shock. He saw the whiteness of her hair and the lines around her eyes, and before he could find his voice, she was in his arms. Through watery eyes, Arlo watched Hank and Jim silently wave good-bye and leave.

"Hold me, darling. Don't ever let me go again. I can't believe this is happening. Just two weeks ago I was hiding in the jungle afraid I'd never see you again..."

"It's all over now, my love. Oh, you feel good in my arms where you belong. When you left, there was a part of me that went with you...now, I'm whole again." Arlo choked with emotion, burrowing his face in her hair.

It took a while for the reality of the moment to sink in to their hearts. Their prayers had been answered. Hopes had just became reality, and dreams, at last, had not been in vain. They clung to each other communing with each other's souls. In the background, Lieutenant Matthews asked Maria if he could take her bag. She was reluctant to release it until the Lieutenant explained that this was going to be their new home for a while.

"Before anything else is said, dear Arlo, I want you to know that through all of the years and months, I have remained true to you and true to our vows to each other. I could not betray the trust that we've cherished all these years."

"It's been the same for me, Michelle," Arlo whispered in her ear.

"My constant companion throughout all this time has been the young lady standing behind you. I owe my life to her. Her name is Maria. I've talked so much about you that you're not a stranger to her."

Arlo looked down at the slender girl next to him. She seemed so small and fragile! Her eyes were bright, and he saw a trace of fear in them as if she was about to take off in flight. He crouched down before her and reached out for her.

"Hello, Maria. I'm Arlo, Michelle's husband, and I'm indebted to you for bringing my Michelle back to me. Would you mind if a thankful soldier gave you a hug? I need that right now." Holding out his arms for her, she seized the moment and fell into them. She closed her eyes and felt acceptance and security in his strong embrace. She had come home!

"Aunt Michelle has told me a lot about you, Sir. She's been worried that you would not want her after all this time."

"What nonsense," replied Arlo, standing to confront Michelle. "How could you ever think such a thing. Erase those kinds of thoughts from your mind, dear lady. Nobody could ever love you as deeply as I have for all these years. If I had it to do over again, I'd do the same thing. Don't you ever dare to question my feelings for you, Michelle."

"I knew in my heart that you'd say those things. I love you, Arlo. Fear and doubts and uncertainty gnawed at me so much that I questioned everything, including my own self worth. Forgive me. It was foolish and I'll never doubt again," she cried. "Hold me some more."

Later that night, in a small apartment on officer's row, dreams came true and prayers were answered for Arlo and Michelle. The war was forgotten and their love became one again. Maria was given Lieutenant Matthew's room, while he cheerfully moved into bachelor's quarters across the compound. Marie slept deeply and dreamed of a better tomorrow. A sense of well-being surrounded her. She drew strength and contentment from the love shared by Arlo and Michelle. Her expectations for tomorrow were high.

The next day, Arlo excused himself from the planning process that was a daily ritual for the advancement of the campaigns then underway. Arlo, Michelle, and Maria spent the day together exploring the many lovely sights of Oahu. Early evening they drove back to Pearl Harbor to visit with Bright Cloud and Mark at the hospital. Michelle was rediscovering the sheer pleasure of simply being with her husband. She was lucky. The ordeal she had experienced strengthened the love they held for each other. They had discussed the situation about Maria. She did not want to force Maria upon Arlo, but she had strong feelings about providing a good home for the orphan. She was confident that it would work out for the three of them. Arlo and Maria were starting out well with each other. Michelle was pleased to see how readily Maria was drawn to him. Arlo had that way about him. Michelle secretly prayed that this was the way God intended the two of them to share their lives with a child of their own...

Bright Cloud was later than usual getting to the hospital. She had spent the morning composing a letter to Chief Collin Montgomery's parents. She described the circumstances of his death to them, and his last wish for the Navy Cross. The letter left her in a somber mood. The war keeps taking and taking from them... When she posted the letter, she was told that she had a letter in her mailbox. It was from DJ. She nervously took a seat in the hotel lobby to read it.

November 3, 1944

Dear Mom and Dad,

It's quiet on the ship tonight. Most of my platoon are sleeping by now. I can't tell you where I am, but I can say that we'll be in combat sometime soon. That's what I went to West Point for, and I'll be glad to do my share to end the war as soon as possible.

You were right, Dad, I am afraid, like everyone else in the company. I honestly think that I'm more afraid of failing my men than I am for myself. There are several things I wanted to say to you because I never said it as often as I should have. If something should happen to me, I want both of you to know how much I've always loved and respected you.

Mother, I know that you were sometimes offended by unkind words and actions of thoughtless people who saw strangers of a different culture as unequal. They could not know what was in your heart, or they would have repented their deeds. I have always been proud of the heritage and legacy you and father have passed on to me. Whatever my own shortcomings are, you have been an absolute angel in human form.

Dad, no son has ever loved, or been as proud of his father, as I have always been of you. Your support and positive thinking, softly expressed, has always been a source of strength to me. I'll try to do my best, as you've taught me to do.

The legacy from both of you that means the most to me, and is a constant source of inspiration, is the wonderful love you two have for each other. I treasure it and wish for such a love to be a part of my life. It's important for me to tell you these things tonight.

I think often of all our good times together.

Love you both,

Daniel-Joseph {DJ}

He had that way of making you feel good about yourself, Bright Cloud thought. Walking to the hospital, she could not get rid of the words "we'll be in combat soon". They had an ominous sound to her. When she shared the letter with Mark, he had similar feelings of misgiving.

Bright Cloud was busy massaging Marks inert legs when Arlo and Michelle walked through the door. Mark saw them first and could not believe his eyes.

"My God, you've come back to us..."

"Dearest Mike," cried Bright Cloud, running to them with open arms. "Our prayers have been answered." It was an emotional reunion. They shared a similar disposition and a long-standing friendship for each other.

Michelle reached out to Mark and wept openly in his embrace. "Welcome home Michelle, you've had us worried," Mark said in a low voice. "Macarthur's forces must have reached you."

"Thankfully, the American Rangers escorted me to safety. It's so good to be back with my husband. Seeing the both of you here is incredible," exclaimed Michelle, filled with excitement. "From the looks of you, Mark, I'm not the only one that has caused some worry."

"He gave us some difficult days, Mike, but thanks to his special guardian angel, he's eventually coming home."

"I've heard about your special guardian angel," said Michelle excitedly. "Having been at Fort Lewis for several years, I can easily believe that it was divine intervention through Flying Eagle. What a wonderful gift. The gift of life."

"There's someone I'd like to have you meet," continued Michelle. "Arlo and I have agreed to adopt a young girl from the Philippines by the name of Maria. Maria honey, meet two of our best and dearest friends, Colonel and Mrs. Leroux." Maria was self-conscious and shy, but stepped out from Arlo's protective arm and shook Mark's and Bright Cloud's hands. There was a big smile on her lips, but that smile disappeared when she saw the seriousness of Mark's disposition.

"Young lady, you remind me of our own Bright Star. If you don't mind, I'd be pleased for you to call me Uncle Mark."

"That would be fine with me, Sir...Uncle Mark," Maria responded, feeling more at ease.

"Uncle Mark can't get out of bed to hug you, so I'm going to do it for the both of us. You can call me Aunt Danielle or Aunt Danny. Welcome to the family, Maria," Bright Cloud warmly embraced her. "I'm happy for you. You're coming into a home filled with love. This is a nice surprise, Mike and Arlo. I'm happy for you."

"Did Arlo tell you that Bright Star is here at the hospital?" asked Mark.

"Yes, he did. I don't know what's happening. For over two years I was isolated from the whole world, sneaking away from Japanese patrols, living in the jungles and feeling rejected. Now, within a few weeks, I find myself back in the arms of my husband and surrounded by my most wonderful friends. I can't ask for anything more." Bright Cloud put her arm around Michelle's shoulder. There was a feeling of contentment and an air of thanksgiving in the room.

"Well, gang," said Arlo. "It looks as if we're going to be here for a while. Mark still has more treatments ahead of him, and the planning which I'm involved with is just beginning. We should have time to get together often."

Bright Cloud noticed Michelle's clothing and came to the conclusion that she and Maria were due for a shopping spree, at least for clothes. She had been using Star's clothes ever since she arrived at Pearl Harbor.

"I don't know what you've got planned, but I've got to shop for clothes. I lost all of mine and I'm sure you and Maria could use a new outfit or two. It would be fun to get together for that," Bright Cloud suggested to Michelle.

"What a luxury that would be for me, Bright Cloud. I do need a lot of things. I'd love to go whenever you're ready. How about tomorrow morning?" asked Michelle energetically.

"Tomorrow morning it is."

"I could put Lieutenant Mathews at your disposal with the staff car if you'd like," suggested Arlo. He was pleased to see Michelle starting to get back her familiar zest for life. Bright Cloud will be good for her right now, he thought.

"Rank has its privileges," laughed Mark, winking at Arlo.

"We could celebrate our being together again, by spending money on ourselves. What do you think about that, Maria?" asked Bright Cloud playfully.

Maria didn't really know what to say. "I would like that if Aunt Michelle wants to do it," she answered haltingly.

"We've never been able to enjoy freedom of choice like this," admitted Michelle pulling Maria next to her. "Everything is going to be an adventure."

Bright Star was notified by Lieutenant Barkley that her Uncle Arlo was visiting her father, accompanied by a woman and a young girl. As soon as she had a chance to take a break from her wards, she ran down one flight of stairs to the sixth floor and burst into her father's room. She recognized Michelle, even though the white hair gave her slight pause.

"Aunt Michelle, we've been so worried about you, and here you are out of the blue. It's been five years since we've seen each other. It's so nice to have you back with us. Thank God it's all over for you." Star affectionately embraced Michelle.

"You've blossomed into the lovely young lady we all expected, Star. You look great in your uniform. It has been a while, hasn't it?" Michelle's lips trembled. "I still can't believe my good fortune...this is Maria. I would not have made it if it hadn't been for her."

"Welcome Maria, and thanks for taking such good care of her. She's one in a million and we all love her very much."

"I call her Aunt Michelle, the same as you do," admitted Maria impressed with Star in her uniform.

"Since you took such good care of our Aunt Michelle, that makes us special friends." Bright Star was pleased to meet Maria, but she was nervously preoccupied. "I hope that you all can forgive me for my unusual behavior at this wonderful gathering of dear friends. I know it must seem irregular, but, please, I beg you to bear with me for a short time. Then everything will be explained to you..."

Everyone in the room was puzzled at her unusual statement. "First of all, Uncle Arlo, may I speak in private with you in the hallway?" Star asked in a wavering voice.

"What's wrong, Star?" asked Mark sharply.

"Later, Dad. Please, don't be alarmed, I can explain later. Trust me, please. Especially you, Aunt Michelle."

"If you must..."

Star escorted Arlo out into the corridor.

"This is highly unlikely, young lady," said Arlo, disturbed by her abrupt actions.

"I know that it's irregular, Uncle, and it must look as if I had lost my mind, but I have to ask you some questions that are important to you and especially to Aunt Michelle. Do you remember the details about the adoption of Michelle's son before she met you? As I understood the situation, the original adoption took place in Glens Falls, New York. Their name was Stevens."

"That's correct so far."

"The Stevens family was killed in an automobile accident when the baby was still very young."

"Yes."

"Then, the child was adopted by another couple," stated Bright Star breathlessly. "The detective who checked on the incident told your Aunt Michelle that their name was John Stevens."

"So far so good, Star. No trace of the other couple could be found after the accident, so Michelle and I decided to drop it years ago. Why are you so interested in something that took place so long ago, and why is it important at this moment in our lives?"

"I have good reason to believe that the detective was only partially correct. The child was readopted, as he said, but the name was Steven Jackson. He was raised in Utica, New York, by the Jackson family. They both died natural deaths a few years ago. Before they died, they told Steven that the adoption agency people had told them that Steven's biological mother was a nurse from the Lake George area."

"My God, Star. What are you trying to tell me?"

"I'm telling you that I sincerely believe Aunt Michelle's son is here in this hospital as we speak."

"It can't be possible..."

"Think about it, Uncle. All of the facts fit together except the name. Maybe the first family did give him the name of John Stevens like the detective discovered. Also, maybe the Jackson family decided to change his first name from John to Steven in remembrance of the expired couple. It's logical and the time frame is perfect."

"I don't know what to say."

"There's more. Steven Jackson is a lieutenant in the Army Air Corps. He was badly burned and injured when his airplane crashed near Leyte Island. I believe that it was Aunt Michelle who reset his broken legs in the jungle, before he was evacuated. If what I have been thinking is true, then it's a miracle of fate."

"I can tell you, in confidence, that two old friends confirmed some of that information to me weeks ago. However, I could never imagine such a coincidence..."

"Before we do anything, come with me up one flight and see this young airman. He's a remarkable person."

Lieutenant Steven Jackson was sound asleep when they walked into the room. His eyes were still bandaged but his cheeks and jaw were exposed. Arlo had seen enough. They hurriedly left the ward and returned to the sixth floor.

"He has her facial features, that's for sure, Star. My God, I can't believe this coincidence after all those years. The probability of being here at the same time staggers the imagination."

"I've been going crazy, Uncle Arlo, since I put all of the pieces together. I really believe that he's her son."

"I can't fault your logic, Star. I don't know how Michelle will take it. She's been through a lot!"

"I think it will put an old pain to rest. Steven Jackson is a good person. He's a teacher. I honestly believe that this knowledge will enrich both of their lives."

"I support whatever you think is best, Star."

"I wouldn't want to hurt her for the world, you know that," admitted Star.

"Of course I do."

"Come then. There's no time like the present to spread some joy in their lives." They anxiously returned to the room under questioning stares.

"Aunt Michelle," Bright Star explained carefully. "There's a man in the hospital who was injured in a plane crash in the Philippines. He was taken to a jungle compound where a nurse helped to care for his burns and set his two legs. Do you remember a wounded man who fits that description?"

"Oh, yes, I remember him well. He was terribly hurt. There was something special and significant about him. I'm so glad he's getting good care," answered Michelle with a strange look on her face.

"He remembers you as a lady of mercy who appeared out of nowhere and made him feel better. Would you like to see him? I know he'd enjoy your visit."

"I'd like that, too."

"Come then, we'll be back later Mom and Dad," called Bright Star over her shoulder.

Lieutenant Jackson was still sleeping when they entered the ward. Star leaned over his bed and whispered in his ear. "Do you want to talk or do you wish to continue sleeping, Lieutenant Jackson?"

"Hello, Ensign. I can rest anytime. I didn't hear you come in. Is there someone with you?"

"Yes, there is," answered Bright Star, turning to Michelle who was pale and nervous. "Is this the man you worked on in the jungle compound, Aunt Michelle?" Star removed some of the white sheets that covered his bandaged legs. There was an awkward silence in the tension filled room.

"I remember you, Lieutenant," answered Michelle, haltingly.

"That voice. I'd recognize it anywhere. It's my own angel of the jungle. Thank you for helping me. I may not look much better, but I'm improving, Ma'am."

"Aunt Michelle. I have something that is wonderful and very important to tell both you and Lieutenant Jackson. I don't understand how God arranges such things, but I'm convinced of something that will influence both of your lives. My dearest Aunt Michelle, I fervently believe that Steven Jackson is your son. Steven, your angel of the jungle who miraculously helped you, is actually, your mother

Chapter Fifteen

Bright Cloud celebrated Thanksgiving, 1944, with Mark and the two wounded sailors in his room. Neither of the young men could sit up in their beds, so she helped the nursing staff feed them some of their traditional Thanksgiving meal, consisting of turkey with all of the trimmings. Bright Star dropped by to check on her father and visit a few minutes. She was still pulling the same duty on the floor above. Michelle, Arlo, and Maria visited for a short time. Everyone was in a festive mood. Mark was joking and laughing the way he used to do.

Mark was beginning to be his old self again. The cast on his arm had been removed, and he was attending therapy sessions for the injured limb. There was some disfigurement to his left arm and hand. The bone from the elbow to his wrist was slightly shorter than his right side, by about an inch and a half. His left hand was also turned several degrees away from his body so that he could not clasp his hands together easily. He was lucky to have his arm and readily accepted the limitations. It could have been worse!

Michelle was filled with reverence and a sense of fulfillment that she had found her son after all the agonizing years she had searched for him. Her recovery from the experience in the Philippines was remarkable. The ordeal was replaced with the rapture of being with her husband, and discovering Steven Jackson. She had much to be thankful for. The routine of being a wife to Arlo and a mother for Maria and Steven was fulfilling to her. Michelle and Star wheeled Steven Jackson to Mark's room as soon as the cast was removed from his legs. It was the first time they had ever met.

"Welcome to our circle of friends, Lieutenant Jackson," greeted Mark, shaking his hand. "This Thanksgiving, we really do have something to be thankful for. You're one of them. Your mother has been a very dear friend for many years."

"I'm still shocked by the discovery of my maternal mother. God works in strange ways."

"Since Michelle has found you, Lieutenant, I swear, she has grown younger by ten years. We're happy for all of you," Bright Cloud wrapped her arms around him.

"Your voice sounds a lot like Ensign Leroux."

"I expect so, Lieutenant," admitted Bright Cloud softly.

"I'm anxious for the bandages around my eyes to be removed so that I can see who I'm talking to." Steven told them.

"You and Mark are lucky to be at this hospital. I understand it's the best in the whole U.S. Navy," said Arlo. The last several days with his beloved Michelle at his side were some of the happiest times he had ever known, and it showed in the relaxed way he accepted things around him. He was bursting with pride at being the head of a family. He spent hours with Lieutenant Jackson. They were developing a friendship with each other that promised to grow. They shared a common set of values.

Bright Star had worked at her position at the hospital long enough so that she was fully comfortable with the demands placed upon her. She monitored Lieutenant Jackson's condition and was pleased at his progress. The infections, which had been out of control for a long time, had been arrested, and the healing process was starting to show around his eyes. Every time Star cleansed his eyes, he said the blurred objects were less and less clouded. He freely admitted to her that the main reason he wanted to see was to compare his mental image of her with her real self. Star was constantly fighting her feelings for the gregarious airman.

Now that he had become a member of Michelle's family, she was more conscious than ever of some possible dangers ahead. Personal feelings under the conditions that she and Lieutenant Jackson found themselves, could easily be misinterpreted. Love could be misconstrued for infatuation and/or transference. Appreciation for kindness and other acts by a nurse or a doctor frequently were misplaced when their situations changed.

Lieutenant Jackson was doing remarkably well for a young man so badly injured. He attributed much of his progress to Bright Star. She was afraid that he was thinking too much about her. She was not blind to what he was thinking, and she tried hard not to give him any encouragement. She maintained a very professional manner around him, the way she did with the other patients.

One day after Thanksgiving, Lieutenant Jackson had an operation on his eyes to correct some of his clouded vision. Two days later, the doctors removed the bandages from his eyes and tested him. The right eye was better than expected. The left eye was weaker, but could be improved with corrective glasses.

That night, after Bright Star had reported on her floor, he was looking forward to seeing her for the first time. He was wearing a thin layer of gauze over his eyes that could easily be removed. The doctors wanted him to use his eyes as much as he could, but warned him to refrain from straining them for the first few days and keep them out of bright lights. They provided him with a pair of dark sunglasses to wear until they could prepare a set of corrective lenses for him.

As soon as he heard Bright Star in the ward, he removed the gauze bandage and put on the glasses. She saw him place the glasses over his eyes and smiled as she approached the bed.

"So this is what the surgeons have done to you."

"I expected you to look the way you do, Ensign. Are your eyes really brown or is it the dark glasses that make them look that way?"

"They're brown, Lieutenant. It's wonderful that you can see at last. Aunt Michelle will be pleased for you, too."

"That's something I've wanted to thank you for. If it hadn't been for your keen observation and deduction, my mother, and I would not have found each other. We would've finished out our lives wondering, yet never knowing. It was a wonderful thing that you did for us, and I appreciate it."

"Aunt Michelle has been transformed by the certainty of your identification."

"Are you happy for me, Ensign Leroux?" It was a question that should not have been asked. It just slipped out, and he regretted the impulsiveness of the remark because he knew that it put her in an uncomfortable position.

"Yes, of course I am. The two of you deserve any happiness that comes your way." The answer didn't give him what he was hoping for so he let it drop.

Lieutenant Jackson's physical condition was improving daily. Now, the doctors had to concentrate on his legs. The cast was scheduled to be removed the next day. The burn wounds still demanded daily attention but they were healing more rapidly now that the infections had been controlled. As he continued to improve, his relationship with Bright Star remained on a professional level, but she was more distant and aloof towards him than she had been. He was hurt by the perceived rejection, because she was in his thoughts day and night, and he didn't want to make a fool of himself unless he saw some sign that she was interested in him as a person, instead of as a patient. He had a feeling that she was uncomfortable around him, and his obsession grew.

Down one flight of stairs, Mark was also doing remarkably well. The therapy routine for his arm was helping him to use it like he did before the injury. He could, also, maneuver himself out of bed and climb into a wheel chair. It was a feat of pure pleasure and dogged determination on his part to be able to get away from the bed and the room that had been the center of his life for weeks. The mobility of the chair cured his "cabin fever." His therapy treatments took place in the basement level of the hospital, where he ran into Lieutenant Jackson one morning.

"Good morning, Lieutenant," greeted Mark, happy to see him. "How's the leg therapy coming along?"

"Good morning, Sir. It's slow going. Watch out for that blonde therapist at the end of the room. She likes to hurt you. She keeps telling me that if it doesn't hurt, it's not helping us, and man it does hurt, Colonel."

"My arm's doing great. I wish I could say..." Mark was interrupted by a patient speeding around the corner in a wheelchair that bounced Mark off the wall, spun him around and slammed him again against the hallway wall. It startled him and he began to cry out hysterically, "I felt something in my legs! It hurt when I hit the wall! I felt something in my legs..."

"Easy, Colonel," said Lieutenant Jackson, reaching across his chair to calm Mark.

The blond therapist ran to him at the same time and wheeled him into a dressing room, calling immediately for a doctor. In the meantime, she removed the silk stockings from Mark's legs and tested him with a small pin on the ball of the feet. He could feel it plainly in his right foot! The left one was not so distinct, but he could detect the prick of the pin. It was another miracle to be thankful for. He was anxious to share the news with Bright Cloud. The fear of never being able to walk again had been a bitter pill for him to swallow. The ability to feel some stimuli in the legs was a triumphant beginning for him.

The doctors told him that they could start a strenuous regimen of leg therapy very soon. They mentioned a new electric stimulation therapy which worked well for some patients. It could be ordered for his situation. They were encouraged by his remarkable determination. He had the stamina and perseverance to do what was necessary to walk again! Bright Star playfully called it "good old fashioned Leroux stubbornness."

As soon as Mark started therapy on his legs, the staff told him that he was going to be sent back to the States soon. He requested a hospital near his home in Maine, so they agreed on the Portsmouth Navy Yard Hospital, which was only a few miles from Wells.

Shortly after Thanksgiving, Mark was officially notified that he had been granted the nation's highest award for valor, the Medal of Honor. It was customary for the President of the United States to place it around the neck of those who had earned it, so Mark was notified that it would take place after the first of the year, when he was transferred home.

Bright Cloud was surprised when Mark failed to show very much enthusiasm for the Medal. He was quiet and reflective for the rest of the day. She tried not to intrude upon his private thoughts. Only those who have experienced combat are bound together for a lifetime in an exclusive brotherhood. The frightful losses his regiment had suffered on the day of the assault would always haunt him. He refused to talk about it, but Bright Cloud knew the sorrow that was in his heart. His ability to feel the pain of others was very much a part of the person she loved so dearly. It was that vulnerability that made him feel responsible for the losses. Those same character traits made him an exceptional regimental commander who was respected by his men. If she could, she would have gladly lightened the weight of the grief, but she knew, realistically, that Mark would probably carry the emotional scar to his grave.

There was one aspect of Mark's last day in combat that did please Bright Cloud. He would always mourn the heavy price that his regiment had to pay, but he did not blame himself for the situation that the regiment found themselves in after they hit the beach. It was an act of God, the luck of the draw, which put him on that spot at that time. Mark relived the events of those few hours over and over again, wondering if there had been something he could have done differently. He always came to the same conclusion, he'd make the same decisions again. He found some comfort in that fact.

Michelle came to the hospital everyday after she dropped Maria off to a special school on the outskirts of Pearl City where she could be prepared for entry into regular grade school later in the year. Michelle was saddened to learn that the two men who had been instrumental in her survival were listed as killed in action. Major Carlisle, the proud capable West Point officer who had sheltered her in more ways than she dared to think about, and Lieutenant Harvey, who had courageously carried her to safety from the jungle, were both killed during an offensive action in the Philippines. She cried for a long time when she heard the news from Arlo. It was a bitter piece of news to accept, and Michelle hoped that her sadness did not show when she visited Steven.

Lieutenant Jackson looked forward to her visits as much as Michelle. She told him exactly how she became pregnant with him, and carried the shame with her until she met Arlo, who helped her regain her self-respect. They talked a lot about the past. The future was less clear. Steven was unsure what was ahead for him. Michelle had a suspicion that he felt something for Bright Star, and she said nothing that would encourage or discourage that part of his personal life. That was between the two of them.

One day Michelle found Steven looking at himself in a mirror with a dejected look on his face. He had been showing symptoms of depression for the last few days. He thought the burns looked terrible and would always show, leaving him permanently disfigured! Michelle was unable to elevate his spirits, even though she pointed out the fact that he could have died in the plane crash, and his survival, under any circumstances, was preferable to the alternative.

That same evening, after Michelle left the hospital, Lieutenant Jackson withdrew to the point of becoming sullen about his condition. Bright Star saw the change the moment she came into the ward. He laid quietly in the bed and stared at the ceiling with a defiant look on

241

his face. It was not the same Lieutenant Jackson she had come to know, and she was concerned about his condition.

"Good evening, Lieutenant," said Star. "How was your visit with Aunt Michelle today?"

He waited a few seconds before responding. "I guess I'm beginning to face reality for the first time, Ensign." Bright Star picked up on the change in his attitude and his voice. There was a sullen, mocking tone in the way he spoke that alarmed her. "I can't wait to get out of here. I should request a move to the States. I'll probably be able to walk eventually, but my burn scars from the fire will always be a part of what I look like. I'm not the same person I used to be. I can remember, as a kid, the presence of World War One veterans who had been wounded and disfigured in the war. We were afraid of them, and some of the more brazen and unruly kids even made fun of how they looked. I can imagine how I'll look when it's all over..."

Bright Star was taken aback by the intensity of his bitterness. She wanted to reach out and tell him something, anything that would bring back the friendly, gentle person she knew.

"I can hear the words that you're speaking, but I can't believe it's the same Lieutenant Jackson that I have come to know."

"War changes people, Ensign. I don't have to tell you that. I'm not going home the same person that I was. Am I?"

"No, but you still have much to be thankful for, Lieutenant. You can have a life exactly the way you want it. Many veterans can't say that. It could have been worse."

"Considering what some are going through, you're right, Ensign," answered Steven, watching her closely. "I guess I got myself down in the dumps about what I see in the mirror every day."

"Don't do this to yourself...," interrupted Star nervously. Suddenly, an urgent call for her came from a patient across the room. She left in a hurry.

A couple of hours later, during her daily medicine routine, Bright star found him more reticent and in a better mood than she left him.

"I'm going to change your bandages again, and bathe the wound with an antiseptic solution. Your conversation earlier this evening was uncharacteristic of you, Lieutenant. That attitude won't help you get well."

"I apologize if I upset you. I've been doing a lot of thinking about the future. I let my feelings sway my better judgment and I took the liberty of making assumptions which I had no right to do. It won't happen again, I promise, Ensign."

Bright Star removed his soiled dressings and was quiet while she worked on him. Her hands were gentle as ever, but it took all of Star's discipline to keep her hands from shaking. The resolute way he spoke about himself frightened her even more than his outbursts earlier in the evening.

"It's not very pretty, is it?" he asked calmly.

"Compared to two weeks ago, I'd say it has improved a lot. Pretty is not a word I'd use to describe a burn. When it's completely healed and your hair has grown back, it's going to look much better. Yes, there will always be evidence of your accident, but you survived the ordeal, Lieutenant. Listen, I don't know what has happened to you. Sure, you're one of the unfortunate soldiers of this war, but there are others less fortunate than yourself. Don't let yourself wallow in self-pity or condemnation of your misfortune. If you're going to let your wound dictate your acceptance to the world, then you're being unfair to yourself and others around you.

"There are some individuals who object to me because I'm an Indian and have dark skin. I can't do anything about my birthright. However, I'd like to hope that when people look closer at me, they can see what's in my heart and judge me on the basis of who I am, instead of what I am. You should think about that, Lieutenant Jackson."

"You're right, Ensign...I've been selfish lately."

"You're just being human, and that makes us all imperfect. Give it time, Lieutenant."

Arlo, Michelle and Bright Cloud were excited about celebrating Christmas together for the first time in several years. They planned a Christmas Eve gathering for the whole gang at Arlo's apartment. By mid-December, Steven Jackson was able to walk around with the help of a cane. Mark was still confined to a wheel chair, but he could be helped into the staff car and driven to Schofield Barracks. Michelle even hired a carpenter to construct a ramp to the house so that Mark could enter the front door with dignity.

The celebration of the birth of Jesus Christ was a welcome opportunity to put the war to one side for a few hours and rejoice in the salvation of mankind. Everyone was buoyant about getting together outside of the confining walls of the hospital. Michelle and Bright Cloud teamed up to produce a feast worthy of remembrance. They scoured the stores for supplies and settled on a varied menu of chicken, ham, and roast beef as the staples. They baked several pies and breads that filled the apartment with mouth-watering aromas for days before the event.

Christmas Eve at the hospital was as joyous as a hospital can be in wartime. Bright Star was able to swap her schedule with another nurse on the floor so that she could have the day off. Lieutenant Mathews was sent to pick up Mark and Bright Cloud, and Lieutenant Jackson. Bright Star told them that she had some errands to run in Pearl City and would take a taxicab to Schofield Barracks, later, when she was finished.

This was the first time that Mark and Lieutenant Jackson had worn a complete uniform since they were wounded. It felt good to get out and around like other people did. The ride up into the mountain regions was a tonic to the two men's disposition. They came to an understanding on the ride up to Schofield.

"I've got a proposition for you, young man," said Mark, sitting beside Lieutenant Jackson in the back seat. "We're going to be seeing a lot of each other from now on. You're an important part of the gang, so why don't we drop the formality of rank? After all, we'll be discharged soon and will hang up these uniforms. I'd like to call you Steve, because us Maine folks have a lazy tongue and don't like to use anymore vowels than we have to. I'd be proud for you to call me anything you'd like, except Colonel or bad names." Mark chuckled.

"I was hoping that we could come to some understanding, Sir. I'd be glad to have you call me Steve. All of my friends and classmates called me that. If you don't object, I'd prefer to call you Mr. Leroux for now. I haven't been in the military for too long. However, I know how much work and dedication it takes to earn a full colonelcy. I respect that ability and will feel more comfortable calling you Mr. Leroux. I was raised to be respectful to my elders, and especially, a Medal of Honor recipient. It's my privilege, Sir."

"Then its settled, Steve."

Everyone was present and accounted for except Bright Star. Bright Cloud had apologized to everyone that Star would be a little late. By the time she was escorted by the guards through the gates to Arlo's quarters, the sun was beginning to set. She could smell the food from outside on the walkway as she knocked on the door. Arlo answered the door and stepped backward with a flourish. "I do believe we're being visited by a lady from Venus. Merry Christmas, Bright Star." She blushed as he proudly put his arm around her waist and escorted her into the large central living room, where everyone was in a festive mood. There was a palm Christmas tree and even a fireplace going in the cheerful room.

Bright Star was later than usual because she had stopped to have her hair set in a different style. It was commonly called an "updo". Instead of her hair hanging loose over her shoulders, it was swept upwards, leaving her neck visible. She wore a red dress with white trimmings and a white lace collar that covered part of her neck. She presented a stunning figure that would have turned anyone's head. She wished everyone a Merry Christmas, and embraced the whole gang as she went from one to the other around the room. Steven Jackson was sitting on the far side of the room next to the fireplace, his eyes aglow at the apparition before him. He stood up when she entered the room and balanced himself with the help of his cane. Bright Star was different than he had ever seen her. Not just the new hairstyle, there was a sparkle in her eyes he had never noticed. He thought she was the most beautiful human being he had ever known. There was an awkward silence between them as she approached him.

"Merry Christmas, Steven," she said softly. "Tonight we leave the hospital behind us." Steven was unprepared for the warm rush of feelings that flowed through his body when she put her arms around his neck and intentionally kissed him on the burned side of his face.

"Merry Christmas, Bright Star...you're beautiful tonight." Their eyes met and for the first time, Steven knew what was in her heart... Those soft lips against the sensitive skin of the burn scar, almost caused his legs to buckle and collapse. He held her with his free arm and kissed her gently on the mouth. "My prayers have been answered," he whispered in her ear.

The room was silent. Everyone in the room knew what was in their hearts. They just needed an opportunity to express it. Everyone rejoiced in their discovery of each other. Arlo drummed the glass in his hand with a knife and proposed a toast. Steven had almost forgot that they were in plain sight of the other guests. A smile covered his face. Bright Star, still being held by Steven, turned to see the happy faces of her family circle. A small tear of joy dropped down her bronze face and disappeared, leaving her watery eyes sparkling like jewels. She had never felt happier in her life than she did at this moment. Christmas, 1944, would be a day of remembrance for her and Steven.

Bright Cloud tried out an old piano left in the apartment by a previous tenant. She found that a few of the keys were off tune slightly, but nobody noticed. The guests gathered around the piano and sang some of the familiar Christmas songs of their youth. Mark and Bright Cloud were enjoying the camaraderie of the evening, but in the back of their minds, they were never totally free of their concern for DJ. If only he could have been present, their joy would have been complete. After they had partaken of the memorable meal Michelle and Bright Cloud fixed for the occasion, they gravitated to the living room again. Arlo and Mark lit up their favorite pipes. Arlo asked Steven to join them if he smoked.

"Most of my military experience has been flying airplanes. Smoking was a dangerous habit around so much volatile gasoline, so I never got interested in it," he answered, watching Bright Star help Michelle and her mother clear the dining room table.

"I think you're smart to leave it alone, Steve," commented Mark, sending a smoke screen over his head. "It does have its moments though."

As the evening wore on, Steven and Bright Star couldn't keep their eyes off each other. Star knew that Steve would be going home soon, while she was committed until the end of the war at the hospital. The eventual separation of them was one of the reasons that she wanted Steven to know what she thought about him. The hospital ward was no place for such announcements. Tonight, in the presence of loved ones, she bared her heart to him.

Maria was fascinated by the guests at her new home. She sat in her chair and drank in every word spoken around her. There was an air of peace and security within her new world. She radiated a wondrous feeling of contentment, and smiled more often.

The apartment had a lovely terrace that overlooked a picturesque view to the west. In the distance the Pacific Ocean could be seen beneath the tropical moon. Very few lights shown at night during the war. The night was cool and clear and the air was filled with tropical aromas. Bright Star and Steven were shown the view by Maria, who self-consciously excused herself and returned to the living room. Steven slipped on his uniform jacket. Michelle gave Star a warm shawl to place around her shoulders. The two of them were glad to be alone with each other.

"There's much that I want to say to you, and I don't know where to start," admitted Steven, leaning against the terrace railing. "It won't be long before I'm sent back to the States. I expect they'll discharge me at the same time. Under normal circumstances, I wouldn't be as bold as I may sound tonight. My feelings for you have been building in my heart from that first time you came to me in the ward. I tried to deny them, but it didn't work. I have to be true to myself. I love you, Star."

"We've both felt something for a long time, Steven. My feelings have been suppressed, too. I thought a lot about giving you a gift tonight, so I decided to be honest with myself and to you. I wanted to show you what was in my heart. You can do what you wish with it. I love you, too, Steven. The gift of our love for each other, will make this a Christmas to remember..."

They found each other's lips again and counted their blessings. High above the tragic memory that was Pearl Harbor, Bright Star and Steven were awakened to the thrill of love given and love received in equal measure.

Two weeks after the unforgettable Christmas gathering, Steven was transferred to the Presidio at San Francisco. He would undergo further evaluation and therapy at that institution and ultimately be discharged when his condition was stable enough for him to function on his own. He still used the cane to walk. In time, that too would be unnecessary.

Mark was flown out of Pearl Harbor the same week Steven left for San Francisco. He was transferred to the Portsmouth Navy Yard Hospital, a mere fifteen miles from home. He could use his left arm well enough. It was noticeably unlike his right arm, but he still had a long ways to go with his legs. New muscles had to be developed, even though Bright Cloud had been unrelenting in massaging his legs ever since she arrived at Pearl Harbor. There was some progress. He could feel things through his legs and feet, and was starting to work out on the parallel walking bars. It was going to be a long difficult road back to full recovery. He didn't deceive himself, full usage may not be attainable for him. He had to learn to walk all over again.

Bright Cloud could not accompany him on the medical evacuation plane, so she booked passage on a returning freighter. She stayed with Michelle and Arlo until the boat left Pearl Harbor. Bright Cloud was saddened to hear that the submarine commanded by Captain Evans was lost at sea with all hands on aboard. The men on that gallant ship had touched her heart with their generosity and courage. She still had a pair of pants given to her by Captain Evans.

Bright Cloud arrived a couple of weeks behind Mark. She was pleased to be at home at last. Now she could visit Mark every day and look forward to his eventual homecoming. She was happy to hear the news that Mark told her on one of her visits to the Navy Yard hospital. The President of the United States wanted to award the Medal of Honor to him and six other recipients at a meeting in mid-March. The Navy would provide a VIP plane for the trip to and from Washington, D.C. for both of them.

When the designated day arrived, Bright Cloud proudly accompanied Mark to the presentation. Mark was still confined to his wheelchair. The Marine Corps supplied them with a courtesy escort of three enlisted men, who ushered him in and out of the Oval Office of the White House without any incident. Mark was dressed for the occasion in his best green Marine uniform.

There were seven recipients in all, two soldiers, two sailors, two air corps flyers and one marine. Mark sat quietly in his wheelchair with Bright Cloud standing behind him. She steadied herself with one hand on Mark's shoulder. They both thought that President Roosevelt looked extremely tired, even ill. Mark was the last to be decorated. President Roosevelt rolled his high-backed wheel chair in front of Mark and shook his hand. He read the following citation:

"The Medal Of Honor automatically enrolls you in an exclusive club. Membership cannot be obtained with money, power, government decree, or birthright. It can only be earned on the field of battle where valor and courage are universally admired. Wear it with pride, Colonel Leroux. All Americans, with your President included at the top of the list, admire and respect Medal of Honor recipients more than any other members of our population.

"Congratulations, Colonel Leroux. I understand that you'll someday be able to shed your wheelchair. I envy you for that. On behalf of a grateful nation, I thank you."

After those short words, the President was wheeled out of the room and the Medal of Honor recipients were besieged by a battery of photographers and reporters. They snapped pictures for ten minutes. The recipients then attended a rally at the new Pentagon Building where they were the center of attention and adulation. Bright Cloud was proud of the way Mark handled the busy day. On the flight back to Portsmouth, via Grenier Field at Manchester, New Hampshire, Mark slept most of the way.

Bright Cloud was helping Mark get settled into his small private room at the Portsmouth Navy Yard Hospital, when a knock sounded at the door.

"Come in," said Mark.

"Congratulations, Colonel Leroux," said Commander Fisher, Commandant of the Navy Yard. "I'm sorry to intrude upon your day of celebration, but a dispatch arrived earlier for you. I held it here until you returned from Washington." He handed an official telegram to Mark, who had a fearful premonition of its contents. He unfolded the message with trembling hands and read...

"We regret to inform you that your son, First Lieutenant Daniel Joseph was killed in action while defending a position in Belgium against a powerful German force..."

Blood drained from Mark's face. He handed the sheet of paper to Bright Cloud without saying a word. She was afraid. A silent cry of despair formed on her lips as she fainted and fell to the floor. Commander Fisher had prepared for such an emergency. Just outside the door a doctor and two orderlies waited in case they were needed. They placed Bright Cloud on a stretcher, and attempted to revive her.

Mark was in shock, unable to help Bright Cloud. He stared at the walls not believing what he had just read. He clasped his injured hand with his good right hand and squeezed until they were mottled white. Smelling salts brought Bright Cloud around. She awoke and screamed from the depth of her soul, unable to accept the unthinkable horror. Her own flesh and blood, a product of her womb, now lay dead, never to be held in her arms again. She could not accept what was happening to her. Mark heard her cries in silence. Tears ran slowly down his blanched face. He wiped his cheeks with his disfigured hand and repeated over and over again, in shock: "It's not fair...It's not fair...It's not fair..."

* * *

About the same time that Mark and Bright Cloud received word of DJ's death, Michelle and Maria left Pearl Harbor bound for Diamond Point, New York and her old home. She and Arlo had purchased it from her brother, Peter Gurney. It had been closed for several years. Now they were going to fix it up and establish a permanent residence beside the blue waters of Lake George.

Arlo left Pearl Harbor with the staff of Tenth Army, to attend rehearsal amphibious assaults with the large number of troops soon to be involved in the capture of Okinawa. Shortly after the invasion of Okinawa, the world was stunned to hear about the death of President Roosevelt. One month later, the world was given a blessed piece of news. The Allies had defeated Germany. Victory in Europe, V/E Day, sent an electric bolt of hope and thanksgiving to the peoples of the world. Only Japan remained...

When Okinawa was finally secured in late June, 1945, the American people saw, to their horror, what the price was going to be in order to defeat the Japanese. The losses on Okinawa were brutal and extreme. 500,000 American men killed or wounded! The Japanese lost 1,000,000 men. American blood was turning the Pacific Ocean into a red sea. Visions of hundreds of thousands of American men's lives could be lost, the Joint Chiefs of Staff estimated, when Japan proper was invaded. Japanese losses could conceivably be most of the male population of the nation.

August 6, 1945, the world was informed that the United States had dropped an atomic bomb on the Japanese City of Hiroshima, obliterating the entire city. Three days later, on August 9, 1945, another atomic bomb was dropped on the City of Nagasaki, and the Japanese government asked for peace.

The United States celebrated the outcome with abandon. Those relieved the most were the military leaders. At last they didn't have to send untold thousands of American sons and husbands against the fanatical enemy. Their lives had been spared by the two bombs!

The guns were silent! The killing had stopped!!!

Chapter Sixteen

The early morning sun slowly rose above the majestic spruce trees that lined the eastern shore of Lac Diamante at the small village of Fort Lewis in the Canadian North Woods. There was a touch of fall in the cool air as the warm sun burned off the dampness of a rainy night. Dark shadows rimmed the edge of the lake where the blue waters released a wispy plume of vapor into the air. Scattered among the unbroken barrier of green trees was a myriad of colors that accompanied the transition of the northern forest into its most demanding season of all, winter. Wherever you looked, the landscape reached out to touch the viewer with bursting torches of flaming red, and brilliant splashes of yellow and gold, against a scattered background of dark green sentinels of spruce and balsam fir.

The long wharf at the eastern end of the lake was still being used by the village inhabitants. A lone figure, standing in the middle of the dock, scanned the eastern horizons, shading his eyes from the sun. It was Inspector Gerard Clough of the Royal Canadian Mounted Police, standing proud and erect, meticulously dressed in his best field uniform. Strength and character radiated from his presence, even at his advanced age of seventy years. After several minutes of waiting and watching, a speck appeared on the horizon and grew larger and larger. It had to be the float plane that the Inspector was anticipating.

He was filled with mixed emotions. His job as a policeman, and his natural reticence, did not allow him to cultivate many close friends. The occupants of the plane headed towards the lake were the closest thing he ever came to being part of a family. When they were happy, he was happy. When they were devastated with grief, he felt it in his heart, also.

Inspector Clough had spent a lifetime in the service of his native Canada, loving every minute of it, with the last thirty years spent in the northern forested regions of Quebec Province. He felt a kinship with the hardy native tribes and for the adventuresome independent-minded people who were starting to populate the vast timbered region between the St. Lawrence River and the Arctic. No one ever touched his heart the way Bright Cloud and Mark had done. Their friendship had stood the test of time. The float plane drifted into the wharf where the Inspector secured it with a rope. Bright Cloud was the first to climb from the cabin of the plane into the waiting arms of the policeman.

"Inspector Clough, it's wonderful to see you again. I'd forgotten how much I missed this place until I saw you standing here."

"You're as lovely as ever, Bright Cloud. Welcome home, Lass," said the Inspector, holding her close to him.

Looking over her head, he saw Mark for the first time since the war started. His heart ached when he saw what the war had done to his American friend. The distance from the rocking plane to the dock was short enough that Mark refused help from the pilot. He wanted to return to Fort Lewis under his own power. It was a tricky move from the plane, but the two crutches helped him. He couldn't move without the crutches, and was still a little unsteady, but in time, he was determined to walk without them. Mark wore his uniform and the ribbon for the Medal of Honor. It was good to be back where he had been reborn after the First World War. He and Bright Cloud were both hoping that it would renew their commitment to life once again.

Mark proudly made his way to the spot where Inspector Clough was standing. "Glory be to God, Yank, this old soldier is glad to see you. My prayers were with you every day. Welcome back..." said the Inspector from the heart. "I've always been proud of you, Yank. The Medal of Honor lets the rest of the world know what your friends here at Fort Lewis have always understood. You've made us proud!"

"Thanks, Inspector. A lot has happened since we last saw each other. Bright Cloud and I had strong desires to return to this place that we love so much. Maybe we can plot a new course for our lives and find ourselves again...," replied Mark bravely.

The Inspector saw the sorrow that Mark and Bright Cloud carried with them. He knew about the death of DJ and let his thoughts about the young lad he had come to love, go unsaid. It was shocking to see how much Mark had aged. But then, he thought, Mark had lived a lifetime in a few minutes on the battlefield. He understood what Mark had been through, and his heart cried out in a desire to comfort both of them.

The small group walked slowly past the newly enlarged police station, the church, and the infirmary that Bright Cloud had established. Some things had changed. Many of the faces they met were unrecognizable. They had been away for too long. Yet, there was still a timelessness about the village that remained as they remembered it. It was reassuring. Mark apologized to the Inspector for taking so long to get to the cabin.

"You still have that gentle tenacity that has always been a trademark of yours, Yank," said the Inspector, proudly. "Last night we received a call from Michelle and Arlo Korsman. It seems as if they're coming later today. It was pleasant news. Our angels of the North Woods are returning to see us once again. I look forward to seeing them."

"We knew they would come sometime," answered Bright Cloud, pleased to hear the news. "I do hope that you're going to be able to spend some time with us, dear friend. We all need some time to help put yesterday behind us. Tomorrow will just have to take care of itself."

"I can understand your need for that. It's a privilege to be included in your circle of friends. I'm going to be relieved from the service very shortly. Now that the war is over, the service thinks that I should resign and let new blood take over. I'm ready to go. My old joints are starting to creak more than ever."

"You've left a rich and proud legacy in the North Woods, Inspector. It'll take a big man to fill the shoes you're leaving behind," Mark smiled at his friend.

Later in the day, a two-engine float plane flew over the village, circled around "lookout rock", and banked to the east prepared to land in Lac Diamante. The plane had unfamiliar markings. The Inspector did not recognize the pilot either. Arlo and Michelle emerged first from the plane's cabin. Michelle quickly ran and embraced him excitedly. Arlo shook hands with a warmth that came easy and naturally towards the towering policeman.

Bright Star, holding Steven's hand, stepped from the plane onto the dock. The Inspector's eyes watered as he rushed towards her. "I thought that I was seeing a vision from heaven, Lass. You're lovelier than I remembered. Is this young soldier the reason for the sparkle in your eyes?"

"He is, Inspector. I'd like you to meet Steven Jackson. Steve, meet our dearest friend, Inspector Clough," announced Bright Star proudly.

"I've heard a lot about you, Sir," said Steve, shaking the large raw-boned hand of the Inspector. "I've never been this far north. It's intoxicating."

"The North Woods does have its strong points, young man. Welcome to Canada and to our tiny settlement of Fort Lewis. I see that you're a pilot," said the Inspector, making a mental note of the burn scars on the side of his face.

"Yes, Sir, we rented the plane at Lake George from a charter air service, so that all five of us could fit in it and make the trip together."

"Inspector, I'd like you to be the first to know. Steve and I are planning to be married by Father Lamontagne here at Fort Lewis," Bright Star breathlessly announced.

"No wonder your eyes glow, Lass. Congratulations to both of you. There's nothing like happiness to put a shine in the eyes and color in the cheeks. If you're happy, Lass, then I'm happy for you. Be good to her, Steven. She's a rare jewel."

"I will, Sir. I know that I'm a lucky man."

In all of the excitement, the Inspector had overlooked little Maria, who stepped shyly from the plane while he was busy meeting Bright Star and Steve.

"And who do we have here?" asked the Inspector, surprised to see her standing beside Arlo.

"This is our new addition to the family, Inspector. Maria comes to us from the Philippine Islands. Maria meet Inspector Clough of the Mounted Police."

"My Lord, Maria," exclaimed the Inspector, kneeling down to her level. "You remind me of two lovely girls of the North Country that I have watched grow up before my own eyes. I'd like to be your friend. We can never have too many friends, you know."

"I'd like that too, Sir."

"Ah, yes. Our circle of friends expands to include new loved ones, and that's as it should be, but..," remarked Inspector Clough thinking of DJ. "But the gap left empty, is a heavy burden on this old ticker of mine. I loved that boy as if he was my own and I can't get him out of my mind..." Bright Star reached out to comfort him. It was the first time she had ever seen tears in the Inspector's eyes.

"I was in Pearl Harbor when I received the news from Mother about DJ," explained Bright Star with a tremor on her lips. "The war was almost over by then. When I was discharged a few days after the surrender, I flew to Lake George where Steven was waiting for me with Aunt Michelle and Uncle Arlo. We all agreed with mother's suggestion that we gather here, where so much of our lives have been filled with happy events. I'd like for Steve and I to start our lives together from Fort Lewis."

"I think it's a great idea, too," confirmed Steve. "We've thought a lot about our future, and we want to look into the prospect of a school for the region. I'm a teacher by profession. Who knows, we may be able to make a difference."

The next day, Mark insisted on walking the pathway, without help from anyone else, to the cenotaph for Flying Eagle. He didn't want to hold everyone up, so he started out earlier ahead of them and set his own pace. Bright Star explained to Steve the significance of the towering spires that still stood beside the trail, and showed him the weathered wooden crucifix carved by Flying Eagle. It was the same cross that had played such a powerful role at the Tomb of the Unknown Soldier.

Steve and Arlo dug a small hole in the ground next to the log holding the cross. Bright Cloud, with shaking hands and trembling lips, placed a small wooden box, filled with some of DJ's personal belongings, in the hole and gently covered it with soil. Bright Cloud asked Bright Star to help her scatter rosemary, the herb of remembrance, over the site. It was an ancient custom of their people.

They all observed an emotionally packed moment of silence. Finally, Bright Cloud said aloud in a shaky voice, "My Lord, you now have our son at your side. Our hearts are heavy with sorrow, and we are asking for only one wish from you. In your boundless mercy, would you let Flying Eagle, who has shown us his compassion in striking and powerful ways, take the time to let DJ know that we miss him and will always love him. Show him how things are done where you are. Don't let him feel alone..."

The walk back to the cabin at the village was a time for quiet reflection and remembrance. In the distance the drone of an airplane broke through the stillness of the forest, as the procession, led by Mark and Bright Cloud, slowly approached the settlement. Mark, exhausted by the trek, was glad to sit down in the great room of their cabin. He was oblivious to those around him. His sorrow was almost more than he could handle. Sitting alone and silent, nothing but time could heal the scar in his heart. Suddenly, a knock came at the door.

Bright Cloud answered the door and screamed with delight. She entered the room to introduce Mark and the others to Robert Holden, Jr. Mark, aroused from his despair, thought that Robert, Jr. was the spitting image of his father when they first met twenty-five years ago. Robert Holden, Sr., had been the U.S. Consul representative who had arranged the trip for Mark to present the Distinguished Service Cross to Flying Eagle's family.

"When I came home from the war, I thought about all the times my father talked about the beauty and the feeling of peace he had found in this small village. I've been trying to put my life back together since the war and wanted to see this place. I understand now why my father found it so unforgettable."

The small circle of friends and family that gathered together at the head of Lac Diamante were looking for a beginning, and an ending, to a period in their lives permanently marred by the savagery of war. The war could claim another casualty to its long list. A way of life had passed beyond recall...mourned by those who had lived its dream.

It was a time when the immortality of ideals and truths were defended by the innocent blood of thousands of young men.

It was a time of shared sacrifice when the dreams and aspirations of a generation were put on hold, and a collective effort rang the bell of freedom around the world.

The End

Other Historical Romance Novels
BY
Clifton LaBree

A Song for Lisa   A Historical Romance

This is the story of a young American woman captured by the Japanese in the Philippines, 1941. Like most prisoners, she was brutalized and sadistically treated with a cruel disregard for human life. Three years later, Lisa and her companions had reached the low point of starvation and abuse .....

Lake of Three Sorrows   A Historical Romance

A warm spiritually uplifting story of courage, commitment, and sacrifice. This is the story of Dale Cooper, a battle-weary American soldier who served in two world wars.

Flickering Flame (Colonial Series Book One)

A historical novel, about the Cullen family who settled in Portsmouth, New Hampshire, and their participation in events prior to the French and Indian War. Freedom and opportunity were on the march, but it extracted a heavy price. Frontier settlers were ruthlessly killed and butchered by rampaging Indians lead by French officers and Jesuit priests who frequently incited them to greater levels of inhumanity...

Raising the Torch (Colonial Series Book Two)

A continuation of the saga from Flickering Flame, Colonial Series book one, of the Cullen family in Colonial Portsmouth. This is a moving story of love and sacrifice when a small colony had the audacity to fight for independence from their motherland...

Non-Fiction Books

By

Clifton LaBree

New Hampshire's General John Stark, Live Free or Die: Death Is Not the Greatest of Evils

Publisher - Fading Shadows Imprint

A fresh look at one of America's staunchest defenders of liberty and freedom. John Stark was a courageous New Hampshire citizen-soldier who fought in both, the French and Indian War, and the Revolutionary War. His pursuit of leadership excellence on the battlefield distinguished him as one of the most successful combat commanders of the war, and one of the least appreciated.

His selflessness, modest life style, and devotion to the cause of freedom are an inspiration that time has not diminished. He remains today the embodiment of the frugal, independent, and cantankerous New Hampshire Yankee.

Gentle Warrior, General Oliver Prince Smith, USMC

Published by - Kent State University Press. Kent, Ohio, 2001

The Story of one of the United States Marine Corps best General Officer. His flawless performance in Korea is a story that needed to be told.

www.ingramcontent.com/pod-product-compliance
Lightning Source LLC
Chambersburg PA
CBHW072211170626
46813CB00003B/886